HACKNEY LIBR

Please return this book to c
before the last date stamped. F
Avoid fines by renewing the book

Call the renewals line

People who are over 60, under 18 or registered disabled
are not charged fines.

D0541288

LONDON BOROUGH OF HACKNEY

9130000878620

CHECKERS

Alex   k Parham

Published by
The X Press
PO Box 25694
London, N17 6FP
Tel: 020 8801 2100
Fax: 020 8885 1322
E-mail: vibes@xpress.co.uk
Web site: www.xpress.co.uk

Copyright © Mark Parham, Alex Wheatle 2003

The right of Mark Parham and Alex Wheatle to be identified as the authors of this work
has been asserted in accordance with the Copyright, Designs and Patents Act 1988.

The characters and situations in this book are entirely imaginary and bear no relation to
any real person or actual happenings.

This book is sold subject to the condition that it shall not, by way of trade or otherwise, be
lent, re-sold, hired out or otherwise circulated without the publisher's prior consent in any
form of binding or cover other than that in which it is published and without a similar
condition including this condition being imposed on the subsequent purchaser.

No part of this publication may be reproduced or transmitted in any form or by any means,
electronic or mechanical, including photocopying, recording or any information storage or
retrieval system, without either the prior permission in writing from the publisher or a
license, permitting restricted copying.

Printed by Bookmarque, Surrey, England

Distributed in UK by Turnaround Distribution
Unit 3, Olympia Trading Estate, Coburg Road, London N22 6TZ
Tel: 020 8829 3000
Fax: 020 8881 5088

Distributed in US by National Book Network,
15200 NBN Way, Blue Ridge Summit, PA 17214
Tel: 717 794 3800

ISBN 1-902934-29-6

ACKNOWLEDGEMENTS

The first people who Alex and Mark would like to acknowledge for their help with this work is each other. Ten years of friendship and respect made *Checkers* possible, helped along the way with lots of beer and the occasional cake.

Our families put up with us living in each other's pockets, our friends were pestered for their opinions as the work progressed, so they too must get a mention.

Mark would like to shove a pint of Wallop into the hands of the following people: Mim, Mike, Kyoto, Ted, Dug, Scott, J.M.H. and the General, along with the folks in the V.P.U. and Chaplaincy of H.M.P. Wormwood Scrubs, London.

Alex would like to thank Clive Banton, as well as the inmates of H.M.P. Wormwood Scrubs, London, and H.M.P. Highdown, Sutton.

Lastly, both Mark and Alex would like to thank P.C. Robin Short of Barking nick, Commander Brian Paddick of Lambeth nick, Dr. Burkhard Sonntag and Jimmy Mann for their technical assistance, Barking's Spotted Dog public house for the best beer in London, the real (and sadly deceased) Eddie Maynard for the inspiration, Joan Deitch for bringing us together all those years ago and Laura Susijn for not complaining about harebrained projects like this one. A friend must remain nameless who gave his insight into life in the R.A.M.C. (God bless 'em), and a thought must be spared for those misguided individuals from across the colour rainbow whose penchant for spreading disharmony and fear through the medium of race hate served as a sickening motivation to tell this story.

Other novels by Alex Wheatle:
Brixton Rock
East of Acre Lane
The Seven Sisters

DEDICATION

Mark and Alex would like to dedicate *Checkers* to all those who oppose the Death Penalty; particularly Dug, Scott, J.M.H. and the General.

We raise a glass to Dion.

Mark and Alex would like to assert that all events and characters in this work are purely fictional and that any similarities to real persons, either living or dead, are purely coincidental; except for in the case of Eddie Maynard, who really was the landlord of the Spotted Dog pub and killed by a train at Barking Station, but since this tragic event happened over one-hundred years ago, we don't think that he'll mind.

Prologue

There was only one good thing anyone ever said about Barking town centre, and that concerned the number and diversity of its public houses. It was said that if a drinker began his night out in the Captain Cook and was so inclined, he could crab-foot a drunken half circle around the dingy precinct and tilt at least eleven other hostelries without staggering any more than forty paces between each. Pawn brokers, bookies, games arcades and a pie and mash shop lined the belittered route, but if the drinker could abandon such retreats as the White Horse, Red Lion and Britannia and managed to toe-inch past the more-often-than-not puke-decorated Barking Station, the last post on the Barking pub crawl was the Spotted Dog Public House; residence and only legitimate business venture of Careful Eddie Maynard.

Dick Keating read the name on the awning above the pub and hoped that he'd made the right choice before he stepped inside. Part of him was almost delirious with the expectation of what he hoped to experience here, but there remained the small voice in his head that reminded him of the guilt that had always followed his past transgressions, along with the advice of his counsellors and fellow 'registered' paedophiles.

Inside the Spotted Dog it was dark and smoky, where the only sounds to be heard were the murmured conversations being held in its many discrete enclaves. There was no jukebox, no beeping fruit machines, and the sawdust that covered the floor dampened all but the most determined of footsteps.

Dick stepped across to the bar nervously, where he was confronted by a long-legged, brunette bar maid before he had the time to harbour any second thoughts.

"What's your poison?" she asked, her tone suggesting she was fed up about something.

"Ah - I'm here to see the manager," Dick mumbled, his face and gaze angled to the floor in the manner he always adopted when talking with adult females. "I have some fags to sell and… and…"

The bar maid cut him off. "I'll get him," she said, turning away, whereupon she took the stairs to Eddie's office and stuck her head around the door. "Eddie," she said, speaking like she was addressing her favourite uncle. "He's here."

"Thanks, Yvette, love."

Eddie Maynard was grey-haired, fat, fifty and hadn't tasted so much as a spoonful of porridge in any of Her Majesty's penitentiaries during his thirty years with the firms. He followed Yvette back into the main saloon and recognised Dick Keating without introductions. They were of an equal build and about the same age, although Dick's face looked slightly older; with stress lines and haunted eyes that belied a man used to living his life in fear. Well, Eddie realised, you got like that fast when you were doing bird as a child molester.

His own face showed no emotion as he waved for the man to follow him and he went back upstairs to his ramshackle office.

When they were inside and Eddie had closed the door behind them Dick offered a hand, but Eddie did not shake it. "Sit, Dick," he said in a gruff monotone.

Dick was used to doing as he was told, and right now was no exception. Eddie had already seated himself behind a large desk and was pouring two glasses of whisky from a large bottle that was supposed to be an optic for the bar.

"Our friend said I was to come tonight..." Dick managed to mumble, his chubby hands knitting his fingers together until they resembled a pack of loose sausages. "He said tonight was special and... and..."

"How long have you been out?" Eddie interrupted, getting straight to the point as he handed over a whisky.

"Six days."

"So you're out on Licence, which means your staying at a half-way hostel for men of your, er, *persuasion*?"

Dick sipped at his whisky and felt a warmth grow within his belly that went some way to calming his nerves. "Yeah, my parole officer and counsellor say I've got to stay there another eighteen months," he sighed, rolling the glass forwards and backwards with his palms. "They say that..."

"So you're on a curfew?"

"Yeah - Nine at night"

"And do you have an electronic tag or anything else I should know about?"

Dick pulled back his sleeves to show bare arms, then did the same with his trousers. "There ain't nothing on me," he said.

Careful Eddie Maynard nodded. "So who knows you're here?"

"No-one. I told the duty social worker at the hostel that I was going to..."

"And you're certain you weren't followed?"

"Erm - yeah, I'm pretty certain."

Eddie leant back in his chair and scrutinised Dick while he sipped at his drink. Had he worked out in the prison gym, he wondered? Unlikely, given his age and the nature of his crime. Guys like Dick weren't big on socialising at even the safest of places, and the prison gym was far from that; with the weights, metal bars and dozens of young, healthy men who were only too willing to forfeit some remission in exchange for performing every inmate's solemn duty to concave a nonce's head. So, all that weight he carried would just be blubber, Eddie told himself. Well, that was at least one point where the pair differed.

"So the fun is... er... *tonight*?" Dick asked, dragging Eddie back from his contemplation.

Eddie nodded. "You'll have to break your curfew," he admitted with the apologetic gesture of spread, open hands. "Still, I think it'll be worth it. Do you agree?"

A moment passed as a thousand small voices chorused in Dick's head; all warning him of the dangerous and *some* would say distasteful path he was about to rejoin, but drowning out the voices was one all consuming need and Dick knew that this need would be sated no matter how many voices, counsellors and parole officers shouted to the contrary.

"You're on," he said.

Thursday 29th of November, 2001; 04:30pm.

"I ain't working wid no blood claat white man," spat Ali, waving his huge hands to emphasise the point. His Nike baseball cap barely fitted his basketball-sized dome, so he took it off and threw it to the couch as a further indication of his displeasure.

Ali was as big as Mike Tyson, albeit not so muscular. Infant locks sprouted from his head and his narrow eyes seemed to expose a violent history. "Who's dis Careful Eddie, anyway?" Ali resumed, still gesturing mockingly with his hands. "And why'd he wanna rope in some rarse white gang from de east side?"

Professor K, who was sitting in an armchair with his legs crossed, studied Ali's massive frame and wished he had the intelligence to answer his own question. K was no more than five foot seven and he owned a face full of analytical energy that his rectangular glasses only added to. He only required the spectacles to drive, but wore them at all times. Mixing with the crew he needed any little confidence he could get and the glasses provided some fraction of it. "Because Eddie don't know us," he explained. "He's only given us the job because he's at a loss on finding a pilot. My guess is that Baron's the only Top Gun he could find."

K looked over to Baron, who was parked at a smoked glass coffee table constructing a seven paper, Mersh-grass spliff while he watched a Road Runner cartoon on a silent television. He was wearing a furry, black Kangol beret to cover the ugly scar that ran across his hairline and K once considered asking him about it, but decided it probably wasn't such a good idea. He didn't even want to think about how many men Baron had killed. Baron was taller than everybody in the room and the darkest. K guessed he had some Maroon blood in him, and he wouldn't have had to hear Baron's accent to establish he was one hundred per cent Jamaican - it was there in his lean face, especially those clinical eyes. Eyes that had witnessed too much and had now become immune to any feeling.

Colin X was lounging on the sofa with a sawn-off shotgun in his hands; its aim trained on the head of a Tupac Shakur poster that adorned the wall above him. His bald head reflected the sun as it shone through a cracked window and his shoulders displayed the results of endless work-outs in the prison gym. Colin had the type of face that seemed to be begging for an argument and his eyes were dark pools of disdain. It irked K that Colin tried to talk like a Jamaican when he was born in London and the nearest he had ever been to Jamaica was on a childhood family trip to Littlehampton. K recognised Colin's advantages though. On a few occasions, incidents reported by the hysterical media of yet another gun-related Yardie incident were in fact involving Colin, who was as British as anyone. Operation Trident won't find him with a suspect passport at Heathrow coming in from Jamaica, K thought.

"I'm wid Ali, man," Colin said. "Colin X nah work wid de devil." He trained his shotgun on the Road Runner. "Fucking pork-yamming swines, man. Since when de fuck 'ave we done a job for a focking white man, anyway? K, tell Eddie to fock himself, his wife an' his focking white bitch of a mudder. Eddie can look for anoder focking gang to do his shit."

Baron had finished gift-wrapping his joint, so he secured its end and shook it until the tobacco and herb mingled. Then he set his powerful gaze upon Colin X. "Let me tell yu somet'ing, yout'. Don't try an' speak fe me name, y'hear? Fockin' blood claat liberty. Who de fuck are yu fe speak 'bout do dis an' do dat?"

"I'm jus' sayin' me nah working wid no rarse pagan man," Colin retorted.

Baron ignited his spliff with a throwaway lighter and, upon digiting the remote control, he switched the television over to a wildlife programme. "If de dollars are sayin' somet'ing, me nuh gi' ah fuck inna whorehouse who me work wid. An' besides, me cyan work wid Eddie 'pon me own. Don't fockin' need nuh raas 'elp from yu brudders."

K stood up, checked his watch and joined Ali at the window where they both looked down from their 14th floor vantage point. Well, if Colin don't work on this job I'll enter it with Baron, K decided. Baron switched the T.V. channel back to the cartoons as Colin ran his right index finger along the length of his shotgun.

"We're talking four grand each for a day's work, and Eddie's courier will be here with the up-front payment of two grand," K reminded, trying to get over his point that the monetary gain outweighed the race issue. K checked his watch again. "He'll be here in ten minutes, so what am I gonna tell him? To take the money back?"

"Four grand, yeah?" Colin thought about it. "An' all we 'ave to do is escort a liccle plane wid Baron flying it somewhere? Where does dis Eddie gangster want de shit to be taken? An' where does de plane land?"

K gazed out of the window once more and took in the ugly skyline of South London. The grey tower blocks resembled broken teeth. I *have* to escape from this place, he willed himself before stating: "Eddie will phone and tell us when the courier gets confirmation."

"An' what about dis gang from de east sides?" queried Ali, moving from the window and joining Colin on the couch.

"We'll know more in ten minutes or so," K answered.

Baron had smoked enough of his spliff to make his eyes redden. He threw his head back so he could focus on the ceiling then examined his smoke as it dragon-danced around him. "Me nuh business wha' yu do, but as fe me, me teking de raas appetiser, an' de pay off. Char, boom boom claat! Me cyan do dis mission 'pon me own."

"You wouldn't last a fucking tea break," laughed Ali, rubbing a hand across his vast belly. "When your back is turned for one second, dem swine 'ead white man will mek your back look like a tea strainer wid der gun an' shit."

"Yeah, man," Colin concurred. "You might as well 'ave a rarse target 'pon your back."

Baron inhaled mightily on his spliff by way of a response. "Rubbish yu ah talk!" he dismissed. "De same t'ing might gwarn if me work wid you bredrin. Me nuh trus' any mon, nuh even me own black mon. Nuff ah dem fock me up in de past. Yu nuh know 'ow nuff black yout' fire 'pon each uder dese days fe nutten!"

There was a knock at the door so K went to see who it was while Colin hid the shotgun underneath two cushions. "Look like de courier reach," grinned Colin. "We should tek de money anyway an' don't do de rarse job."

"Are you fucking sick?" berated Ali. "From what I hear of him, Careful Eddie will 'ave de whole of de fucking east sides after us an' dey got some serious hardware; all kinda gun an' shit."

"Yeah, mon, ah true dat," interrupted Baron. "An' der more low profile dan de Yardie dem. Black yout' nuh care who der-'bout 'pon street when dey fire dem gun. An' dem idiot man waan everyone to sight it. Show off dem ah show off."

Colin, Ali and Baron assembled near the doorway to see if it was the courier who had arrived, but were disappointed when they saw K return with two boxes of hot pizza. "Raas claat. Ah Eddie sen' us dinner?" Baron inquired.

"No," K answered. "This lot is Ali's. He ordered it before you arrived."

Ali finger-wrestled the lining of a pocket until it gave up a crumpled bunch of bank notes that he used to pay K for the pizzas, then he returned to the sofa all wet tongued and expectant. "It better 'ave no swine 'pon de top of it,' he stated sourly. "If it has I'm gonna concuss dat delivery bwai permanently."

"Give me some of dat rarse pizza," Colin demanded.

"If you want a cut, you gimmi two pound."

"Fock you, you craven shit. You ever 'ear 'bout hip, batty an' t'igh diet?"

"You're always yamming my food, man. Buy your fucking own."

Colin delved into his pockets and found some loose change. He threw it over to Ali who was sampling the food. "One pound fifty is all me 'ave. Gi' you de rest later."

Baron tossed a pair of pound coins in Ali's direction. "Cut me some ah dat pizza, mon. Me belly ah tickle me."

The front door clapped again so K returned to the short hallway, opened the door and was confronted by a helmeted man in leathers. He had a brown envelope in his gloved right hand. "Tony, right?" K asked. When the man nodded K ushered him into the lounge, where he observed Ali, Colin X and Baron devouring a pizza as a pride of lions gorges upon zebra. Apprehension seeped into his mind. *Yardies*, he thought. *Fucking hell!*

The courier wrenched off his helmet to reveal a blond head. He had a blotchy face and was tall enough to play in goal for Manchester United. He sat in a vacant chair opposite Baron. "What's the story, mate?" he asked, his accent betraying his Australian origin. "Is everything set your end?"

K searched the faces of his gang. Colin was ignoring the courier; preferring, instead, to watch a Tom and Jerry cartoon that had just started. Ali seemed more interested in crocodiling his meal, but suddenly he glanced up and nodded. Baron was carefully re-lighting his three quarter smoked spliff as he surveyed the courier. "Wha' kinda bike yu 'ave? Yu 'ave ah Ninja?"

"Nah, Suzuki."

"It's affirmative," confirmed K, who had noticed Ali's agreeable nod. I have to remember this next time, he noted. If I want Colin to do something, I'll have to sweet up Ali about it beforehand. Get him on board first.

The courier rose to his feet. "Eddie will phone you as soon as he hears from me, and he'll fill you in about the job and where to meet the other crew."

"Hol' on, hol' on," checked Colin. "Before you go, I wanna see a whole 'eap of Queen 'eads."

Tony presented the brown envelope to K and excitement filled his head as he felt the crispness of the money inside. This is the reason why I put up with this lot, he told himself. Just do this last job and I'm out of *this* country. He ravaged the package to reveal three wads of used money bound by elastic bands. The Queen's head on the twenty and fifty pound notes were all facing upwards and K realised the truth of what was said about Careful Eddie; he was a neat and tidy man. He began to count the cash and his crew joined him, adding in their heads.

"Yeah, safe. It's two grand alright."

"Right, I'm done," said the courier, heading for the door. K followed him.

Ali returned to the window; his eyes feasting over the whole of South London and bits of pizza stretching from his mouth, while Colin set the shooter's gaze on a framed picture of Malcolm X that was hung on the wall behind Baron. Baron didn't seem to notice, his attention having returned to where Tom was receiving a severe beating from Butch the dog while Jerry watched, laughing.

They all heard the front door shut and moments later K returned with a glass of orange juice in his hand. "Right," he said. "Let's hope Eddie 'phones quick; I wanna catch the library to pay my fine."

As Colin shook his head, the telephone rang.

Thursday 29th of November, 2001; 05:00pm.

"I tell yah, man. I wouldn't think twice about wasting some cunt what was daft enough to get in my way," the youngest of the trio said. "Gimme a shooter and they're wasted, absolutely fuckin' wasted. Zero fuckin' tolerance I have for people what get in my way."

The man sitting opposite him leant across the beer-puddled table and dropped his vocal tone so that only those who sat around him could hear: "We're in Eddie's fuckin' pub, Lee. Keep that shit to yourself."

"No, Danny – fuck him. Fuck everybody. I don't give a shit what anyone thinks. If Eddie sends in the firm because I speak me mind in his pub, then they're fuckin' wasted too."

Lee was slim and sporting a blond crew cut that made him appear even younger than his barely twenty years. His D.M.'s displayed blue laces while his olive-green bomber jacket was a vexed advert proclaiming to all his fanatical political bias.

Patches and badges covered his sleeves and chest; inciting all who beheld them to join in the imminent race war, while his shoulder-worn swastika informed all to which side they should rally.

Danny, in his mid-thirties and of a slim build, had long ago perfected the art of cautious sideways glances. He used this skill now to scan the clientele of the pub, his mop-top brown hair hardly stirring as he did so. Satisfied that no-one was heeding the youngster's words, he turned his gaze and locked it upon Davie; the only member of the crew who was near his own age. A look of understanding passed between them that said let the boy spout his shit, no-one in the pub would bother to pay attention, then their ineffable discourse was broken as Matt, the fourth member of their party, returned with some drinks: two pints of Wallop for the Jones boys, a Guinness for Danny and a still water for Davie.

"I wish Eddie would hurry up," Matt complained as he sat down beside Lee. Matt looked older than Lee despite being two years his junior; his face wore a haunted expression constantly and his hooded, pin-ball eyes emphasised his nervous disposition.

Davie shook a pill from a bottle, swallowed it, then tracked it down with a gulp of water. He looked at the crew around him to show he didn't want to be questioned about this ritual. "Eddie's your old man's friend, Lee. You shouldn't talk of him that way," he said, coughing at the bitter taste of the Benperidol. "He'd also blow your face off if he found out, and your dad couldn't do sweet Fanny Adams about it."

"Have you worked with him before, then?" Matt asked quietly as he glanced around the pub.

Both Davie and Danny nodded. "He's a good boss," Danny informed him, "but he's *waaaay* too cautious. Eddie wouldn't put a pound on a one horse race. Then again, maybe that's what makes him a good boss. It's certainly why they call him Careful Eddie. He keeps everything on a need-to-know basis until the job is ready; then he dishes out the info just before it kicks off."

"Yeah, you kids are about to hit the big league now, you know, rubbing shoulders with the likes of Eddie Maynard," Davie added. "We ain't going to knock over some late-night Seven

Eleven for a few quid. If Eddie Maynard sets you a job you know you're in for some serious work and some serious readies."

"You never know," Danny went on. "If this job comes off kosher he may even put some more business your way. If Eddie thinks you're loyal he makes sure you're kept well oiled." Danny knew this last statement wasn't exactly true, but felt some reassurance about the job in hand was required.

"When do we get the shooters?" Lee asked eagerly.

Danny went to tell him to shut up, but stopped as an endlessly tall man wearing bike leathers approached and leant into their shadowed booth. "Eddie's ready," he stated in a hazy Australian drawl.

Lee and Matt rose first, but the tall man raised a hand to halt them. "He only wants to see Danny. The rest of you stay put."

A hateful scowl betrayed Lee's anger at being left out of the briefing, but Davie's hand gripped his elbow and pulled him back to his seat. "Do as Tony says," he commanded. "You'll learn that way."

Danny said nothing as he rose and followed Tony across the spit and sawdust, through to the back of the bar and up a staircase that led to Eddie's store-room-come-office.

Eddie was parked behind his battered M.F.I. desk leafing through the results of a recent stock take and smiled when Danny entered. "Danny-boy," he intoned good-naturedly. "The pipes, the pipes are calling."

Danny took a seat and mirrored the smile nervously. I haven't seen the fat boy *this* happy before a job, he noted. "What tune are they playing?" he asked.

"Oh, a sweet one, Danny. You'll think it's the angels."

"In that case, I can't wait to hear them and neither can my boys. Speaking of which; they wanna know why they ain't up here too."

Eddie sat back in his chair and pulled a face. "He who pays the piper calls the tune, Danny-boy. You'll find out why if you let me get a word in."

Danny plucked a packet of Bensons from his jacket, took one out, lit it, then used its filter to indicate zipping his mouth. He was glad that Eddie wanted to do all the talking, because the less he spoke the less chance Eddie had of noticing that he was more than a little wary of being left alone with him. I hope he hasn't got something else for me to do on my own.

"Okay. Are you sitting comfortably?" Eddie asked as he adjusted the hearing aid that served as a reminder of a kick-in he'd received in the Sixties. "Then I'll begin. Imagine, Danny-boy, you've heard that some crew have been using a beat-up old sky-bucket to smuggle in some top quality merchandise to our beloved home counties and that you knew when the next drop was gonna be. What would you do?"

"That depends. Who are the firm?"

"That's the beauty of it, Danny-boy. There ain't no firm. I've checked all over London and even with those hay-chewin' tossers in Kent and none of them have a handle on these guys. It would appear they're flying solo."

"So if we paid them a visit, there'd be no come-back?"

"Exactly."

Danny puffed on his cigarette and watched as the smoke snake-charmed upwards to engulf a shelf laden with boxed beer-mats and other brewery sundries. With no firm to protect them it would be like stealing a mobile phone from a nine year old, he reasoned, but then he thought of the necessity for two crews and realised there must be a catch. "Why the South London muscle?" he asked.

"I'm getting to that part," Eddie told him; fiddling with the hearing aid once more. "It would appear that my source; a Yid who goes by the name of Harry Green; has been getting leant on by this crew who've been using his farm like fuckin' Heathrow over the last couple of months. Any road, he wants them stopped and says the contents of the plane are for whoever does the stopping."

Eddie paused, stared out of the window for a time, then continued: "Here's the catch. Old Rabbi-chops can't be left with a fuckin' hot aircraft on his plot, so the deal is that the bastard's gotta be shifted too. Savvy?"

"Yep, I follow. But I can't see how we'd do it, unless you're offering us a crash course in the arts of flying planes... In which case, you'll have the F.B.I. sniffing our arses like we're bin Laden's bum chums."

Eddie always enjoyed Danny's humour and smiled generously. "Well, to get that side of things sorted I had to go to a mate of mine called Elizabeth Richardson who helps organise jobs for the lads south of the water."

"Elizabeth? A bird running a firm?"

"Nah, Liz is a bloke, but it's a long story," Eddie laughed. "Anyway, Liz told me of a crew down Brixton way who have a fly-boy in their ranks. I've enlisted them to work on the project."

"Brixton?" Fuck me, Danny thought. Is Eddie chancing his toes in unfamiliar waters? This could go wrong.

"Yeah, Brixton."

"These guys, they wouldn't be - er - *blacks*, would they?" Danny knew it was the silliest question he had asked in a while.

"As they're from Brixton, there could be a slight chance, Danny-boy."

"But… but, Eddie. Christ, why didn't you say so before? Have you met Lee Jones? He wouldn't talk to a coloured if his life depended on it, and this is his first job. I was hoping to ease him in slowly."

"Exactly, Danny-boy, exactly. That's why I pulled your crew in for the job. I heard that Alan Jones had asked you to take his kid into your crew after he and Wayne got sent down for that job. Stupid bastards. I told them not to do it. I also heard that his boy is going through a fuckin' stupid Nazi phase or some such Nationalist shit. Anyhow, you know me, Danny. I'll work with anybody who'll do the job and keep his gob stapled, whether he be black, white or fuckin' sky-blue-pink. I don't give a shit. Unless, of course, it affects business – or he's a shirt-lifter."

Eddie paused and almost shivered as he uttered the last words; scratching at his lager-abused belly as though this would somehow purge the air of his mentioning bad business and homosexuality. He then concluded his monologue with a statement: "Tony tells me there are two youngsters downstairs," he said.

Danny nodded. "I replaced Wayne with a kid called Matt; he's Lee's cousin. He's only just twenty, but he should learn fast enough. Alan writ me that he's smart."

"That makes me edgy, Danny. One kid in the team can be looked after, but two? Why didn't you pick someone a bit older and more established?"

"You know how I like to work, Eddie. I'm set in my ways. Davie and I have worked together so often we both know what to do and with these youngsters, well, they'll get taught my way 'cos they won't know no better. Know what I mean? I mean, I won't have to keep telling them to fuck off when they spout shit like: this is how we did it when we blah, blah fuckin' blah, 'cos there won't be no blah, blah fuckin' blah."

"And of course Alan will always be around to kick their arse if they don't toe the line."

"Well, as much as he can kick arse now that he's at our dear Majesty's pleasure. He won't sniff the dog shit in Barking 'til Prince William's a grandad."

Both men succumbed to a maudlin silence and looked out of the window to the trains leaving Barking Station as they thought of their erstwhile colleague.

"Anyhow, it's because you have Alan's boy under your wing that I thought of you for the job," Eddie stated.

Danny chugged on his Benson before speaking. "How so?" he asked.

"Well, apart from the fact that we both owe Alan big-style, it's because I heard about his boy getting in with that National Front mob. Now I ain't never worked with these African boys before, so I don't trust 'em as far as I could spit 'em. However, I need 'em because of the fly-boy, so what do I do? I'll tell you what I decided. I decided to pair 'em up with another crew – to baby-sit 'em, like, and more importantly, to pair 'em up with a crew what I could trust one hundred percent."

"You know me, Eddie."

"Sure I do, and you know I think you're diamond – and Davie for that matter, but with this fuckin' Nazi as well? We're sorted."

"How'd you reckon?"

"I see it like this: no matter how much money these Africans wave under his nose to do a dirty on us he ain't gonna do Jack Shit. He's young, see? He believes all that N.F. bollocks, and idealism makes a prick of a man – especially a boy. On top of that, he'll be so fucked up with hate for the South London crew that he'll have his eyes on them like Elvis clocking a burger, so if they try anything funny he'll be the first to know."

"You mentioned we'd be getting tooled. How much heat are we expecting?"

"Fuck knows. The guys ain't in no known firm, remember? Who knows what they'll be packing? But I tell you one thing - if I was bringing in that much gear I'd make sure I was well tooled - very well tooled indeed."

Danny leant forward over the desk and steepled his fingers. "And how many notches on the barrels?" he asked.

"Danny, Danny, Danny - you'd think I'd shit on you?" Eddie gasped, feigning shock. "None of the hardware has been used on any jobs before. I'm a careful man - you know that - and that's why I want them back. It's the only way I can guarantee they're disposed of properly."

Danny wondered why he had asked, knowing of Eddie's reputation. He also reasoned that Eddie was now probably the proud owner of a consignment of Heckler and Koch firearms that had been swiped from Barking Container Base the previous month. "In that case; when can I pick them up?"

"You can leave with them. The South London boys have theirs already - you know how their type like to play with guns - fuckin' idiots, have you heard how they're all killing each other? The way they're carrying on there won't be a black face in sight come twenty years and they're so indiscreet they might as well pose with their shooters for the tabloids... Anyway, you've gotta take 'em now. After all, the job is tonight."

"What the hell?"

"That's why I called all the crew in when I only wanted to talk to you. Tony's down there right now giving them the M.O. for tonight; and the South London boys have been given their instructions and are already on their way over."

"For fuck's sake, Eddie. That's cutting it a bit fine even by your standards."

"These guys we're jackin' ain't Securicor, Danny, with a shiny, typed-up schedule and shit. I knew the job was coming up, but couldn't get confirmation from Harry until this afternoon. I ain't no fuckin' Mystic Meg - bless the powder on her face."

"And your source is clean?"

"Stand on me, Danny-boy. Of course he is, and that's why I called you up here alone, 'cos I don't want no other bugger to know who he is and go blabbing. The only reason I'm dropping his name in your shell-like is so you know I ain't setting you up with no grass or ponce or nothing. Fuck, if I told every crew member what was going on, my jobs'd go pear-shaped quicker than a wop in a pasta shop."

Danny understood the reasons why Eddie wouldn't want Lee and Matt to know the name and origin of his source, but was agitated that Davie had not been included in their meeting. "Screw the kids, but what about Davie?" he demanded, his frustration overriding his fear of the firm. "I don't like leaving him out of it, Eddie."

"Look, Danny-boy. Davie's all messed up – we know that," Eddie replied in a fatherly tone. "I mean, it's shitty what's happening to him and everything, but it means he ain't got his full quota of cards no more. Sure I trust him in the crew, but since the syndrome kicked in... well, you know what I mean. Maybe we'll see him sorted once the job's over – get him bunged into a nice clinic surrounded by nice fields where pretty nurses can molly-coddle him and give him a few tests or something - but until then we can't trust his marbles to stay in the bag."

Danny's anger intensified at Eddie's discussing his friend in such blunt terms, but he knew that business was business. The pills and the syndrome made Davie fuzzy around the edges and, as such, the intricacies of the job were better left to a keener, more stable mind. "We'll sort him out afterwards," was all that he managed.

"Good man. I knew you'd understand," Eddie said in a conciliatory manner. "Now on with the plan."

Eddie produced an A-Z from a desk drawer and leafed through it until he found the page he was looking for. "Right," he said. "This is the job: two crews, four cars, two sawn-offs and two pistols. It'll be a bit of a notion for our South London gents, seeing as they're more used to Uzis and Kalashnikovs... I want three men from each crew to drive here," Eddie indicated a deserted area on the Isle of Sheppey near Harty with a stubby, nicotine-stained finger. "Harry tells me the plane is always met by a pick-up car with two blokes in it and this is your first obstacle. Find it and take 'em out of the picture. The fourth member of each crew will drive to here," Eddie pointed again, this time to the Isle of Grain, which was a short way across the Thames estuary. "Once you've dealt with the pick-up car and jacked the plane two of you dump the cars somewhere well away from our Mr. Green. One from each crew, right? The rest of you get in the plane and fly it to... here, on the Isle of Grain where the other cars will be waiting. And don't for Christ's sake get outnumbered on the plane. Two of you, the fly-boy and whoever they want to hold his hand, Okay? Once you've unloaded the stuff into the cars meet Tony at my lock-up and hand over the guns along with the merchandise."

"Is that the lot?"

"There's one other thing. You might want to torch the plane. Better for fingerprints, but it could cut down on your time for getting clear. What do you reckon?"

"Davie could sort that out – you know how he likes to burn things."

"Has he got the stuff with him?"

"He doesn't need to. He puts that shit together out of B&Q. We'll make a stop on the way."

"Right, that's it, then. I'll see you back here after you've been to the lock-up. As long as I'm happy, you get the rest of your money then."

"Sorted," Danny smirked as he ground out his cigarette on a chipped Guinness ashtray.

"Sorted," Eddie agreed.

Danny rose and prepared to leave, but was stopped with a last remark from Eddie. "Tony tells me your young Fascist is wearing his colours downstairs," he stated. "If that's true, tell him to get changed before the Africans get here; I don't get paid to be no Henry fuckin' Kissinger – Tony will lend him a jacket – and, for the future, tell him to keep that shit outa my pub."

Thursday 29th of November, 2001; 05:15pm.

"Why can't dey come an' collect us," queried Ali, squeezing into the front passenger seat of K's Polo.

"'Cos the place where the party's swinging is closer to Barking than South London," answered K. "Besides, we've got to pick up the cars. No way I'm using *my* wheels."

Ali nodded then satisfied himself with a packet of smokey bacon crisps.

K pulled away once Colin X and Baron had made themselves comfortable in the back; heading for Camberwell. Busta Rhymes' *Get High Tonight* blasted from the car stereo and Ali bobbed his head in time with the beat while Baron tried to capture sleep. Colin contented himself with glaring at the driver behind him. The overhead clouds were ill-tempered, threatening a deluge, and a hostile wind forced pedestrians to walk with squinted eyes.

"So which way you heading, K?" asked Colin.

"Through Peckham and Deptford, up through Charlton way. Then go through the Blackwall Tunnel."

"Peckham," enthused Ali. "Bwai, dat brings back memories, innit, Colin?"

"Yeah, when was it? Summer ninety-two? When I dealt wid Kangolman?"

Ali bellowed an ugly laugh that was made worse by the crisps he had in his mouth. "He jus' weren't expecting it, was he? Right outside de hot chicken take-away. His own mudder couldn't 'ave recognised him."

"He made a serious shit of a mess on de window, innit, an' in my friggin face, man. I 'ad to rinse it after dat shit, wiping away bits of his rarse face. Bloodclaat, who gives ah fock, he was one ugly brudder anyway. De so-called Yardies got de blame for dat shit as well," Colin smirked.

"Yeah, you remember the local papers: *Yardie Gun War*. And as for Kangolman's face. It kinda reminded me of an undercooked pizza."

"You're focking gross, man. 'Ow can you compare his fucked-up face to a rarse claat pizza?"

"Dat's what it looked like to me… Yeah, try an' t'ink 'bout dose pizzas wid dose black things on it."

"Olives," corrected K, disliking the conversation. Sometimes he wondered if Colin and Ali were in this game just for the kicks and *not* the money. He would love to tell them they were just a couple of braggers, but he knew he would never do so. What he did know was that if they implicated him in any criminal deed by their loose talk he would set them up for the Police like a row of skittles.

K drove past Camberwell Green, checking his wing mirror and trying to mask his humour of the fact that Ali was munching *Smokey Bacon* crisps. Uneducated fool!

"It weren't jus' blood dat came out, was it?" Ali resumed. "Der were sort of… bits."

"Kangolman 'ad it coming, man. Rarted cheek of 'im, 'bout he's bruking into my lock-up an' teking my Crispies."

"Crispies?" K wondered. "What's that?"

"K, man. You got to sniff de streets more often an' get your backside out of your books. Rice Crispies, you know the cereal, snap crackle an' pop? Crackle? Does it ding a rarse bell? Crack?"

"Oh yeah. That's kinda smart for you guys." Especially *you* guys, he wanted to add.

"Fuck you," munched Ali.

"Zip your blood-claat beaks, mon," Baron decreed. "Yu cyan't see dat me trying fe ketch ah sleep?"

"I could arrange fe Ali to gi' you ah right-hander," laughed Colin.

"Yu try an' touch me face wid your big paw an' see me don't tek me Stanley knife an' etch yu cheekbone!"

"Backside," cooled Colin. "You Yardie man 'ave no sense of 'umour."

Ali kept quiet, not wanting to test the Jamaican's temperament.

K entered Peckham and Ali laughed as they went by the hot chicken take-away, while Colin continued to scowl at the miserable-looking people they passed. Spots of rain appeared on K's windscreen. A slow-walking African woman nearly got run over by a tint-windowed Saab.

Ali had started on his second bag of crisps by the time they reached Deptford.

"Don't your mother feed you at home?" K queried.

"Yeah. Shit, I forget to ding her an' tell 'er I won't reach home 'till late. She's gonna kill me."

Colin laughed out loud, disturbing Baron once again, so he kissed his teeth and closed his eyes; leaning his head against the window.

"Your mudder's rough, innit," commented Colin. "She cusses like a Brixton fishwife. No wonder your fader made his departure. If I know how she stay, she's gonna blast your ears when you reach 'ome in de morning. An' don't boder say you was out wid me. You know she don't like me from time, blaming me for you ending up inna jailhouse."

"Yeah, it's dat," Ali concurred. "She come up de school once an' lick up a teacher to rarted, an' to dis day I dunno why. Don't fuck wid my mudder."

"So you've never left home?" wondered K, driving through Blackheath.

"Only when I've been inna jailhouse."

K shook his head; thinking it's not right for a man over thirty to live at home. Colin went back to his passion of staring out other motorists.

It was dark when K entered the Blackwall tunnel. He checked his mirror above him to steal a glance at Baron and found he was sleeping fitfully. The Fugees' *Ready Or Not* rapped out from the stereo. Oblivious to his surroundings, Ali began to devour a melting Mars bar that he had found in his name-brand anorak. "Forgot 'bout dis, bought it dis-morning," he exclaimed. "Could do wid a Pepsi to wash it down, though."

After emerging out of the Blackwall tunnel, K turned right onto the A13. The Millennium Dome, looking like a gigantic grey ladybird receiving a course of acupuncture, was momentarily visible between the gaps of various buildings.

"What a waste of money *that* was," remarked K, hoping for a proper conversation. Something he could debate about. "Could've built all sorts of useful things rather than that eyesore. I for one am glad I never went there. Think of the schools and hospitals, man!"

The rest of K's crew failed to comment, opting to give each other curious glances.

Twenty-five minutes later, K, after consulting his brand new A-Z twice, had reached the Spotted Dog in central Barking. "I'm parking on a side road," he announced. "No way I'm parking right next to the pub. Colin, grab the exterminators from the boot and *don't* unzip the bag. Baron, *wake up*, man. We're here."

Baron opened his eyes, focused, then observed K turning past an abandoned cinema and into a terraced street. K parked behind a B.M.W. then turned to his crew. "I know you lot don't frequent these parts often. Basically, be suspicious of everyone, keep a good watch, and remember they are not friends nor ever will be. This is just a money thing, pure and simple. Have that in mind when this white crew show themselves."

"You're too right der," Baron agreed. "But yu t'ink me 'fraid of dem?"

"We'll walk in two at a time," K advised. "It'll look too obvious that something is going down if we all walk in together. *Capish*?"

"Yeah, dat makes sense," Colin agreed. "Me an' Ali go first. An' if any pagan man look like der twitching to use somet'ing, den dey are gonna fart 'cos dey don't know me's as fast as Clint Eastwood."

"Stop your bragga," cussed Baron. "Yu t'ink bullet cyan't trouble yu cah yu blast ah nobody? Carry on dem way an' see dat bullet don't ketch yu bombaclaat."

"Stop your arguing, man," soothed K. "Remember - think *money*."

Colin collected the holdall that contained the arms from the boot of the car and set off towards the rendezvous with Ali. K and Baron slouched on the car, tasting the East London air, before starting for the pub themselves.

Colin entered the pub first with Ali close behind him. Before heading to the bar, where they both recognised the towering figure of Tony, they took stock of their surroundings. There was no music, not even a jukebox, Colin noted. Arcade games were another feature missing from this particular pub. Not like a South London drinking hole, Ali thought. All they could hear were the mutterings of the clientele and the chinking of glasses. Colin then spotted four men huddled together in a shadowy alcove towards the rear of the pub; their furtive glances in their direction suggesting that they were the other crew. Ali noticed that one of the younger crew members was staring at him so he returned the glare defiantly, but before the eye-ball battle grew too intense Tony had come around from the bar and presented himself to the South Londoners.

"Where's your fly-boy?" he greeted, scanning the entrance.

"Don't worry yourself, man," Colin replied. "He soon come."

"Can I get you two a drink? On the house, as they say in England."

"Yeah," nodded Colin, answering for Ali as well. "Hol' us two lagers."

"No worries."

K and Baron entered the pub as Tony, Colin and Ali reached the bar, but, after little more than a few steps, K looked down at his name-brand trainers and noticed the floor's sawdust had taken up residence on his soles. He cursed venomously. It was not like this on *his* side of the river. "Do you want to try the house speciality?" offered Tony congenially when he and Baron joined them. "It's called *Wallop*, really popular drink around here, mate."

Ali and Colin nodded, but Baron ignored the barman and flamed a cigarette. K studied the East London crew and came to the conclusion that the slender blond one might prove a problem; his eyes were full of hate, not your normal hate, but a kind of hate deeply entrenched. "I'll have an orange juice," K instructed, superiority in his voice. He lifted his head a little and stood up to his full height, wanting the patrons of this place to read his body language and conclude that *he's* in charge.

Tony tried to grab Baron's attention, but Baron was examining his smoke kiting towards the ceiling. "What can I get your friend?"

"Nothing," answered K. "If he wanted something he would have ordered it. Besides, he's working machinery tonight."

Tony served the drinks then disappeared somewhere behind the bar, while Ali hailed Yvette the brunette barmaid and bought a packet of cheese and onion crisps; his hate for white people momentarily forgotten as he appreciated the curve of her backside. "Hey, sweetness, what should I call you?" he asked lustily, waving a crumpled twenty in his hand as though it was a mating signal.

"Unobtainable," came the coquettish reply. "But everyone else around here calls me Yvette."

From beside him, Colin scrutinised the East London crew scornfully as K sipped at his orange juice; spying the amount of cigarettes the other gang were smoking. Nerves, he thought, then he realised that he shouldn't be so condescending since he wasn't feeling so fresh himself. He stole another look and white trash almost whispered from his mouth.

K returned his attention to his companions, who were laughing at a tale Baron was relating concerning his former life back in Jamaica, and once his back was turned Lee felt free to jab an accusatory finger in their direction. "I tell ya - he's fuckin' lucky we're doing the same fuckin' job, otherwise I'd waste the dark one what's trying to stare me out," he insisted.

"Keep your gob shut," commanded Danny, lipping the head of his Guinness. "You've got a lot to learn." Danny now wished he wasn't so loyal to Alan, Lee's father.

"Yeah, you have," agreed Davie. "You ain't going to ruin my chances of earning some serious readies... I wonder which one is the fly-boy."

"Can't be the fat one," answered Matt with feigned joviality. He ran a nervous hand through his lank, dark hair. "Look at the size of him. He could never sit in a pilot's seat. And if he travels in the plane he might get that deep bone thromb-what-you-call-it."

"I bet his old girl's one of those big mommas," laughed Lee.

Danny thumped his pint down on the table to symbolise a full stop to their conversation. "You two young herberts wanna serve us up a little race riot, or something?" he berated. "If you can't talk sense, then keep your fuckin' gills still."

Lee and Matt recognised that Danny would take no more of their chat, so they concentrated on their pints while continuing to fish-eye the other crew.

Tony reappeared and stopped by the black gang, who he then brought across to Danny and his companions. "Alright, mates," he said, wielding a plastic smile. "Meet your fellow flight attendants on Blagger Airlines. K, this is Danny, Lee, Matt and Davie. Guys, this is K, Ali, Colin and Baron, our very own Bomber Harris."

The eight men exchanged handshakes like boxers touching gloves and after a few rounds of uneasy silence Davie chose to speak. "We hear from Eddie that you're a top notch crew," he said, having heard nothing of the sort. "I feel safe working with you."

"Yeah – better wid you dan against you," Colin told him.

Now that they were close, K scrutinised the other crew. The blond one looked even more unhinged than he had appeared at a distance, his eyes thin slits of disdain and his mouth set into a tight, mirthless line. The other youngster had made a wall of his fellow crew-members between himself and the South Londoners as though he feared he'd catch something, while the older men were trying to make a brave face of it. One was offering cigarettes around and K appreciated the comment Davie had made about feeling safe, knowing it for the perfectly calculated, deliberate line that it was, and knew that he was the one to turn to should trouble arise between the crews.

While the two crews chatted; the East Londoners only catching a word of each sentence that Baron spoke, Tony finalised the plans and then returned to where they stood. "Okay, mates," he twanged in his smooth, Australian rhythm. "Time for work. Just to recap the route. Drivers, head to the M25 and go over the Dartford crossing. Take a left onto the A2 and look out for the A249, which takes you to Sheppey. If any probs, follow the other lot. Now, I know you don't know each other, but try to keep in touch on the road, especially Colin and

Danny. You'll find mobile phones in the glove compartment of each car – chipped, naturally, and we'll want them back. The other crew's phone number is speed-dialled hash-one. Each crew's pick-up car is speed-dial hash-two. K, Matt, happy? Know where you're going?"

Both men nodded so Tony made a vague directional gesture with his arms.

"Your motors are outside. Head right when you come outa the pub and take the first left. K, you've got the red Sierra and, Colin, you're the light Cavalier. Lee, you've got the Nissan and, Matt, you've got the Rover. Now get out there and I'll see you in a sec with the keys."

The two crews downed their drinks then left the pub. Outside they were met by rioting wind and horizontal rain. They found the cars parked bumper to nose. "Put on your gloves," ordered K.

A minute of uncomfortable silence followed until they saw Tony jogging towards them while attempting to pull an anorak over his head. "Give us de keys, man," Colin insisted. "You wan' me to catch a rarse cold before I get a job done?"

"Yu t'ink dis weder is rough," Baron laughed. "Yu waan see de rain inna Jamaica when hurricane come."

Lee looked at Colin with oblique eyes, but was fascinated by Baron's Jamaican patois. Monkey talk.

Tony passed on the keys to the drivers then handed a crisp twenty pound note to Davie. "That's to cover the shopping," he said. "Eddie wants to make sure you do a real neat job."

"Don't you mean a right messy one?" laughed Lee. "From what I hear off my old man, Davie here can blow just about anything to Kingdom fuckin' Come."

Vinegar glances from both crews indicated that Lee should not talk shop outside, but he was saved from a dressing down from Danny when Tony said: "Just get in the fuckin' car."

"Hey - has the wheels got a stereo?" Colin X demanded before stepping into the driver's seat.

Tony nodded as Ali and Baron followed Colin into the Vauxhall. The East London crew's Nissan was parked on the other side of the road and Lee clambered, scowling, into its driver's seat while thieving glances across the road. K climbed into the Sierra that would serve as the South Londoner's pick-up car, studying Matt, who was the other pick-up driver, in his dripping wing mirror. The East London crew pulled away first, pursued by Colin, and as K shifted into first gear he wondered why Eddie was using two inexperienced boys to do a man's job. He'd have to box with tactics and gauge the other men's strengths, he realised. After all, he didn't want to get knocked out in the first round.

Thursday 29th of November, 2001; 07:30pm.

By the time the two crews had crossed the aged, lever bridge that led to the windswept, estuarine Isle of Sheppey, both Danny and Davie were tired of Lee's maniacal rants. "I mean, for fuck's sake, man," the youngster complained; having abandoned his Combat 18 ensemble for a black bomber jacket that was too big for him and a ski hat. "Why the fuck didn't you tell me we were workin' with fuckin' niggers? Banana munchin' fuckin' retards. Cunts. I mean, they're bound to screw the job up, ain't they? Too fuckin' busy thinking about their coon baby-mothers and ways to fiddle the Benefits. I'm surprised the big momma's son didn't try and rape Yvette! You see his eyes all over her?"

Danny shook his head, but Davie leant forward and tapped Lee on his shoulder with a map. "And what about you, grasshopper? We ain't gonna need nappies now, are we?"

Lee's face flushed red with rage and he attempted to draw attention back to the South Londoners and away from himself by venting forth another fresh tirade, but Danny's raised hand prevented him from doing so. Danny had been trying to relax by focusing his attention upon the rain that rapped against the windows and the gentle swoosh, swoosh, swoosh of the windscreen wipers, but it was impossible to do anything when Lee had something to prove. "Just keep your eyes on the road,

Lee," he admonished quietly, clearly exasperated. He decided that this journey would be the furthest he would ever go in a car with Lee. "So long as they get the job done," he answered finally.

To hinder Lee's discourse Danny slapped home the tape that was jutting out of the car's cassette player and was relieved when he heard that the erstwhile owner of their stolen Nissan had nurtured similar musical tastes to his own. The Jam proceeded to blast out a barrage of clashing chords while Paul Weller shouted about some woman's private hell.

"Hey, Davie," Danny said after a time. "Can you check that the hardware's up to scratch?"

Davie pulled a sports bag from under the passenger seat and opened it carefully. From within he withdrew a sawn off shotgun that he checked quickly and expertly. "This is a H.K. M4 Super 90 tactical shotgun," he said quietly. "It's criminal to have sawn it off this way. Eddie's ruined a beautiful machine."

"There should be a pistol in there too."

After hiding the shotgun, Davie retrieved a small, black handgun from the holdall and pulled out its magazine, which he checked thoroughly. "Yep – a H.K. Custom Sport .45 with a full metal jacket," he replied, clicking the magazine back into place. "It just goes to show that the word on the street was the truth for once."

"Eh?"

"Well, we've got two Heckler and Koch firearms here and it was rumoured that Eddie'd half-inched a load from Barking Container Base last month."

"Oh yeah – I see what you mean. In that case, we know full well that they're clean."

From his comfortable position on the back seat, Davie replaced the pistol then checked the components of the timed incendiary he had assembled in the car park of Barking's B&Q. It was a plastic petrol container attached to a cheap alarm clock. Two wires led down through the nozzle, which was sealed tightly with putty, while the container was filled with a mixture of petrol and Vaseline. He worked mechanically and smoothly as though hypnotised, but his eyes were keen and fired up with the prospect of imminent confrontation. "On the left," he grunted hoarsely.

Almost sleepily, Danny turned his head and noticed the dark blue Ford Escort that was stranded on the A249's bepuddled lay-by and he smiled when he saw the two dejected travellers who were changing its front-right tyre busily. "Poor bastards," he half stated, half laughed. "Not the best night to have your motor conk out on you."

"Probably workers at the Power Station," Davie intoned gravely. "In which case they deserve it, messing up the atmosphere an' all."

Danny was about to ask what Davie was going on about, but was prevented from doing so by the annoying, beeping refrain of a mobile phone that he took from the Nissan's glove compartment and answered. "Yeah?" he asked. "Yeah. Scuse me? We'll take the 2231. Yeah. Say that again... Past Eastchurch then that road heading south. No – it ain't got no name on my map neither, but it says it heads down to Harty. Yeah, I saw 'em too... What? Poor fuckers. Sure, Baron. Sweet. Catch you later... Do Jamaicans speak English? That fly-boy sure ain't got the vocal charms of Trevor McDonald. We could do with an interpreter. I think I caught about three words and they were man, man and man!"

After clicking the cover of the mobile back in place, Danny tucked it into his pocket. "E.T.A. five minutes," he said. "Just make sure we take the next right, Lee."

Davie nodded solemnly, while Lee jerked his thumb over his shoulder to indicate the South London crew's stolen Vauxhall Cavalier, which was about one hundred metres behind them. "And fuckin' mobile phones," he growled. "You ever seen a mud monkey *without* a mobile phone? With any luck it'll give 'em all fuckin' brain cancer. Fuckin' proof that God's a white man."

Their Nissan passed through Eastchurch, turned off the B road, then continued through the rain until the crews travelled along what was little more than a muddy, industrial track. With no streetlights and the further harassment of the eddying pockets of rain, Lee had some difficulty keeping the car on the road, but soon the stark silhouette of a large farmhouse loomed visible through the nothingness. Danny knew the farm to be the residence of Harry Green, Eddie's source and owner of the land upon which the plane was to make its clandestine rendezvous. He wondered if Harry was receiving a cut of the cake as well.

"Okay, get off the road and head towards those trees," Danny commanded. "Kill the lights."

Lee did as he was bid and the last quarter mile of their journey was undertaken by instinct and guesswork. They drove into a tight cluster of trees and when Danny thought the car was properly concealed he told Lee to pull over.

The South London crew drew alongside them and Baron wound down his window. "Rain falling like it waan to be Hurricane Gilbert," he said, showing his teeth. "Where' yu t'ink der car der-ya?"

Danny took a few seconds to digest Baron's question, then thrust his arm out of the window and circled it in a vague motion to indicate the vast expanse of soggy fuck-all that surrounded them. "We're gonna have to go search this lot," he said. "The landing field is definitely over there," he pointed. "So their car has gotta be someplace yonder."

Colin X stepped free of the Vauxhall's passenger seat and laid his sawn-off on its bonnet. Davie noticed that like the East Londoners, the South Londoners' sawn-off was a H.K. M4 Super 90.

"We gonna split up?" Colin asked.

"Okay. You boys sweep right and we'll go left. If you find their motor don't do shit; just phone us so we can all rumble together."

Colin X nodded and cradled the shotgun under his arm, while Baron pulled back the safety on his pistol. Ali had opted for the comfort of a baseball bat and he swung it in a leisurely arc while the others looked at him feeling dwarfed.

Danny cocked his own pistol then the two crews separated. Davie followed close behind Danny, saying nothing, but Lee yapped around them like an expectant terrier demanding attention. "Why the fuck ain't I tooled?" he complained as he hefted a pair of catalogue-bought nunchaku from hand to hand. "I wanna carry the shotgun."

"Will you shut the fuck up?" Danny demanded, rounding on him. "Now we know this crew are met by a car and we know they're waiting somewhere near the clearing. You wanna wake the fuckers up so they'll be all ready and waiting for us?"

"Nah, I'm just saying..."

"You just say fuck all. Christ, if your old man was here he'd kick your arse from here to Mile End and then bounce you over Upton Park."

Danny stomped off into the darkness before Lee could riposte, mumbling something about Alan and loyalty and Davie followed him in a bizarre, scuttling half-crouch; his shotgun ready.

"*Fuck*," Lee muttered before trudging after them.

The three men searched the trees that lined the left side of the makeshift landing field cautiously, but found no trace of the pick-up car. "Are you sure the time's right?" Davie hissed from the corner of his mouth. "Eddie ain't got his pants in a rinse, has he?"

Danny shrugged. "Buggered if I know. Maybe the others have found it." He dialled a pre-set number on the mobile phone and realised that Colin X must have had his finger ready on the receive button, because it did not ring before he heard a "Yeah?" from its tiny speaker.

"You found what we're looking for? What? No – no sign of it neither. Yeah – that's what Davie said, but I ain't never known Eddie to be wrong about a job. Okay – yeah – back at the cars."

He snapped the mobile closed and stuffed it back into his jacket, then the trio returned to the cars where Colin X, Baron and Ali were already waiting.

"Dis is fucked up, to rarted," Ali exclaimed. "If der ain't no pick-up car den der ain't no rarse job. *Believe.*"

"Fe real." Colin agreed. "An' I could ah been sexing a fit bitch tonight! Like dat one me sight at Eddie's pub."

Davie broke his shotgun to make it safe then nodded at the weapon Colin held to suggest that he should do the same. "You're forgetting one thing," he said quietly as he wiped rain from his gaunt face. "That car we passed. What if *that* was the pick up car?"

"Bloodfire!" Baron exclaimed excitedly. "Idiot mon dem! Kiss der foolish backside. If you're right, bwai, we've controlled one easy, raas pay day. Dey nuh even finish tek off de flat when we passed, so der gwarn be at least anoder twenty minutes."

As the two crews conversed, Lee stood apart from them and leant with one elbow upon the roof of their stolen Nissan. He tapped the nunchaku against his thigh nonchalantly, by all appearances lost to the world, but everyone looked to him when he said: "I hear something."

Each man cocked his head to one side and at varying intervals nodded his concord. "It's the plane," Danny acknowledged, feeling adrenaline rush through him, the excitement he could feel in his fingers. "Lee, pull the motor out over there and flash the lights. Let 'em think we're their friendly reception committee."

Lee went to open the car door, but Baron prevented him with a raised hand. "Tek time an' don't be so fas'," he commanded, evoking a sulphurous glance from Lee. "Use your fockin' brain, mon. Yu coulda fuck up de programme big time, getting carried 'way an' t'ing. Dat der bucket affe land *inna* de wind, y'hear me, bwai? An' I'll bet yu dem 'ave ah system wid der bredrens 'pon de ground fe knowing wha' way is de right way."

"Well, you ain't got long to work out what that system is, fly-boy," Danny answered.

Baron sucked on his teeth then left the cover of the trees to jog a hundred or so metres into the clearing. He licked a finger and held it in the air, then made a brief study of the angle that the rain was blowing.

When he returned to the others he was panting. "Yeah, mon, me t'ink me 'ave it. Me cyan't be certain wid all dese trees an' being so low to de ground, but me feel so me know de programme," he said.

"How'd you think they'd signal? Launching a firework?" Danny wanted to know, annoyed that his excitement could be suspended.

"In the army you'd use a few lights," Davie suggested, but then Baron threw up his arms in a gesture that suggested he was out of patience.

"Ah fuckery dat," he said. "Dey mus' use de car 'eadlights as ah beacon. We jus' drive de car out to where we waan de mek-up runway to finish an' dem will 'ead straight fe it."

"That or they'll fuck off," Lee cut in.

Baron didn't bother to acknowledge what he said and bullfrogged into the Vauxhall. He then drove it upwind into the clearing and turned it about, its lights switched to full beam.

Danny, Davie and Colin X ran to join him, while Ali and Lee returned to the Nissan that remained beneath the trees. By the time they were all in position the sound of the light aircraft's engine was distinct and it was possible to discern its bearing despite the rain and darkness.

"The bastard's turning." Danny exclaimed. "We've blown it."

"Char!" Colin X agreed.

Baron guffawed and shook his head at their dismay. "Dey gwarn do ah lef' circuit den forward dis way," he said. "Yu, bwai, don't know how fe fly nuh raas plane. 'im affe get *inna* de wind, an im affe turn lef so he can sight wha' de fock 'e is doing." He paused then pointed straight ahead. "Me say yu 'ave one minute to get buried inna de mud. 'bout ah t'ird of de way in."

Davie nodded, cocked his sawn-off, then motioned to get out of the car. "Who's coming?" he asked.

Colin X cursed then readied his own weapon before joining him in the rain. "De party start from *now*. Let's get dis shit over wid," he demanded.

Both men skulked off into the night then laid down in the mud about two hundred metres away from the car. Colin X pounded the ground in frustration at getting his tracksuit all dirty then nudged Davie in the side. "You know how to use dat t'ing, white bwai?" he asked, indicating the shotgun in Davie's hands.

Davie nodded and grinned, seemingly untroubled by the veiled put-down. "I've seen shit that'd make you whiter than the pet Nazi we have over there," he stated by way of a riposte. "Two tours of Bosnia, the Gulf and more stints with the bog-trotters than you can shake a stick at."

"You was in the army, den?"

"Spot on. I was a Full-Screw in the R.A.M.C.."

Colin X grew silent, save for a mumbled curse that was too low for Davie to discern, but as the whine of the aircraft's engine grew louder he spoke again. "You kill off any of me bredren in Islam out der in de Gulf?" he probed in a monotone.

"Only those who deserved it."

"Char bloodclaat. You don't know wha' you fighting for just like dem Yankee fools in Afghanistan."

"But I saved a few too. R.A.M.C. means 'Royal Army Medical Corps' – it means I was a medic."

"Medics don't know how fe use no focking guns."

"Well, you'll find out if that's true soon enough."

At that moment, both men thrust their faces into the mud instinctively as the aircraft came in for its final approach. It passed low over them and at only a few metres to one side, so Colin expressed his concern with a barrage of 'Fucks' and 'Shits'.

Seated in the comfort of the beacon car, Baron kissed his teeth while he fiddled with his Heckler and Koch pistol. "Dat's ah Piper Cherokee," he stated. "Wicked, wicked-style bucket. Nuff Miami smuggler use dem. An' me fly dem nuff time back ah yard."

Danny looked up from his weapon and nodded, wondering where back-ah-yard was. "So long as you can fly it," he said.

The Piper bobbed and rumbled along the uneven field as it taxied to a halt about fifty metres from the car. Danny put his hand on the door-handle then turned to face Baron. "You'd better stay put," he advised. "In this light they won't recognise me as different, but I don't think they're gonna be so dumb as to think their contact's changed colour since they last met."

"Ah so it go, bwai," Baron replied, not offended. "Black me black."

Once Danny had pulled on a navy blue bobble-hat that all but obscured his face he levered himself from the car and waved at the Piper's cockpit cheerfully. This is a bitch of a place to end your days, he thought. For a short second, the image of his six year old son grew large in his mind. He walked over to the aircraft slowly while its engine spluttered and died and from the corner of his eye he could see Colin X and Davie prizing themselves from the mud before making their own stealthy advance upon the plane from the rear.

Despite the cold, miserable night Danny felt hot and his hands were sweating so much that he feared he would drop his pistol once he drew it. He was always like this before a job that necessitated his being tooled, but the thought of the prize money that lay waiting in the Piper overrode any doubts he had about getting on with the job at hand. He thumped on the aircraft's door eagerly when he reached it, then put a hand in his pocket that soon gripped the cold, hard reality of a gun.

Davie and Colin X had reached the tail of the Piper. Danny risked a quick glance in their direction. Davie nodded his readiness and he and Colin both levelled their shotguns. Danny knocked again. Somewhere in his brain he heard his son say 'daddy'. Colin tightened his grip on his weapon. All of the hijackers stopped blinking.

"Yeah, hold up, Sean," a voice said from within.

A slight feeling of relief caressed Danny's quickened heart when he realised that the occupants of the plane had no idea that he was not their usual contact, so he continued with the plan that he and Colin X had hatched via the mobiles *en route*. After attracting the attention of the pilot he pointed to himself and then made a vague gesture in the direction of the car as though he needed to return to it for some reason. The pilot acknowledged the signal, whereupon Danny turned and walked away so that they could not see his face until it was too late.

He had almost completed the journey back to Baron and the Vauxhall when the Piper's door opened with a metallic creak. Davie and Colin X were hidden behind the Piper's tail, but were more than ready for action when two men dressed in combat fatigues clambered unsteadily from the aircraft, using the Piper's wing as an improvised stair. One queried: "What's up, Sean?" and Danny felt an intense desire to turn around; his exposed back screamed for him to avert it from the gaze of the men he was soon to rob, but he knew that this could not be done, so without looking back he replied to them with a waved arm that symbolised 'wait a minute'.

From the safety of the hidden Nissan, Ali and Lee watched Davie and Colin X as they crept up behind the two men with their shotguns ready. Throughout their wait, Lee had said nothing to Ali, preferring instead to wish death by obesity upon him though narrowed, hateful eyes, but he could not maintain his Trappist stance when he heard a grumbling sound to their left. He turned his head so he could see out the passenger's side window and beheld a car with no lights that was weaving slowly through the trees some way in the distance. "The fuckin' Escort's turned up!" he exclaimed, and at that moment the occupants of the Escort saw the Vauxhall with the plane and realised its intent. Within seconds, the car the crews had last seen laying wounded by the bridge flicked on its headlights and James-Bonded through the trees to its beset companions.

Thursday 29th of November, 2001; 07:35pm.

"Where the fuck are we?" asked Matt, entering K's Sierra and shaking the rain out of his hair. Reaching the rendezvous had led to a jolting realisation of the job in hand and he felt a surging apprehension. K watched his accomplice with increasing alarm, his own face a mask, then cursed as something forced Matt to abandon the car with clumsy haste. Bent double, the youngster clutched at his midriff and retched twice before a gooey concoction of chipsticks and bile waterfalled from his mouth; some of it clinging to his lips and chin. With splutters and gasps, he waited a few seconds until his convulsions had died then wiped his face with the cuff of his tatty jacket before stepping back into the car. "I had a dodgy burger for lunch," he stated.

K acknowledged the lie without comment and recalled the time before his first major heist – a payroll number out Wembley way. As he sat in the beat-up old Cortina with Cyrus, Pogo and The Dong he hadn't puked, although it felt like he would, but bad wind had plagued him something rotten and their jibes at the stench only made him feel worse. He could still see their laughing, mocking faces as they waited for the job that would see two of them imprisoned for their twenties. He couldn't recall seeing them laugh since. Prison had a way of taking the laughter out of a man and K had decided after visiting Cyrus and The Dong in their respective prisons, he would never see them again. He was summoned from his reverie by Matt jerking a thumb out of the window to the Rover he had only just parked. "The motor should be safe there, you reckon?"

"Well, we've reached the end of the road," K answered after a time, analysing Matt's face. "That big building with the floodlights we just passed was a power station and if we go any further we might fall into the North Sea. I think they call this place the Isle of Grain, or something."

"Can't see shit," Matt exclaimed, peering into the black horizon "You sure your fly-boy can find this place alright? It's fuckin' black out there… Er, no offence."

"None taken. He'll find it. My only fear is he might mistake one of those islands we passed for the landing site. Back in Jamaica, Baron tells me he flew light aircraft in all sorts of weathers and the wind can blow there a bit. He used to spray crops in the rural areas, but soon realised that wouldn't buy him a Goldeneye."

"A what?"

Doesn't he even watch James Bond films? K asked himself. "Ian Fleming's place."

Matt used the car cigarette lighter to torch his Benson. He inhaled deeply then blew his smoke over the dashboard. "How long'll they be? You reckon they jacked the plane alright? We might be waiting here for fuck all. They could be Hovis for all we know."

K killed the engine, but spared the radio on account of good behaviour. As he did so he took stock of Matt's pale features and noticed the sweat forming on his upper lip, while his cigarette was already in its death throes. "Ever played cowboys and Indians with the big boys before?" he asked.

"Yeah… Sort of. Er, no, nothing like this shit anyway," came the reply.

K laughed. "Don't worry about it. My crew haven't exactly jacked a plane from the continent and flown it over the Thames Estuary before."

Matt's breathing down-tempoed a notch as he ground out the cigarette. For some reason he could not discern, K's words had soothed his nerves. He observed K's calm countenance and thought Lee's assertion that niggers didn't have as many brain cells as whites well off the beam. "No offence, but you don't talk like the rest of your guys. Seems like you had good schooling, know what I mean?"

Well blow me down, K thought. He's an observant one. "Yeah, right, but I only ever learned one thing," K replied cautiously. "And that was the more you educate yourself, the more you realise the world is fucked up with corrupt politics and run by corrupt men. In short, I learned that ignorance is bliss."

"So you became a blagger?"

K's mind flashed back to his dismissal from Lambeth social services for harbouring a criminal; a young person on his files who he had grown fond of. At the time he thought he could have talked sense into the angry eighteen year old who had just shot his father. Just as he felt he was getting through to the teenager, the Police arrived, ransacking his flat and, to his dismay, discovering heroin in the bedroom where the fugitive slept. This was nothing compared to how he felt when his mother, believing the Police charges, accused him of dealing with drugs and corrupting the young. He still heard his mother's voice ringing inside his head: 'Me work all the God-sent hours to mek you go university and you bring shame on us all!'. Although he had escaped the drug rap his employers found him guilty of gross misconduct and he hadn't spoken to his mother or seen her since.

Radio Five was broadcasting the News Flash of George Harrison's death as the howling rain lashed the exposed car, causing tiny zigzagging canals to caper all over the windscreen. The breath of the sea could be heard in the distance and the floodlights of the power station seemed to be in peril. If this is the garden of England, K thought, then they should call in Prince Charles for a serious talk with the soil.

"You could say that," K replied finally, noting that his long silence preyed on Matt's nerves. "Reckoned I could get what I want with a couple of years hustling… What about you?"

"I'm a trained mechanic – used to be an apprentice at Ford's - but you get more for this shit than a fuckin' month of overtime getting greased under a motor."

K chuckled again.

"Yeah, it's better than coursework in anthropology."

"What?"

"Don't worry yourself."

Matt lit another cigarette, not liking to be patronised. Fucking nigger, he thought. He probably learned that big word today – probably got word-a-day bog paper. His emotions blazed a fierce red, yet he was surprised at his reaction. He'd never called *anyone* a nigger before, not even in his thoughts, and that realisation belittled him further.

"Where the fuck are they?" he demanded in an effort to assert himself. "What's the fuckin' time? What direction d'you think they'll come in by?"

"You're a man of questions, innit. The worse that can happen is that we don't see no plane and we just go home. All intact. That's the first rule - you go home *intact*. Stop fretting, we've only been here five minutes. Remember that they had further to go than us, then they've got the job, then they've gotta get here. Be patient. But to answer your question, Baron will be flying over the Estuary, so keep your eyes clocked right."

Matt looked to where K pointed, but only saw the rain trickling down the window, so after a few moments his patience upped and left him. "Fuck this for a game of soldiers," he complained. "I'm going out to have a butchers."

He donned a baseball cap then prowled around in the forty-five degree rain, glancing up occasionally to the wrathful sky as K watched him keenly, taking stock of the tasteless, market-bought clothes and no-name-brand, pair-for-a-fiver trainers that typified the terminally skint. The poor bastard certainly ain't doing this for kicks, K realised.

Having been defeated by the downpour, Matt threw away his now-irrigated cigarette and returned to K's car. "Bloody weather; it just had to rain tonight, for fuck's sake," he complained. "For all we know they could've crashed in the fuckin' sea."

K chuckled. "Be glad you ain't flying in this deluge."

Matt fiddled with the radio dial to try and receive a more musically inclined station and was satisfied when he found Capital F.M.. It was playing George Harrison's *My Sweet Lord*. "You ever wasted someone?" he asked. "With a shooter, I mean."

No I haven't, K's inner voice replied, but he wouldn't let Matt know that. "I take it by your question that you haven't?"

Matt ignited another Benson. "Glassed someone in a pub once. His face was a right mess, and me and Lee and some of his mates had a baseball party with some Pakis in Whitechapel. They were coming out of their church."

"You mean a mosque if, indeed, they *were* Pakistanis. Most Asians are, in fact, Indians; and Indians and Pakistanis get along about as well as Ian Paisley and Gerry Adams on a blind date. But getting back to the point, you've never *shot* anyone?"

"Er, never had to. Had hold of a shooter when we done a post-office, but didn't need to fire the bastard. Would've done, though. It's only a piece of metal with a lever after all."

K recognised Matt's second lie and, like the first, let it drop. "That's a dangerous assumption," he said in a fatherly manner. "So take this piece of advice. If ever you see before you the end game of your life, and you've got a piece of metal with a lever in your hands, don't hesitate, you'll get gun shake. Draw and fire in one swift movement, lift up your arm and fire immediately – don't care too much where the bullet lands, so long as you down the foe you're shooting at."

"Nah – me?" Matt scoffed, pointing a finger at his chest. "I'm more of your surgical type. Like to kill 'em sure and clean. If I ever have to waste someone I'll be sure to take 'em smack-bang between the eyes so they don't get up no more."

"You reckon?" K twisted his back around to grab a holdall from the back seat then from it he took a pistol.

"What the fuck?" Matt exclaimed.

"Safe, safe," K consoled him. "It's a replica. If some boy racer gives me grief on the road I just wave this about and let off a few blanks to make 'em think twice. It creates quite a din, but as safe as a Labour majority – unless you put it up to your ear, of course."

"I thought Eddie had given it you."

"Nah – from what I hear Eddie only allows his own guns on jobs, to save them from being traced. He uses them once then destroys them - that's one of the reasons he's called Careful Eddie. Anyway, back to my point. Take a hold of the gun."

Matt accepted the thoroughly convincing nine-millimetre replica and hefted it in his hand. It was certainly far heavier than he had expected.

"Stick it out the window and aim at the Rover's front-right tyre," K went on. "Easy does it."

Matt wound down the window and did as he was asked, drops of rain pattering from the glistening, black barrel. He closed an eye and used the sight to train his aim on the Rover's silver hubcap, but by then he could feel the weight of the gun pulling his arm down and the muscles in his wrist twitched spasmodically.

"You see? You see?" K affirmed. "Your hand's wobbling like an inmate doing solitary with only a snap of Kylie Minogue for comfort. Let go of your hesitation and just let rip, as a captain says to his quickest bowler." He paused as he sought further explanation. "Look at it this way – why take out the tyre when you've got a whole windscreen in front of you? The same goes with people. Hesitate and you're dead. There ain't no time to be like Lee Van Cleef or what you see on telly. If you take your time with your aim you won't get to squeeze the trigger."

"No – not when the shit hits the fan – there's no way I'll get fuckin' gun shake. If I can use a blade I can use a fuckin' gun, and I'll get the same result - a fucked up face."

K turned down the radio then retrieved the pistol, which he returned to the holdall. "Bullets don't disfigure faces. They mess up the insides. Sometimes all you see is the entry hole, but beyond that it gets sloppy. And of course it depends on what kinda gun you use – boy, if you had a Magnum…"

Matt reclined in his seat, appreciating why K's companions also called him the Professor, and watched as he wound down his own window. Once this was achieved, they both quarter-mooned their eyes, since the rain greeted him without introductions, and tried to make out the dark clouds to the right of them. They could see nothing and K meditated on whether Baron would make it; laughing to himself when he realised that he was ignoring the advice he had so recently offered the kid.

"No offence, but I'd be shitting myself if I was inside a small plane with a Jamaican pilot and it was pissing down cats and dogs. Bet he's more used to flying in the sun... I mean under the sun."

K grinned wryly, unable to take offence at the remark. "And I'd be uneasy myself if I was flying a small plane in this weather with only three white brothers to back me up," he stated by way of a rejoinder.

"You'd be more safe with white guys than black," Matt persisted, recalling snippets of propaganda he had received from Lee as statements of fact. "You lot are always shooting each other. Every week in the News you've got some schizo black guy wasting another black guy in Brixton or Harlesden or somewhere. Tell me it ain't so."

"And every day you have white guys, who are supposed to be religious, bombing and shooting each other all over the U.S.A., Bosnia, Northern Ireland and loads of other places all over the world. Don't you tell me about black on black violence when you have worse white on white violence no further than your own back yard."

Matt thought about his next words, realising K would have a smart retort, but could not help himself. "Nah - that's different. Lee says..."

"No – who cares what Lee says? There's no difference," K stated, this time tinting his tone with assertion. "Men still get killed and widows still weep the same salty tears. Reality is reality – just goes by different names."

"But Lee says..."

"Lee says this, Lee says that." K thought of his own crew and how he would love to have this type of conversation with them. "What do *you* say?"

Matt faltered for a moment. According to Lee, people like K weren't for talking to, they were for baseball-batting. He couldn't very well express that particular sentiment any more than he could deny his second-hand beliefs.

"I know one thing, if it wasn't for all the blacks I wouldn't be sitting in this motor waiting to rip off some poor bastard."

"Now, how do you make that out?"

"Well, you come over here, taking our jobs – I'd be a mechanic by now if it weren't for the blacks."

"Taking your jobs! You really think a black man put you on the dole?"

"He fuckin' did! Desmond Higgins his name was. The guvnor kept him on and gave *me* the boot."

Here's an opportunity to teach some wisdom to the young, K thought, turning into social worker mode. "No chance he was a better mechanic than you, I suppose?"

"What's that got to do with anything? If he hadn't been there he couldn't've taken my job, could he?"

"Jesus! The brother was probably born two streets from you. I'll bet you anything you like he didn't come over here for some Y.T. slave labour."

"Doesn't matter. His fuckin' parents came, didn't they?"

"My God, you must have had some bad influences. What do you know about that?"

"I know what I need to know. I'm on the dole and he's in my fuckin' job."

"Let me tell you something. My mother came here from St. Lucia. She was asked to come; the British were all over the Caribbean with their reps, saying how much the Mother Country needs workers. All you white boys spent the Second World War putting each other in the ground and there was no-one left to do the unsavoury jobs. She keeps a photo on the mantelpiece at home of herself all done up in her London Transport uniform. She was a bus conductor. You ought to see the smile on her face, it'll do you good. She was so damn proud of that uniform. Ironed it every time before she went on her shift. But she wanted better for her children. And she saw us as British children, not black or anything else. If I was naughty in school and told to stand in the corner of the class, she would come up to see the teacher and give he or she hell for depriving me of an education. Everything I have learned I have learned here. So like my dear mum, I believe that entitles me to have an equal chance of any job I go for."

"That ain't the point…"

"What is the point? Where are you from, Matt? Your parents, I mean."

"They're Irish."

"Irish! Excuse me! You ought to have a bit more respect, then. The way I hear it, the Irish were the niggers until we got here. No dogs, no blacks, no Irish?"

"I've heard my old man talk that way. He got treated like shit when he came over… and Lee's mates call him a bog wog when they want to wind him up."

"And you still haven't got any further than the colour of a man's skin, have you?"

"What do you mean?"

"Well, that's a good East End accent you've got there. Nobody knows you're just some mick on the make, over here to nick jobs from the English. Probably planting bombs as well."

"You don't know anything about me! I ain't no fuckin' terrorist!"

"Ease yourself. The point I'm making is this. I'm the same as you. The brother who's got your so-called job is too. Difference is, him and me can't hide what we are with a cockney accent. There's nothing wrong with hate, Matt. Just make sure you're hating the right enemy."

"What?"

"Black men didn't take your job, Matt, that was good old Maggie Thatcher. Not even a touch of the tarbrush there. It was every yuppie who grabbed the money when they privatised everything. Think they gave a monkeys if you were black or white? There ain't no colour of money. That's why you're in this car, same as me. Because for the men with the money, we're *all* niggers. It's a capitalist's world and you'd better get with the programme."

Matt looked up to the half-monsoon, raven skies and wondered what Lee would say. Nothing, he realised. The only thing he'd ever heard Lee say to a black was some variant of 'Oi, coon', and conversation tended to go downhill after opening gambits like that.

"You're right - it's all shit," he answered.

Thursday 29th of November, 2001; 07:40pm.

When Danny saw the Escort's approach he completed his journey to the Vauxhall in a mad dash; diving into the passenger seat just as Baron fired up its engine. "Bloodclaat, pussy'ole job," Baron growled once he had gotten the car in gear. "Me 'ere to fly de bombaclaat plane, nuh de raas getaway car!"

Davie and Colin X were obscured by the length of the plane, so they were unaware of any problem until they noticed a change in the movements of their prey. Both turned to look into the forest where headlights blinked as they criss-crossed trees. "Old Bill?" one asked, and it was then that Davie knew he should strike before his quarry attempted to flee. With one bound he was behind the closer of the two men and had swung the butt of his sawn-off H.K. M4 around the back of his head. Colin X was close behind and while Davie dealt a similar fate to his second victim, Colin X pummelled the first into submission with the butt of his loaded weapon.

The Escort entered the clearing as Baron succeeded in getting the Vauxhall into second gear, and it was then that Davie noticed the yellow-blue muzzle flashes from the passenger side of the oncoming vehicle. A quick glance between he and Colin X was all the pair needed and, bellowing a fierce curse of aggression, Davie darted into the clearing to position himself between Baron's Vauxhall and the Escort, while Colin X ducked inside the Piper.

"Ah party, you pussies!" Colin roared as he bounded into the Piper to confront a startled, middle-aged pilot with blond curly hair and glasses who was already holding his hands in the air in a gesture of submission. Colin took a hold of the pilot's shirt-collar then dragged him from his chair to the floor, whereupon he beat him about the face. "I'm cool. I'm cool. I'll do anything you say," the pilot blurted as he was dragged through the cabin and cast unceremoniously into the mud.

The front panel of Baron's car gave a brief, thudding protestation as two point nine calibre bullets punctured its hide. He turned the vehicle to one side sharply in an attempt to avoid Davie then reset his course in the direction of the Piper.

"Come on, you cowsons!" Davie yelled as the Escort approached him. He held the sawn-off at his side and knew that to fire too soon would prove futile, but as another muzzle-flash punctuated the darkness of the night he realised that to wait for them to draw close enough could result in his being left behind. "Danny!" he yelled, turning about to behold the Vauxhall reaching the Piper, then he joined them in their race to the plane.

Colin X kicked at the three men who lay at the bottom of the plane while he watched the Escort bear down upon Davie. "Bloodfire! De white bwai gwarn ketch ah tribulation!" he exclaimed before reaching down and hefting one of the concussed men under his brawny left arm. The man squawked in pain and terror, but his protests dwindled to silent sobbing as the sawn-off was levelled at his head. Colin X then carried him like an errant child out from the cover of the Piper and into plain view of the charging Escort. "Allahu akbar," he muttered to himself repeatedly, holding the battered, whimpering man out for the Escort to see. He hoped that the hostage he held was a friend of the men in the car, because if he wasn't they'd both soon be ventilated by bullets.

Baron braked their Vauxhall a short distance from the Piper then ran at a crouch to clamber onto its wing then into its cabin. Danny followed, struggling to carry the home-made incendiary, but he, too, reached the Piper safely. Colin thought then of dumping his blubbering captive and leaving Davie to his fate – why the rarse should he draw heat for a white man? – but he maintained his defiant stance against the Escort until Davie had lurched, rasping for breath, to the safety of the plane.

While Colin, Davie and Danny fired their weapons at the charging Escort, Baron set about revving up the Piper's engine. "Remember wha' me say 'bout landing inna de wind?" he asked frantically; his eyes wide with gallows' excitement. "Well, did me mention yu shoulda tek off dat way too? Me affe turn 'round an' rhino dis ya mob, so me say yu better 'old on to your seedbags, 'cos dis gwarn be one bitch of ah raas tek-off."

Colin X slammed the door as Baron wheeled the tiny aircraft about. "Seat belts ah mus'," he whinnied maniacally as he prepared for a hasty departure.

Danny did as he was commanded then tossed his mobile to Colin X. "I hope you left your mate with the phone, 'cos we've gotta tell them to get the fuck outa here!" he exclaimed, his face showing signs of his distress.

Colin X pumped a number as the protesting Piper picked up speed. It was answered instantly and a distraught voice demanded: "Wha' de rarse ah gwarn, brudder?"

"Ali?" Colin X barked into the mouthpiece as the plane juddered him from side to side. "Yeah. Remove from de area, man. Yeah. Fuck dem and set your speed seriously. Yeah. See you wid K and de white boy." He slapped the mobile closed then eye-drilled Baron. "Get dis fuckin' t'ing in de air, man!" he screeched.

Baron nodded and failed to see the increasing apprehension that clouded his companions' faces when the plane did not leave the ground. It taxied to the far end of the field and then slowed before Colin finally lost his nerve. "Wha' de rarse you doing, man?" he demanded. "You t'ink you ah fly model plane? Fly up like Luke Skywalker an' lick de hyper speed!"

"Chat to me in dem tone again an' see if me nuh boot yu outta de raas plane... Boom boom claat! Me affe get dis t'ing *inna* de wind," Baron explained as he swung the Piper in a wide arc to face the direction in which it had landed. Once achieved, he noticed the Escort bumping its way towards them. "Now it's time fe play ah liccle chicken," he smiled.

The Escort had lost valuable seconds by picking up its hijacked companions, but now made up for this momentary lack of pursuit with renewed ardour, angling itself directly in front of the oncoming aircraft.

Baron recognised their intent and wrestled with the throttle as he sought sufficient speed for the Piper to achieve lift, but it was slow in coming over the rough, muddy terrain. He adjusted the flaps with reckless haste, but this sent the Piper into a frenzied St. Vitas Dance accompanied by metallic groans, creaks and shudders that terrified Danny and Colin X. Davie appeared unmoved by their plight and focussed his attention out of the window to where he could see the Escort's thunderous advance. "They're gonna smack us on the kisser," he said mechanically.

Baron was used to the workings of a plane, but even *he* was showing signs of distress when its wheels finally lurched free from the groping mud. The Escort was still over twenty metres away, but the ascending Piper's wheels only missed its roof by a whisker. "Me never done nuh fool amateur flying fuckery like dis before," he complained in a high-pitched squeal, like a pig on its way to the slaughterhouse. He turned to Danny, who was occupying the co-pilot's seat. "Me need some raas 'elp up 'ere so. Yu know ah liccle somet'ing 'bout planes, white bwai?"

"Only that when they crash people don't usually walk away with slight cuts and bruises," Danny replied, expecting the worst.

Davie nodded warily. "I've been in the front of loads, but they were all military," he stated.

"Well, dat' will affe do. Get your backside up 'ere so."

Davie unbuckled himself and reached Baron via a series of staggered, tenuous steps, whereupon he swapped places with Danny.

As the Piper picked up speed so the aircraft's shudders and jolts increased until beads of sweat were visible upon Baron's plough-lined brow. He fought with the controls mercilessly, taunting and threatening them with a barrage of Jamaican expletives that roasted the air as he spat them. "Right, yu know wha' an altimeter is?" he asked between insults.

Davie pointed to an illuminated dial. "Yeah," he said in his cautious monotone.

"Yu know how fe work ah radio?"

"Yeah."

"Like de one der so?"

"No."

"Den learn quick time. Me need fe get de weder report so we cyan adjust de altimeter. Any of yu 'ustlers know any airfields der-'bout?"

Danny, his mind in the middle of a silent prayer, opened his eyes and nodded. "Rochester – not far at all," he said casually, as if nothing mattered any more. He looked around the plane for any lifebelts and wondered if he'd be brave enough to open the door and plunge into the estuary - if the plane reached that far.

"Right, soljie-bwai, try fe get de Rochester Control Tower an' listen fe dem talking to some pussy."

Colin X was giving the Escort the finger as they passed overhead. "Wha' de fuck do we need de weder for?" he demanded. "Wha' do we wanna do? Tune in to de rarse fishing report? I dunno 'bout you but I kinda noticed it's raining, so we don't need no rarse weder report an' we ain't got time for dis kinda fuckery. We're only going ten bloodclaat miles."

"Cah we're gwarn be flying at less dan five 'undred feet, yu raas fool. Me t'ought dat K tell me dat Inglan' is good fe education? Anyway, to do dat an' stay in one piece me affe know wha' de pussy-claat weder is like. It affects de altimeter reading an' we nuh know if de last fly-bwai tek ah reading from Rochester or from de bloodclaat Nort' Pole. Boom boom claat! If it nuh set right we coulda be flying way too low an' end up wrapped around ah bloodclaat pylon!"

"Allah 'ave pussy-claat mercy," cried Colin X.

Danny crossed himself and looked out of the window to where he could see the occupants of the Escort arguing with their three hijacked companions and the Nissan containing Ali and Lee roaring into the darkness. "The others look like they've made it," he commented.

Davie was busy fiddling with the radio, but could find nothing save for whining, scratching static and high-pitched beeps. Visibility dwindled as the plane rose, until distant street lights and the glow of London were the only illumination to be had and this made Baron fret again. "Yu nuh find nuh raas Tower?" he complained.

Davie ignored him, preferring to keep on with his work, and Baron was too preoccupied with turning the Piper to persist. Once the plane had completed its circuit and was angled towards the Isle of Grain the buffeting that had beset them slowed and Baron was able to adjust to what he hoped was a suitable altitude.

"If you're so focking 'fraid 'bout de rarse pylons why don't you fly high?" Colin asked him.

"Lord me God! Your mama never teach yu any sense? Yu waan de radar to pick us up?" Baron asked haughtily by way of a riposte. "Five 'undred feet is our ceiling an' we're pushing our luck even den. Wha de altimeter say now?"

"Nine Nine Three."

"Bloodfire!"

Davie put on a set of headphones so that he could listen to the radio without distraction, while Baron attempted to corroborate the altimeter reading by judging their altitude above the shimmering black and silver water of the Themes Estuary.

Now that they were airborne Colin X felt a little safer so he craned his neck to look about the Piper's cramped confines. "Man, but we got ourselves de marching powder," he said.

Danny nodded. "Is that what it is? I did wonder."

Colin smacked his lips then his brow crumpled in thought. "So I reckon. Didn't Eddie tell you what we were picking up?"

"Nah – he just mentioned 'gear' and I assumed he was talking about Charlie."

Colin's brow furrowed further. "Come to mention it," he said. "Dat's all Eddie said to us too. We'll 'ave to check it out when we land."

The Piper picked up speed as Baron grew confident with their altitude and soon Sheppey was nothing but nostalgia as they travelled the short distance over the Thames Estuary to the Isle of Grain.

"Bloodfire! We showed dem, innit," Colin said, letting out a sigh.

Danny peered out of the window and waited a moment before responding. "Yeah, but Eddie won't be pleased with us when he finds out we left a motor at the scene. We were supposed to leave it clean."

Colin shrugged. "Fuck him. He don't need to know if we don't tell him nutten."

Danny thought of Harry Green and his demand of Eddie that there be no trace of the jacking left on his estate, then his thoughts turned to Eddie's seemingly psychotic need for perfection. "We'll be for the high-jump, 'cos Eddie'll definitely find out," he stated. "He don't need us to tell him."

A fresh cloudburst beset the Piper as Davie took off his headphones. "Just got Rochester," he said.

Baron snatched the headphones as he groped for a tatty flight plan that was shoved in the Piper's door-pocket. "Ah, Rochester, dis is Golf - Alpha Bravo Charlie Kilo," he said in his best British accent, reading the Piper's call-sign from the ragged flight plan. "Requesting Q.N.H.."

Danny, now confident that he would indeed live, had to bite his bottom lip to stop himself from laughing.

"Roger, Golf - Alpha Bravo Charlie Kilo. This is Rochester. Q.N.H. is currently nine nine five."

"Roger, Rochester. Q.N.H. is nine nine five. Out."

Baron swore as he handed the headphones back to Davie.

"Wha' dat mean in English?" Colin wanted to know.

Baron twiddled with the altimeter then bent his neck to face him. "Ah change of one digit in de altimeter means it's misjudging de altitude by t'irty feet. We coulda been ah blip on some pussy's radar fe ah minute or two, but dey 'ave nuh chance of finding us now."

Colin smiled then took out his mobile phone. "You want me to ding de Professor an' get him to do de wind t'ing?" he asked.

After flicking some switch or other Baron nodded, so Colin jabbed the pre-set number. As he spoke with K, Davie pointed out of the window to a floodlit area some way ahead. "That there is the power station," he said. "Baron, steer the kite that way."

Baron nodded and the remainder of their journey was undertaken in silence until it neared the time to land. "Seat belts on," Baron chortled, flashing his teeth. "We t'ank yu fe flying wid Yardie Airlines an' kindly remind yu nuh to smoke your spliff, rape de stewardess or leggo gunfire while de red sign is on."

Danny grinned and stubbed out his cigarette on the arm of his chair. "No offence, but I'll have to be dead cargo before I fly with you again… I just hope your mate on the ground got the wind direction right… Eddie should have brought in a T.V. weather bird on this job."

"Well, Me see der lights already, so we nah 'ave long fe find out."

The Piper slowed as it began its circuit of their makeshift landing field and tension grew once again in the hearts of the clandestine travellers. "Nuh such ah bad place fe land," Baron consoled his passengers. "We 'ave ah nice, long piece ah runway an' untold sof' mud fe land inna should we crash... Boom boom claat!"

Coughs and splutters rasped from the Piper's engine as it made its descent and Danny crossed himself as he had done before take-off, but his fears were replaced by relief before they had time to take a proper hold as the Piper plopped into the mud, bounced a few inches, then came to a gradual halt some sixty or so metres from the pick-up cars, where K and Matt were waiting.

It took a few moments for them to realise they were safe, explosive releases of breath and head-wide grins emphasising the incredible truth.

"Top Gun, to rarted!" exulted Colin X, pounding a startled Danny on the shoulder.

"We sure did, didn't we?" he agreed in tones of soft wonder, hoping that it was the right response to Colin's incomprehensible statement. "Come on, we'd better shift the gear."

They clambered unsteadily from the confines of the Piper's cabin as K's Sierra drew up alongside the cargo hold.

"Your batteries flat or what, X-man?" asked Davie jokingly.

Colin stiffened momentarily before he realised it was banter rather than abuse. "Me never short of juice, pagan. Ah wha' you ah say?"

"Wanna give your mate a tinkle? See if they've got lost, or what?"

Colin grumbled to himself, embarrassed at being recalled to duty by a white devil, and took out the phone. "I bet my bredrin is slamming dat bitch from de bar," he retorted, hoping it would hit a nerve. "She look like she could do wid a big, black man to keep her warm in dis shit weder."

"Well, he'll have to join the line," came the reply. "Tony 's been trying it on with Yvette for ages with no joy yet."

Colin bit his lip and said nothing as he punched in the number, realising with distaste that the leggy brunette from the Spotted Dog caused a twitching in his white-hating loins. He recollected her casual put-down to Ali and anger flared, but then that anger transformed into satisfaction as he pictured her begging for mercy as he - Colin X - claimed her lithe body for nothing more than the slaking of his lust. After all, what else were the devils for? he reasoned.

His fantasy remained unchallenged in his mind until his call was answered by Ali. "Wha' 'appen, my brudder, where you der-ya?" Colin asked excitedly. "Safe, we're down. K's on the spot. We're gonna load up with the white boys…"

"Keep it short," urged Davie. "That cellular stuff gets picked up by anyone with ears."

Colin made an annoyed gesture, but took the sense of it.

"How long fe get here? Two minutes? Safe, brethren. You mus' 'ave flew quicker dan us. Laters."

He clicked off the mobile and turned to confront an agitated Davie.

"Listen, *mate*," Davie snapped, and Colin thought he'd only just managed to avoid using the word *boy*. "Never give out anything specific on an open line."

"Wha' you bitchin' on now? You're too para."

"*We're down – You musta flown quicker than us.* That's what I mean. If anyone's listening you've shown our arse. Even plod will know it's a plane."

"Rarse claat! No bloodclaat somebody ah listen."

"You'd better be right."

They were almost squaring up to each other, the euphoria of moments earlier replaced by a rising tension, but K stepped between them quickly. "Put your handbags down, ladies, we've got other fish to fry. Let's see to the gear."

Danny nodded and pulled Davie away to the cargo hold, turning his back on Colin X's outraged figure.

"Boom boom claat," murmured Baron, slapping Colin on the shoulder. 'Mind your business, yout'."

Colin shook his hand off, then went to help unload. Davie had figured out the complex locking mechanism and he pulled the sliding door back to reveal a multitude of packets jammed tightly into the hold.

"That's an awful lot of gear," said Davie. "Let's get on with it."

"Ah true dat. Ah Piper cyan hol' two-'undred pounds ah baggage," Baron told him.

Danny pulled out the first of the packets, which was brown-papered and tied up with string.

"Bloodfire! Me affe know wha' it is," said X. "Let's open dis one."

"Maybe we ought to get on with it," said Danny dubiously, but the way his eyes crawled over the packets belied his true opinion.

"Just one," urged K.

They stood there, irresolute, and the tableau might have held indefinitely, but just then headlights appeared in the distance.

"Dat's Ali," said Colin, thinking no white bwai would dare apprehend him now his bodyguard had turned up.

"Make sure," stressed K, but by the time Colin had keyed the number, Ali's Nissan was pulling to a stop beside them.

Ali and Lee jumped out and came over, the distance between them reflecting their essential differences.

"Man, dat's a fucked-up devil," muttered Ali to Colin. "Telling me dat he an' his kind would gladly pay my fare an' gi' me something to live on if I went back home." Ali paused and a wide smile split his broad face. "Ah tell 'im I already 'ave de money fe a bus pass back to Brixton, but 'e could top up me D.S.S. money if 'e felt like it." He paused once again and looked around. "He could do wid a rarse lick in 'im fore'ead... You 'ave anyt'ing fe yam? 'unger is killing me."

"Fuck your belly, Ali. When de white boy dem get you on Death Row, dey ain't never going to pull de rarse switch – you ain't never going to finish de condemned brudder's last meal."

"I wanna reach 'ome quick," asserted Ali. "My mudder was preparing a serious curry goat dis morning."

"We're just checking," put in K, looking at Danny. "What do you say?"

In answer, Danny produced a penknife from his pocket and applied it to the string of a packet. Fuck it, he thought. I'll tell

Eddie one of the packages was already opened. There was an ear-lashing ping as the string snapped, then he wrestled the brown paper wrapping to reveal a tightly-wrapped box that was shiny in the reflected light of headlamps and covered with strange hieroglyphics.

"What the fuck is *this*?" he wondered aloud, turning the odd package over and over in his hand. Colin X moved forward with a grunt of recognition.

"Give it here, white boy," he said. "Me could ah swear already you pagans nah gwarn' recognise de word of Allah."

He took the packet and scrutinised it closely.

"Dis somet'ing Arabic, seen?"

"What's it say?"

"Hol' it up a sec. Ali, ah wha' dis say, brethren?'

The two wannabe Moslems went into a huddle over the package with much head-scratching and turning over of the object of confusion; Ali feeling proud that he was displaying a learned knowledge to his audience. I'm *not* just muscle, he smiled to himself. To his onlookers, Ali seemed to be arguing with some conviction for a solution that Colin obviously found unacceptable.

"Nah, can't be… Fuck dat shit! De Moslem brudder inna jailhouse teach you bad," spat Colin X.

"Ah true dat,'" insisted Ali. "If I'm wrong I'll treat Rammadan serious an' begin me fasting proper."

"What? Fuckin' what?" howled Danny. "We just got ourselves a load of bin Laden's anthrax?"

Colin was tearing the wrapping from the package feverishly to reveal a greyish powder, then he started laughing, but there was no humour in the sound.

"Charlie?" asked Lee, forgetting his self-imposed restriction on talking to anyone from the South London crew in his excitement.

"Charlie? Nah, bwai, and dis ain't no anthrax neider. This here de finest rhino horn."

"Rhino fuckin' *what*?"

"*Horn*. You know, de t'ing you white boys have a liccle trouble getting. So you go chop up de creatures of Allah fe steal theirs."

"What? Are you telling me we just ripped off a fuckin' consignment of Spanish Fly?" cried Danny in disbelief. "Eddie'll be as sick as a parrot."

"Rhino horn, elephant's seedbag, fuckin' wing of bat or a hamster's whiskers for all I fuckin' know!" retorted Colin X. "The Chinee man love dem sort of t'ings, though."

"What the fuck we gonna do with it?" asked Matt.

"What we were told to," said K. "Seems to me I heard this particular merchandise is worth a fortune. And Colin's right, the Chinese pay the earth for this sort of thing. Punting is Eddie's problem, but I'll reckon he'll take it up China Town. Let's get it in the cars."

All of a sudden everybody felt they'd been hanging around too long and they burst into vehement activity. Matt's Rover took the bulk of the packets and the rest was split between K's Sierra and the Nissan's capacious boot.

"I'll just take care of the laundry," said Davie, testing the weight of his home-made bomb in an assured hand, then running to the plane for a final check-over. As he peered into the darkened interior he made out the indistinct figure of Lee crouching over in the depths of the hold, apparently stuffing something into his jacket.

"What you got there, grasshopper?" he asked, causing Lee to jump.

"Er, mob - mobile phone," he replied quickly. "Right tasty one too. It's one of them what vibrates. Why should the fuckin' niggers be the only cunts with top gear?"

"Better leave it, Lee. Shit like that's traceable."

"Bollocks. I'll take it down Romford market, get the memory wiped. No cunt'll be any the wiser."

Davie considered arguing the point, but thought better of it.

"Just don't get caught with it," he said, abstractedly. He laid the incendiary close to the seats and quickly connected the two wires to the hands of the clock. As he did so he sent a silent prayer of gratitude to the Heavens for sparing him from the shakes of the syndrome that he was finding more difficult to control every day.

"Now come on," he said eventually. "Time we wasn't here."

He had enough time to notice, as Lee crab-walked to Ali's waiting Nissan, that whatever he was holding was far too big to be a mobile phone. Danny was already in the car, obviously wanting the boy under his direct control. Matt and Colin X were in the Rover, and Davie ran to join K and Baron in the Sierra. The mixture of the crews between the getaway cars was a deliberate one, each crew guaranteeing their good behaviour with a hostage.

"How long we got?" asked K as Davie pulled the car door shut.

"Seven minutes."

"Sure?"

"You think I don't know what I'm doing?"

"Easy, I just don't want to get caught out here.'

"Then drive. The clock is ticking.'

"No offence, man."

Davie thought about it. "None taken. I just don't like my judgement being questioned."

"Okay."

The other cars had pulled away, Matt in the lead since he already knew the road and K slipped the Sierra into gear, following the convoy away from the Piper. There was no traffic at that time of night and they made good time, although Matt was sensible enough to keep to acceptable speed limits. K checked the rear view mirror repeatedly as Davie watched in amused silence.

"Now," he said finally.

"Now what?" asked K.

"That explosion you've been looking for."

"I don't hear anything."

"Then we're sweet. Believe me, if I tell you it's burning, it's burning."

Soon after they rejoined the A2 the convoy ate up the road, less conspicuous now amongst the late night traffic. Forty minutes later they pulled up outside Eddie Maynard's lock-up.

Tony was alert and had the double doors open before the engines died and the three cars eased into the spacious interior.

"Everything alright?"

"No worries," said Danny with a smirk.

"Right, let's unload the gear and get back to the pub. You've earned a drink and Eddie's buying."

Thursday 29th of November, 2001; 10:15pm.

Matt was happy – well, at least he was as happy as he ever was, and this happiness was on account of the unaccustomed bulge in his right trouser pocket. It betokened his percentage of the neat bundle of notes that Eddie had distributed amongst the crews. Most of Matt's advance money was in a shoebox stowed under his bed at home. He'd peeled off a tonne for splash money in the Spotted Dog, but when Eddie coughed up the rest he'd have nearly four K - more money than he'd ever seen! And it had all been so easy...

The crews were relaxing in the Dog House at the rear of Eddie's pub; lager bottles and pint glasses littering the tables, but they might as well have been in different pubs for all the socialising they were doing. The Brixton boys were at one table talking animatedly and laughing loudly amongst themselves while, by contrast, the East Londoners were subdued, almost moody.

Matt didn't like it.

"What's everyone having?" he asked, anxious to lighten the mood. He couldn't hide his surge of pleasure at not having to worry about standing his shout; he'd often had to drink halves or go without in the past, just so Lee wouldn't take the piss.

"Wallop," said Lee shortly, breaking off his scrutiny of the South London mob. Danny signed for Guinness and Davie for organic orange juice, but as Matt ambled across to the bar an impulse made him turn and head back to the other crew.

"Who wants a drink?"

Ali and Colin X looked at him in frank amazement, while Baron only smiled. K was, for once, lost for words, but not displeased.

"Come on, K, what's that? Fosters?"

"Not in this life," K replied with a smile. "I'll have a pint of Becks. Thanks, Matt."

"Colin?"

"Hol' us two lagers, bwai," replied X, indicating Ali with a jerk of one callused thumb.

"An' a bag of nuts," interjected Ali.

Baron swirled the last eighth of an inch of rum and coke around the bottom of his glass then tossed it back.

"Rum, mon. Mek 'im large, me done workin' machinery dis night."

There was another bubble of laughter and Matt crossed the sawdust to the bar while trying to avoid Lee's furious glare. He was relieved to notice that Danny and Davie didn't seem bothered by his gesture, but he still felt as though he was some kind of extra on *Schindler's List*.

Careful Eddie was behind the jump; a most unusual occurrence in the everyday running of things, but an activity approaching tradition on job nights. He had a vague idea that was culled from a long-ago viewing of *The Godfather* that it was the done thing for bosses to add some personal appreciation to their retainers' payoff. After all, Vito Corleone had served Luca Brasi a drink so that was good enough for Eddie. It didn't cost anything and, more importantly, it put him on the spot to keep an eye on lippy types.

He began pouring drinks as Matt reeled off the order, but checked him as he reached for his wad.

"That's alright, son. These are on me."

"You sure, Eddie? It's a big round."

"Yeah, right. Too big for you to pay for, get me? You're supposed to be brassic."

This last statement was in an undertone, a custom-designed Careful Eddie whisper that just about made it to the one ear it was directed at. Lee was hovering in the background, ostensibly to help with the beer delivery, so after Matt had organised the drinks onto two trays and when he thought that Eddie was out of earshot he pounced.

"What the fuck are you doing, buying drinks for fuckin' dance-monkeys?" he hissed as he scooped up a tray.

"Eddie bought 'em."

"Yeah, right.   But you were gonna, weren't you?   You shouldn't even be fuckin' carrying them.   Catch me carrying a coon's drinks?   Fuck!   Have you forgotten that it was a black momma who got my dad put inside?   A black bitch who *grassed*?"

Matt wondered whether a bank teller with a gun in her face was actually grassing when she was called to Court as a prosecution witness, but said nothing.   Instead, he carried his tray through to the Dog House and set it down at his own table; whereupon he took a seat and looked expectantly at K.   There was a moment of charged silence before K stood, picked up his glass, then dragged his chair across to join them, then there was another pause before the rest of the Brixton crew joined him.   In the confusion of arranging chairs and shifting glasses, Lee arrived with the second tray; a weird expression on his face that seemed an admixture of tight-lipped disapproval and open-mouthed amazement.   Matt had never seen anybody with an open mouth and tight lips before and a nervous giggle bounced around behind his teeth at the sight of it.   Lee was getting Danny's sternest glare, so he put down the tray and slouched into his seat as far from the nearest black guy as he could, which wasn't far enough.   Tokyo wasn't far enough as far as *he* was concerned.

"Wha' 'appen to me nuts, bwai?"   demanded Ali, searching amongst the crowded tray desperately as a shipwrecked man gropes for a floating mast.

"Sorry, mate.   I forgot them."

"Nah, man."   Ali's face adopted a forlorn expression that made his friends laugh.

"Ali could have lived without the beer," said K.   "But never tell him you forgot the food.   It's a comfort thing."

"I'll get a packet on the next round."

That wasn't good enough for Ali, who grumbled off to the bar.

"What are you guys doing at the weekend?"   asked Matt, pleased at his melting pot, but worried that it wasn't quite on the boil.   The line wasn't much better than 'do you come here often', but even Colin X could see Matt was trying.

"Allah, it's only Thursday. Me nah think 'bout it, yet," he replied. "Dis business open up a few rarse doors though, innit?"

Ali was back with his peanuts and munching on a handful. His anorak crackled like a giant crisp packet, suggesting that he had some reserve rations squirreled away to cover himself against damn fool white boys with fucked up priorities. "We could check out Crumbs's blues," he said between mouthfuls. "Nuff man tell me dat Crumbs's blues always has nuff women. So we should forward down der an' celebrate."

"Ah true dat," agreed Colin. "Wha' you saying, K? Up for mixin' wid de ghetto people dis Saturday?"

I'll go just to keep up appearances, K thought. "Why not? I haven't been to a blues in years." K had never been to a blues party in his life. "Baron?"

"Yu know me, long time me nuh rub de skirt of ah fit woman an' *feel* her fitness 'pon me black rod of correction."

Colin laughed out loud, while making a mental note of Baron's latest phrase for his later use.

"Ain't we invited, then?" asked Danny with a slight lilt of humour in his tone. Wonder why they call it a blues? he thought. Maybe they got some old, dirt- poor black man from Jamaica and he entertains the revellers by singing about some bird who left him when he was young while playing a dodgy, home-made guitar? A smile caressed his face. "Well, a bit of Muddy Waters never hurt anyone," he added. "I might fancy a bit of that myself."

Ali guffawed in a manner that sprayed K.P. debris everywhere and Lee glared between him and his pint on account of the chewed peanut now floating in the beverage. No way he was drinking it now - no fuckin' way – and he was even more disturbed to notice that Ali was unaware of his petit *faux pas*, or at least he was acting as such. Uncouth bastard, he said in his mind. Didn't his fat momma teach him no table manners?

"Tink we're out of place here?" Ali grinned to Danny. "Dis is nutten'. Stockwell sides is definitely a no-go area fe you white devils. Especially in the Stansfield Road."

"Who needs a drink?" demanded Lee. K looked at him, held his gaze, then lowered it to Lee's full pint where he saw Ali's souvenir pogoing around therein like a skinhead on uppers. He smiled, because he was damn sure he wasn't included in the offer.

"I'll get these," he said. "Same again?"

"The fuck you will!"

"*Easy.*"

"I ain't taking no drink off no fucking…"

"Lee!" snapped Danny. "Behave yourself!"

He nodded towards where Eddie Maynard stood at the bar, all flat-eyed and expressionless, and noticed him give Tony the Australian barman a slight nudge with an elbow. Lee knew he'd gone too far.

"I'm going for a piss," he growled as he stomped off in his outrage.

"Sorry about that," said Danny.

Colin X was coiled, wary, and Baron looked as if he could give a shit, while Ali was busy nosing around the bottom of his packet of nuts.

"Yeah, me too," replied K. "That kid's got a big mouth and no brakes. He's gonna cost you one of these days."

"Maybe."

"So why'd you put up with it?"

Danny considered the question and saw no reason not to answer.

"His old man and me go way back and he asked me to watch out for him." Why the fuck did Lee's old man have to ask me to do the honours, Danny bemoaned inside his head.

"Dead?"

"Might as well be. *Life.*"

"You make a habit of raising other men's kids?"

"Like I say, we go back a long way."

K nodded and cast an eye over his crew.

"I heard *that*. What you having?"

He took their orders, picked up the polluted pint and went to the bar.

"Same again, is it?" asked Eddie, and there was a hint of coldness in his voice that offended K more than Lee's ranting. Kids like Lee were easy, he reflected. Better to have them out in the open where you had a chance of seeing trouble coming, but this guy was much more dangerous. This had nothing to do with colour, or anything else as ephemeral. It had everything to do with keeping his own arse intact.

"Please," K said.

"You don't want to take any notice of that Lee Jones," said Eddie, rounding off the head on a pint of Guinness expertly. "His old man just got a hefty stint of bird and a coloured lass helped put him there."

"You see me getting upset?"

"No – that's what I like about you."

"Aw shucks."

"Smart too, eh? Well, okay, I also like that. Means I won't ever regret bringing you in."

"Just so long as I never regret coming in. Speaking of which: when can we expect the balance?"

Eddie grinned to reveal a rack of yellowed teeth then beckoned Danny over with a waved hand. When he had reached the bar Eddie handed him a set of car keys, then cast his eyes to the floor.

"Out back you'll find a blue Sierra," he grunted hoarsely. "Under the back seat you'll find two canvas bags and in them you'll find your payoffs. Envelopes contain the balance for each guy in your crews."

Danny tossed the car keys from hand to hand then glanced at the Professor. "Shall we go?" he smiled.

K nodded and Danny led him from a side door of the pub that led into a deserted street lined with parked cars.

Colin X saw the two crewmen depart and wondered for a moment whether Danny intended to beat the Professor up. He glanced at the bar and saw Eddie smiling as he set drinks on a tray. It was K's order, so Colin stood and strode over to the bar.

"Why would my brethren choose to leave good soapsuds when he ain't no designated driver?" he demanded accusingly.

Eddie answered without bothering to look up. "He's just gone to settle our business. It's been great having you guys over for a visit and everything, but as they say, all good things must come to an end." Eddie paused as he poured the last drink and set it on the tray. "You guys did good tonight, and the lads have gone off to discover how I express my appreciation."

Colin tried to read Eddie's demeanour and part of him hoped to smell the scent of a double-cross. It would almost be worth losing the money to reinforce his hatred of white men, but all he gleaned from Eddie was a sense of preoccupied nonchalance.

Danny found the envelopes bulging with cash exactly where Eddie had told him they would be. A boyish smirk covered his face as he counted his own notes. K, who was waiting outside the car, decided to enter the vehicle when a few drops of rain appeared in the air. He made himself comfortable in the front passenger seat as Danny tossed him the envelopes for his crew. "So what you going to spend your cut on?" K asked.

"Set up a trust fund for my boy," Danny answered proudly. "Don't trust giving it to the ex to look after for him."

"Oh, so was you married?"

"If you can call it that."

"So what happened?"

Danny thought for a moment that K was being too intrusive, but he didn't mind. It wouldn't be likely that they would be crossing paths again. "Aaaahhh, dear Vanessa. Before I married her I didn't really get to know her. But when I did, I found out she put the bark into Barking, has the glare of the Terminator, spent money like she's the offspring of Elton John and Jackie Onassis, and to top it all, she can spit further than the whole West Ham first team squad put together... Quite a woman."

"Why did you get with her in the first place," K asked, suppressing a smile.

"Like any other normal bloke does. She's as pretty as anyone and I couldn't resist her Kylie Minogue-like arse - she could go clubbing up West dressed in a dustbin suit and a Tesco bag for a hat and still look more fuckable than Posh Spice." Danny smiled, enjoying a pleasant memory. "Sex with her was like West Ham winning the Cup every night."

K admired Danny's honesty and this time he let himself laugh, guessing that Danny's humour got him far with women. "So why did you get involved in this sort of career?"

"I can ask the same about you," Danny countered. "Excitement, I suppose. Wasn't much at school - I was the model for the first dunce's hat. Couldn't even get into any of the sports teams. Loved football, but I was crap at that. All my mates used to take the piss. I just drifted along not knowing what the fuck to do with my life. Then I sorta got sucked into *this*." Danny gestured with the notes. "It gave me a buzz. Now I don't feel like the wanky guy who got picked last in the Sunday football game in the park... Funny enough if I weren't in this game I doubt if I woulda had my son. Vanessa wouldn't have looked at me once if she knew I was just a normal Joe. I think my career choice was a buzz for her an' all. Silly tart... What about you? You're a bit of an unlikely one in this game. What's your S.P.?"

K heard his mother's voice in his mind again: 'you had all the opportunities I never had and you just wasted them'. "I was a social worker," he answered with a tinge of bitterness. "I got framed by my superiors on a case I was working with. I'll never get a job with any social services again."

Danny studied K's face and guessed that K didn't want to elaborate on this matter.

"So I'm in this just to make some quick money and forge a new life out of this country. Away from it all." Away from his mother, his inner voice whispered. She'll have to look for me one day and apologise. I didn't let her down. *She* let me down by not believing in me in my time of crisis.

Danny noticed K's vacant stare and decided it was time to return to the pub. "Let's go back," he said. "Otherwise Lee will probably think you kidnapped me."

K laughed again, forcing himself out of his melancholy. Once they had banked the envelopes underneath their jackets, they returned through the pub doors. Colin was still in conversation with Eddie at the bar. Danny recognised the back of a man who had just entered the premises before they did. He tugged on K's arm and ushered him away, facing the wall.

"Well, I guess it's true wha dey say about you," Colin told Eddie, finishing off their discourse.

"And what's that, then, Eddie?" asked a new voice. Colin turned to see a man in his early thirties; thick set, dark haired and suited approaching the bar. He knew him for the Law without even thinking about it. An air of Police hung around him like old aftershave.

"Nothing to concern you, Detective Sergeant Powell," said Eddie, pushing the tray of drinks at Colin and urging him away with his eyes. The newcomer didn't miss it, nor Tony's coming to stand behind him. Colin took the tray and sauntered back to the table.

"Heads up, everybody," he said in a low voice. "Beast at five O'clock."

Colin had to admire the way Davie took the news. He failed to give so much as a surreptitious peek at the interloper, whereas Ali grew decidedly and visibly uncomfortable. Like himself, Ali had porridge-eating on his C.V., so the Law always made him skittish. Baron looked bored, for which Colin gave silent thanks to Allah; because he didn't want the entire crew to look like pussies in front of the pagans, and he was pleased to note that Matt appeared in the worst state. He was staring at the newcomer with ill-concealed terror and the bulge in his pocket felt suddenly obvious, like an erection at a heavyweight championship weigh-in.

"'im don't know nutten', yout'," said Baron. "Dis 'as nutten' fe do wid us."

"He's right, Matt. Powell comes here regular just to piss Eddie off," agreed Davie. "Think nothing of it."

There was a pause while the men sipped their drinks and Davie wondered where Danny and the Professor had got to. Had they set them up? He looked around and spotted them talking amicably while facing the wall, obviously aware of the situation. Davie rebuked himself for having had such thoughts.

"He's coming over. Everybody keep schtumn," Davie said through unmoving lips as the Detective Sergeant approached them.

"Well, now, what have we here, then?" said Powell. He enjoyed using the opening gambit of the Bobby stereotype, since it made him feel part of some kind of admirable urban folklore. "Little Matty Jones, eh?" he went on. "All grown up and getting into bad company. Never seen you in here before. Didn't your mother tell you about mixing with strange men?"

Silence confronted him like a runaway cement truck. Matt, Colin and Ali stared into their beer, while Davie and Baron ignored him.

"Davie Thompson. Why do I always think about paperwork and overtime whenever I see you? You still raging against the machine?"

Davie took a long sip from his orange juice.

"So," said Powell. "What's going on?"

"Just a quiet drink with a few friends, D.S. Powell."

"That's all, is it? I thought I knew all your friends, Davie. I've locked up most of 'em. Why don't you introduce me."

"I don't think so."

"No matter. I'm sure we'll be discussing their habits at the Station soon enough."

"If you like. You still do those tasty bacon rolls?"

"Hmm. We'll have to see about that. Where's your other half, Jones?"

"Wh-what?"

"Lee. Can't say I think he'd approve of the company you're keeping. Where is he?"

"I'm here, pig," hissed Lee, crossing the floor from the toilets.

"Now you want to watch that. Didn't your old man teach you no manners?"

"What do you want?"

"Me? Maybe I just wanted to find out how your dad's doing in Wandsworth. Maybe I want to know what your nasty little mind is up to."

"Like he said, we're just having a couple of pints."

"Is *that* all? You've come a long way in a short time, then, Lee. Nelson Mandela would be proud. I mean, what would your old man say if he knew you were partying around with these guys? Have you told them of your hobby?"

Colin X stiffened, but Baron put a restraining hand on his arm. Ali kissed his teeth in a drawn out sound of contempt.

"Don't you talk about my dad!"

"Fair enough, son. It ain't him I'm interested in these days, anyway. But I must admit, I'm intrigued... Last I heard you were fighting the race war. Taken to sleeping with the enemy, have you?"

Lee stared into his pint.

"*Remove,*" said Colin. "Just remove from de scene. Leave us alone, man."

"And who might you be?"

"I'm de brudder of all those people *you* killed in cells! Dat's who me is."

Ali felt bolstered by Colin's confidence and decided to join in the fray. "Yeah! Arrest us, then. Go on," he said, raising his pint at the Detective Sergeant in a mocking toast. "Tek us down de sty an' see where dat gets you. But know one t'ing right from de start. I'm not some scared brudder wid a five-pound draw in his pocket. You'd better be sure dat you've got wha' you need before you start, 'cos if you open up on me, I'm up for it. All de fuckin' way. I know de Law an' it ain't behind you on dis one."

"That a fact? Then why have you and little Matt here been shitting yourselves since I smiled a greeting? I know your lot don't appreciate gays, but I'm not one of those, so what else could it be that's causing them inner hysterics?"

"Oh, you beastman can make it hard on us," growled Colin. "Every black man knows dat. But times ain't wha' dey were, pig. Der ain't no sus laws dis side of the Eighties, so eider do wha' you 'ave to or *remove* from de scene, because you're putting me off my drink."

Powell looked at him and his face showed a mixture of emotions as he leant his face in close to that of Colin. "Sus laws, get real," he spat. "You were still in short trousers when that shit was going down and so was I for that matter. In that event, what the fuck do *we* know about the sus laws? You're talking ancient history, my friend, and the quicker you learn that it ain't the black man but the bad man we're after the quicker your kids as well as my kids will be able to sleep safer in their beds at night." He paused and took a moment to take in the faces of the men at the table. "People like you perpetuate a myth that stops us getting the job done," he went on, "and when we can't get the job done it makes people like you look like they're talking sense. So, let me tell you, my friend, that sort of comment is just the sort of thing that pisses me and the Law off."

Powell turned on his heel and as he left the pub Colin released a long, drawn-out breath. His knees felt like liquorice and his glass chattered against his teeth as he took a grateful swallow of lager. From the corner of his eye he could see K and Danny observing the proceedings and as Powell left the pub the two of them came back to the table.

"Me and the Law? Who's he think he is, Judge Dread or something?" K managed in an attempt to disperse the stress that smothered them.

Everybody laughed, a raw sound with the hiss of escaping tension, but it was some time before Colin joined them.

Friday 30th of November, 2001; 12:45am.

It was close to one in the morning by the time Eddie was finally able to head up the stairs to his office, where Dick Keating had been kept waiting in expectant and clandestine solitude. The bottle of whisky that had been set on his desk some six hours previously had been drained by a half, but Eddie didn't mind that as it served his purposes all the better.

"How's it going, Dick?" he asked amiably.

Dick looked up from the portable television that Eddie kept in his office to keep an eye on the racing and raised his glass. "I'm getting a bit excited," he confessed earnestly, his voice tinged with nervous expectation. "When are we going to start?"

"Soon," Eddie acknowledged, plucking a bottle of tonic from a packing crate and cracking it open. Unlike Dick, he'd only had one sniff of alcohol all day.

He sat in his chair and drank the tonic water straight from the bottle; enjoying the bitter taste as it puckered his palette. He had one more job to do tonight and he wondered whether or not he was up for it. After all, it had been such a long time...

"You know," Dick said, turning from the television to face him for the first time, "I haven't thanked you yet for bringing me in on this... you know... *fun*. I mean, I know I'm on their books now and so I'm probably a risk, but I just want you to know that I'll do my bit and make sure we all have some fun - I mean that. You'll come to trust me, Eddie, I can promise you that."

"Our friend said you were perfect for the job. I trust his judgement without question."

Dick Keating nodded and a nervous smile developed from the corners of his mouth. "You know, I never knew our friend shared in the fun until he came to me about you, saying you wanted me for something special," he explained. "I can't wait."

There was a pause while Dick wiped a hand across his chubby face. "I tell you, though, our friend is good," he went on. "No-one back there knows of his hobby, and he even joined in with those guys who like giving grief to the offenders in the Vulnerable Prisoners Unit..." Dick winced and shivered at the thought.

Eddie twiddled with his hearing aid more out of habit than need until he was satisfied with the result. "Oh, I share the views of our friend alright when it comes to your idea of 'fun'," he said, "and like him I'm just as good at hiding it."

"That's good," Dick admitted. "I tell you something, though, he never spilled the beans about what you had in mind. So, are you gonna tell me all about this something special before I burst with excitement, or what?"

Eddie sipped at his tonic and whether his grimace was due to the bitter taste of the quinine or the prospect of the special thing Dick could not tell.

"Oh, you'll find out what I have in store for you soon enough," Eddie stated after a pause, "and it's so much *fun* I'm sure it's something you'll remember for the rest of your life."

Friday 30th of November, 2001; 05:45am.

Detective Sergeant Dudley Powell was not in the best frame of mind as he descended the steps that led to platform eight of Barking Station. Fifteen minutes short of finishing his night shift he had been summoned to a suspicious death, and that meant overtime at a time when a bed was already overdue.

Detective Constable Scott Hain was already on the platform to meet him, along with a station employee who was wearing a black donkey jacket and Day-Glo orange waistcoat. He carried two spare visibility jackets in his hands, and Dudley knew that he'd soon be wearing one of them as he tip-toed through the mud that lined the tracks.

"Wotcha, Sarge," Scott said, feigning a smile. His fine, blond hair appeared darker than usual on account of the rain that had drenched it and his face carried the pinched look of someone who had spent some time standing in the cold. "This is Andy Fredericks, and he's safety manager for the station."

Andy; a swarthy, dark-skinned man in his early thirties, held out a hand that Dudley accepted. He flashed a weather-beaten smile. "Not exactly the best morning for it," he said, glancing up at the clouds that were just becoming visible with the first light of dawn. "Here, put these on and I'll take you down. You wanna lend of some boots?"

Dudley took the Day-Glo waistcoat and tugged it over his jacket. Now he was wet, cold and had tight clothing irritating his armpits. He looked down at his shoes; new shoes that still had the smell of the shop on them, then he thought of the dirty, second hand and undoubtedly smelly boots with which they would be replaced. No. He would sacrifice his shoes for the sake of avoiding further discomfort. "I'm fine as I am," he replied wearily.

Andy shrugged and waved for the two C.I.D. men to follow him along the platform, Scott pulling on his own visibility jacket as they did so.

"Why are we here?" Dudley asked, feeling slightly annoyed that he was out in the elements when he didn't need to be. "This is a job for the B.T.P.."

"My fault, Sarge," Scott informed him. "I was in the station checking out a routine disturbance when the shit hit the fan, so they asked me to pop down here and take a gander because I'd get to the scene before the Transport Police. Maybe the D.I. wanted you to baby-sit, because he thought you were in need of some fresh air and exercise?"

"The B.T.P. won't like it," Dudley reminded him, "stepping on their toes like that."

"Well, all we have to do is secure the scene before they turn up."

"The incident is about four and five hundred metres along the Fenchurch Street to Tilbury Line," Andy interrupted them. "That's about half way between here and Upney Station."

Dudley nodded and wondered why rail deaths were always called 'incidents' by staff. He guessed it was to spare the frayed nerves of any eavesdropping passengers, in the same way that all fires on the tracks were simply referred to as 'smouldering'.

"What do you mean, four *and* five hundred metres along the tracks?" Scott Hain wanted to know.

They had walked to the end of the platform and were just about to descend onto the tracks themselves. Andy turned around to face the young Detective Constable and his expression betrayed both surprise and humour at his question. "It sure shows that you ain't with the B.T.P.," he grinned.

Scott nodded and at the same time shrugged his shoulders in a 'so what' gesture.

"Well," Andy began, having abandoned their rail-track rambling for a moment so that he could gesticulate with his arms, "when you get hit by a train you don't get flung over the bonnet as you do when you're hit by a car."

He paused and ran his palm face down in a line that ran parallel with the tracks. "You sort of… *smear*. Bits of your clothing get caught up in the machinery and drag bits of you in one direction, while other bits of you get caught in other things that pull you the other way. You kinda get ripped apart in the process and where those different bits of you land depends upon what bits they got caught up in, or how tough your clothing is, *et cetera*."

"So you're saying that our body is smeared along a hundred metres of track?" Dudley asked, the bacon and eggs he was planning an hour ago now off his agenda.

"Yeah - there or thereabouts. I ain't no tape measure."

Andy turned and led the two officers down the stairs that led from the platform to the track. There was a short tunnel for them to walk through that ran under the station itself, but then it was all over-ground until the track terminated at Tilbury. "These tracks ain't live," Andy said amicably. "These are for trains, not for the tube, so you can step pretty-much where you want." He stopped yet again and flung out an arm to indicate other sets of tracks that ran alongside them to their left. "But keep away from *that* lot," he went on. "This line has been closed due to the incident, but that lot ain't and the tube is soon to open. So, we've got live rails there *and* passenger tubes will be along at any minute. Don't say I didn't warn you."

Dudley nodded and as they left the tunnel he felt fresh drizzle on his face. "Do you know what time the incident occurred?" he asked.

"Nope," Andy replied. "It's strange. Usually suicides kinda jump in front of the trains, so the drivers get to see them and report in straight after, but not this time. We woulda known bugger all about it if it hadn't been for a maintenance crew checking the tracks. They do that every night. Rather them than me in this shit weather."

"And they informed the station how long ago?" Scott enquired.

"About eight minutes."

Dudley checked his watch. It was now five forty-five a.m., and soon the first commuters for the Tilbury to Fenchurch Street line would learn that an 'incident' was to put a crimp on their day. Network South East would get the blame, since it usually *was* their fault, but how was it their fault that someone had decided to throw themselves in front of a train? Maybe the rail companies should stop being so coy, Dudley realised. Instead of referring to 'incidents' they should just come clean and say that some idiot had decided to cash in their chips in a melodramatic and, ultimately, selfish manner by cutting one of London's steel arteries - albeit temporarily - to hasten their own demise.

A question from D.C. Scott Hain brought him back to the cold, wet reality of the dawn. "This line closes pretty early, doesn't it?" he said as he wiped rain from his face.

Andy nodded. "Sorta. Yes, the good people of Tilbury get short changed by a train service that stops earlier than almost everywhere else, but goods trains heading for Barking Container Base and Dagenham Dock keep rolling throughout the night. So, in truth, the incident could have happened at any time because this track is used twenty-four seven."

There was a pause while Andy stepped over a puddle then he pointed to some flashes of orange in the distance. "That there is the maintenance crew," he said. "Right nasty job that is, walking from one end of the line to the other every bleeding night. They should be knocking off soon, but seeing as there were no witnesses to the incident we thought your mob would want a dickie-bird with them first."

"I might just need to take their names," Dudley confirmed. "After all, these sort of things are usually pretty-much open and shut. Just tell them to leave their names with Scott here."

The three men lapsed into silence as they trudged the last few sodden steps of their journey. Dawn was reclaiming the sky with a fist of red and orange fingers, but it had not quite emerged as the victor, so they had to be almost on top of the incident before they could see it. Even then, it took Andy's indicating the evidence with a waved hand before Dudley and Scott could recognise it for what it was.

Dudley had been expecting a body, a bashed up body for sure, and after what Andy had said maybe a mangled body but with an arm or so missing. What he hadn't expected to see was a head to crotch *bisected* trunk with an arm and a lower leg missing, presumably resting somewhere further along the track. The bisection was neat, as though the victim had been laying along the rail itself, and the two halves of the body were separated from the groin to the head, with each half having fallen to either side of the rail. The head itself was little more than mush, having crumpled in upon itself as it was crushed and snapped in two, so that it looked as though the one eye that remained was seated like a boiled egg atop a nest of uncooked mincemeat. Dudley knew little about physiology, but he thought he recognised the grey and pink remnants of a tongue amidst a cluster of yellow, loosened teeth and what appeared to be a patch of skin covered in pubic hair that had come to rest on the pulverised remains of a nose. The corpse also emitted a vile smell.

"Jesus bloody Christ!" Scott exclaimed, his hand raising to cover his mouth and nose. "What a fucking mess."

Andy, too, seemed shaken despite his experience with such matters. He cupped his hands and covered his lower face. "I ain't never seen one like this before," he confirmed before anyone could ask. "Either that's a one in a million hit, or the sod just laid there on the rail waiting for a train to run over him family jewels first."

The rail was a distinct silvery-blood-smeared line running between the two halves of the corpse that indicated its absolute bisection. Bits of spine could be seen with either set of remains, while the neck was little more than a crimson splatter that stretched for about ten feet along the rail.

"Erm… Okay… what can we tell?" Dudley asked, not just so he could get on with the job at hand, but also so that he could break the numb stupefaction that kept him staring mindlessly at the bloody mass of offal that was before him. He stopped breathing through his nose and opened his mouth, but couldn't rid himself of the stench. They still don't pay us enough, he thought.

"Jeans, blue waterproof jacket," Scott said mechanically as he scribbled in his notebook. "White trainers, black socks and dark red - no - erm - *white* - T-shirt."

Dudley noticed that the detective constable was concentrating upon the clothing of their victim, no doubt in an effort to take his mind from the person who lay amidst them and to rid himself of having to study the physical remains. Well, I guess that makes it my job, he said to himself.

"Okay," he mumbled, in his last attempt at putting off the inevitable. "Male - erm- Gawd knows - about five foot seven? Caucasian, middle fifties and - what's that stuff?"

"Fat," Andy Fredericks added helpfully, before walking off to talk with a workman who was waving at him down the track.

The ribs that remained were either jutting out at peculiar angles, crushed to splinters, or pushed deep into the body, so it was difficult to determine a build for the victim. The only indication was the brownish-yellow blobs of adipocere, or body fat, that were bestrewn about the corpse and, indeed, the next twenty feet of rail.

"You reckon there was a lot of this guy?" Scott asked, his biro poised.

Dudley thought about it for a time, his mind trying with utmost reluctance to imagine the mess that was daubed around the corpse back on its smashed frame so he could take a guess at its weight. "I'd say a little on the large side," he managed eventually, thinking that this was the safest bet given the grey hair and, thus, presumed age, of the victim. After all, most grey haired guys of his height were a little on the large side, weren't they?

Andy returned and although he tried to keep his eyes fixed on Dudley his gaze kept flicking to the mauled corpse that lay before them. "I just got word on my radio that the Ambulance Service have turned up and that one of my boys is bringing them down here," he said. "I've also written the names of the maintenance crew down to save you a bit of time."

Scott took the piece of paper that Andy offered him and tucked it into his pocket before the rain could turn it to pulp. "Thanks," he said. He then looked at Dudley and raised an eyebrow. "What about S.O.C.O.?" he asked.

Rain dribbled down Dudley's chin while he scratched at it ponderously. "Well, the guy couldn't be more dead, so S.O.C.O. *have* to turn up," he said. "Not that I think it'll do much good. If we were to put a tent over this corpse now, I think it's still too late for them to find any prints - that's if there are any. The rain will've washed them all away."

"Policing by numbers. You never know, they might find something," Scott consoled him.

"Tell me," Dudley said, turning to face Andy, who was standing around feeling a bit like a fifth wheel. "Is it unusual for a suicide to top himself like that?"

"Gawd, I don't know," the transport worker admitted. He took a cigarette from his pocket, lit it, then wagged it at Dudley while he elaborated. "The thing is, jumpers can get themselves under a train in any number of ways, so they can end up in any bloody position. I even heard of a woman once who laid down in front of a train while it was *stopped* at a station and just waited for it to start up. Silly tart - like the driver was gonna move off with her just lying there... Anyway, the point is, I can't say to you 'Sure, that looks like a suicide to me', because the only certainty about being hit full-on by a moving train is that you're gonna end up brown bread. Where you land, and how many bits you land in, depends upon gravity, momentum and a whole bunch of other things best left to the likes of Sir Isaac Newton to worry about."

"It looks to me like whoever it was laid there on the rail deliberately, Sarge," Scott cut in as he accepted a proffered cigarette from Andy. "I mean, I'm aware of probability and all that, but what are the chances of some fruitcake jumping in front of a train and getting spliced clean through from the nuts to the nut right centre over the rail like that? Not even Ladbrokes would put odds on it."

"Yeah - I think we can agree that our victim wasn't pushed. In which case, I don't think we need to worry about S.O.C.O.'s problems," Dudley agreed.

Dudley stopped talking when he heard footsteps kicking up the puddles and mud behind him. Two members of the Ambulance Service were being led along the track by a transport worker who appeared to be a carbon copy of Andy. They carried boxes of medical equipment between them.

"Hi, I'm Peter Ellison," a black, broad-smiled Ambulance crew member said in a cockney accent. He looked down at the victim, grimaced, and his once polite expression wilted like a chocolate flake in a microwave. "I don't think you need us here," he stated, his voice dropping down a tone. "You just want me to confirm death so S.O.C.O. can turn up? I don't think we need to wait for the F.M.E. to make the call when the victim is cut in half."

"Sure."

"In truth, I prefer 'em dead, " Peter admitted earnestly while his crew mate radioed in that their cause was a lost one. "What most people don't realise is that when someone jumps in front of a train they're more likely to come out of it alive, but minus a few limbs. The tube has what's called a suicide trench, see? They just fall into that, but any stray arms or legs that flail around outside of it get lopped off P.D.Q.."

"So why do you prefer them dead?" Scott asked.

"Because if they're dead we just leave the body for your S.O.C.O. people, but if they ain't then it's *us* who have to pick up the loose arms and legs and take them with us back to the hospital… It stinks out the whole van and if I was to carry *this* one it would've been mask time and a lot of cleaning up."

The second Ambulance crew member - a ginger-haired guy called Steve - looked up at his superior. "I told you we'd need a couple of body bags for this one if he was alive," he said.

"Yeah, and you'd need at least another two as well," Andy told him. "My lads have found the arm and the leg and they're marked out by those traffic cones up yonder." He pointed with his soggy cigarette. "What a right bloody two 'n' eight, eh?"

The two Ambulance men were glad their work ended here and that they could soon beat a bedraggled path back to their vehicle to await their next shout. They watched distastefully as internal sludge dribbled and slurped noisily from the chest cavity of the corpse as it waited in the gravel and mud. "Hold on a sec, what's that?" Peter Ellison asked. He was pointing at the left half of the victim's head, which was not attached to the body and resembled little more than a bloody clod of skull, skin and hair. "Looks like a post-aural aid to me," he added, indicating a strange twist of clear plastic that was mostly obscured by the victim's seeping grey matter.

"A what?" Dudley asked.

"A type of hearing aid, like. The sort that's worn behind the ear."

"Well, at least it's evidence for the identification," Scott interjected. "But is it safe for us to take it? I mean, it's got bits of brain on it after all."

"Now? No," Peter replied. "But I've worked with your S.O.C.O. before. Manky stuff like this can't just get left on some C.I.D. desk, but your forensic department know how to deal with it. S.O.C.O.'ll take it back to the morgue at Oldchurch Hospital for the post mortem and then your forensics can do the rest."

"Will you do me a favour?" Dudley wanted to know.

"Shoot," Peter said with restrained reluctance. The eager and desperate timbre of Dudley's voice meant that whatever he was going to ask, Peter wouldn't like it.

"Will you have a quick rummage around in the pockets for me?"

Peter Ellison bit on his lower lip as he thought about it. Plod are forever getting me to do their dirty work, he mused. It wasn't against the law for him to do it, especially at the behest of a suit from C.I.D.; it was just that he didn't really fancy touching the squelchiness of such a mauled corpse. Sure he was wearing the thick gloves, but the copper could borrow a pair too and do the job himself if he asked. Better yet, he could just wait for S.O.C.O. to turn up, who were paid to do that sort of thing. He glanced at Steve and judged by his facial contortions that he was about to be reacquainted with the soup he'd eaten an hour ago, so he knew he couldn't delegate.

"Does it have to be now?" Peter enquired.

"That aural wotsit has given me a hunch, and it'd save me a whole lot of time if I could confirm it with some I.D.."

There was a moment of silence while Peter's gaze flicked between the bolognese of organs and the young Detective Sergeant, whose face was showing a variety of shades of green despite his best efforts to the contrary. Why put him through it? Peter wondered. "Sure, man," he said.

"Be careful not to move the body, though. It'll need to be photographed as-is."

The left half of the corpse was bereft of an arm, so the bloodstained jacket it wore was attached to its owner with little more than a shredded stump of shoulder. With careful movements, Peter peeled the sodden jacket from the bloody tangle of pulverised flesh and patted it to see if he could feel anything that indicated the contents of a pocket. "Nothing there," he said after a time.

The right side of the corpse was laying between the two rails of the track on the sleepers and he crab-stepped towards it gingerly, trying in futility to avoid the pools of rainwater that were stained a grisly red. He did the same as before, his hands patting the ripped and blood-stained jacket, but this time he felt something. "What's this?" he asked, pulling a square of leather from an inside pocket.

"Wallet," Dudley stated excitedly. "Open it."

Peter flipped open the wallet and from it he took out a credit card.

"Well, guys," he said, casting his large, brown eyes about the expectant men. "Say a wet morning to one Eddie Maynard, but don't be upset if you don't get no reply."

Friday 30th of November, 2001; 09:40am.

Danny hopped off the 87 bus at the stop nearest Barking shopping precinct then crossed the grounds of the old abbey to the unkempt tower-blocks that made up the Gascoigne Council Estate. The looming grey monoliths that housed the poorest and most deprived of Barking's denizens seemed all the more bleak due to the portentous clouds that hung like bloated corpses overhead, and Danny had to orientate himself before he could locate the block he was looking for.

Once found and entered, he was amazed to discover a lift that had not succumbed to the fashion of wearing an 'Out of Order' logo, and while it creaked and groaned to the 13th floor he held his breath to mask the stench of nappies and piss.

Despite Danny's agitation, Davie's flat was not difficult to find; it being the only one that proclaimed its tenant's unwillingness to accept any local papers, flyers, junk mail, official/governmental mail, canvassers, religious zealots, council officials, gas men, provost, councillors, counsellors or priests on a tatty piece of paper that was sellotaped to the front door. The bell had been stolen, so Danny knocked twice.

"Go away," came a voice after a short delay.

"Davie, it's me," Danny stage-whispered through the sellotape-sealed letterbox. "Get the wood out the hole, we need to talk and it's serious."

"Danny?"

"Of course it's me, for Christ's sake. Get the bloody door open, will you?"

There was the clank of a deadlock before the threshold of Davie's demesne revealed itself, and, notwithstanding his anxiety, Danny felt a moment of curiosity when he crossed it, because this was the first time he had dared approach Davie's self-confessed hermitage despite their ten years' of friendship.

He wondered what would be revealed and as he was led along the hallway to the sitting room he took the opportunity to take in his extraordinary surroundings. The floor and Spartan furniture were clean and neat – almost obsessively so – but they did not capture Danny's attention – not when he had the walls to gaze upon. As Davie murmured something about not expecting any visitors, Danny was preoccupied with reading the newspaper clippings that enclosed the flat more completely than the wallpaper they concealed: Afghanistan, Northern Ireland, the Gulf, Tiananmen Square and countless other wars, conflicts, atrocities and 'troubles' fought for column inches against natural disasters such as hurricanes, famines and floods and not so natural disasters including Piper Alpha, Chernobyl and Hillsborough. They screamed from the walls like a Munch exhibition; with journalists proclaiming the distress of the countless photographed victims, some of whose tortured faces were circled in red biro with scribbled notes beside. Fuck me, Danny thought. Either Davie thinks he's the second coming of St. John or he's the mother of all sadists. He tried to read the scrawl that entombed in ink Davie's reaction to the photograph of a Buddhist monk who had set himself ablaze in response to the Chinese occupation of Tibet, but he could discern not a word of it, nor a letter for that matter, because Davie had written in a cipher; but whether it was a cipher gleaned from his time with the Forces or a cipher of his own conception Danny could not say.

"So what's the problem?" Davie asked eventually.

"Get your coat," Danny replied, trying to ignore the walls.

Davie pushed aside a yellow newspaper upon which ran the legend "*Gotcha*" and from under it he pulled a crumpled camouflage jacket. "Man, you should get a phone," Danny told him as the duo walked back to the front door.

"Not in this life," Davie answered.

They took the stairs and were soon walking in the direction of Barking Town Centre. "I just got a text message from Tony on my mobile," Danny said after a time. "He said for us to meet him in the abbey grounds at ten O'clock, which gives us about five minutes."

"Did he say why?"

"Nope, but he didn't sound too chuffed."

"I don't suppose he is, otherwise he'd've got us to meet him at... that place... at the - eh - you know... the... the..."

"The *pub*?"

"Yeah, that's it, the pub. Thanks, Alan."

Alan? Danny knew that Davie hadn't seen Alan Jones since he'd been sent down to Wandsworth over a year previously and he noticed that Davie's voice was slurred, as though he was drunk. Not for the first time he was concerned for his friend and as he turned around to face him his fears grew worse. One side of Davie's face had slackened as though he'd suffered a stroke, while his right shoulder twitched spasmodically.

"Davie?" Danny said in an unsure manner.

"Yes, Danny?"

"Are you alright?"

"Sure. Never felt better."

Danny had seen the shoulder tic before and knew that Davie would be able to mask it by the time they reached Tony, but he wasn't even certain that Davie *knew* what had happened to his face. He was good at hiding the symptoms of the syndrome, Danny admitted, but he also had to admit that Davie's erratic behaviour, forgetfulness and increasing spasms were becoming more than a bottle of Benperidol could hide.

"You'd better take one of your tablets, pal," he said. "We need to get into character."

They returned to silence until the abbey, or rather what was left of it, came into view. The abbey had been reduced to ruins centuries before and had long been replaced by Saint Margaret's Church, but the locals still referred to it as the abbey and a nearby school bore its name. "You know, I've always loved this place," Davie said once they had stepped through its old iron gates. The tablets had tightened his face a little and his shoulder had stopped twitching. "Did you know it was built in the year six-six-six?"

Maybe Davie *does* think of himself as the one to tell the world of its imminent doom, Danny pondered, only partly in jest. He looked around and all he could see was some broken down walls and a lot of moss-covered gravestones. "Churches give me the creeps," he answered, his disinterest apparent in his tone. He thrust his hands in his pockets to combat the cold and hunched his shoulders. "Come on, let's just look around until we see Tony and find out what's up."

They walked through the graveyard until Davie spied the Australian barman sitting on a park bench that was ensconced within the walls of the derelict abbey itself. He was holding a cheeseburger in his hand, but didn't look like he had any intention of eating it.

"Wotcha, Tony," Danny said, patting him on the shoulder before sitting down next to him. "So what's the morning glory?"

Davie, as ever, was willing to let Danny do all the talking and he sat down on the bench beside him.

"Christ, mate, don't you know?" Tony whined, and now both men could see the dark crescents that hung under his eyes and the tormented look on his face. "Last night? Did you know that Eddie was going to top himself?"

"What?"

"Eddie. I got called by the cops this-morning before even the bloody milkman was up and now they're crawling all over the pub. It seems that Eddie took a dive under a train last night after I'd left." He paused and stared at his cheeseburger as though it could somehow offer him some advice. When none was forthcoming he carried on of his own volition. "The fuckin' brewery gave them my number as secondary key-holder, and I've been answering questions to D.S. Powell since six bloody thirty and had to open up the pub for him."

"Shit," Davie managed, his unaccustomed use of profanity emphasising his concern. "Was any stuff left over from the job there?" he added. Despite what Eddie had called his *'fuzziness'* he was always the first to think of operational matters.

"No, mate, no," Tony consoled him, his blue eyes still focussed upon the cheeseburger. "I was doing the clean-up job with Eddie last night and we both made sure that everything was sorted. Even his lock-up is empty, with a courier having picked up the gear within an hour of you lot dropping it off. We even washed the place down for prints."

"What about the shooters?"

"They're safe. Trust me. Bottom of the Thames. There's nothing in the pub that the Law will pick up on, even if they were looking for it, which they ain't. They're looking for suicide notes and shit."

Much to everybody's surprise, including Tony's, he found himself offering around a carton of fries. He hadn't touched them, and they had already grown cold. Davie declined with a contemptuous sneer, but Danny took a handful.

"Mates, I've got something to say," Tony mumbled nervously while Danny chewed. "What if I was to tell you that something bigger than the job last night was going on? What if I told you I had some information. What would that be worth?"

"That depends upon the information," Danny spluttered with his mouth full, still digesting the news about Eddie. The realisation struck him that soon every Herbert from Shoreditch to Southend would be on the manor, wanting some of Eddie's spoils. "But at the moment I'm more preoccupied with the Sweeney crawling all over the gaff of my boss," he said eventually, still trying to erase his shock.

"Well, you'll soon forget about the Old Bill when I tell you that my information has something to do with more fucking wonga than you can shake a stick at."

Danny and Davie exchanged glances. "Well, let the rat out of the fuckin' toilet! Give us the S.P.!"

"First off I want to say this," Tony whimpered, and now it looked as though he was scared of their reaction to what he was about to tell them. "First off, I want to say that I had no part to play in Eddie's deal and that it wasn't me who was fucking you over. I heard this information by mistake, and Eddie didn't know it. So, you'll give me no grief, right?"

"You'd better spit it out."

"Well, second, I want to make a deal with you. If I give you the information and you can pull it off, I want to be cut in on the readies. I can't do it on my Todd, and I ain't got a clue about running with a crew, but you can't do it without the information I have, so I think it's a pretty fair trade."

Davie noticed that Tony's hands were shaking as he spoke. He was out of his depth - a no-balls courier and errand boy sparring with the trigger-men - and he knew it.

"We'll give you the going rate," Danny replied, knowing that the going rate would depend entirely upon how he felt at the time - perhaps a few hundred to party in Amsterdam or somewhere - Aussies love travelling. "Now spit out the dummy before we all catch our deaths out here. What do you mean about Eddie stitching us up?"

An arc of lightening raced across the sky and its near-instantaneous boom indicated that the cloudburst was almost directly overhead. Tony pulled the collar of his leather jacket tighter about his neck. "I heard Eddie speaking on the dog a few days back and he was talking about your job. He was saying that he didn't give a shit about not knowing where to flog the Chinese medicine, because all he was interested in was shifting the diamonds."

"Diamonds? What bloody diamonds?" Danny demanded, his expression radiating his surprise like heat from a bulb.

"That's the whole point," Tony explained. "In the jacking there was a double bluff. One of the crew we done over was stitching the rest of his crew by bringing in some extra stuff that his mates didn't know about. They thought they were bringing in about sixty K's worth of rhino bollocks or whatever, but within that rhino bollocks was a nice little bag of diamonds that only this one guy knew about."

Davie was suspicious and he held up a callused hand to halt Tony's discourse. "And how did Eddie find out?" he wanted to know.

"From what I can gather, one of the crew rumbled what was going on and needed some muscle to get the gear for himself, so he called upon Eddie to provide it. That's where you and the Brixton lads came in."

"Then there was an inside man who knew all about our jacking them?"

"I guess so, but who it was I haven't a clue."

"What about Harry Green?" Danny asked. "Eddie told me that he was the source. We could take him out for afternoon tea and gently persuade him to be on-side."

"Oh, he's legit alright. I was their go-between and I know for certain that he knows fuck all about the diamonds. Eddie and him went way back, and when Eddie asked whether he could rumble on his turf he was only too pleased because he really *was* getting leant on by those guys. That ain't complicity - it's just common or garden circumstance."

"So it was someone on the job."

"I don't know. At this point your guess is as good as mine."

Davie slapped his palms on his knees and let out a small chuckle. "Boy, but that takes some balls," he admitted. "We went in there tooled up to the nines and a guy inside the plane knew it all along? He knew he could've ended up as a worm's dinner."

"It could've been someone in the car," Danny remarked. "After all, they did have that blow-out, didn't they? It might've been part of a set up to keep the heat from us."

"No, Danny," Davie corrected him. "If that was part of the plan Eddie would've let us in on it. You know how careful Eddie played everything. He wouldn't have done anything that was unexpected for us, because that might've sent the plan tits up. That flat was a real one, so we can rule its occupants out of the running for inside man. If Tony here says that Harry Green ain't in on it neither then that just leaves the guys in the plane itself."

There was a pause while the three men allowed an old lady walking her dog to pass by, then Tony turned to face the two crew men. "There's one other thing about the diamonds that I can tell you," he murmured. "And that, mates, is that according to Eddie there was eight million quids worth stuffed in them there boxes."

"What?" Danny exclaimed, his surprise making his voice louder than it should have been. His mind stopped computing for a long second and his mouth gaped and stayed gaped. "If you're telling me a whopping great Jeffrey Archer I'm gonna boot your Aussie arse right back across the ocean to the land of upside-down."

"You heard me. Eight million smackers. I need a fucking calculator to work out how much that is in Aussie dollars."

The usual emotionless expression remained painted across Davie's gaunt face and he popped a tablet into his mouth before speaking. "There's one thing we're forgetting," he said after he'd swallowed. "Eight million beer vouchers are most definitely worth killing one firm-member-come-publican over. Maybe it was the inside man what did for Careful Eddie? Maybe it wasn't suicide at all."

"You reckon?" Tony asked.

"Well, would you turn up your toes voluntarily on the very night that you'd just made your first million?"

"I guess not."

Danny looked up at the darkening sky and stood. "We've gotta split," he said. "Tony, you leave it to us and we'll see what we can do."

Tony nodded and Danny led Davie away from the ruins of the old abbey without further comment. "Come on, I'll treat you to some pie and mash," he said as they crossed Barking's shopping precinct.

The windows of the pie and mash shop were lacquered with condensation and inside it was steamy despite Danny and Davie being the first patrons of the day. "Double pie and mash with plenty of liquor," Danny asked amicably of the stout, middle-aged women who was serving.

He looked at Davie and raised an eyebrow. "Stewed eels," came the reply.

"Yeah - and two cups of cha while you're at it," Danny added as he fished around for some money. "*Clean* cups!"

After paying, they grabbed their food along with some cutlery and sat at a chipped table that was far away from the door.

"Well?" Danny probed as he poured vinegar over the mashed potato and pale green liquor.

Davie clocked the door before he answered. They were still alone and the woman who had served them had retreated back to the kitchen. "I think we might as well forget about Tony's information," he said. "Someone did for Careful Eddie and we have no clues, so them diamonds might as well be on the moon for all the good it'll do us. I mean, where would we start looking?"

"The pub? The lock-up?" Danny answered excitedly, the thrill of the chase upon him.

Davie shook his head as he sucked the meat from a chunk of eel, and he took its bone from his mouth and laid it beside his bowl before speaking. "You know Eddie," he said, wiping his mouth on the back of his hand. "He scrubbed his place clean of prints if he thought a cop show was gonna come on television. The same goes for his lock-up. There'll be nothing there."

Danny was stirring the liquor into his mash and he looked down into it while he thought as though it was an oracle. "Do you reckon Tony was right about Harry Green? We could lean on him a little."

"Nah - if Harry was involved Eddie would've dealt with him direct and not had Tony as their go-between. I say we keep him out of it, or we could end up with a 'too many cooks' situation."

"Then that just leaves the crew we jacked and the Brixton boys."

Davie spat out another eel bone. "I've been thinking about that," he mumbled. "I'd lay money on the Brixton crew having nothing to do with Eddie turning his toes skyward, but they may know something we don't. Contacts, leads, something like that. As for Eddie's murder, well, at the moment it's odds on that his source in the jacked crew did the proverbial honours."

There was a pause while both men rottweilered their breakfast; with each scouring his mind for schemes that would get their hands on the diamonds. If only... Danny thought dreamily. Images of a trust fund for his boy filled his mind, along with his ex-wife's facial expression when she realised that she'd jumped ship just before it discovered the promised land. Wouldn't have to worry about *her*, though, he realised. I'll even have Barbara Windsor wanting to entertain me if we can pull this off.

"So shall we pay our friends a visit?" Danny asked eventually.

"I think it's a must," Davie replied. He took a slurp of tea. "On top of the information, we need to let them know about Eddie, because if they don't hear it from us first they may think we did for him and get nervous. You never know; they might even think they're next, and try to pre-empt us in a little gang war, which is the last thing we need."

Danny didn't like the idea of revealing any information to the South Londoners, but he knew that to *not* do so could put his crew in their firing line. By their reasoning, the South Londoners would have to take his crew out before they did to them what, they would assume, they had done to Eddie. "Man, we've got to make peace with those guys fast," he said, not relishing the prospect of unnecessary conflict. "But where do we find them? I guess we could ask Tony whether he couriered anything to one of their addresses."

"I think we should leave that as a last resort," Davie replied. "Let's keep him at arm's length until we have to. There's a way we can contact the South London boys without Tony getting involved."

"And that is?"

"Don't you remember? Last night they mentioned about going to some kind of party down the Stansfield Road. We could pay them a visit there."

The door to the pie and mash shop clapped as a teenage mum dragged in a pram that housed a crying toddler, and the sound summoned the women who had served them out from the kitchen.

"Okay, I'll get on the blower to Lee and Matt and we'll get this business sorted," Danny said surreptitiously, his eyes flicking in the direction of the young woman, then flicking back to Davie wearing an expression that indicated 'enough said'.

Davie had finished his stewed eels, so he popped two tablets into his mouth and swallowed. "I have to take these with food or drink," he said, his face contorting at the bitter taste that he washed away with some tea. Their former conversation was now as dead as the Kray twins.

"Any news?" Danny asked.

"Not yet, but soon. I've gotta go to Oldchurch Hospital for the results of some tests next Thursday."

"Are they any closer to knowing what it is? I ain't no expert, but I thought the Government didn't even *admit* to Gulf War Syndrome being around yet."

Davie laughed; a raw, tired sound. "Nah - all they can tell me is what it *ain't*. It's not Parkinson's and it's not mad cow disease. My bastard G.P. thought I had the shakes, because I was an alcoholic, though. I mean, I ain't touched a drop since nineteen ninety-four and didn't drink much even then. They put chemicals in it, see?"

Danny spooned the last of the liquor from his plate and concluded that it was Davie's intimacy with Gulf War Syndrome that had sparked his obsession with Government conspiracies, global corporations and ecological warfare. Maybe Eddie was right, he thought. Perhaps Davie does need the attention of one of those private clinics. When this is all over I'll sort Davie out. "You want a lift on Thursday?" he asked.

"No thanks. I won't pollute the atmosphere when I can get a bus."

"It's no bother. I need to go to that neck of the woods to speak to a man about a dog anyhow. Coming with me would halve the petrol and help save the planet."

Davie smiled and Danny realised with sadness what a rare sight that was. "If I'm saving you from yourself, then I think I'll take you up on the offer," Davie said. "Can you pick me up around ten?"

"Sure I can. Providing we get back from our trip to Stockwell in one piece first."

Saturday 1st December, 2001; 02:30am.

Danny noticed that the bickering and debate behind him had quelled somewhat since he had emerged on the south side of the Rotherhithe Tunnel. He rebuked himself for hauling in Lee on his quest, but felt he had to be loyal to Alan. Besides, Lee *was* in on the initial heist. Maybe with wads of money in his pocket he'll forget about his prejudices. The streets leading up to Elephant and Castle were deserted apart from the boisterous queue awaiting to gain admission into the *Ministry Of Sound* night-club. A night bus was motoring over the urban speed limit ahead of him and a Police patrol car was stationary by the roundabout. For a moment, he wondered whether the car within which they were travelling had been reported stolen yet.

"I still can't believe it," Matt commented, his vacant eyes staring out the window. "Eddie fuckin' *dead*!"

"Shit happens," answered Danny. "I s'pose his luck had to run out one day. It's funny, though. No one laid so much as a finger on Eddie for over thirty years until he must've thought his bollocks were charmed. Then in one go his fat arse is no more but squelch."

Davie scanned his crew's faces and guessed that no-one felt any great sense of loss. Danny spotted a road-sign for Brixton and found himself increasing his grip on the steering wheel and placing his foot over the brake pedal while checking his speed. He glanced at his watch. 02:30am. "Right, Kennington Road leads off this roundabout - how far is the Clapham Road, Davie?"

Davie, sitting in the passenger seat, peered into his dog-eared A-Z with his nose nearly touching the yellowing pages. It rustled in his gently trembling hands. "About half a mile - it carries on from this road. Go straight through all the lights. Turn left when you come to Stockwell Tube and Stansfield Road is on the right about half a mile down there."

Danny nodded, feeling *that* buzz again.

Davie looked behind at Lee who was peering out of the window contemptuously, as if these streets were beneath him. He had been strangely subdued on the journey thus far.

As Lee pulled hard on his cigarette he reminded himself of the joke he once heard about niggers commuting to work via the trees. "Now, Lee," Davie counselled, keeping his tone calm. "You've been running close to the edge with the South London mob since this thing started. I ain't gonna warn you again - any wise-cracks and I'll put my knee into your B.N.P. gob. We *only* want to know if they know about the diamonds. Got that?"

"It's fuckin' obvious the niggers know!" Lee spat, flinging his cigarette butt out of the window and challenging Davie momentarily with his eyes. He then glanced at Matt for some kind of support, but Matt looked down at the car floor; exhaling his cigarette smoke softly and not prepared to back Lee up on this one. "I dunno what the fuck Eddie was playing at having those niggers on the job," Lee ranted. "He should've known they can't be trusted. Fuckin' coons. They probably killed

Eddie themselves. They're probably having some sort of jungle party celebrating they got one over all of us!"

"If they did con us," Davie reasoned, "then why would they tell us where they're gonna be celebrating tonight?"

"Cos they're fuckin' idiots!" Lee returned, lighting another cigarette.

Three minutes later, Danny parked alongside a skateboard park; its concrete hollows and mounds appearing like a primitive burial ground in the dark. This was backdropped by the vast Stockwell Park council estate where it was a guess where one flat's border started and another finished. Across the street from the brickwork maze was the back-end of the Brixton Academy; five stories high and its brown brickwork plastered with advertising boards and graffiti. A siren could be heard in the distance. Stansfield Road, full with three-storied terraced houses that were much more expensive than the East Londoners could guess, was opposite the skateboard park. The lamp-posts glowed yellow except for one at the end of the street that flickered erratically, showering light on an orange, road-side skip. The crew could all hear the faint rumble of music.

Davie climbed out of the car first, taking in his alien surroundings for a few seconds. The sensations he felt within his chest were the same he sensed whilst on operations in Ulster, although from first glances he thought this place was like any other inner-city area at night. He didn't allow his feelings to show on his face, but he was angry that the syndrome was causing the muscles in his left hand and forearm to twitch slightly. He hoped no-one thought it was fear as he fought to control them. Lee jumped out next, showing a hyperactivity in his head movements. His breathing accelerated and he shifted from foot to foot as if he needed the toilet in a manner that made Davie wonder whether Lee's antics were nerves or bravado. Matt climbed out of the car slowly and reluctantly, thinking there must have been a better plan than *this*. I'm glad for the money I got already, he thought. Fuck this for a game of soldiers. Eddie's fuckin' dead, *who* might be next? Once Danny emerged from the car he stared ahead into Stansfield Road, thinking how best to confront the situation. He found himself hoping that K was at the party. "Let's turn into the road and park the car on the corner. We should keep the motor in sight - nothing is probably safe 'round here."

"You can say that again," Lee sniped. "Niggers nick cars from their old ladies!"

Davie caught Lee with a disapproving frown. "Get in the car, grasshopper!" he ordered menacingly.

Danny pulled up three car lengths within Stansfield Road and the music was now audible enough to discern the words. Matt took in a deep breath, while Davie peered down the street. Lee wound down his window and stuck his head out, curiosity overcoming any fear of Davie's rebuke.

About fifty yards away a number of black party-goers were shooting the breeze, downing drinks from paper cups and smoking cigarettes along with other incendiaries outside a residence. Sounds of laughter split through the night, accompanied by a soul tune infected with a deep, reverberating bass that seemed to resonate underground. In the street outside the rave, cars were double parked causing, in effect, a one-way street at this part of the road. The lamp-post at the end of the street kept on blinking.

"So, what's the plan?" Danny asked himself aloud. "Might look a bit dodgy if we pretend we're invited to this gig... Christ, do you hear that music? Have they booked the road crew from a U2 stadium gig?"

"They're all probably beating drums," quipped Lee.

Davie thought about his next move. Matt slithered down his seat, feigning tiredness, while Lee checked something in his jacket inner pocket; his eyes darting here and there. He lit another cigarette, unable to keep his feet still.

"We'll wait," Danny decided finally. "Who knows what knida commotion we'll cause if we go up there. Don't wanna get Keith Blakelock'ed. One of them is bound to come out eventually and pass our way."

"Yeah, that's best," agreed Matt, wondering who Keith Blakelock was.

Danny switched on the car radio, tuning into Capital Gold and turning the volume down low. Davie stared out of the front windscreen, drumming his fingers on the dashboard. Matt closed his eyes. Lee was fidgeting with the zip on his jacket.

Inside the rave, K had felt like a jockey in a basketball players' locker room. He didn't like the mocking smiles when he asked for orange juice from the kitchen and was embarrassed by the gyrations of sexually-charged females. Clad in rainbow-coloured wigs, short skirts and nipple-yielding, Lycra tops, they had caused a constant stirring in his boxer shorts and he found it hard to accept that these 'ghetto girls' had such power over his manhood. The loudness of the music was a torture for him, especially when the D.J. upped the tempo with Jamaican dancehall tunes by the likes of Bounty Killer and Merciless. Most of his time he spent against the walls, peering through the smokey dark and observing what he deemed as lewd behaviour. He failed to see that everyone was simply having a good time and that no-one took offence - apart from him. He spotted a smiling Colin with Ali, who was emptying a bottle of Dragon Stout down his throat. They approached him, Ali not keeping a straight line.

"K!" Colin called. "Hey, K! Tek me bredrin to de cab office near de Academy - he's seriously buzzing."

Music to K's ears! Before he had a chance to appreciate his good fortune, Ali was already tottering into the hallway nearing the front door; party goers kept out of his way.

Two minutes after Capital's 04:00am news bulletin, Davie spotted a large man emerge into the street from the party. He was walking unsteadily and was humoured about something. It was Ali, stumbling along the street towards Danny's car. Another shorter man was behind him, pausing for a moment to wipe his glasses with a handkerchief - Professor K. He adjusted the lapels on his knee-length leather jacket.

"Matt, Lee, you two stay put," ordered Danny, his eyes not leaving Ali's broad chest. Matt peered ahead and upon seeing Ali found his breathing gathering pace. Lee had stiffened, with only his eyes moving. Danny climbed out of the car, taking care to close the door gently; not wanting to attract attention from other ravers who were now all inside. Davie leaped out of the motor and left his passenger-side door ajar. Ali was twenty yards away, his joviality fuelled by drink. K spotted the East London crew first and he stopped as though he'd run into a chain-link fence. "Ali!" he called.

Ali focused and the sight of the East London crew sobered him a little. "Wha' de fock are *dey* doing 'ere?"

K quickly scanned Danny and Davie and was satisfied they presented no danger, although something was obviously urgent. He stepped forward cautiously. "Ali, I'll talk to them."

Ali looked at Danny and Davie with increased suspicion. Danny sat on the bonnet of the car, trying to appear relaxed, happy that K had appeared, while Davie stepped forward a few paces to meet K; his hands spread in a gesture of good will. "Eddie's dead," he revealed matter of factly. "Old Bill found his body, or what was left of it, on the tracks of Barking train station."

K studied Davie's body language and guessed the East London crew hadn't come necessarily to blame his crew. His face managed to disguise the alarm he felt at the news.

"And what's more," Davie continued. "There's a little matter of diamonds involved in this whole business… Eight million quids worth. You wouldn't know anything about any of this would you?" Davie tried to read K's eyes and facial expression but, like his own, they offered no clues.

"So you're trying to say it's us!" Ali interjected, pacing towards Davie. "Who de rarse you t'ink you are? Coming down to our sides an' accusing us of some shit wha' happened up your sides! Tek your fucking white arse an' remove from 'ere. We don't know nutten so *fock off*!"

"Ali, I'll deal with it," pacified K.

Davie backed up a yard, unintimidated by the sheer size of Ali and his ranting, but unwilling to appear confrontational during what he knew to be delicate negotiations. Danny slid off the bonnet of his car in a manner he hoped would appear nonchalant, wondering what would happen next. He clenched his fists without realising it. K stretched out his arms in a gesture to cool the situation.

"Fucking pagans!" Ali spat. "Fock off an' tek your white arses from a place you don't belong!" He stepped towards the car.

"But we need to talk. There could be…"

"Nah - fock you!"

Ali squared his shoulders and his gaze flicked between Davie and Danny as one of the car doors opened. Lee jumped out. He shrugged off Matt who was trying to restrain him then moved his right hand within his jacket. Davie spun around. "Oh, *shit*!" he managed.

"*Get down*," screamed K as he dropped to the asphalt.

Ali, immersed in his own hatred, failed to register K's command.

Two hands gripping a 9mm handgun, Lee shot Ali in the left shoulder; then in his chest, while a third bullet shattered his collar bone. Blood sprayed and Danny, Davie and Lee launched themselves back into the car before Ali's body could topple forward, face first. His head bounced off the kerb an inch, altering its final resting position. K was laying still on the pavement, his face down. He heard a wheel spin and a frenzied acceleration, then the sound of a door opening. A scream cut the air as frantic footsteps echoed off the pavement. K lifted his head to look at Ali and saw his face kissing the kerb, his mouth open and dribbling with saliva. His eyes were closed and his body lay infinitely still.

Davie finally managed to slam his passenger side door shut as their car screeched past Stockwell tube station. Shouts could be heard in the distance. Danny was driving, his hands gripping the wheel so tightly that white islands of bone could be seen in his knuckles, while Lee and Matt huddled in the back, their eyes cast to their shoes. "What the fuck?" Danny raged, glancing over his shoulder at Lee. "What the fuck!" It was all he could manage through his fury, confusion and terror.

Davie peered out of his side window coolly. "We need to ditch the car," he asserted. "Pronto."

Kennington Road seemed to be an extremely busy place despite the late hour and Danny felt that each passer by he saw was taking a good, hard look at him for any forthcoming identity parade. He tried to shake off his paranoia by driving very, very carefully.

Muffled snuffles coming from the back seat indicated that Matt was crying; a timid, wretched sound that was almost snuffed out by his face being thrust into his tatty anorak.

Davie craned his neck to look at Lee, who was now staring out of his window vacantly. "Is that hardware from the plane, or one of your dad's?" he asked quietly.

Lee mumbled something about 'finders keepers', then squirmed around to face Matt. "Don't be such a big girl's blouse," he snarled, his eyes slit windows of glass. He prodded his whimpering cousin in the side with a finger, which only made him shrink further into his anorak, then returned his gaze to the fleeing pavement.

"Give me the gun, Lee," Davie said. "Now!"

The gun was handed over without comment. It was still warm. Davie recognised the weapon as a Heckler and Koch USP Compact 9mm, with its snub nose and light frame, and he checked its safety before thrusting it into his coat pocket. "I'll rat-file the rifling to screw up ballistics tests when I get home," he stated confidently. "I'll dispose of it later."

Davie's calmness under pressure made Danny realise quite how nervous he felt. He wondered whether he was now capable of coherent speech, and decided to find out by haranguing Lee. "You're a fuckin' idiot!" he shouted, spittle flying from his mouth like venom to spray against the windscreen. "You realise what you just did, you bloody fool!"

"Yeah - I just got me a nigger!" Lee shouted back.

"Got yourself a fucking nigger? Got yourself a fucking nigger? What the fuck? Let me give you a swift bloody lesson in the English language, boy. You didn't just get yourself a nigger, you just *killed* yourself a *man*, and that means the Law are gonna be all over us like a rash!"

"It wasn't me," Matt murmured, as though he was already preparing for the dock.

"Gurtcha, cowson!" Danny growled as his response, his hand raised to indicate a slap. "I'll swing for you!"

The Rotherhithe Tunnel swallowed them and once it spat them out the other side Davie let forth a long, drawn-out exhalation. "The whole of Brixton are gonna be looking for our arses now," he sighed resignedly. "Not to mention the slight chance of a race war if word gets out about this."

The realisation of a war hit Danny like a sockful of wet sand, making his shoulders slump. "Christ on a bike," he groaned.

He blamed himself for a short second. Perhaps I was too greedy going after the diamonds. Or just the buzz of it all. "You really think they'll come up east looking for us?"

Davie nodded. "I think they're gonna come at us with a little more than Jamaican harsh language, that's as sure as Americans slamming their doors to Afghan travel reps."

"Then gimmi my fuckin' gun back!" Lee blurted, reaching between the two front seats for Davie's pocket.

A fist snapped back to hit him on the nose and he was knocked into his seat. Davie hadn't even turned around. "You're out of this now, grasshopper," Davie told him. "Once we dump the motor I don't want to see hide nor hair of you again. You're bad for business, and your old man would be the first to kick you out on your arse if he were here, on account of all the stupid things you've done."

"Bollocks. You can't do that to me. My old man'll... he'll..."

"He'll tell you that trigger happy young thugs who don't do as they're told get kicked into touch pretty bloody sharpish," Davie interrupted. "You're lucky you're your old man's son, grasshopper, because if you weren't you'd be learning the hard way as soon as we stopped the bloody car."

Lee grew incandescent at Davie's impassive rebuke and leant forward in his seat. "Yeah? You think you can take me on, you trembling fuckin' spastic?" he screeched. "I'll shove those fuckin' pills of yours right up your shitty arse!" He pulled a knife from his jacket and slashed it at the back of Davie's head, its keen blade reflecting the passing street lights. "Come on then!"

Davie leant forward sharply so that the blade sliced into his seat's headrest, while at the same time drawing the H&K. He pointed its snubbed, black barrel at Lee's startled face and clicked off its safety. "Not so fast, grasshopper," he growled.

Matt screamed and Danny almost lost control of the vehicle as he glanced over his shoulder at the panicked tableau that was beside him. Lee was pressed back into his seat, his eyes wide and his mouth hanging open, while Davie sat twisted in his seat with the gun pointing at Lee's open mouth.

"I could pull the trigger and end our little gang war here and now," Davie cooed silkily, seemingly oblivious to the tension that pressed in from all around them. "I could serve you up to our South London friends and they'd probably eat you for breakfast. After all, they're all cannibals, ain't they, Lee? That's what you say, innit?"

The knife tumbled from Lee's trembling fingers to rest on his lap and his jaw slackened further.

"*Ain't they*, Lee?" Davie demanded, and Danny realised that it was the first time he had ever heard Davie shout. Davie, *don't lose it.*

"Yeah, they're all…"

The pistol slapped Lee about the side of the head so that a welt of blood showed. "I ain't taking no more of your programming, Lee," Davie snarled at him, levelling the gun back at his face. "Are they cannibals or not?"

"Well, nah, they ain't actually…"

"So stop spouting it, then!"

Danny thought about pulling the car over, before his shattered nerve caused him to lose control of the wheel, but there were too many people on the street for him to risk a brawl out in the open. He wanted to say something to calm the situation, but Davie's determined bass continued to reverberate about the swerving vehicle.

"People like you make me sick," he ranted, the muzzle of the gun not swaying an inch to either side of Lee's nose. "White Power this and Black Power that. Girl Power, for Christsakes! Gimmi a break! You ain't part of the final solution, grasshopper, you're part of the final problem! You've swallowed all the crap that gets thrown at you about how you ain't happy, because some other poor cowson has stolen whatever it is you want, and then you do their dirty-work by causing such a bloody fuss that everybody is too busy dealing with *you* to see that *they* are getting away with it."

Davie paused for breath and Danny noticed the lustre of madness that glowered from behind his sunken eyes. His face had also slackened on one side as it had while they were in the graveyard. Oh my God, he's lost it again and this time he has a gun! Danny realised as he sought for a place to park. He thought about asking Davie to take one of his pills, but while he summoned the courage to do so Davie resumed his tirade.

"We've got global warming! We've got banks who have more money than half the Third World!" he snarled. "We've got famine, we've got the C.I.A. and we've got A.I.D.S.. But what do you care about? I'll tell you what you care about, so help me! You care about flags and skin colour and whether or not the Hammers are gonna stay in the Premier League.

"It doesn't matter that none of these things put bread on your table. Oh no! You've watched the telly and read The Sun. You know what's important, because they've bloody-well told you so. It's too much of an effort to find out for yourself, so while you pull your hair out over their latest shock horror headline, they quietly skin you alive by selling *you* your season ticket to Upton Park, putting up another fast food restaurant that sells *you* B.S.E.-stuffed offal, and by flogging *you* England kits that were made in a sweat shop in Pakistan by homeless, unionless children!

"But you're happy, grasshopper. You're happy because they've told you what you should be angry about. It isn't *they* who are doing it to you with their greedy shareholders, spin doctors and brown-enveloped lobbyists; it's the blacks and the queers along with Johnny-bloody-foreigner and his nasty Euro what don't have the Queen's head on it, God bless her!"

Davie's voice had become a frenzied babble and although his eyes flickered about the car seemingly at random his aim remained steadfastly locked upon Lee. His breathing was heavy, his face slack, and while he summoned up the energy to pour forth a fresh torrent of vitriol Danny managed to park the car in a deserted alleyway.

"Davie," he said, placing a gentle hand on his friend's arm. "Come on. We need to torch the car."

The mention of business appeared to snap Davie from his diatribe, so he clicked the safety back on the gun and thrust it into his pocket; whereupon he jerked his passenger door open. "Let's get this over with," he snarled.

Lee wasn't sure whether Davie meant torching the car, or taking him up on his earlier offer of a showdown, so he slid out of the car reluctantly after a few shoves from Matt. His younger cousin was still snivelling and once he had followed him out onto the pavement Danny wagged a finger at them both.

"Okay, here's the deal," he said while Davie got to work picking the lock of the car's petrol cap. "The fun stops here. I said to Alan I'd look after you, but I didn't say I'd do time because of your fucked up prejudices. In fifteen years I ain't never seen anyone wasted what didn't deserve it, and I was hoping to retire the same way. So, the pair of you can hop it right now and I don't want to see either of your boats around my manor again. You got that?"

Matt rubbed some snot from his nose and looked like he was going to run, but Davie glanced up from the now-picked lock to give them some final instructions. "You both stayed in tonight," he said. "If Powell comes snooping around keep your gobs shut, and if he asks why you were with me in the pub on Thursday it's because you had some bent car stereos to sell. I didn't buy one, got that?"

Matt nodded like a toy dog in the back of a Fiesta, while Lee stared around the darkened alleyway vacantly. "There's a night bus that stops just around the corner. Take it." Davie commanded them. "And be sure to avoid any C.C.T.V.s on your way home."

Danny tilted his head in the direction of the street-lit main road and it was all the encouragement that Lee and Matt needed. They were soon lost to the metropolis.

"Start wiping the prints," Davie instructed Danny. "I'm almost finished here."

While Danny rubbed down the vehicle's external handles, Davie opened its bonnet and pulled a tube from the engine, which he then used to siphon out some petrol into a paper cup to pour over the car's interior.

"We can guarantee the forensics are smoke before the Fuzz gets here this way," he informed Danny. "We don't want big petrol tank bangs to wake up the world before we're history."

Danny nodded and lit a cigarette as Davie wound down the driver's side front window then closed the doors. "Game on," he smiled, whereupon Danny posted the glowing cigarette into the car's interior.

Blue flame danced around the mock leather upholstery and both men felt the urge to flee, but they waited around shifting their weight from one nervous foot to the other until they were certain that the interior of the vehicle would burn thoroughly. Once the plastic of the dashboard had begun to blister they shrank warily into the night and neither looked back.

Sunday 2nd December, 2001; 05:00am.

Detective Chief Inspector William Wiley had been watching C.N.N. in his boxer shorts and vest while lipping a mug of black coffee when his bleeper sopranoed. It was 05:00am. He responded to the call and learned that there had been a fatal shooting of a black man in the Brixton area and that it could be gang related. He washed and dressed hastily, not wanting the C.I.D. from Brixton Station to get a march on him. Meddling bastards, he thought.

In his twenty-three years in the Force, Wiley had seen four riots, investigated over a hundred murders, numerous suicides, four attempts on his life and seen the exit of two wives. Three years ago he had been promoted to Detective Chief Inspector to work with Operation Trident investigating black on black gun crime in the capital. Wiley hated the term 'Yardie Buster' with which a few of his former peers had labelled him. He had been invited by his commander to recruit black celebrities in his organisation's campaign to wipe out gun crime. Wiley thought this act of public relations a desperate measure. After all, if a lengthy prison sentence was no deterrent, those gun-crazed idiots were hardly going to listen to the pleas of a voluptuous R&B songstress.

His six foot four frame clad in a navy-blue suit, white shirt, red tie and black-polished lace-up shoes, Wiley climbed into his Rover deciding to head straight to the crime scene. He checked his face in his rear view mirror, running his fingers over his clean-shaven jaw line. He cursed himself as he realised he had left his squash racket on the back seat. Before setting off he built himself a roll-up cigarette, smiling at the assumption of his commander who had once told him: you seem to get on well with the community and you have an understanding that many of the young officers lack. Wiley had to laugh at that. *Understanding*? It had nothing to do with understanding and everything to do with the fact that he was one of the few black officers assigned to Operation Trident. Of course he was going to get along better with the '*community*', which was another politically correct term that he'd always hated.

Wiley knew his commander was in effect saying: if any of us are going to make the blacks talk and give us some evidence about gun crime, it's going to be you who extracts it, yet he knew this was preposterous. The main reason why blacks were not forthcoming with evidence was because they were shit scared of reprisals.

From his flat in Streatham it only took him seven minutes to drive to Stansfield Road. Blue and white striped Police tape cordoned off the street and one of the residents was arguing with a constable about vehicle access. Wiley parked on Stockwell Road and as he stepped out of the car, he noticed the sun creeping over Stockwell Park estate to herald a fine morning. He ducked under the tape and, about thirty yards down the street, saw the familiar sight of a white S.O.C.O. bell-tent straddling the pavement and half of the road that concealed the dead body. Next to this was an ambulance and its crew, waiting around drinking coffee from polystyrene cups, appearing impatient. Two Police cars were abreast on the street, acting as another barrier and Wiley noticed the flashes from an S.O.11 photographer within the tent. Two forensic experts were scrutinising something on the road and a uniformed constable was ordering residents to remain indoors, particularly from one house where soiled paper cups and plates were strewn across the pavement.

Wiley, displaying his badge in his right hand, approached a constable in the street who had been glancing uneasily at the residence where the party had been.

"So, what have we got?" Wiley asked. "Any witnesses?"

"Victim was shot three times at point blank range, Detective Chief Inspector," the constable answered. "He seems to have been making his way from a party." He nodded to indicate where this was. "No witnesses have come forward with specific evidence, but a couple of guys from the party said they heard gunshots and a car screeching away. Forensics are looking at tyre tracks. We've conducted a search for the murder weapon, but as yet we've found nothing."

"Those two guys still around?" Wiley asked, thinking if they were he'd probably get nothing out of them.

"Yeah, they're both members of the sound system and they're not best pleased because they can't get access to their van driver to take home their equipment."

"I'll talk to them soon," Wiley assured. He nodded his thanks and walked on to the S.O.C.O. tent where the photographer was still at work, seemingly unmoved by the lifeless body that filled his lens. A forensic expert was beside him. Wiley looked at the corpse automatically, searching for clues. He trained his eyes on Ali's head where it was nestling against the kerb and then turned to the forensic expert. "I'm from Trident," he greeted. "Have you got a spec for the gun?"

Detective Sergeant Sexton, who had been working in forensics for seven years, pointed to the bullet entry holes in Ali's upper body that were covered in blood. "My guess is a 9mm handgun, fired from close range. He never stood a chance."

Wiley turned to the photographer. "Have you finished? I want to go through the victim's pockets to establish identity."

"Yes - go ahead."

Wiley dropped down to his haunches, not wanting to blemish his trousers on the pavement. He searched the zip pockets of Ali's name-brand fleece jacket where he found a bunch of keys, cigarette papers, a small polythene bag of cannabis, a lighter and fifty pounds in cash - new bank notes. The officer then searched Ali's tracksuit trousers and noticed that one zip was only halfway pulled up; the lining of the trousers was caught in the zip. The inside of the pocket appeared as if it had been rifled through hastily and apart from the remains of a forgotten tissue, the pocket was empty.

Strange, Wiley thought. Someone's obviously gone through the trouser pocket. What did they take? Perhaps a mobile phone? And why didn't they take the cash and cannabis from the jacket? Wiley knew about the current spate of street robberies of mobile phones, but these offenders were usually kids. Surely they wouldn't shoot somebody for a mobile phone? And if it was a gangland killing, why did they stop to go through his pockets when they knew there could be witnesses from the party? Even if it was an opportunist, why did they leave the cash?

Wiley wrestled with the possible motives of the killing until he heard a commotion from further down the street. He turned, walked out of the tent and saw four black men in a residence doorway who were arguing with three constables.

"How long do we have to stay here?" one black guy demanded. "I've told you what I know. I just want to get my stuff and fuck off home! My van man is waiting around the corner."

"As soon as they take the body away you can go," interjected Wiley. "About five minutes. I just want to ask a few questions on whether you saw or heard anything that may help us. Or perhaps one of you will know who the victim is? There is the terrible matter of having to inform the next of kin... Can I come in please? Mr..."

"I'm known as Crumbs, but it's Mr. Grogan."

"Okay, Mr. Grogan. I'll be grateful for your time. May I call you Crumbs?"

The besieged sound engineers looked at each other and perceived that Wiley was more polite than the previous constables who had spoken to them on this chaotic morning. He even seemed genuinely concerned about the loss of life, but they just put that down to his being a fellow black. "Yeah, I s'pose so," Crumbs answered, stepping aside to let Wiley through. Wiley looked at the two other black men and sensed a deep intolerance. He recognised their eyes accusing him of being a traitor to his race, but he was used to that. I'd better address my questions to Crumbs, he thought as he gave a mental shrug to their disdain. Then if he co-operates it'll be easier to question the others. Crumbs looked very smart in black slacks, maroon shirt and a corn-row plaited hairstyle. Just get this over and done with, he willed. I wanna go home.

Wiley took in his surroundings as he stepped into the wooden-tiled hallway. A woman was sweeping the stairway carpet with a broom, ignoring the presence of the Inspector. At the end of the passage was the kitchen where two girls were busy washing up pots and pans and emptying waste food into black bags in silence. Quite a nice house, Wiley thought. "Who's the resident of this abode, Sir?" Wiley turned to Crumbs.

"My woman," Crumbs answered with a tint of pride, noticing Wiley's agreeable nods. "She's kinda upset 'cos her party mash up when we heard the gunfire. Everybody panicked and a lot of people ran out. She's upstairs in her bedroom, not quite believing that someone got killed near her gates."

Crumbs led Wiley into the front room where two young men were carefully replacing the furniture. Sisqo was performing his 'thong-song' on the wide-screen television that stood in a corner. Wiley was invited to sit in a leather armchair. "Thank you."

Crumbs settled in a sofa opposite Wiley, wondering what he'd be asked. Tiredness crept over his face.

"So… the victim," Wiley began, feeling the urge to build a roll-up, but thinking this action could prove impolite. "If he was a friend of yours then you have my condolences."

"I didn't know him *that* well," Crumbs returned, glancing at the doorway and checking if anyone was listening to the conversation. "Friend of a friend business, you know what I'm saying?"

Wiley nodded.

"I'm not sure of his real name, but he's known as Ali," Crumbs revealed. "He was enjoying himself at the rave, I can tell you that."

Wiley's eyebrows shot up. At last! Someone willing to talk. He leaned closer towards Crumbs, his eyes now keen. "Who was he enjoying the rave with?"

"Don't know their names." Crumbs wiped his mouth and scratched his nose. This action didn't escape Wiley. "He was with a short guy wearing glasses and two taller guys - one of them was really dark wid a scar 'bout his forehead." Crumbs checked himself, realising he was presenting more information to the Inspector than he wanted to.

"Did you hear or see this… Ali gentleman row with anyone?"

"Nah, he was just enjoying himself, dancing wid girls an' t'ing."

They both heard a frantic banging on the front door. Crumbs went to investigate and Wiley followed, inwardly cursing the interruption. Crumbs opened the door to reveal his van driver, who had slipped under the Police tape and evaded the constables who were in pursuit. Half a dozen or so black men had assembled at the top of the road and were looking down the street with vexed apprehension. "Crumbs, man!" the van driver called, looking aggrieved. "I ain't got all fucking day! When can I drive the van down the street to load up the gear? I *want* my bed!"

As Crumbs was about to reply, the van driver was grabbed by three pairs of Police hands. In the ensuing scuffle, he tripped and fell to the ground. Wiley came out into the street. "All of you calm down," he stressed, glaring at the Police officers. Just as he was about to help the van driver to his feet, in his peripheral vision he saw another two black men duck under the Police tape and run towards him. Crumbs went back inside the house, cursing to himself and wondering if he'd ever be able to drive his gear home. More heads peered out of upstairs windows. The van driver got up to his feet, dusting himself down. He wondered who these two guys were who were fast approaching, obviously upset.

"Fucking liberty!" one of them yelled. "The brudder weren't doing nutten an' you beast 'ad to blast 'im to de ground!"

"Now, just calm down," Wiley pacified. "We're trying to investigate a murder and we need no hindrance. So can you please go away quietly so we can get on with our job?"

"Go away quietly! After you jus' brutalise a brudder? Go fuck yourself, you coconut pig!"

The other black man who had raced to the scene and up to now had remained quiet, thought about the peril he was now in. He backed off a few paces, not wanting to get arrested.

"Now, I'll ask again, *Sir*, if you can just move along quietly and let us get on with our job," Wiley addressed the rabble-rouser. "Or I'll be forced to arrest you."

"Arrest me! 'cos I was a witness to Police brutality? Fuck you! I'm gonna see the C.R.E. about this shit. You pigs still 'aven't learned your lesson from de past. I ain't going nowhere 'til someone senior 'ears my complaint about the brudder."

Wiley grew impatient. "What are you? From rent-a-mob? Do you always try and make elephant crap out of dog piss? Your brother is perfectly alright and if he wants to make a complaint I'm sure he's able to make it himself."

The van driver now regretted his rush of blood in his attempt to air his feelings to Crumbs. He glanced at the agitator not wanting to lose face, and wished he could tell him that it was all an accident and he had come to no harm, but while he thought on the best way to go about it the rabble-rouser turned to Wiley again. "He's too scared to speak for himself," he raged. "An' he fucking knows dat if his complaint comes to somet'ing you pigs will lie t'rough your teet'."

Wiley had tolerated just about his fill from this dissenter. He communicated something with his eyes to his fellow officers and suddenly the insurrectionist was grabbed from behind and hauled away to a Police car as he screamed Jamaican expletives. "You're arrested for a breach of the peace!" Wiley called out. "Someone read him his rights!"

The van driver and the other black man hot-footed up the road. Crumbs appeared at the front door, shaking his head. Wiley turned to him. "Look, I've just got to see to this idiot, but I promise we won't keep you longer than ten minutes."

Crumbs nodded and wondered who the hell was this abrasive character who was just led away? Storms in teacups were the last things he needed. The arrested man was now sitting in the back of a Police car, still cursing. He was flanked by two officers. Wiley, having collected the keys from another constable, climbed into the driver's seat, started the car and drove to the end of the street opposite the Stockwell Road entrance. He turned a right and left before pulling up, whereupon he spun around to face the black man. "Morning, Michael," he greeted. "That was a bit strong, weren't it?"

Detective Sergeant Michael Hooker had been working in covert investigations for Operation Trident for the last two years. He was wearing a baseball cap and a name brand anorak. The latest Nike trainers caressed his feet.

"Yeah. I have to make it believable, innit," Michael grinned as he scanned the street. "Don't park here for fuck's sake. Go on a bit further."

Wiley, recognising his colleague's need for caution, restarted the car and drove on, finally stopping in a back street in Clapham North.

"So, Michael," Wiley resumed. "You find out anything?"

"No. I only got the call half an hour go. Most of the guys who were at the top end of Stansfield Road were just nosing around. They were talking about the shooting, but no-one was too sure who the victim was."

"Do you know of a Crumbs?"

"Yeah – M.C. Crumbs - he runs a popular party sound system in the area. He's also a D.J. for a pirate radio station."

"Well it was his girlfriend's party... I managed to get a little info from him but he was also holding back something. He mentioned the victim was with a short black guy with glasses and two other taller black men - one of them really dark with a scar across his forehead."

"Really dark and a scar?" repeated Michael. "I just wonder?"

"Wonder what?"

"It's a wild guess."

"What's a wild guess?"

"It could be Baron. You remember? A Jamaican import - early forties - I used to be his handler."

"Baron! Oh yes. I know who you're talking of. Now there's a man who's kept a low profile for the last few years."

"Well, wouldn't you if you were in his position?"

"Yeah, I suppose so... Is he still on our books as an informer?"

"Of course."

"You'd better arrange to see him. Even if he wasn't at the party he might know something."

"Will do... You'll hear from me when I know something. Oh, and one more thing, don't call me on my mobile! Haven't you heard of texting?"

Wiley dropped Michael off at Lavender Hill Police Station, still cuffed and flanked by the two grinning constables to make everything look convincing in case they were being observed. He then headed back to the murder scene. If Baron was at this party then it probably *was* a Yardie-related killing, he thought, and, what was more, Baron would be only too willing to tell them all about it; providing the price was right, of course.

Sunday 2nd of December, 2001; 07:00am.

"Look, you can't just go up there in that East London pub and fire your Uzi at will," K stressed, shaking his head.

"Watch me!" Colin X replied, with acid on his tongue. He was checking and cleaning an Uzi sub-machine gun that Baron had secured from a 'friend' within two hours of Ali's death. "Dem focking pagans came down to *our* sides *blatantly* and killed my brethren!"

K looked out of his front room window, his mind whirring furiously on what to tell Colin to make him see sense. From his 14th floor vantage point he could see the London Eye in the distance. His gaze diverted to his coffee table where three soiled dinner plates were waiting to be washed. "This pub is on a High Street," reasoned K. "There's bound to be closed circuit cameras all over the place. On top of that, I don't think it was the entire crew, Colin. I think they were as surprised as I was. That B.N.P. kid just went psycho."

"I don't give a fock!" stormed Colin. "You t'ink me 'fraid of jailhouse? You don't even feel anything, do you?"

Colin paced quickly towards K and pulled his right shoulder in order to face him square on. He glared at him unblinking. K held his gaze. "All your t'inking 'bout is how to keep your focking backside safe in all dis. Dat's why you tek Ali's mobile when he was still warm... You didn't give a shit! The difference between me an' you is dat I 'ave lost a good bredrin, but you 'ave lost just ah somebody who help to mek you money... I should shoot your focking backside an' den sen' your arse to de B.N.P. pagans for dem to piss 'pon you."

Colin raised the gun in his right hand and trained it on K's forehead. K closed his eyes and felt a tightening of his stomach. His head was still and was warming by the second. He found himself taking in a huge gulp of air and felt nauseous. Surely he won't, he hoped. K had to admit to himself that after the shock of Lee gunning down Ali, his thoughts centred on retrieving Ali's mobile. God! What have I become? he asked himself. A small part of him wanted Colin to pull the trigger as he heard his mother's voice resonating inside his head again. 'You shame us all'. He imagined her regretting her words at his graveside.

Colin grinned a sadistic grin, satisfied that with all K's education and big words, it was *he* who had the power. Look at him! He ain't nutten but a fucking pussy.

"Bwai, you're a dogheart, mon," interrupted Baron, seizing Colin with his eyes and smoking a spliff, laying horizontal on K's sofa. "Yu cyan't kill ah man who jus' serve yu ah wicked fried plantain, callaloo, dumpling an' t'ing!" Watching the confrontation, even *he* wasn't sure whether Colin would have killed K. He had seen unpredictable affects on many men following the slaying of their brethrens. After Ali's murder he had made a mental note for himself to get 'packed' with a weapon, but now wondered of his own judgement on handing over the weapon to Colin. "Cah if yu out K's light, den yu might as well out me own light cah me nuh go 'pon nuh killing spree inna dat der pub. Me nuh waan nuh boom boom claat C.C.T.V. fe catch me backside 'pon tape. Me also 'ear so wha' 'im say 'bout de uder crew. 'im did-der an' sight wha' ah gwarn, so if de Professor say de white bwai fly solo, den me believe 'im."

Colin thought about it. His mind drifted back to his seven year incarceration where he first met Ali. Indeed it was Ali who suggested that they should listen to the words of a Nation of Islam teacher who provoked protest in the prison amongst the blacks because of the lack of ethnic historical books. He had witnessed Ali's once low esteem change into a man proud of his race and its achievements. It was Colin himself who planted the seed of hatred towards white people in Ali's head. He blamed *all* whites for the social state of the blacks all over the world. If K was telling the truth on the moments leading up to Ali's death, then that same hatred killed Ali just as much as Lee's gun. He would never admit it to anyone, but Colin blamed himself for Ali's murder. He wondered if the Police had identified the body and worst of all, how could he face Ali's mother again? He assured her many times that Ali will be 'safe' with him and they were not getting up to no good. *Lucky dat she don't know where I live,* he thought. He recognised her unconditional love for her son, a love denied Colin from his own parents. *I was jealous of that,* he reasoned. *Blatantly* jealous. From when they had reached K's flat after Ali's murder, Colin felt the tears well up inside of him and felt a sickly cramping sensation inside his stomach; but he couldn't shed tears in front of Baron. *He'll think I'm a pussy.*

Colin threw the gun in an armchair. He looked at K, his anger still apparent, but directed towards something indistinct, not at K. "Alright, K. What's your focking great plan?"

K breathed out hard. "Give me a second. I... I just want to get myself a drink."

K went to his kitchen and returned with a glass of orange juice. He drank the full contents within three seconds and then cleared his throat. Mentally, he tried to rid himself of the image of the gun aimed at his face. "We have to find out where Lee lives," he stated, regaining his confidence. "Like I said before, I think the other guys were as shocked as me. I reckon that courier guy, Tony. He must know where all of them live because he was handing out all the payments... We should stake him out."

Colin nodded, his eyes trained on the Uzi. "Alright. For now I will follow your plan, but *I* want to kill dat racist focker. An' I want *him* to see who's pulling de rarse trigger!"

K looked at Baron, searching for agreement. The Jamaican sat up and killed his spliff in an ashtray. "Yeah, whatever. Ali was alright y'know, 'im deserve ah response fe 'im murder. From me sight dat ball'ead white bwai me feel so 'im looking war, y'know?"

K sat down on the sofa and held his head in his right palm, thinking of a way to wreak his crew's vengeance. "We need to acquire a van," he said finally. "Don't want to drive up there in my own wheels. Also I don't want you two to be seen. Once we get Lee's address out of Tony, we'll go for Lee early in the morning. I'll use that old postman's outfit of Sceptic's if he'll lend it to knock on the door with a parcel. You know the routine, Colin."

"Yeah, once he opens the door you get flat and I'll burst from the van an' sen' him to de Devil."

"Boom boom claat!"

Sunday 2nd of December, 2001; 07:05pm.

Lee had told Matt to arrive at seven thirty, but he turned up outside his decrepit council home on Bastable Avenue at just past seven on account of his frayed nerves. He'd wrestled with a sleepless night, where every time he closed his eyes he witnessed once again those few seconds that had resulted in the taking of Ali's life, and each time his tortured subconscious replayed the memory he thought of fresh ways in which he could have prevented it. Lee had shown him the gun once they'd got back from the heist, saying that he'd taken it from the plane as a souvenir. Why hadn't Matt told him to get rid of it there and then? Why hadn't he told Lee of his conversation with Professor K, where he'd learned so much of what Lee believed to be misguided? Why hadn't he just held on to Lee's jacket a bit harder when he'd leapt out of the car?

The front door was opened by Lee's mum, who was a short, pale woman in her mid thirties that had fallen pregnant with Lee at fifteen. As she ushered him inside with one cigarette-wielding hand she ran the other through her peroxide perm in a pointless effort to hide its brown roots. "He's in his room, Mattie," she said, once again indicating with her cigarette as though Matt needed directions.

"Thanks, Auntie Michelle."

"Ain't I gonna get a kiss, then?"

There was a moment of painful stillness while Matt conjured up the courage to confront the inevitable, then the sanguine stench of stale liquor wafted past his face as his Auntie Michelle stumbled forward to plant a wet smacker on his cheek. She gripped his shoulders as a fulcrum to force herself upright then took a long, slow toke on her Benson.

"I don't know what's got into Lee today, Mattie," she said as she adjusted her bra strap under her Marks and Sparks blouse. "Miserable cunt. Maybe you can cheer him up, *eh*? Hey, how's your mum? Tell her she still owes me that quid from Bingo."

Matt mumbled an affirmative as he stomped up the carpet-less stairs to Lee's room. He knocked, heard the music that was coming from within turned down, then waited for Lee's "Yeah, come on in," before he stepped inside.

It had always surprised Matt that Lee's room was the tidiest in the house. Matt's mum was always having a go at him about picking his clothes off the floor and taking down his dirty mugs to the sink, but Lee kept his room as spotless as the mould on the walls would allow. There was his bed with its West Ham United quilt cover, a cupboard with a photograph of Lee's dad on it and an old record player with a row of L.P.s beneath it. His C.D.s were kept on the paint-peeling windowsill along with a cheap, Tandy-bought player.

"What ya listening to?" Matt asked as he sat down on the edge of the bed. "I don't know it."

"A band called the Small Faces."

"Yeah?"

"Yeah."

"Never heard of 'em."

Lee tossed an L.P. cover to the quilt then proceeded to tie up his knee-length Doctor Martin boots. "We've gotta split in a bit, I wanna take you to a special pub," he said.

"Can't we just sit around and listen to some music? After last night I don't feel like going out."

"Not tonight. Mum started early today." Lee closed his eyes tightly for a moment, while Matt looked down as though he could see his Auntie Michelle through the floorboards. The last thing he wanted was to go outside, but he knew that Lee didn't like staying in when his mum was on a bender. The bender,

Matt knew, had been going on for as long as he could remember, but according to Lee some days were worse than others. "Is it far?" he asked.

"Mile End."

Lee had managed to tie one blue-laced boot and as he wrestled with the other Matt learnt forward towards the row of records. He pulled one out at random, some band he'd never heard of called the Yardbirds, and when Lee spotted what he was doing his face burst into varying shades of crimson and he snatched the L.P. away. "What the fuck are you doing?" he demanded urgently, punching Matt on the arm. "They're my *dad's!*"

"Er, sorry," Matt murmured as a means of consolation, while he rubbed at his smarting arm. "I ain't never seen them in here before."

"Nah - I just got 'em down from the loft, but keep your fuckin' mitts off 'em, 'cos no-one touches my dad's stuff but me."

Lee placed the record back amidst its companions carefully then finished tying his boot. "Sorted," he said eventually, standing. "Come on - I hope you've brought enough money for a travel pass."

Matt nodded and soon the pair of them had taken a westbound District Line tube from Barking Station heading for Mile End. East Ham, Plaistow and West Ham passed by in silence, with Lee seeming to prefer staring out of the window to conversation, but as they passed through Bow he grew more excited. "Man, you're going to *love* where I'm taking you," he said.

"What's so special about this pub?"

"It's a surprise."

Matt shrugged and returned his attention to his shoes. Lee was great and everything, but Matt always felt a bit nervous when he was out with him in public, because his haircut, jacket and inflammatory badges drew an awful lot of stares, particularly from blacks and Asians, and this made Matt feel incredibly uncomfortable. Attention was the last thing he wanted, but it was something that Lee sought in abundance.

Eventually, they were out of the tube and walking along some road that Matt didn't know. Brown tower blocks stood like dominoes all the way to the Thames and the roads were thick with black cabs and red buses. Peeling posters seemed to cover every wall advertising anarchist newspapers or underground clubs and every bus stop they passed had its glass kicked out onto the pavement to resemble a tiny hail storm. Lee turned into a side street then put on his black woolly hat. "You got yer titfa?" he asked.

Matt shook his head. "It ain't raining," he pointed out somewhat redundantly.

"Then put this on yer bonce."

Lee pulled a newspaper from his inside jacket pocket and handed it over. It was a copy of *Freedom*, the British Nationalist Party rag, and it was one of the few things that Matt had ever seen Lee read. "What for?" Matt asked, holding the paper over his head as if to shield himself from a downpour.

"Just do as your told," came the reply.

After tugging his woolly hat down low over his brow, Lee ducked into a shabby side street then scuttled towards a ramshackle and graffiti-adorned pub that was called The Saint George. As he neared, his attention was drawn to the second floor window of a derelict building that was on the other side of the street, which he waved at for a few moments, but with his face tilted to the belittered pavement.

"What you doing?" Matt wanted to know.

Lee laughed and his wave transformed into the two-finger salute, which he jabbed at the window mercilessly. "Say '*Hello*' to S.O.11," he chuckled. "And be sure to keep that paper on your nut."

"What?"

"S.O.11 - the Met's Intelligence bastards. That's where they take their photos, so be sure to keep your boat outa sight."

"What?"

"Oh, for fuck's sake! Just get into the pub!"

His head still bent low, Lee grabbed Matt's arm then tugged him into The Saint George, whereupon they were confronted by a bouncer of elephantine dimensions. He wore an olive green flight jacket similar to Lee's, a Union Jack T-shirt and blue, ripped jeans; while his muscular, tattooed forearm blocked their passage more effectively than a crow bar.

"Alright, lads," he said. "You know the drill."

Matt didn't, so he was relieved when Lee took the lead. He stood in front of the bouncer and raised his arms as if to be searched whereupon Matt coughed slightly, because he knew that Lee carried a knife. Within a moment the bouncer knew too, because he took it from Lee's inside jacket pocket and studied it closely. It was a replica S.S. dagger that Lee had bought in Camden market.

"Sweet," the bouncer admitted in a brutal Bethnal Green growl, holding the blade up to catch the light. "A nineteen thirty-three model?"

"Yeah."

The bouncer's eyes narrowed suspiciously. "Tell me: what's the motto written on the blade?"

"*Meine Ehre Heisst Treue.*"

"And what's it mean?"

"My Honour Is Loyalty."

"Spot on. So you *are* a true believer. You can go on through, *mein bruder.*"

The bouncer smiled and handed back the weapon, much to Matt's surprise. It was then his turn to be searched, so he held up his arms and waited for his own knife to be found; a fruit knife that he'd taken from his mum's culinary drawer, and when the bouncer did so he just chuckled and handed it straight back.

"Excuse me," Matt asked nervously as the bouncer nodded for him to follow his elder cousin. "Why'd you bother searching us if you return everything?"

"What?" the bouncer replied, and this time his laughter was loud and full. He turned to Lee and pulled a contorted face of astonishment. "This his first time?"

"Yeah. Sorry about that."

Lee pulled Matt away from the bouncer and through a set of double doors that led into the pub. Loud music now confronted them like a fist as the Sex Pistols belched out *Belsen Was A Gas* and the air was clogged with cigarette smoke. "They ain't looking for blades, you dozy great pillock," Lee chided gently as he shouldered his way through a cluster of drinkers. "They're looking for wires. Under cover cops, you moron!"

"What for?"

Matt could half answer his own question, because now that they had orbited the vista-consuming shoulders of a group of bikers he could glance around the pub. Union Jacks and Saint George crosses hung from the walls like towels on a line and everywhere his eyes roamed he beheld crew-cutted young men in flight jackets, crombies and leather trench coats, along with youths clad in the designer-casual image of football *'firms'*. A small stage was situated by the pub's lavatories and upon it a microphone was erected draped in the red flag with white circle and black lightning strike of the *British Union of Fascists*. A drum kit and amps suggested a band.

Lee strode across to the bar and ordered two pints of Guinness from a walking tattoo with an Ulsterman's accent and as Matt followed him his eyes jiggled around in their sockets like lottery balls in a tombola. Part of him wanted to take in all the strange sights that pressed in from all around him; the clothes, the stern faces and the countless flags and banners, but another part of him, a part that he could not ignore, urged him to keep his gaze locked on the floor so that he could avoid making eye contact with anyone.

"Oi! That's a good one, innit, eh? *Eh*?"

An elbow in the side indicated that the statement was directed at him. Matt turned to see a group of skinheads chugging pints and smiling broadly. They wore a mixture of band logo T-shirts, but their boots were all black, toe-capped and courtesy of Doctor Martin.

"Eh?" he replied, trying to sound as inoffensive as possible, without appearing a pussy.

"What? You deaf, ya cunt?"

In the millisecond that followed, Matt prayed that Lee would arrive with the pints and save him from the beating of which the skinhead's hard, poxed face foretold, but the moment passed before his blood had the chance to drain from his face.

"Ha hah!" a member of the group brayed. "You don't wanna give a fuck about what Spider here says. He's just pullin' yer leg."

"Yeah. Didn't you hear me joke?" Spider asked. "I said... I said..." Spider paused as giggles escaped him like bubbles. "I said: the reason I like chainsaws, is because... is because when you start 'em they go: *'Run, nigger, nigger, nigger'*."

Spider mimed sweeping a chainsaw before him with his hands, spilling lager to the bare floorboards as he did so, while his companions laughed obligingly. Lee arrived with two pints, one of which he handed to Matt, then joined the conversation without introductions. "I got one. I got one," he chortled. "Did you know that I actually *like* black people? Sure I do. In fact, I think all whites should *own* at least one!"

Laughter rippled about the group and as the next would-be comedian fought to get a word in edgeways Matt found his thoughts receding to his own internal world. Lee's joke had unsettled him. Sure, he found your average black or Paki joke as entertaining as the next man, but K's fatherly and compassionate countenance hovered in his mind's eye like Marley's ghost and his knowing him now made the abstract corporeal. How, Matt reasoned, could anybody *own* someone who could think and act and feel like the man with whom he had sat in a car that dark and rain-swept night? How could anyone dare to possess another man's life and identity? The joke, Matt realised, and he hated himself at the thought, suddenly wasn't that funny.

Skrewdriver were now playing, a Neo-Nazi band Matt knew because Lee listened to them, and as he tried to recollect the name of the song someone silenced the juke box. All eyes swivelled to the tiny stage and locked upon the short, black-clad Londoner who stood there with one hand cupping the mike and the other a pint of lager.

"Politics, Politics, Politics..." the man began with an air of tired resignation. "Where I live politics is a load of crap." He paused as he shook his head. "Whenever I come here all I hear about is politics, but nobody where I live has the time to even *think* about politics. We spend our nights banging our heads against a brick wall because us white British volk are getting overrun by Pakis."

The man swigged his lager in an aggressive gesture and as he did so Matt wondered what 'volk' meant, while the majority of the throng encouraged the speaker with a chorus of *'Too fuckin' right'*s and *'Yeah'*s.

"We live in a Britain that has a Paki-loving government," the speaker continued. "That's it. End of story. Electing the Tories or Lib pussy Dems wont change that. The B.N.P. is the next best bet, so we vote for the B.N.P.; but to become even a *threat* to the other parties will take *years*... maybe a hundred! But we can't wait for years, because the Pakis are right here right *now*!"

The speaker's tone intensified and now his words were spat out with vitriol. "And don't even start me on that fifty-five years of freedom bollocks!" he scowled. "Anyone with a brain cell knows that the troops bound for Normandy on that fabled 6th of June would've turned around if they'd foreseen the pathetic excuse for a country we live in today and said '*Nice one, Adolf! Why don't you come on over*?'! So stop all that plastic flag waving patriotism, and have a walk around Birmingham or London these days! You'll see that we're *still* at war! I tell you, the fuckin' inner cities are under *siege*!

"So why bother to talk about politics, *eh*?" Now the speaker's voice lowered to a sibilant purr. "Our government and future governments will still look on we Aryan volk as the beast that must shoulder the mud man's burden; feeding their starving and funding their Benefits.

"Now is *not* a time for politics. Now is a time for *action*!

"Now is the time for stopping these parasites from spreading, because in another hundred years they'll be in control of over half of England, and by that time it'll be too late; and the struggle for an All British Britain will be out of our grasp!

"Talk, talk, talk all you want, but you won't change a thing!

"What we need is action, action, *action*!

"Make a stand. Drive them out *now* while we still can! White Power! White Power! White Power!"

As the speaker's voice rose, so too did the cheers of those who listened to him. A young skinhead near the front appeared to be frothing at the mouth, such was his frenzy, while others nearby resembled the hypnotised goons of an American T.V. evangelist; their arms punching the air above them and their eyes feasting upon the apostle who brought with him the Commandments of hate and fear.

"White Power!" they chorused, part hymn, part mantra, as each partook of the communion of beer and crisps. "White Power!"

The black-clad man left the stage to be replaced by four skinheads, three of whom wielded guitars. After jacking the instruments into the amps and waiting for the drummer to settle behind his kit, the bassist leant towards the mike and growled an introduction: *"Gott steht uns bei, dem Volk zugute, meine tapferen Keltischen Krieger!"* he hollered as the guitarist slashed free his first stinging, whining chord. *"Macht der Weissen Rasse!"*

Matt was pushed closer to the stage by the pressing throng of fans who wanted to pogo about the improvised mosh pit. Young men jostled him this way and that, spilling his drink, while Lee's frenzied war-cries lanced through his ears like glass splinters. He could sense the thumping bass of the song through his feet and the surge of adrenaline as the singer vocalised his feelings of frustration, helplessness and anger that so closely matched Matt's own. The intensity of the raw, surging emotion intoxicated him and Matt thought of his job at Fords, his redundancy, his subsequent descent into crime and the eventual murder of Ali. K was wrong, a part of himself raged. He now realised that it wasn't *his* fault that he had lost his job. It wasn't *his* fault that he had been forced to descend into crime, just so that he could get some money to buy some clothes. It wasn't *his* fault that he'd needed to mix with the criminal likes of Ali who, through his own animal aggression, had hastened his own death. If it was *anyone's* fault Matt knew it was the fault of Desmond Higgins, the black fitter who had stolen his job at Fords.

As this notion cemented itself in Matt's mind, a small voice wondered whether this was all just an excuse aimed to rid himself of any guilt in the death of Ali. Suddenly nauseous, he felt his stomach and heart sommaesalt with self loathing. No, he retaliated with bitter anger. This had to be the answer, for there were no other options available. Matt knew himself better than anyone, and he *knew* that he was no thief. He *knew* that he was no killer. There *had* to be another explanation, because there *had* to be someone else upon whom he could lay the blame for all the terrible things he had been forced to do.

Why was Europe this way for the working White? the singer demanded shrilly, dragging Matt back thankfully from his painful reverie. Why must we suffer in poverty while the mud races take our jobs? Matt now understood that other people wondered as he wondered too - the men who surrounded him - and it was clear that they were ready to fight to get back what was theirs by blood right.

As the song continued Matt realised that he was not alone with his sense of angst and isolation and once the final, screaming chord of the song had died away he acknowledged his kinship with those who surrounded him by joining them in their chorus of "White Power! White Power! *White Power!*"

Sunday 2nd of December, 2001; 10:30pm.

K, wearing a donkey jacket, dark wool hat and black gloves, was waiting in the driver's seat of a white van that Colin had 'acquired' from a friend in the building trade. He had parked almost opposite the Spotted Dog in Barking and strained his eyes on the exits. He had taken off his glasses and put them in a case on the passenger seat, taking no chances on being recognised, even in the dark. Behind him, amongst power tools, pieces of wood, decorating equipment and ironmongery, sat Colin and Baron. Colin was sporting a New York Yankee baseball cap and a leather jacket. His eyes were trained on the Uzi sub-machine gun that was resting on his lap and he caressed the length of it with his right index finger as if in a trance. Ridiculously, he found himself thinking what he would say to Ali's mother if their paths crossed again. At least I can kill dat racist focker for her an' Ali, he thought. After dat, I don't care what happens to me.

Baron, clad in an ill-fitting polo-neck sweater and a suede bomber jacket, still felt the cold. He peered out the front windscreen impatiently.

"You know," began Colin. "If I sight dat pagan Lee I'm gonna drill him wid nuff holes 'pon dis very street... I don't give a fock." He still fondled his weapon.

Baron and K didn't reply.

Twenty minutes later they saw groups of men in twos and threes leave the pub; none of whom the South London crew recognised. Colin was now crouching directly behind K. Baron was still sitting on the floor of the van, pushing his knees close to his chest and obviously not liking this experience. Just then a light-blue Ford Focus pulled up twenty yards ahead of where K had parked. A young woman emerged from the car. Topped by a neat brunette hairstyle, she was wearing a belted leather coat and dark trousers. Her boots resounded off the asphalt as she tottered to the pub. Colin recognised her as the barmaid Yvette, who had rebuffed Ali on the night of the heist.

By the time that Colin had smoked a cigarette, he saw the woman in the leather coat again. She was walking towards her car with a tall man; Tony.

"Let's deal wid 'im now," insisted Colin, preparing to exit the van.

"No," stressed K. "That woman could be useful... We'll follow them." K had spotted that Tony and Yvette were linking arms. "Baron, when they pull up, go for the girl. Don't do nothing to her, but pretend that there is some intent. You get my drift?"

Baron nodded. "In uder words *terrorise* de gal."

"Yes," K agreed. "Colin, don't do anything stupid. Remember, we need to find out where this Lee lives."

"Don't talk down to *me.* I ain't a focking idiot."

Keeping a distance of about sixty yards, K tailed the Ford Focus. Checking the road signs, he realised they were heading towards Leyton.

"Lose dem an' I might use dis Uzi 'pon you," Colin stated quietly into K's left ear. K, ignoring the threat, drove on carefully; respecting the speed limit. Five minutes later, K found himself approaching the Whipps Cross roundabout. He followed the Ford Focus into Wood Street and it turned right into a car park that served the residents of twin tower blocks.

"Ideal," smiled K. "Right, get ready. Baron, remember to get the girl."

K watched the car reverse into a parking bay that was part of a grid marked in white paint. Yvette switched off the engine. Tony was the first to get out. He was holding a plastic bag. Yvette climbed out of the car, placed the straps of her handbag over her shoulder and locked the car doors. "I just can't, Tony."

"Why not?" Tony replied, exasperation written on his face. "You know I like you. You like me. What's the problem?"

Yvette looked up at the block of flats, longing to escort Tony to his place, but she knew she couldn't. She then felt a black-gloved hand smother her mouth and an arm seizing her waist. She glanced at Tony and saw there was a Uzi sub-machine gun concentrating on his left temple. Her eyes widened and her mouth opened wide. Her sound was muffled.

"Move, now!" Colin ordered Tony. "To the van."

Colin gestured where the van was with his gun. Tony, scared by the intent in Colin's eyes, co-operated; wondering if Yvette would come out of this situation alive. He saw her being hauled away by Baron and she was dumped unceremoniously into the back of the van. K was still in the driver's seat. Colin ushered Tony into the passenger seat. He glanced into the rear of the van to see if Yvette was alright. "Yvette!"

"Quiet your focking mout'!"

"Tone!" Yvette managed to blurt out.

Baron pulled her left arm to drag her towards him and viced his right arm around her neck. "Shout out again an' de bloodclaat windscreen turn red! Boom boom claat!"

K glanced back to study her face and was satisfied that Yvette was sufficiently intimidated. He turned to Tony. "Now, my Australian friend. You're going to give us some information. I don't know if you know that Lee gunned down our brother Ali?"

"I don't know nothing about that," answered Tony rapidly, shaking his head. "I ain't got nothing to do with that. I just worked for Eddie."

"Where does Lee live?" interjected Colin, his gun aimed at Tony's head.

"We know you do all Eddie's deliveries," added K.

"Bastable Avenue on the Thamesview council estate," Tony revealed, having no qualms about betraying the East London crew.

"The *full* address," stressed K. He took out a notepad and pen from the glove compartment. "Write it on this and it better be right. Otherwise..."

"Alright, alright... Just don't hurt her."

Tony wrote Lee's full address in capital letters on the notepad, glancing at Yvette intermittently. Colin looked on with suspicion. "I've done what you wanted," said Tony. "Can we go now?"

"Not quite yet," said K. "What can you tell us about diamonds? Please don't excuse yourself with ignorance, because you *must* know something."

"I... I eavesdropped on a telephone call that Eddie was having. He mentioned something, er, something about eight million pounds worth of diamonds on the plane that you lot jacked..." Tony paused and swallowed. His mouth was dryer than a Bond Martini. "When I told the other guys, they wanted to find where Eddie had stashed them, and they said they'd bring you in on the deal too if you helped them look."

"See, I told you," said K, glancing at Colin.

"So what the fuck is going on?" Tony demanded suddenly. "Isn't eight million enough to keep us all happy?"

"It ain't now," Colin sneered at him, his revenge still the first priority.

An uneasy silence choked the air of the cramped van like a miasma of Sarin while K thought about Tony's answers. "Alright, you can go," he said finally, "but *she* stays with us. A little insurance, you understand? I hope you're not telling fibs... Anything you might have forgotten or perhaps want to add?"

"No, no! She's no part of this. Why don't you take me? Let her go."

"No. We prefer female company and my Jamaican friend wants, as he calls it, a slam from a *real* English lady... I take it you made no spelling mistakes in Lee's address?"

"*No*, no." Tony worked out quick what K meant by the term 'slam', but before he could protest he was bundled out of the van by Colin. "Feel lucky I ain't drilling your fuckin' white behind!" he growled.

Yvette was too scared to twitch so much as an eyebrow. She dared a look at Baron's features and saw the ugly scar that crossed his hairline. She tried desperately not to think about it, but a vision of gang-rape entered her mind. Tears were falling down her cheeks that she didn't dare wipe away.

K started the van and soon pulled away. In his rear mirror he saw Tony looking as helpless as a fat turkey weeks before Christmas. Colin span around to have a good look at Yvette. Her green eyes were moist, looking down at the cluttered floor in disbelief. He could smell her perfume and noticed a gold cross hanging from a rope chain around her neck. Pretty, he admitted. And fit too, he decided, gazing at her breasts and the rest of her body. He remembered times in prison when Ali and himself pleasured themselves by flicking through porn magazines. He wouldn't admit it to anyone, but in different circumstances he would happily give up his embargo on dealing with anything pale-skinned if he had the chance to fuck her... He *could* fuck her! he reasoned. Right now. What's to stop him? Baron wouldn't give a shit. If he'd wanted her he would have already made his intent obvious; Jamaicans were like that. But K? He would say something sarcastic. Or he might not say it, but he would *think* it. K wouldn't see him as a proper member of the Nation of Islam if he fucked her. Colin looked at Yvette again, appreciating her even more. Forbidden fruit is always tempting, Colin recalled someone once telling him in prison. Maybe I can fuck her if K gets out of the way for any time, he thought. Yeah, give her a good fuck. Let her feel the power of a black man.

Thirty-five minutes later, K parked outside his council block. He checked his watch and saw it was now just past midnight. He turned to Yvette who was still staring at the van floor. Her mouth was open and her lips trembling. Baron, no longer feeling the need to hold her, sat next to her; eyeing her with fascination. "Don't do nothing stupid," K demanded, but his tone was soft.

Yvette was allowed to walk unaided to the lift of the council block. Unnerved by the road signs that informed her she was in

South London, she dreaded what would happen to her now. The driver seems calm enough, she guessed, but that guy with the heavy accent. Jesus Christ! Baron was walking with K close behind Yvette and Colin strutted at the rear extravagantly, his gun concealed by his leather jacket.

K opened the door of his flat and stood aside to let his crew and Yvette enter before securing the mortice lock. He led them to the lounge. Baron gestured Yvette to sit down in an armchair. Tears were still bowling down her face as she seated herself, holding her arms tightly around her stomach, not even thinking about unbelting her coat. Colin unbuttoned his jacket, took it off and flung it on an armchair opposite Yvette. He sat down on the same chair, legs apart, staring at her. "You can tek off your coat, you know?"

Yvette didn't respond, opting to study the carpet. Using the corner of her eye, she spotted Baron making himself comfortable on the sofa. What are they gonna do to me? she asked herself.

"Anybody want a drink?" offered K, addressing Yvette with his eyes.

"Yeah, hol' me ah beer," answered Baron.

"An' me too," concurred Colin, his eyes not leaving their brunette captive.

"And... what is your name?" asked K, looking at Yvette.

She was afraid to answer.

"Look," K said. "We're not going to hurt you. If Tony gave us the right address you ain't got nothing to worry about. Now, do you want a drink? A mug of coffee perhaps?"

"Nnn... No."

"Suit yourself," K replied, feeling slightly insulted. "But I need to know your full name."

He walked over to her. "Your handbag, please."

Without looking at him, Yvette handed over her designer-labelled bag, a gift from a man she knew. Colin and Baron looked on curiously as K rifled through its contents. He picked out a filo-fax and proceeded to leaf through the pages. "Yvette Walters," he smiled. "Welcome to my humble home, Yvette."

Yvette ignored the greeting.

"Now, let's see," K added, turning more pages over. "Aaaahhh! Mummy and Daddy Walters. They live in Plaistow - in a council estate. But you're dressed like an Essex girl, Yvette? Trying to move up in life, are we? Let me write this address down so next time I happen to be in Plaistow I can perhaps pay them a visit."

K walked off with the filo-fax in his hands. Trying to keep still, Yvette was unable to stop her whole being from shaking.

Baron took out a Stanley knife from his trouser pocket and eyed Yvette with fascination. "K, mon," he called. "We affe mek sure she nuh talk to anyone."

"I'll deal with it, Baron," K answered, guessing that Baron was promising violence. "This filo-fax is very interesting, its got *all* of her friends addresses in it."

Baron put the knife back in his pocket and switched on the television. By the time he tuned in to a repeat of *The Bill*, K had returned with the drinks; including a glass of orange juice for himself. He placed them on a chess board that covered a smoked-glass table and sat on the limb of the sofa. "You sure you don't want anything?"

"No, I'm alright," Yvette stuttered, now hating K's politeness.

Baron started to construct a spliff, his eyes not diverting from the television. Colin was still watching Yvette, captivated with her obvious dread and struck by her beauty.

"We'll leave about quarter to seven," K announced. "I'm going to have a little lie down. I've morticed the front door and the key's around my neck, so you can relax. Treat the girl kindly, we don't want her to think that black guys are all sexual predators." The phrase was meant for Yvette's ears and he grinned to himself as he left the room.

On hearing K's last remark, Yvette was even more alarmed. She saw Baron approach her, spliff in mouth. She pushed her knees close to her chest, wrapping her arms over her calves. Colin watched her intently.

"Yu smoke 'erb?" Baron asked.

"Wh… What?"

"Yu smoke de good 'erb?"

Yvette thought about it. Yes, she did smoke dope, if that's what he meant. I'd better say yes. It might put 'em off what they might do to me. Or it might upset him if I refuse… Don't wanna upset *him*. "Yeah… Why not? You're not gonna do anything to me?"

Baron cackled. "Bwai! Yu nuh easy gal. Me nuh like fock gal who put up resistance. An' besides, yu too maaga fe me liking."

Yvette couldn't understand Baron's patois, but judging by his laughter she thought the Jamaican at least wouldn't ravage her yet. "Can… Can you roll it for me? Please?"

"Nuh problem, gal."

During the small hours of the morning, Yvette smoked four spliffs and downed three cans of beer. She found herself giggling at the cartoons on the television and heard Baron apparently telling strange tales about his life in Jamaica. She hardly understood a word of it, but laughed anyway. Colin was subdued throughout the night, his mind drifting to better times with Ali. *Maybe if we can find those diamonds I'll give a cut of the take to Ali's mum*, he thought. *Just post the notes through her letter box and make a run for it. Don't want her to see me.* He also contemplated whether he should just drag Yvette to the spare bedroom and fock her there and then. *At least it will stop her focking giggling*, he reasoned.

By the time K's alarm clock had sounded at 06:15am, Yvette was now higher than the top floor of K's tower block. When K entered the lounge, he found her sprawled across the armchair, her leather coat on the floor and a butt end of a spliff between her nail-varnished fingers. Baron was sleeping on the sofa and Colin was wide awake, audibly breathing through his nose, staring at Yvette with a face full of sexual frustration. The *Flintstones* had just started on the T.V..

"Baron! Wake up!" K called. "Colin, get yourself ready - wake up the girl."

"*You* wake her up. I ain't putting my hands on no white bitch!"

K roused Baron and Yvette, then went off to the kitchen to switch the kettle on and make some toast.

Twenty minutes later, K was driving the white van through the Rotherhithe Tunnel. He was wearing a postman's outfit, complete with cap, and on the passenger seat was a red post bag and a brown parcel. Now and again his eyes flicked to the notepaper on the dashboard where Tony had scrawled Lee's address. Colin was seated in the rear of the van, close to the back entrance. His eyes stared ahead blankly as his gloved right hand caressed the Uzi sub-machine gun. Yvette, now sobered by a mug of black coffee that K had given her back in the flat, dared to glance at Colin, not quite believing the situation she found herself in. She felt worse now than at any time since she was incarcerated in K's flat. Baron was opposite her, apparently more concerned with the chill of the morning.

K reached the Thamesview council estate at 07:15am. Taking in his surroundings he concluded that this estate was in a far worse state of neglect than anything around his South London home. He drove slowly, reading Lee's address and the names of the council blocks. "There it is - Bastable Avenue," he said as they crossed a set of lights. "Seems like Tony's word was true. Colin, ready?"

Colin simply nodded, still gazing ahead blankly. In his mind he saw Ali's bullet-ridden body, slumped in the road. K pulled up as close as he could to Lee's residence. He picked up the brown parcel and pulled his cap down to almost cover his eyes; then he strapped on his red postbag. He climbed out of the van and walked towards Lee's lair. He wondered what his mother would say if she knew he was an accomplice to murder.

Colin, who had tucked his gun underneath his jacket, stepped out of the van and tailed K keeping a fifteen yard distance. He stood by a wall as he watched K rattle Lee's letter box. K kept his head down, shifting uneasily from foot to foot. A hand stirred an upstairs net curtain. He knocked again. Colin began to unbutton his anorak slowly. Footsteps could be heard from within Lee's hallway. K gestured to Colin with his free hand. The door opened and there stood Lee in his boxer shorts, his face contorted and blinking with a hangover. K hit the ground as Colin sprayed Lee with a maelstrom of bullets. The young skinhead fell back into his hallway, his eyes still apparently in shock at recognising K despite his uniform.

As K got up to his feet he saw Colin hot-stepping to the van and heard the bubbling, wheezing sound of Lee's lungs fighting for breath. He took one last glance at Lee's blood-covered torso before running himself. He jumped in the driver's seat and heard Yvette muttering something that made no sense, her whole being was shaking and her eyes were locked in a vacant stare.

"Baron, shut her up," K ordered, before turning the ignition and screeching away. Baron smothered her mouth with his left hand. K had driven two miles before he pulled up suddenly. "I think it's time to sever our relationship, Yvette."

Baron opened the back of the van as Yvette, still in shock, moved towards the rear gingerly.

"Hurry up, bitch," threatened Colin.

Yvette jumped out, saw the doors close and the van pull away. She stood still on the spot, oblivious to what was happening around her, still not believing what she had witnessed and what had happened to her in the last ten hours or so. She didn't even notice Colin leaping out of the back of the van and stepping into the passenger seat, complaining of a sore backside.

Monday 3rd of December, 2001; 09:30am.

Detective Sergeant Dudley Powell was sitting at his desk in Barking Police Station and staring out of his third-floor window at the shoppers who were milling around the Vicarage Field shopping centre when Scott Hain entered the office. The young Detective Constable grinned at a blonde W.P.C. as he wove his way through the banks of paper-piled desks that crowded C.I.D.'s under-staffed office then kicked off his shoes for comfort. "Wotcha, Sarge," he said, slumping down at the desk opposite Dudley. He held a Styrofoam cup of coffee in one hand and a bacon roll in the other. "Any news?"

Dudley shook his head and continued to stare out of the window. "Fuck all," he replied.

"What? Not even from the snouts?"

A disgruntled "*Hmph*" was Dudley's only answer. For two days he had drank endless cups of tea in endless cafes talking with Barking's endless supply of informants, but none of them knew of anyone who had had it in for Careful Eddie Maynard. In most murder cases the prime suspect was usually the spouse, but Eddie didn't have one and, considering his line of work, it wasn't too big a leap of the imagination to turn to his dubious business associates instead, but even *that* was leading to a dead end.

"You know, I really am starting to believe that it was a suicide," he said eventually.

Scott swivelled his chair from side to side like a toddler on a swing while he waited for his P.C. to boot up. "Have Forensics come up with anything?" he asked when the Windows logo pinged into view.

"From the post mortem? No. Other than that he was pissed and stoned at the time, but wouldn't you be if you were about to throw in the towel the way he did?"

"I guess so. What about the confirmation of identification?"

"Nah - not yet. We know Eddie's prints aren't kept by S.O.4 on account of his clean record, so they've taken what's left of his jaw to a Forensic Orthodontist to see what he can make of it. I know they've already pulled his records from that dentist's down Longbridge Road, so pretty soon it's gonna be a simple case of compare and contrast to make a positive I.D., then case closed."

"Couldn't S.O.C.O. lift any of Eddie's prints from the pub to save time?"

Dudley shook his head ruefully. "Nah. Not a sausage," he sighed. "Upstairs was wiped clean, and the bar and optics had too many prints on 'em to get anything reliable."

"*Man*," Scott exclaimed in exasperation. He whacked the Enter key on his keyboard as he logged on. "I thought we had a double whammy there - getting Careful Eddie out of the picture, *and* being able to lock up some scrote for doing it."

"Well, we're still a few weeks away from Christmas presents, so maybe we should content ourselves with just Eddie."

Scott frowned as he ran a hand through his fine blond hair. "That don't sound like you, Sarge," he admitted cautiously.

Dudley shrugged. "The thing is, we're fresh out of leads and, on top of that, Careful Eddie didn't win his moniker at a raffle.

He was one careful so-and-so and despite his being with the firms for as long as I've been alive, we ain't never bagged him for so much as a parking ticket." Dudley paused as he sipped at his own Styrofoam cup, then grimaced at the plastic taste of tea á la vending machine. "That means," he continued, "that even *if* his untimely demise *is* the result of some deal gone bad, then we'll be lucky if we pick up any pieces. The guy's just too flippin' good at covering his tracks."

"Yeah," Scott laughed with his mouth full of bacon roll. Bits sprayed onto his desk. "He covered those tracks at Barking Station for a good thirty feet."

It was too early in the morning for Dudley to find that joke funny, but he forced a chuckle anyway for the sake of office politics.

"'ere, I know what'll cheer you up," Scott said after a few moments of silence. "You'll never guess what I heard in the Canteen just now."

"What?"

"D.S. Conway just came in from the Thamesview Estate after having cleared up what's left of that thug Lee Jones. It seems that someone saw fit to rip him in half during the small hours with an Uzi or something."

"An Uzi? You're pulling my leg. That's hardly Barking style."

"Well, some kind of automatic, anyway. According to Mike, the little Nazi was almost cut in half by the lead they'd pumped into him." Scott paused as he swallowed a mouthful of bacon roll. "Not exactly a loss for the community, is it?"

Scott's carefree use of the phrase *'cut in half'* dragged the unwelcome memory of Careful Eddie's bisected corpse back into Dudley's imagination and he realised that the last time he had seen both of the deceased men alive was in the Spotted Dog pub five days before. Lee had been mixing with some unusual company for someone S.O.11 said was a member of Combat 18, as well as a few other faces well known to Barking nick for their penchant for night work. Dudley smelled a connection.

"Here, Mike," he shouted across the office. "You got any leads on Jones yet?"

Detective Sergeant Mike Conway swung around in his chair to face him. "Nah - I've just got Frank going through a shit load of C.C.T.V. footage to see if any of the usual suspects turn up," he replied. "S.O.C.O. are still tidying up the scene and Lee's mum is too Brahmsed to talk, so I don't have much to work on. All we know is that Jones was blasted to Kingdom Come smack bang on his front doorstep while still in his boxers."

"You had much joy with the C.C.T.V.?"

Mike shrugged and jerked his thumb to where a young Detective Constable was harassing C.I.D.'s battered video player. "Maybe. At the estimated time of death, there's a white van that entered Bastable Avenue first from the lights, but when it comes out the other end its dropped back about ten cars behind, so it must've stopped for half a minute or so. I've just phoned through for the technical lads to try and make out the registration and Frank's trying to track the van's path through Barking."

Dudley nodded. "Give us a shout if he sees anyone," he said. "With any luck I might just be able to take that case off your hands."

Monday 3rd of December, 2001; 09:40am.

Baron had just emerged from a Jamaican baker shop in Acre Lane, Brixton, eating a coco-bread and chicken pattie sandwich when he spotted a man standing on the pavement who he knew from his past. Baron acted as if he didn't notice him.

"Long time nuh see, brethren," Detective Sergeant Michael Hooker hailed, giving Baron a friendly punch on the shoulder. Michael was dressed in jeans and name brand anorak. "You want ah lift?"

Baron thought about it, taking another bite of his morning meal. He nodded as he looked on Michael cautiously. He walked to the unmarked Policeman's car and hesitated momentarily before climbing into the passenger's seat. Michael got in on the other side, started the car and the latest hot reggae tune blasted out from the car stereo system. As Baron finished his breakfast nonchalantly, nodding to the music, Michael drove towards Balham. He pulled up in a side-road off Balham High Street, opposite the local leisure centre. Immediately ahead of Michael was a parked Rover; where a black man, dressed in a tracksuit, was apparently waiting in the driver's seat. It was Detective Chief Inspector Wiley. Michael stepped out of his vehicle and gestured Baron to join him in Wiley's car. Baron co-operated.

Wiley, holding papers in his hands, swivelled to greet the Jamaican. "Good morning, Baron. Or should I say, Mr. Perry... Mr. Malakai Perry?"

Baron turned to Michael. "Who de raas is dis?"

"Detective Chief Inspector Wiley," Michael answered. "One of my colleagues at Trident. He's bona-fide."

"Wha'? Ah black Inspector?" Baron didn't look convinced.

"These things can happen," interjected Wiley, injured by Baron's mocking expression.

"So yu do dem dutty work?" Baron laughed in contempt, never feeling threatened by any British Police.

Not amused, Wiley began to read his papers. "Malakai Alphonso Perry. Born in Kingston, Jamaica, 1959. Raised in the Denham Town area of Kingston and your family moved to Tivoli Gardens, another area of Kingston, in 1971. In 1976 you saw your father murdered on your front door step by assassins under the control of Manley's P.N.P. government." Wiley paused and glanced at Baron, looking for some kind of reaction, but he didn't get any. He resumed. "You joined the death squads of Seaga's J.L.P. party and killed a number of your counterparts from the P.N.P.. After an attempt on your life, one where you sustained a scar on your forehead from a glancing bullet, you moved to the Jamaican countryside where you were involved with the guns for ganga trade. At this time you were recruited by the C.I.A., who wanted to destabilise the Manley government, and was trained by them in guerrilla warfare in Florida along with how to fly light aircraft; thus enabling you to bring back to Jamaica the guns for your ganga."

This last statement did get a response from Baron. Surprise was on his face like a politician being hit by a thrown egg.

Bloodfire! He thought. Dem C.I.A. mus' ave been 'pon me backside fe long time. Wiley smiled and continued. "You returned to Jamaica in 1980 prior to the election in the country and, again, you and your death squad executed a number of goons from the P.N.P. party."

"Dem did deserve it, mon. Dem kill off ah whole heap of me bredrin."

Wiley put the papers down. "I know everything about you, Malakai. I even know about your girlfriend; Carol Lindus is her name, and two teenage sons in Miami."

"Is dat ah bloodclaat crime? Ah man cyan't 'ave ah family? Instead ah yu gi' me ah tale fe me life why yu nuh tell me wha' yu waan?"

Wiley was not deterred and wanted to finish off Baron's life story briefing. "After Seaga gained power the C.I.A. had no further use for you. So, you came into England in the mid 1980's under the alias of Menelik Joseph. Thereafter you played a big part in establishing the so-called Yardie crack trade in South London and North West London."

"So yu know 'bout me! Yu waan ah tick fe yu 'omework? Or yu waan ah liccle information... An' dat will cost yu ah liccle somet'ing, y'understand?"

"I reckon you owe *us* something," interrupted Michael. "We've already paid you more than you're worth."

"But me gi' yu wha' yu waan. An' cah wha' me tell yu, de judge sentence t'ree Jamaican fe life. Me owe yu nutten!"

"Well, you can't leave the country without our say so," stated Wiley. "And, of course, we still have the option of deporting you to Jamaica if we say you're a threat to national security... I wonder what our trigger-happy friends the Jamaican Police would do to you? I don't think you'll get to marvel at the inside decor of a Jamaican court. Even if you did, it's Death Row for you, Malakai, and you know what it's like at Saint Catherine's. With your family in Miami there's no-one to bring you food, and with the beef-swill Saint Catherine's provide you'll die of malnutrition long before they got the chance to hang you."

Baron stroked his stubbled beard with his right thumb and index finger, working things over in his mind. An internal voice whispered that it was against European Law for a government to deport a man who might face capital punishment, but he knew that he didn't have the guts to take that risk. A lifetime spent in the V.P.U. of Wormwood Scrubs as an informant was nothing compared to a month on Saint Catherine's Death Row, and Wiley was right; with no family to bring him food he'd starve long before a hangman had the chance to loop the noose about his neck. "Alright. Wha' yu waan fe know?" he asked eventually, thoroughly defeated, but attempting to put a brave face on it.

"We know you was at a party in Stansfield Road last Saturday night," said Michael.

"Was I?"

"You were clearly identified," returned Wiley. "What can you tell us about the killing of a black man outside this party?"

"Nutten. Me nuh know nutten 'bout it. Cah me leave early. Me only did ah 'ear 'bout it when me sight de front page of de Sout' London press de nex' day."

Frustration creeping into his face, Wiley presented Baron with a look to show he wasn't convinced by his explanation. "Did you see a large man who called himself Ali at this party? Was there any incident? People arguing?"

Baron thought that if he was going to make any money out of this investigation, he'd have to give Trident a sweetener, some kind of clue. "Me did nuh know 'im fe talk to but me sight 'im aroun' town an' t'ing, jus' like yu see ah somebody who live inna de local area."

"*Did* you see him at the party?"

"Yeah, mon. But me never talk to 'im. He was jus' enjoying 'imself, dancing an' t'ing wid de girl dem."

"Who was he with?" asked Michael.

Baron glanced quickly out of the car window and then returned his gaze to Wiley. "'ard fe seh. He was talking to plenty people an' it was dark, y'know."

"Do you think you could find out who this Ali used to hang around with?"

"Yeah, mon. In time. But yu know so it could be well dangerous, y'know, asking dem kinda question." Baron made a gesture with his right thumb and two fingers, rubbing them together.

Wiley and Michael looked at each other, whereupon Michael nodded in agreement of something. Wiley put his hand into his tracksuit pocket and it emerged with a mobile phone. "Only use this to give us information," he instructed. *"Don't* use the phone for any other purpose. It's a secure line and all calls will be monitored. Do you understand?"

"Me know de programme."

"We expect results, Malakai," Wiley affirmed, a hint of a threat within his voice.

Wiley handed the mobile phone to Baron, while Michael presented the Jamaican an open envelope that contained five hundred pounds in uncreased cash. Baron banked the mobile phone and money in his pockets. "Stop fret, mon," he said, noticing the anxious looks of the Policemen. "'ave me let yu down before?"

"Just remember this, Malakai," warned Wiley, leaning closer to the Jamaican. "We know you want to return to the States and play happy families, but you haven't got no chance of that without our help. We know you've made an application for a visa, but United States Immigration rejected your application, citing you as an undesirable. And your friends in the C.I.A. have washed their hands on you... So, Malakai, to use your term, you'd better get with the programme."

Baron said nothing, opting to seize Wiley with a murderous stare.

Monday 3rd of December, 2001; 11:35am.

It was approaching lunchtime when Mike Conway shouted his excitement loud enough for Dudley to turn and face him. "That's it, we've got the bastards on tape!" Mike exclaimed. "Here, Dud, you want to come and have a gander?"

Both Dudley and Scott stood and walked over to the V.C.R., where Mike Conway and Frank Whitney were gawping at a television. Frank was rewinding a fuzzy security tape and cursing the sellotaped remote control. "I tracked 'em back to Barking," he said. "Outside the abbey they let some I.C.1 bird out the back and an I.C.3 male gets into the passenger seat. There's not much of an I.D. on the bird, but the bloke gives us a half-decent facial."

He stopped the rewind and pressed play. A white van with a mud-smeared registration plate drew to a hasty halt just opposite the main gates of Barking Abbey and a tall, brunette woman clambered from the back with her face buried in her hands as though she was crying. A well-built black man followed her out onto the street and as he slid into the passenger seat he gave her a fleeting stare of contempt. The van then drove away, leaving the woman to her own devices.

Dudley recognised the look although he did not know the man by name. After all, he had been on the receiving end of that same look himself not so many days before. He recalled the conversation he had held with Lee Jones about his unusual choice of drinking partners and the reactions he had received from the three black men who were with him.

"Well, I'll go to the foot of our stairs," he mumbled under his breath.

"What, Sarge?" Scott asked uncertainly. "You know one of 'em?"

"I've seen the I.C.3 before and he was in Eddie's pub drinking with Lee Jones."

"Pull the other one. It's got bells on."

"Nope - it's true," Dudley replied. "Lee Jones was drinking with that guy last week and I bumped into them doing so. In fact, come to think of it, it was the night when Eddie handed in his library card."

When the van thundered from view Frank Whitney rewound the tape and played it again. "Well, it sounds like this case is yours, not mine," Mike Conway said, who was also staring at the television screen. "You want me to have a word with the D.I.?"

Dudley nodded and for the first time since Eddie's death he felt as though he had something to work with. He went back to his chair without another word and Scott trailed after him like a skinny blond duckling. "Do I have to give ya a penny for 'em, or what?" Scott asked after a time, when it seemed as though Dudley was going to keep everything he suspected to himself.

"I've just got a hunch," Dudley replied. "I definitely saw that I.C.3 in the Spotted Dog with Lee on the night that Eddie topped himself. He was there with his cousin and a local fruitcake named Davie Thompson."

"I don't know him."

"Davie is some kind of an ecological psycho with a long string of minor offences against giants of capitalism like Coca Cola and McDonalds."

"What the fuck?"

"Don't ask me. I only know that, because I was on Court duty when he got sent down last and the stupidity of it stuck in my mind. He did a two year stretch for turning over a warehouse full of Benetton gear, and his warped defence was that he was striking a blow for the sweatshops in Bangladesh."

"Now you've lost me."

"According to Davie, Benetton has little Bangladeshi kids making their clothes for them in Dickensian sweatshops and he claimed in Court that he was doing the robbery to get some justice for *them*."

Scott laughed. "You're right," he said. "He does sound like an Eco-psycho. So are you putting him in the frame for killing Eddie?"

There was a moment of silence while Dudley ran a check on the Police National Computer to bring up his details.

"Not a chance," he said, spinning the P.C. monitor around so Scott could read the screen. "According to the P.N.C. it ain't his style. Davie is purely political. Now if it was Ronald McDonald we'd found dead at Barking Station it'd be a completely different story…"

"So that leaves the I.C.3?"

"So I reckon. I reckon Careful Eddie Maynard bit off more than he can chew. I reckon this is a job for Trident."

Scott drained the last of his coffee then tossed his Styrofoam cup into a nearby bin. "What? Ain't you going to check the local faces first?" he asked.

"There ain't no point," Dudley responded. "First off, we've squeezed every snout in the Borough and come out with didley squat, and second; for someone to get that close to Eddie they'd have to be pretty tough *hombres* with good connections."

"So it's either the Organised Crime Division or Trident?"

"Yeah, and seeing as he's an I.C.3 I'm going with Trident first." Dudley picked up a Metropolitan Police phone book and tossed it onto Scott's desk. "Here, see if you can get one of their D.I.s on the blower; any one of them who's had someone malkied recently."

Scott did as he was asked without comment and as he went through the various operators and cursed at the various answering machines Dudley pulled up Lee Jones's file from the P.N.C.. It didn't make for pretty reading. Eventually, Scott handed him the phone and as he held it to his ear he heard a deep voice state: "This is Detective Chief Inspector Wiley from Operation Trident. Can I help you?"

Dudley smiled as he picked up a pad and pen. "Yes, D.C.I. Wiley, I think you can," was his reply.

Tuesday 4th of December, 2001; 04:14pm.

Colin X was studying the books and pamphlets of a stall owned by a 'Bobo dread' rastaman in Brixton market. He heard tireless tongues advertising the ripeness of their fruit and veg and they were battling with 1970s reggae music blaring out from another market stall; bargain hunters nodded their approval as they strutted by. Colin had noticed the hustlers doing their business in shadowy doorways with quiet whispers and quick eyes, ganga spliffs dangling from the corner of their mouths as though cannabis had never been a banned substance. Colin liked this edginess to Brixton and especially enjoyed a nearby butcher's calling card of a stereo system running a tape of a Jamaican stage show featuring the top dancehall D.J.s of

Jamaica. Despite his paranoia that Ali's mother could suddenly appear at any moment, he felt at home here among his own people, aside the explosion of wine bars, restaurants and gay clubs that were now part of the Brixton landscape. Often, with Ali by his side egging him on, he would take a step over the threshold of these new enterprises and offer anybody who was inside a long, baleful stare, making sure they were not welcomed by *him*. Situated next to the Index bookshop and straddling part of the road and pavement, the Bobo dread stall specialised in selling rasta doctrine and obscure black history. The dread, impressively tall and dressed in a white robe with red, gold and green trims and crowned by a spotless white turban, looked forward to making a sale. "Yu know 'bout de Holy Piby?" he asked.

"What's dat?" returned Colin.

"De black mon bible! It's ban in dis country an' even de Pope himself don't sanction it. Me nuh expose it inna me display cah me could ketch nuff trouble from all kinda Babylon agents."

Colin liked the fact the book was banned. "Alright, but I haven't got the dollars on me today. The next time, yeah?"

To show his respect Colin offered a fist and the rasta smiled and presented his own; almost bruising Colin's knuckles. "Walk safe an' live good," the rasta said.

"Yeah, man. An' dat go for you too!"

Colin turned and started for Brixton High Street when a sudden realisation came to him that this spot was where the Brixton nail-bomber had struck. He reflected on Ali's death and realised he was the only true friend he ever had. His thoughts turned to Lee and he smiled, justifying that his murder of Lee may well have prevented another atrocity. Someone nudged him on his shoulder. Colin stiffened, readying himself to give a right uppercut, but he was becalmed when he realised that it was someone he knew; Keith Worral, the brethren who told him about Crumbs's party. "Yo, X," he greeted. "Been looking for you, man. Bwai, you're a hard man to find."

"Yeah? Wha' you looking for me for?"

Keith took a check around himself and peacocked a few strides, stopping at the entrance of the Iceland store, trying to look like a bad-man. "Bwai," Colin laughed. "You're going on like der is nuff C.I.A. about... Wha' de fock is it?"

Keith noticed the impatience in Colin's eyes. "It's Crumbs, man. One of his sound guys tell me dat he's been squealing to the Police, giving descriptions an' t'ing... You didn't hear dis from me."

"Is dat so?" Colin smiled a violence-promising smile. "Is dat so? T'anks for dat, an' I'll rope you in on somet'ing soon, yeah. Mek you a liccle money for yourself... I have to get mobile now, so laters."

Keith watched Colin blitzkrieg his way through pedestrians and those at the crowded bus-stops, wondering if he was now the cause of more black on black violence. A minute later, Colin was inside the library that was situated opposite the town hall. He looked for a quiet spot and ignored the greeting of one of the library's staff. He took out his mobile phone from his trouser pocket and searched for Baron's number, deciding he was going to deal with Crumbs in *his* way. Fuck K, he thought. I can sort out t'ings.

Tuesday 4th of December, 2001; 05:25pm.

Matt was sitting in his cramped kitchen at a wooden table, enjoying his King Prawn Chow Mein supper that he had purchased from Yung's Chinese take-away. His mother, a stout woman who was sporting a permed hairstyle streaked with grey, was eyeing her son suspiciously while scrubbing a pot clean in the sink. She was wearing a ridiculously small pinafore that could have doubled as a baby's bib. They both heard the boiler, situated on the kitchen wall next to a Rod Stewart calendar, vibrate and click into gear as someone upstairs proceeded to run a bath. The hot water tap serving the kitchen sink relented to a dribble. The woman cursed under her breath and turned to her son. "Where did ya get the money to buy a take-away, then?" she asked, recoiling at the smell of the food. "Stinking out the flippin' place. You were crying poverty last week, but for the last few days you've been scoffing Kentucky, McDonalds and now bloody Chinese. Have I turned a bad cook over-bloody-night?"

"Nah, mum," replied Matt between chews. "I told you the other day that I'm doing some private work on some cars for some bloke."

"Private work? I should bleedin' co-co. If that's true your old girl's a Hollywood sex bomb! Your blue overalls ain't been out of your wardrobe for so bloody long even the moths can't stand the dust on it. And your tool box ain't seen the light of day outside the shed since you got laid off! Private bloody work – my eye! Maybe that's what that bad sort Lee Jones calls his criminal goings on. I don't like you hanging around with him - just like his shifty old man he is, and I don't care if he's my brother-in-law an' all. Mark my words, Lee Jones will be the downfall of you."

Matt looked up to his mother and saw her pointing at him with a saucepan. "But he's family."

"Family? I don't call Lee's lot a family. What with their drunken mother and Lee's old man living at Her Majesty's pleasure. Fine example I say of a family! They shame us all."

"Lee's had a rough time of it," Matt managed. "He really misses Uncle Alan."

"It could be a blessing for him. His old man has a bad influence on him, and it ain't no excuse for his bloody manners, is it? Coming in here the other day shouting and cursing. What was all that about? I'm surprised you ain't with him today getting up to all sorts."

"I rang him twice... No answer."

"That's another thing - I want to pick a bone with you. Calling bloody mobiles on *my* phone. Didn't I show you the bill? Do I have to show you again? Over a hundred and thirty quid it was. You can gimmi some of that private work money towards it... If it's legal."

Just then the letter box rapped fiercely. Matt's mother placed the saucepan in a drying rack and stomped off along the hallway, preparing herself to give a mouthful to whoever knocked her door so loudly. She opened the door to reveal two men; Dudley Powell and Scott Hain of the Barking Police. She looked at them suspiciously, hands on her hips. "And who the bloody hell are you? We're not a family of deaf and dumbs." She checked them over again and soon realised they probably weren't Matt's mates, they were too well dressed.

Both officers showed their badges. "I'm Detective Sergeant Powell and this is my colleague, Detective Constable Hain... Is this the residence of a Matthew Jones?"

"I'm his mother. What do you want with him?"

Powell's eyes dropped to the ground and he shifted uneasily from foot to foot. "I'm afraid I have some bad news for you... Mrs.?"

"Mrs. Gloria Jones. What is it? Has my Matt been up to no good? He hasn't been shoplifting again, has he? If he has I'll beat the living daylights out of him."

"No, Mrs. Jones. It's your nephew Lee. He was... murdered yesterday morning."

Gloria opened her lips wide but no sound came out. She quickly covered her mouth with her right hand but her eyes reflected her shock. Powell noticed Matt approaching from the hallway.

"One of our officers found Lee's mother in a bedroom. She seems to have taken it very badly and is in hospital from shock and, er, drink... We need to talk to Matthew."

Gloria seemed to look through the Police officers and offered no response. It took her three seconds to move aside and let the Policemen enter the house. Matt had overheard the news of Lee's death and he could feel his heart pumping violently within his chest. He led the officers into the front room on unsteady, numbed legs, not daring to look the Policemen in their faces. He heard his mum climb the stairs, preparing to inform his dad, who was in the bath.

Powell and Hain sat down in a two-seater sofa, Hain with notebook out and biro poised. Matt decided to remain standing, staring blankly around him. There were bruises and stains on the woodchip wallpaper and the blue carpet was thin enough to feel the nails in the floorboards with your soles. "I know this is a shock to you, but to help us get Lee's killers we need you to *think*, Matt," Powell began.

Matt responded with a slight nod.

"That night I saw you in the Spotted Dog with Lee, who were the coloured guys sitting around with you? Have you seen them before and do you know why they were in the Spotted Dog that night?"

Matt wasn't paying Powell his full attention. He was thinking of better times he had spent with Lee. He addressed his answer to the window. "No. Never seen 'em before. They just joined us for a drink."

Hain glanced at Powell and communicated with his eyes that Powell probably would not get any sense out of Matt at this time. Powell pressed on. "Did you hear their names? What were they talking about?"

"Dunno…" Matt dropped his head and stared at the carpet. He shook his head slightly, still not believing that Lee was dead.

"I saw you with a man called Davie Thompson. Did he say where he knew the coloured guys from?"

"Dunno."

Hain, who hadn't scribbled one word, whispered to his colleague. "This is pointless. We're not gonna get a dickie-bird out of him."

Powell ignored him. "Did you see anyone having a row with Mr. Maynard on that night? Maybe someone you haven't seen before?"

"Dunno."

Matt's father entered the room, naked except for a white towel held tight around his waist. Steam was rising from his torso and his hair dripped with water. Bubbles of soap still clung to his ears. He peered at the officers looking for some kind of confirmation on the news he had just received from his wife. "My nephew… Lee was murdered?" he managed.

Powell and Hain nodded.

Matt's father paused as he let the realisation sink in. "How? Who?"

"That's what we're investigating," returned Powell, who was now feeling very uncomfortable. He indicated his desire to depart to Hain with a momentary upturn of his eyes and both men stood. "We… we will call again when we receive more information and we might need to talk with Matthew again if something jogs in his memory… Perhaps he needs a bit of time. I'm very sorry."

Still holding his towel to cover his modesty, Matt's father escorted the officers to the front door in silence. When they left he returned to the lounge and found his son still standing in the middle of the room, motionless, staring at the carpet.

Tuesday 4th of December, 2001; 09:25pm.

"We shoulda tell 'im, man," growled Baron, looking out the window of a stolen car in Stansfield Road. "De Professor might be ah weak-'eart but 'im useful in dis kinda situation."

"No, Baron," rejected Colin. "If we did tell him de news 'bout Crumbs squealing somet'ing to de beast, he would've gone all soft 'bout it an' do some shit where he puts his focking arm 'round Crumbs an' explaining de situation. Well fock dat shit an' Crumbs mout' better be silenced 'cos I ain't going no jailhouse again!"

Baron stroked the wispy hairs on his chin with his right thumb and index finger, thinking on a decision. He wondered what would happen to him if Trident caught wind of his involvement in the initial heist and the murder of Lee. At best he'd get life in an English prison and at worst he'd be deported back to Jamaica where an anonymous death in a Police cell would be the only certainty. Even if he *could* escape the jaws of the Jamaican constabulary he'd have to evade the Uzi-toting 'Dons' supported by the P.N.P.. His face creased into seriousness. "Alright, yout'. But gi' me de raas claat gun. Me nuh waan yu get twitchy an' kill off everybody inna de yard."

Held between his feet, Colin looked at the Uzi and his expression informed Baron that he wasn't going to give up the arms without fuss. In one swift movement, Baron snatched

Colin's left arm and held it tightly behind his back and viced his throat with his long fingers, forcing Colin to look at the car ceiling. "Let me tell yu one t'ing, bwai," Baron said in a near whisper. "I *don't* like mon who hesitate. It mek me feel nervous, y'understand? Me get de gun an' from *now* on, *me* control it. Boom boom claat!"

Colin fought for breath as Baron released his grip and picked up the gun. The two of them didn't exchange any words or glances for the next thirty-five minutes until they saw a car pull up with Crumbs emerging from the driver seat. Before Crumbs could make it to the front door of his girlfriend's home he spotted a serious piece of hardware staring at him from under the veil of an anorak. He froze, thinking that if he so much as squeezed a fart he would lose his life. Yardies don't care where they shoot their victims, he thought. Baron walked up to him calmly, Colin a few paces behind. "Now," Baron addressed calmly. "Do as me say or de craven dog dem will be sniffing bits of your brain pon' de sidewalk come morning time... Y'understand?"

Even Colin's guts reacted to Baron's last phrase. Crumbs remained rooted to the pavement, waiting for orders. He looked at Baron and felt his gaze lance into him like two welder's torches. "Now, yu were jus' 'bout to call on your woman. Wha' yu ah wait for?"

Crumbs took nine nervous strides to his girlfriend's front door and pressed the doorbell with an unsteady finger. He felt Baron's breath on his neck. The door opened and Crumbs' face was mournful as he met his girlfriend's eyes. "Sorry, Lesley."

Baron prodded his hostage with the gun and with Colin they entered the house. Colin closed the door behind him. "Yu 'ave any visitor?" Baron asked Lesley, checking along the hallway and the flight of stairs.

Lesley couldn't take her eyes off the gun and she shook her head, unable to speak. "Alright," Baron continued. "Move to de front room."

Lesley led the way as Colin inwardly approved of the way Baron was handling things. He's probably done a lot of this shit before in Jamaica, he thought. "Si' down," Baron ordered.

Crumbs and Lesley both sat in the two-seater sofa. Destiny's Child were performing *Survivor* on the wide-screen television. Colin guarded the door, admiring a wall cabinet full of glasses and china that stood against a wall. To add to the couple's dread, Baron closed the curtains, while Colin switched off the light. Lesley started to weep, staining her eye make-up. Baron slowly walked up to Crumbs, looking at him as if he was the forgotten chewing gum stuck on a sole of a drunken tramp. "Ah liccle bird tell me dat yu 'ave been chatting wid de Police dem. Yu waan fe tell us wha' did mek up de conversation?"

"I told 'em nutten! Dey were jus' asking us questions. I didn't know wha' was going on. I didn't 'ave nutten to tell. Believe me I woulda gone a long time, but I 'ad to stay 'cos de road was seal off. I couldn't move my sound stuff. Dey wanted to know if I knew de guy who got shot."

"Is dat right?" Baron said, caressing his chin with his right thumb and fore-finger. He dropped to his haunches and beheld Crumbs with laser-like eyes. "Dis same bird tell me dat of your own free will, yu gi' de Police dem some descriptions. One ah dem was *me.* Ah true dat?"

"No, no! I can't even remember seeing you guys at de party. It mus' ave been someone else 'cos I wouldn't tell de Police nutten. I 'ate dem an' dey used to trouble me all de time when I was doing nutten wrong. Me an' dem could never agree."

Holding the gun in his right hand, Baron used his left to take out something from his anorak pocket. It was a Stanley knife. He used his thumb to push the lever to make the blade protrude. The metal reflected the television lights. Crumbs pressed his back deeper into the sofa and Lesley gazed at the knife, shocked into stillness. Baron maintained his seizure of Crumbs with his unblinking eyes. Suddenly, there was a rapid movement of Baron's left arm. Lesley loosed a stifled scream that was caused more by shock than by pain. Her right arm was slashed by Baron's blade and the blood swarmed red over the sleeve of her cream pullover. With her left hand she tried to stem the bleeding. Crumbs looked on, not knowing if he should aid her or not. Baron cleaned the blade on the carpet, not letting go of his gaze directed at Crumbs. "Let me tell yu dis, bwai," he said in a low, murderous tone. "If me 'ear 'bout yu talking to de

Police again, me nuh come fe look fe yu. Me coming fe look fe your woman. An' I will kill her an' everybody else me find inna de yard... Y'understand me, yout'?"

Crumbs nodded repeatedly, his frame almost disappearing into the sofa. Baron stood up and turned to Colin. "Come, time fe go."

With a calmness that Colin couldn't begin to understand, Baron tucked the gun inside his jacket and left the house, simply walking to the stolen car. "Mek sure yu tek de car somewhere far an' burn it."

Colin nodded, checking for the Zippo in his trouser pockets, and he acknowledged that he had just received a lesson in how to induce fear.

Baron climbed into the passenger seat. "Dey won't talk," he said. "Yu don't affe fire gun to mek people 'fraid."

Wednesday 5th of December, 2001; 09:20am.

Scott Hain swallowed his mouthful of bacon roll then jerked a thumb over his shoulder at a petite W.P.C. who had tottered by. "What an arse she's got," he stated wistfully, whistling though his teeth.

Dudley nodded as he leant back in his chair and smiled as the W.P.C. ran a hand through her bobbed auburn hair before putting her peaked cap on. While he sipped at his morning coffee he noticed Scott's eyes track her across the office, then saw the colour rising in his friend's pale cheeks.

"For goodness' sake, Scott, why don't you just ask her out?" he demanded after a time. "It's obvious that you're nuts about her. It's written all over your face."

"Who? Heather?" Scott replied somewhat redundantly. His already flushed cheeks blossomed red with a blush and his eyes tilted to the floor. "You think she'd say yes?"

"Well, there's only one way to find out."

Scott stirred his tea with a plastic spoon while he thought about it. W.P.C. Heather Golightly had been consuming his days and tormenting his nights since her transfer from Stratford nick three months before, and he'd thought that nobody, not even Dudley, had known about his infatuation. He decided that complete denial was the best policy, but before he could do so the telephone rang. It was Detective Chief Inspector Wiley from Trident, and he was at the front desk wanting to speak with Dudley.

"Okay," Dudley said after Scott had passed on the message. "This'll probably take me an hour. While I'm gone, chase up that forensic orthodontist and see if he's made a match with Careful Eddie's choppers yet, then start on the paperwork."

Scott nodded his concord, so Dudley donned his dark blue jacket and went down the stairs to meet Trident's only black Detective Chief Inspector.

"Hi, I'm William," D.C.I. Wiley said as he held out a shovel-like hand for Dudley to shake. "I hope you don't mind me dropping in like this."

Dudley had never been asked what he minded by a D.C.I. before, and the notion amused him. "Not at all. Not at all," he replied musically, ushering Wiley past the front desk and up some stairs to a conference room. "Although I must admit that I'm surprised."

The conference room was empty save for a table and chairs, some video equipment and a large white board. William placed a leather document case on the table then sat down, whereupon Dudley joined him. "You want a cuppa?" Dudley asked.

"Coffee, please."

Dudley pulled a phone out from under the table and dialled a number. "Hi, Heather, it's Dudley," he said after a time. "Can you get Scott to bring us in two coffees? Conference Room Four. Yeah. That's it. And when you speak to him, be nice. He's having women troubles, so compliment his hair or something. You know - low self esteem. That's a sweetie. Thanks. Yeah. Thanks."

Dudley was laughing as he laid the receiver back in its cradle, and wished he could see Scott's face when the impossible happened and he found himself in conversation with his amour.

"Something funny?" Wiley asked.

"My D.C. needs a little help aiming Cupid's arrow, so I just moved the target a little closer for him."

Wiley grinned broadly as he opened his leather document case. "What do you know of the shooting near the Stockwell Park estate last Sunday?" he asked, pulling out some papers.

Dudley shrugged. "Only what I saw on the telly, which means not a lot. An I.C.3 got plugged as he was coming out of a party. Crikey, you must have your hands full in your job. Nearly every day some I.C.3 gets plugged by another I.C.3."

Wiley found himself being saddened by Dudley's last phrase and found it impossible to argue against the statistics. "Well, I guess you're right, but on this particular case there are many discrepancies. Ballistics tests reveal that the firearm used was a Heckler and Koch USP Compact 9mm and so far we haven't linked it to any other crimes, which is odd."

"How so?"

"The men we hunt down at Trident aren't known for their common sense, Detective Sergeant Powell. Have you ever dealt with Yardie-related crime before?"

"Call me Dudley, and the answer is 'No'."

"Then allow me to explain. When it comes to gun crime, Trident's work differs from that of the rest of the Met.. On the north side of the river gun crime is comparatively rare, and when it *does* take place it's either some blagger doing a job, or a professional making a hit. Either way, nine times out of ten the perpetrator is smart enough to get shot of the weapon the first chance he gets.

"Down south, however, it's a bit different. Guns are used for a far more general type of crime. They're sometimes used in street robberies, and often fired during gangland disputes. They're even turning up in schools. Because of this, guns are far more likely to be kept after they've been used in a felony, and because of this we're far more likely to find that a gun has been used on multiple jobs."

"I understand you, but I don't see what this has to do with me."

"Ah, but you will. What if I told you that a consignment of Heckler and Koch firearms had been stolen from Barking Container Base last month?"

"Yeah – I know that, but the scene was left spotless... We knew if would be, for a job on that patch would have to be under the auspices of Eddie Maynard..."

Dudley's voice trailed into nothingness as he had guessed the point of Wiley's visit as he spoke. With the realisation came a conclusion that gave him the urge to slap his forehead with his palm, but he managed to resist the temptation. "So there's a possible link between your death near the Stockwell Park estate and the death of Careful Eddie," he blurted eventually.

"Could be. Although, of course, the emphasis is still on the word *possible*. The firearm used in the killing is spotless by South London standards, and, as I said, a batch of squeaky-clean Heckler and Koch *were* blagged from Barking last month. Could the death of my boy be a Barking hit?"

Dudley had to agree that D.C.I. Wiley had a point, but before he could say so there came a thud at the door as someone kicked it.

"Come in," Dudley said.

"I can't," came the reply. "I'm holding your bloody tray, so I can't twist the knob."

Dudley stood and let Scott into the conference room carrying a tray of coffee and Rich Tea biscuits. "I'll swing for you," Scott hissed through his teeth as he placed the tray on the table. "You set me up with Heather."

"Ah, D.C.I. Wiley, meet D.C. Hain – the gentleman I was telling you about, " Dudley said with a grin.

"D.C. Hain, pleased to meet you," William said, proffering one of his huge hands. "I hope you're having a good day."

The realisation that Dudley was in conference with a Detective Chief Inspector, and a Detective Chief Inspector from another department at that, finally clawed its way into Scott's consciousness and he felt his stomach tighten.

"Erm... erm..." he managed.

"See, I told you he was in love," Dudley laughed as he escorted Scott back to the door. "Don't forget to put the wood in the hole on your way out."

"No... there's something else," Scott mumbled before Dudley could shut the door in his face. "I just got off the dog with that orthodontist at Oldchurch Hospital. It turns out that according to his dental records, that stiff ain't Eddie Maynard."

"What?" Dudley slumped back in his chair as though he had been punched, while William's eyes widened until it appeared they would burst out of his head.

"I'm sorry, Sarge, but the choppers don't match up. The forensic orthodontist is convinced that the stiff ain't Eddie."

"Then where the fuck is he?"

Scott shrugged. "Sorry, Sarge. You want me to get him on the phone?"

"No, not the orthodontist – I mean Careful Eddie!"

Dudley pulled Scott back into the conference room and closed the door behind him. "Okay, here's what we do," he said, wagging a finger as though he was scolding an errant child. "Get the prints from the stiff checked out and see if we have them on file. Then I want you to round up all the usual suspects and see if they know where Eddie's done a bunk to."

"You sure we want that released?" Scott replied uncertainly. "If word hits the streets that Eddie ain't holding the reins, then we could be in for a crime wave, not to mention the bloodshed as every blagger from Beckton to Canvey tries to grab himself a piece of Eddie's manor."

There was a moment of silence while Dudley pondered Scott's observation. "You've got a point," he admitted sourly. "Okay, we'll keep a lid on it for now, but bring in Eddie's gopher for a quiet chat. What's his name? Tony something? Well, it's on file, so go look it up."

Scott nodded and left Dudley and William alone in the Conference Room, relieved to be away from the tension that issued from Dudley like a bad smell. "Bollocks," Dudley complained bitterly, letting out a whoosh of breath as he slouched back into his chair. His shoulders sagged. "That's certainly pissed in my cupasoup."

Wiley preferred to be philosophical about the matter. "You're not looking at the bright side," he said by way of consolation. He ran a hand through his tight afro hair. "Before now you had an identified corpse and no murder suspect, but now you have an unidentified body with a suspect smack bang in the centre of the frame. I know which of the two I'd prefer."

"I guess you're right," Dudley confessed. The faintest hint of a smile tortured the corners of his mouth until he relented to let it bloom. "Okay, that's enough of my troubles," he smirked wryly. "A quid says your leather case ain't on the table, 'cos your lunch is in it."

William laughed, and the sound was deep and full. "There are no flies on you, D.S. Powell."

Wiley pulled a sheaf of papers from the document case and spread them across the table until he found the one he was looking for. "Have you had your breakfast?" he asked suddenly.

Dudley nodded, so William handed the document over. It was a photograph taken at Ali's post mortem. Mercifully, it was just a head shot to help with his identification, but the sunken cheeks and waxy flesh of the cadaver still made for an unpleasant sight.

"I'll never get used to this end of the job," Dudley mumbled under his breath. He took a sip of his coffee, but knew he couldn't stomach a biscuit, because soggy Rich Teas looked too much like the serrated flaps of fatty skin left from whence the pathologist had cut Ali's throat open.

Wiley nodded his concord, but was more than willing to knock a dent in the packet of biscuits. "It's always unpleasant, but also always necessary. Tell me, D.S. Powell…"

"Dudley."

"… Dudley. Do you know this man?"

Dudley scrutinised the picture and felt Ali's glazed, rheumy eyes tugging at a distant part of his memory, but its pull was too feeble to force any recollection.

"Do you have another picture?" he asked, frustrated that the cadaver's face evoked in him an itch that he could not scratch.

Wiley slid another post mortem photo across the table. It showed Ali from the waist up; revealing his broad chest, muscular shoulders and bullet-ridden skin. Rulers were laid across his corpse to indicate the width of the entry wounds and a long row of stitches stretched up from his crotch to his throat, where it separated into two stitched lines that circumnavigated his neck to meet at his back. The pathologist had certainly gone to town on him.

Dudley could almost smell the Formaldehyde, so he took a sip of coffee to kick his senses back into touch. The head on its own had done little more that nag at his subconscious, but when he saw the brutal face set above the prison gym shoulders he recalled where he had seen the man before.

One week before, Dudley had entered the Spotted Dog public house with no more of an intention than to just hassle Careful Eddie for a while, but in the seven days that had followed two of the men who he had seen were now dead, and a third had gone missing after presumably killing a fourth.

"Jesus fucking Christ," he stated, more to himself than to Wiley. "It was like the Last fucking Supper."

"I'm sorry, D.S. Powell? Dudley?"

"Erm... yeah... I know him. Sort of. I saw your stiff in Eddie Maynard's pub on the night of his murder – I mean disappearance – sitting with another guy who got sent skyward last Sunday."

"A black man or a white man?"

"A white one. In fact, he wasn't just white; his file says he's a Combat 18 thoroughbred, with a long string of convictions for racial violence."

"I don't follow. They were arguing?" Wiley asked, confused.

"No – that's exactly the point. I saw the Nazi guy's cousin-come-sidekick in the pub talking to some I.C.3s and it made me smell a rat, then the Nazi himself turned up and didn't let loose with a bottle or knife, so I thought either the World's turned upside down, or the little fucker was up to something."

"And you're sure that your I.C.1 was talking to my I.C.3?"

"As sure as I can be. I only saw him the once, but it sticks in my mind because of the unlikelyness of his drinking partner."

Wiley pulled a pad from his inside jacket pocket along with a gold fountain pen. "Let me get this straight," he said, his gaze flicking between Dudley and the pad. "Last week you went into Eddie's pub and you saw an I.C.3 talking to two I.C.1s who have Neo-Nazi links, and within the last week one of the I.C.1s is dead, along with my I.C.3." He paused to drink some coffee, trying to digest these startling facts. "On top of that, the landlord of that pub has done a bunk, and a guy who you *thought* to be him up until just now had to be peeled from the rails of Barking Station?"

Dudley nodded. "Yeah, but it wasn't just the three of them. There were three I.C.1s and three I.C.3s."

"Do you know all of them?"

"I know the I.C.1s. Lee Jones, our latest victim, his cousin Matt, and a local nutcase by the name of Davie Thompson. As for the I.C.3s, there's your body and a guy who we want to question about Lee's murder on account of his appearing in some fuzzy C.C.T.V. footage close to the crime scene. The last I.C.3 is a mystery. All I can remember is that he was in his forties or so and had a strong accent."

"What type of accent? Jamaican? African? Brixtonian?"

Dudley shrugged apologetically. "Sorry. I'm not clued up on that sort of thing."

"Can I see the footage of your suspect?"

Dudley picked up the phone and punched a number. "Heather? Yeah. Speak to Frank Whitney and get me the tape on the Jones case, will you? He'll know what I mean. Yeah. Ta. Thanks." He hung up.

"If you have an I.C.3 in the frame for the murder of your Neo-Nazi, this could be a grudge thing," Wiley postulated. "Could this be a tit-for-tat killing?"

"Jones killed your I.C.3, then one of his mates paid him back in kind? I guess so, but how do we link that up to the disappearance of Eddie Maynard and the stiff we thought was him?"

"Could they have been contracted to make a hit together? Could the deal have gone bad?"

"No. Not Lee Jones. You couldn't pay him enough after his dad got sent down. According to his file, he developed a hatred of blacks when his dad got handed a life term. The key prosecution witness was from an ethnic minority."

"They must be a nice family."

"Yeah – the best of British."

Wiley drew a smiley face on his pad then wondered why he had done it. He scribbled it out before Dudley could notice and thought about taking another biscuit. "I'm gonna go out on a limb here and make a hypothesis," he said. "I'd bet a pound to a penny that Jones is responsible for the Stockwell Park murder, and that his death is Brixtonian payback. Chances are that this has something to do with the disappearance of Eddie Maynard, but what that *something* is could be anyone's guess. So, I say our priorities are to find Eddie or whoever the I.C.3 is on your surveillance footage and ask *them* what's going on."

"That's easier said than done."

"I agree, but we have a place to start. You said you knew all the I.C.1s. We could start with them."

Dudley frowned slightly and picked up a biro to chew. "We went and saw Jones' cousin yesterday and he was pretty-much nonsensical. He doesn't really have any form to speak of, and he's not known to have any right wing tendencies. I doubt he'll know much."

"What about your nutcase?"

"He's so out of the picture that he isn't even in the same movie. Davie Thompson is a political activist, an anarchist or whatever you want to call them. By all accounts, particularly his own, he has Gulf War Syndrome and it's set him on a vengeful collision course with any kind of multinational or authority. In short, McDonalds will start selling wholesome food before Davie Thompson's political beliefs swing any further right than Red Ken's."

"That makes me wonder what he was doing talking with the likes of Jones."

"I've been thinking about that," Dudley replied. "The thing is, I didn't see our suspects straight away when I came into the pub. I was busy talking to Eddie. Now, it wouldn't be a surprise if I found out that Davie clocked me first and went over to the Jones boys and their I.C.3 friends to spread the word of my arrival just out of spite for the Police. He's also a smart cookie who enjoys locking horns, so maybe he wanted to be part of any trouble."

"But you can't be certain?"

"No. He may have been with them all along. I couldn't swear to it."

There was a moment of silence while Wiley lost the battle to resist the last of the biscuits, then he spoke with his mouth full.

"Let me run this by you," he said, wiping crumbs from his lips. "How about we pull in the cousin and sit on the nutcase for a while? We'll see what we can get out of the first one, but if that draws a blank then we still have the other. Meanwhile, we can work on identifying your dead publican substitute and my dead Yardie. Once we know who they are all this might make a lot more sense."

A knock came at the door before Dudley could answer, then W.P.C. Heather Golightly entered bringing with her the video tape of Colin X and the van.

"Thanks, Heather," Dudley smiled, taking the tape and posting it into the V.C.R..

"You getting anywhere with this one, Sarge?" Heather replied as Dudley turned on the television then pressed rewind.

"Why? You think you can help?"

"If only. Anything's better than being a plod."

Dudley chuckled as the tape whirred in the machine. "Nah – you don't want to be C.I.D.. Why bugger up your own clothes chasing villains when you can knacker up a uniform instead?"

"It's not the uniform, it's the work. And this case sounds interesting."

Dudley turned away from the television and realised that W.P.C. Golightly actually meant what she was saying. Her head was tilted to one side in a display of coquettish curiosity.

"You know I don't have the authority to bring you in on this one, Heth, and I've already got D.C. Hain doing all the legwork, so I can't blagg it with the D.I.."

Heather appeared crestfallen and turned to leave the Conference Room, but William Wiley's deep base snagged her like a trout on a line. "D.S. Powell might not, but I do," he said, displaying his enamel like a white picket fence. "Trident moves in mysterious ways. I'll have a word with your Detective Chief Inspector."

Heather's lips bent into a cherry red bow of excitement, while Dudley's formed the extended 'O' of complete surprise.

"Thank you… *Sir*?" Heather managed before skipping out of the room, Dudley's hands propelling her by the shoulders.

When Dudley had closed the door behind her he raised his left eyebrow at Wiley to ask the obvious question.

"What? Have you got the monopoly on playing Cupid around here, D.S. Powell?" Wiley grinned as he pressed play on the V.C.R., and it was then that Dudley knew that the two of them were going to get along just fine.

***

Wednesday 5th of December, 2001; 05:12am.

Eddie Maynard was laying down on a Southend hotel bed, dressed in a blue silk shirt that was unbuttoned down to his flab-hidden navel and blue and white striped boxer shorts. His back was supported by three pillows and he sipped champagne leisurely from a long, flute glass. He had asked room service for it especially, wanting to leave the staff with the impression that he was a sophisticated and cultured man. In his left hand he held a television remote control and he thumbed through the myriad of cable channels, until he settled for the American wrestling. The heavy gold bracelet on his wrist clinked erratically. He placed his glass on a bedside cabinet, next to the bucket that contained the champagne bottle and checked his watch. 05:12pm. He was about to curse something when he heard the door knock. "Mr Michael Hoskins?" a female voice called.

"Yes, come in, love."

Yvette Walters entered the room sporting a long, black leather coat and suede, high-heeled sandals. A brown, suede and reptile-skinned handbag was hanging from her left shoulder. She was wearing no make-up and her eyes were tired, the skin below was swollen and dark. Eddie ran his eyes over her and sensed something was wrong. The silly mare ain't on drugs is she? he thought. "My dear, Yvette," he greeted, gesturing for her to sit down on the bed by patting it gently. "What's a matter, my love? Tony being over keen? You can't blame him, love. He probably wants to send nice little letters to his friends back in Oz telling 'em he's found his English rose. Working beside you while not enjoying intimate moments with you is a torture for him. Especially as he thinks you're of the single persuasion. A cruel torture for any man who's not interested in queer pursuits."

"No, no. It's not that," Yvette shook her head, remembering her ordeal with the South London crew. The sub-machine gun fire. The sound of a body collapsing on a threshold. The screaming of the tyres and the smell of a recently-fired weapon.

"Then what is it, love?" Eddie cajoled, slightly annoyed because Yvette hadn't yet unbuttoned her coat.

"*They* took me," Yvette blurted, a sudden terror in her eyes. She had to inform someone of her tribulation and Eddie was the only one she could tell. She parked herself at the end of the bed. "They fucking took me, Eddie. I thought they were gonna kill me. They killed someone! I heard it all. I was there!" Yvette's voice was becoming more panic-stricken and she tried to get out all her words at once. "I was there in their van! The Police have been on my case. Tony might've dropped you right in it. *They* know where I live and they know where my mum and dad live. Eddie, you have to stop them. Sort them out. I can't sleep. It's doing my head in."

Eddie moved over to her, dropped the remote control on the floor and embraced her; kissing Yvette fatherly on the forehead. He could smell her expensive perfume and felt an erection gathering momentum. God, he thought. It's been too long since I fucked her. "Who took ya?" he asked, feigning deep concern. "You haven't told 'em of any of my daring escapades?" Eddie's relaxed shield suddenly fell and the concern for his own safety was evident as he awaited Yvette's reply.

"No, Eddie. I'll *never* tell 'em that." Yvette sighed silently. "We're in this together, *aren't* we? It was those Yardies. You've got to sort 'em out, Eddie. They scared me to death. I thought they were gonna…"

"Now, now, my dear, Yvette. Have I ever let you down before?" Eddie lifted up Yvette's head with his right thumb and index finger. He gazed into her eyes, his erection now fully matured. "Don't worry, love. I'll sort them out. I'll just make a few calls in the morning and the Africans will be history. A few gentlemen owe me some favours. Besides, we'll be off in a few days. And there'll be plenty more things I will get ya, like that new car of yours. The World can be our playground. And you won't have to worry about anyone while you're with me. You've just gotta be patient for a few more days."

Eddie had said what he felt was what Yvette wanted to hear. Not even with *his* contacts did he know someone or a crew who would be willing to go down south of the river on a Yardie hunt. On top of that, everyone in the firm thought he was dead, and he had no intention of letting them know otherwise.

"Can't I stay here, Eddie? Until we go away?" Yvette asked, taken in by Eddie's spin and the promise of a better life on the continent. Away from fucking Plaistow.

"Now you know that would be silly, love. Just carry on as you are, going to your job and the hours and days will pass quicker than you'll realise. We don't want the planks at the Met putting two and two together if you suddenly disappear from the stage."

"I ain't going back to the pub. No way, Eddie. The Yardies might be looking for me."

"No they won't. If they've got any savvy they'll know that the pub is out of bounds for 'em, what with Mr. Powell and his mob doing their solemn duty and all. Just do what you've been doing. You know, turning up for work, things like that. I don't want anyone to cotten on to something and realise something's up. So you be a good girl."

"Alright, Eddie… But I'm scared. I was even thinking of going back to my mum's in Plaistow. Can't bear staying at the shared flat in Stratford. I don't get on with my flatmates and I don't talk to 'em much. I dunno what to do, Eddie."

"Back to your mum's?" Eddie was surprised. "I thought you don't get on with her?"

Yvette remembered her formative years when untold times she watched her forlorn-looking mother, sitting at her dining table placing leaflets in innumerable envelopes while the family dinner was overcooking in the cramped kitchen. Yvette was petrified to end up like her, but showed little talent at school; ending up in no-where jobs and dating no-where men. Until Eddie came into her life. Sure, she knew that Eddie was too old for her and she didn't enjoy the lovemaking, but at least he gave gifts generously; making her feel better with herself.

Eddie, sensing Yvette's vulnerability, started to unbutton her coat. He lifted her arms to help her out of the leather garment and once he'd completed this task he went over to the wardrobe and hung it over a coat hanger. He stopped by the door, turned the key and locked it before dimming the light from a circular switch on the wall. He approached the bed wearing a grin as wide as Marble Arch and gazed at Yvette, still not believing this beauty actually had sex with *him*. As he admired her, sitting in her black slacks and cream, crew-neck sweater; a gold rope chain hanging tantalisingly between the shape of her breasts, he thought too himself that good looking mares more often than not would rather sleep with a man of means than your average working class Joe. He sat beside her and pulled her on top of him, roughly grabbing her breasts and forcing her mouth open with his lips. He searched for her tongue greedily with his own and slid one hand down to her crotch, grasping it with four fingers and rubbing it with unnecessary force. He then yanked off her sweater, catching her nose with the fabric in the process and threw it on the floor. Yvette offered no response nor resistance, staring blankly ahead. Eddie, now breathing hard, struggled with the button of Yvette's trousers, popping it off in his frustration; the accursed button ended up spinning on the carpet. He guillotined down her zip and tugged the trousers off her legs. Ferociously, he ripped off her pink knickers and slammed his right palm between her legs, searching for a way in with two fingers. Yvette groaned in pain. His other hand was fumbling with her bra strap and impatience getting the better of him, Eddie opted to just pull the straps down, exposing Yvette's perfectly rounded breasts. He locked his mouth on her left nipple rapaciously.

"No, no... I... I can't," gasped Yvette, pulling herself away. "I'm sorry... I just can't."

Eddie looked mortified. "What's wrong?" he asked while sitting up, his arousal still obvious.

"I just can't... I'm sorry. Not in the mood."

She found her knickers and pulled them on and then adjusted her bra to fit her breasts. Yvette hated herself for allowing Eddie to maul her in this way - he was always the same. But it's this route or ending up like mum; she recoiled at the thought. Can't see no other way out in my fucked up life. But I ain't fucking *him* tonight!

"If you're that worried, love, you can stay the night," Eddie offered. "I'll look after ya. I thought it'll be nice to celebrate my last night in this hotel. Tomorrow I'll be going to a hotel nearer the sea front."

"No, no. I'm going to my mum's," Yvette lied, reproaching herself for asking to stay with Eddie until they flew to foreign lands. After what I've been through you'd think he'd be more considerate, she realised. He don't really give a fuck. "Sorry, Eddie, you've been so good to me, but I wanna see my family."

Eddie watched Yvette dress, thinking the incident with the Yardies had really unhinged her. "Well, you go off to your family, love, and come back and see me when I give you a call. Meanwhile, make sure you've got your passport and start packing. The main thing is to stay calm and be patient. By this time next Saturday the business with the Africans will be just like a bad dream."

Yvette nodded as she pulled on her coat. She smiled weakly at Eddie before opening the door and departing. Eddie poured himself more champagne and shook his head. "Silly mare," he said aloud. "She's definitely more trouble than she's worth, but come Saturday *I'll* be the one having fun in the sun, and I won't be with some daft tart who leaves me sitting in a hotel room with nothing to do but wank."

Wednesday 5th of December, 2001; 07:22pm.

Matt had been sitting in his room listening to his parents arguing downstairs when the phone rang. He knew the call was for him even before his mum shouted up from the hallway – the ring had had an ominous timbre to it - and after a brief, taciturn conversation with his caller he tugged on his anorak then trudged with leaden feet to the corner of the road where a car was waiting. His legs were shaking.

"Get in the car," Danny told him, his hands thrust into the pockets of his grey trench coat.

Davie was sitting in the back seat of the stolen Vauxhall Astra reading a paper upon which ran the legend: *Uzi Death Rocks East End*. He put the paper down when Matt slid into the front passenger's seat and forced a mirthless smile. "Good evening," he said.

Danny slumped into the car and throttled the radio. "Okay, I think it's time we had a little talk," he muttered. He lit a cigarette and blew smoke over the dashboard while Matt squirmed further back in his seat as though he hoped the upholstery would swallow him.

"We're sorry to hear about your cousin, Matt," Danny began with smoke spiralling out of his nostrils. More sorry for Alan's sake than mine, he thought. "The deal's certainly gone tits up, but we can prevent it from getting any worse if we all stick to the same story. You got that?"

Matt nodded. His nose was running, so he wiped it with the back of his hand and gave a tearful sniff. He wished he'd brought his cigarettes.

"The thing is," Davie said from behind him. "The local paper claims that D.S. Powell is in charge of the case, and he saw you, me and Lee chatting with the South London muscle on the night that Eddie caught a train in his guts. Now that makes me nervous, Matt, and it should make *you* nervous too."

Danny agreed with a nod. "Do you understand that we could all be accessories to murder, Matt? That we could all be looking at a ten to twenty stretch in Wandsworth or Brixton?"

"I didn't know Lee'd nicked the gun."

"That don't make no difference in the eyes of the Law, Matt. We were there, and if we don't hold our hands up right now and let the Old Bill know what we know then we might as well have pulled the trigger ourselves. That's how the Law works."

"But we ain't going to grass up to the Law, Matt. Me and Danny have come up with a plan, and so long as you can keep your head we can all come out of this smelling like Britney Spear's uncharted pussy."

Matt rubbed his hand across the windscreen to wipe away some condensation then stared down the road vacantly, his hands limp on his lap. "But why can't we just go to the Police?" he asked.

"No!" Danny snarled, making Matt jump. "We can't do that. It'd raise too many questions, and even if we walked away from the murder charge they might be able to finger us for the jacking. On top of that, it'd bugger up any chance we have of getting them diamonds."

"I don't want no diamonds. I just want Lee back."

Danny slapped his knees in exasperation. "Well, unless you're Frankenstein's apprentice that ain't going to happen, is it?" he snapped.

"Look," Davie cooed softly as he leant between the two front seats and waved Danny's cigarette smoke away from under his nose. "All you have to tell Powell or any copper who comes snooping is that Lee was arguing with a couple of black guys in the pub and you tried to break it up. That's all you know. If they ask about me then all you have to say is that I came over to stop them arguing as well, because I know Lee's dad. They'll have that on their files already, so they'll believe you."

"But we weren't arguing."

"Powell doesn't know that. What he does know, however, is that any fool stops arguing when the Law is around and acts like his worst enemy is his best friend. That's just plain common sense, and Powell ain't stupid. He knows Lee wouldn't carry on a race riot smack bang in front of him."

"And you reckon that'll keep us out the nick?"

"As sure as eggs is eggs."

There was a moment of silence and Danny noticed Matt's concentration focus upon his packet of Bensons, which were perched on the dashboard. As a calming gesture, he opened the packet and offered a cigarette to the youngster, who accepted one gratefully. Poor kid, he thought. Should've never got him involved.

"Me and dad went to see Uncle Alan in Wandsworth today," Matt said suddenly, changing the subject. "He's right cut up about Lee."

"I'm sure he is," Danny replied, feeling genuine concern for the distress of his incarcerated friend. "Are they gonna let him out for the funeral?"

"Dad reckons yes, but the Governor ain't said nothing for definite yet."

"What did your Uncle Alan say?"

"Nothing about that, but he did gimmi a message to pass on to you."

Danny and Davie looked to each other and their eyes asked the same question. Was Alan blaming them for the death of his only son? "Okay, then you'd better spit it out," Danny said as he flicked his cigarette butt out of the car window.

"Uncle Alan said that he wants you to come and visit him in the next few days," Matt replied quietly, his gaze drawn to a stray dog that was taking a shit in the road. "He says it's right important and that it can't wait. He says it's something to do with the death of Eddie Maynard."

"What does he know about that?" Davie asked from his seat in the rear.

"I don't know. That's all he said."

A black cab pulled over on the far side of the road and two passengers alighted carrying plastic bags that were stuffed with Christmas shopping. Danny watched them suspiciously with slit eyes until they had paid the driver and decided that it was now time for he and Davie to clear off. "Alright, 'nuff said," he stated tiredly. "It's time for you to hop it."

Matt took a long, ponderous drag on his cigarette then opened his door. Once he had stepped outside onto the pavement he stuck his head back into the car and looked from Danny to Davie. "One last thing," he said, blowing smoke. "It you want me to keep schtumn about Ali and Lee, then you'd better make sure I'm kept in with the chase to them diamonds. I ain't gonna be pushed around no more."

Matt saw the look that passed between Davie and Danny and realised that their unspoken agreement was a sincere one. "You're on," Danny said, then as Matt slammed the car door the Astra pulled away into the darkness.

Matt watched them depart then returned to his home with his shoulders slumped. His mum and dad were still in the kitchen arguing about whether or not they should visit Lee's mum, who had been in a drunken stupor since Lee's death, so he went directly to his room and closed the door behind him. His bed was unmade, with his sheets whipped up into a tangled mess where he had tussled with a sleepless night, so he sat on the crumpled sheets to think about what he should do next.

As he stared at his bare bedroom walls a sullen, cantankerous mood enveloped him like a poisoned gas. He was angry at Danny and Davie for not showing any remorse over Lee's death, angry at his parents because they were releasing their frustration on each other rather than focusing more attention upon *him*, but most of all he was angry at Professor K. Matt now knew that the bespectacled South Londoner had mesmerised him with his easy smile and calming manner, until he had questioned the wisdom of his own flesh and blood – of his own *race*. Lee had been right all along and Matt had ignored him, so now he was dead.

Maybe if Matt had understood that sooner he would have been with Lee when those damned *niggers* turned up, and he would still be alive today, but he had not. Professor K had made sure of that. With that realisation, Matt knew that there was only one person to blame for the death of his closest friend, and he also realised that the guilt of that knowledge would lay heavy upon him like an executioner's axe until K was made to pay for his clandestine, white-subverting machinations. He had known all along what he was doing when he spoke to Matt in the car. He had known that he was filling Matt's mind with mumbo jumbo to steer him from his racial destiny. He had known that he was driving Matt away from his closest friend, and he had done it so that that friend could be killed; martyred like a prophet at the hands of the infidel.

Matt clambered free of his bed then rooted around in a bedside drawer that was full of cassette tapes. He found the one he was looking for, a compilation of the skinhead band *Skrewdriver* that Lee had made for him some months ago, then slapped it home in his player. He had never listened to it before. The music had always seemed too noisy, and he'd never liked the lyrics, but now he realised that it was because he hadn't *understood* the lyrics.

A few seconds of dead tape wound by, then a surging maelstrom of rage and spite exploded into the room at a volume that shook the windows. Within moments, Matt's mum was hollering up the stairs for him to turn that racket off, but Matt didn't care. As the band's singer vocalised his race's defiant and righteous anger at their attempted corruption by the mud races, Matt knew what he must do. He heard his dad's heavy footsteps pounding up the stairs, no doubt to enforce an excessive volume embargo dictated by his mother, as he reached for his anorak and took a flyer from its pocket. He had picked it up at the Saint George pub where he and Lee had met others of their kindred and the recollection made him smile. His bedroom door blasted open as though pushed by a hurricane, his dad's face glowered with a fury that almost matched his own, and as he ranted so much drivel about how he needed his peace and quiet Matt read from the flyer that a meeting was planned for next Thursday. Okay, he thought, realising for the first time how his parents had never really loved him. I now know where I'm going, and my journey starts here.

Wednesday 5th of December, 2001; 11:02pm.

K, simply dressed in a white-stringed vest and boxer shorts, parted the curtain and gazed out of his bedroom window, preoccupied by something. Without his glasses, everything north of the River Thames was a blur to him, but he could clearly see the omnipresent dark shape of Battersea Power Station, its chimneys reaching out to the starless sky. It's about time they done something with that place, he thought. What a waste. And that goes for my education as well. Can't use it in this country no more. He reasoned that his mother's worst torture would be seeing him drive a bus or labouring on some muddy, puddled building site. *That* would score her heart more than if she knew I was an accomplice to a murder, he concluded. No university lecturer for her, he thought, mocking her dream. And if I do teach in Iran I won't tell her about it. No way.

"Keith," a female voice cooed invitingly. "Ain't you coming back to bed?"

K swung around and saw his woman sitting up in his double bed, wearing just a smile. Through the darkness of the room he could make out her breasts, which were trembling provocatively as she patted K's concaved pillow. A recent memory pleasured him and he hoped he wouldn't have to wait long for another erection. He walked over to her, sat down on the bed and cupped her jaw with his hands, gazing intently into her eyes. "You keep me sane, Jasmine."

Jasmine smiled and swept her rich, black hair from out of her face, her dark eyes returning K's appreciation. Her light-honeyed skin the product of a Sudanese mother and Iranian father, K couldn't see a future without her in it. "Won't be long now," he said. "Soon we'll be gone from this country and make a new start in Iran. Once I start teaching there we can get married and have kids. I've got the qualifications and I'll get more respect there. I'll still have to brush up a bit on the Koran, though. I don't want to appear ignorant. If you're right about a more liberal regime in power, we'll do well for ourselves and I'll send Lambeth social services a post card." K grinned, masking his bitter resentment to his former employers.

"I *am* right," cooed Jasmine. "Women can now do what they want to do and the present regime want to modernise things. There'll probably be a whole load of McDonalds opening there soon." She smiled a delicious smile. "Now, stop being so serious and relax." Her hands massaged his shoulders.

K knew Jasmine's last words were a playful jest on him climaxing sooner than she wanted him to fifteen minutes ago. He owed her in a big way. Before he had time to analyse this, Jasmine wrapped her arms around his neck and pulled him down onto the bed, kissing his chest and working downwards to the small tufts of hair below his navel. K closed his eyes, feeling a pleasure overload. For a few seconds he fantasised on what sort of life he could have with Jasmine if he could have a share of eight million pounds worth of diamonds. *Imagine*, he thought. He wouldn't have to bother with any teaching and have time to write a book about the evils of the West. He could take Jasmine to somewhere like Bali for a long holiday. He could purchase a beach-side property in the Caribbean. Yeah, that'll be good, he decided. Make love to Jasmine in the sand and the sea. And their kids would be so pretty. With his West Indian ancestry and Jasmine's middle-eastern heritage, their offspring would have the blood of many cultures running through them; and he would teach them all about it.

K's dream was halted abruptly as Jasmine hit the spot. He moaned pleasurably and felt the life within his genitals stir. I'm gonna make love to you until first light, he willed himself, recognising that Jasmine was his hard drug.

Wednesday 5th of December, 2001; 11:35pm.

Yvette pulled up outside the Spotted Dog under the glare of a lamp-post. Before stepping out of her car she checked behind and in front to see if she was being watched. Apart from a white male teenager passing by while eating a portion of chips and an elderly Asian man who was crowned by a brown turban, the road was deserted. She scanned the parked cars around her and was only satisfied when she detected no movement within the vehicles after a long minute. Thank God, she thought. No fucking van with black gangsters in sight. "Right," she said to herself. "Let's get this over with. I _won't_ be coming here again."

She had been working at the Spotted Dog for nearly four months and had almost yielded to Tony, who kept on asking her out. But she knew she couldn't. What could he offer me? she thought. He's just a barman who'll probably be off travelling the world again. Aussies I've met do that kinda thing. Yvette closed her eyes momentarily and smiled, visualising Tony's tall, naked frame. She had only slept fitfully since her kidnapping and her nerves were frayed when she was in the pub. Perhaps I will go to mum's until I go away with Eddie, sort it out with her. I might not get another chance. At least the silly cow cares for me. She tapped four times on the Spotted Dog's door. A dreadful thought rocked her conscience when she realised that those South London guys knew where her mother lived. The door opened with Yvette looking behind herself nervously.

The pub had three people in it. Tony, who was now behind the bar after opening the door, looked like he had just given three pints of blood. He offered Yvette a stressful nod and a weak grin. Two glasses of water sat in front of him. Dudley Powell swivelled on his bar stool and ran his eyes over Yvette from scalp to toe, appreciating a beautiful woman when he saw one. Scott Hain, sitting beside Powell, only gave a passing glance, not allowing his lust to be detected.

"Good evening... *Yvette*?" Powell greeted. "Looking the way you do tonight you'll give Kate Moss more than a run for her money. I hope you'll remember me when you're strutting your stuff in Milan." Yvette grimaced, not liking the compliment. "Well, you have saved me a journey," resumed Powell. "I need to talk to you. Just want to ask if you've left something out from the last time we spoke to you."

Yvette had halted like a wasp greeting a windscreen the moment her eyes beheld Powell's back; her anxiety obvious. "Tony, give her a drink," Powell ordered. "It'll refresh her memory." He locked Tony in his gaze and took a sip of water. "Now, where was we?"

Hain readied his biro and leafed over another page from his note-book. Tony managed a sorrowful glance to Yvette, who had now taken a seat and was searching for her cigarettes. "I haven't seen the black guys before," reaffirmed Tony, more fearful of the affect of this interview on Yvette than himself. "I just served them drinks."

"What were they talking about?"

"I dunno. I didn't get too close. They looked like..."

"Looked like what, Tony?" Powell sensed a breakthrough. "Trouble? Or even gangsters?"

"No, no. They looked like the kinda guys you don't mess with."

"And why would you say that?"

"The way they looked. And we don't usually get their... their *type* in here."

Tony filled a wine glass with claret and tonic water and was about to set off to give the drink to Yvette. "Scott, take the lady's drink to her," commanded Powell, his eyes not leaving Tony. "Tell her it's on the house."

Scott picked up the wine glass and walked over to Yvette, not daring eye contact with her. Powell didn't say a word until Scott returned. "What's your hourly rate, Tony?" Powell asked, a glint of cunning in his eye.

"Six pound fifty an hour. I'm head barman."

"You're well rewarded for your work, then. Most barmen would be lucky to clear six pounds an hour. You sure your duties only included bar work? Eddie didn't pay you for any other miscellaneous duties?"

"I don't know what you mean."

"I'm sure you do, Tony. So you're saying Eddie never paid you cash in hand for anything?"

"No! He paid me through my bank account. It was all above board."

"Ah, yes, your bank account." Powell leaned closer to Tony and his nose was within touching distance of Tony's chin. "Perhaps you can explain a certain deposit of four thousand pounds in cash to your bank account last week... I don't think it was the Abbey National's interest rate."

Yvette flashed a curious glance to Tony and he tried to ignore it, feeling his face warming. Powell was quick to take up on it. "Planning a Christmas present for Yvette here? Trying to impress her with a surprise holiday in Oz?"

Tony poured himself a shot of whisky, unable to withstand Powell's glare. Scott Hain was busily writing something. Yvette's cheeks hollowed as she pulled nervously on a cigarette. "Now," Powell continued. "Do you want to finish this little talk down the nick or are you going to be more helpful?"

Tony downed half of the contents of his glass before nodding. "You'll have to come up with some sort of protection 'cos my life will be on the line."

Powell turned to Hain and indicated his opinion with a raised eyebrow. "Give us the right information and we might tot up your holiday money back to Oz," he assured, turning back to face the nervous Australian. "You can start off by telling us why two little thugs and Davie Thompson were swapping gossip with a few black gentlemen?"

Tony sipped from his glass again and realised his body language was being scrutinised by his interrogator meticulously. He reasoned that the so-called Yardies could prove more of a peril to him and Yvette than Danny's mob, so he decided to give the absolute minimum information about them. He tried to look Powell in the eyes. "Something was being arranged," he said finally. "Eddie never told me what it was, but on the evening before he died he called several people."

Scott Hain halted his pen and tried to repel a spontaneous smirk. Powell helped his colleague suppress the smile by giving him a glare. "Go on," said Powell.

"Before that night Eddie was always on the phone and all kinds of people were ringing him up. When I answered the phone they never gave their names, just asking for Eddie. Once I heard him talk about diamonds when I was bringing up some beer from the cellar."

Powell raised his eyebrows and gave Hain a look of curiosity. Hain's eyes widened and he scribbled frantically. "What diamonds?" Powell pressed.

Tony paused, glancing at Yvette, who was now engrossed in the interview. Her expression had soured quicker than milk in a heatwave. "I heard him mention eight million pounds worth."

"Crikey!" Hain exclaimed, dropping his pen. Powell presented his colleague another baleful stare.

"I think Eddie was ringing people up about a light aircraft pilot," Tony continued. "That's all I heard. Then a few days later Danny turned up with his mob; a guy called Davie, Lee Jones and his cousin Matt."

"What Danny? I only saw the Jones boys and Davie at the table."

Tony realised that his mouth had opened only for him to put his foot in it. So the Police had known nothing about Danny. "Erm – I don't know his other name," he mumbled.

Powell's expression indicated that Scott Hain should make a note and once he had done so he nodded for Tony to continue.

"Like I said," Tony resumed in an effort to salvage the situation. "I've never seen them before. I wanted to know what was going on, but if you work for Eddie you don't ask questions. Eddie sensed I knew something and that's when he gave me the money. He told me that the owners of eager tongues sometimes find themselves in fatal accidents. He didn't say no more and gave me the money… Would you refuse four big ones if you were a barman?"

"I'll ask the questions," replied Powell, knowing his honest answer would be no. "You sure you never eavesdropped on any conversations between the blacks and Eddie? And for that matter Davie and the others?"

"No. They kept out of earshot."

Powell turned to Yvette. "You're looking alone there, love. Why don't you come and join us?" He stood up and dragged a nearby stool close to him and gestured with his hand. Yvette rose silkily and seemed to float across to the bar. She refused the seat, choosing to stand up while looking down at the floor. Her breasts were distractingly close to Scott's head.

"I'll ask you again, Yvette," Powell began. "Before that evening did you see any of the black men before?"

"No," Yvette replied rapidly, before gulping down a generous portion of her red wine. "I just work here part time. Tony was my boss. I hardly ever spoke to Eddie."

"Just answer the question, Yvette, no need to discuss work relationships. Now, did you overhear anything that maybe you shouldn't have on that night?"

"No, no. I was just doing my job. I haven't been here long and I don't really know the people who come in here."

"You're an attractive girl, Yvette," Powell grinned. "You must've heard all the chat-up lines working behind this bar. I'm sure most of them are pathetic." Powell laughed. "Anybody try to, er, get on acquaintances with you that evening? You might have heard a name via a means of introduction?"

"No! It seemed just an ordinary night."

"What, with our colonial brothers frequenting the establishment? A usual occurrence it is, then?"

"No. I didn't say that. I just never saw anything suspicious."

Powell stroked his left eyebrow in deep thought. "Hmmm. I may need to question you later." He turned to Tony. "So tell me, with Eddie now sadly gone and all, bless his soul," Hain covered his mouth with his left hand, "who do you report to?" Powell insisted. "Who's going to do the books. Who's going to check the invoices and put in the orders for more stock?"

"This bloke phoned up," answered Tony, preferring Powell questioning him rather than Yvette. She looked like she was about to explode. "They're going to wheel in some temporary manager from the brewery. Starts next week. I'm holding the fort until then."

"Do you have an address or phone number?"

"For the brewery? You can look that up in the book yourself, D.S. Powell."

Powell turned to his colleague so that Tony could not see the anger that coloured his face. "Got all that?"

Hain nodded.

"Right, let's clock off, Scott," Powell suggested.

The officers prepared to leave. Tony was anxious about something as he watched Yvette saunter behind the bar to pour herself another drink. "What about the protection thing?"

"Protection from a dead man?" replied Powell.

Before Yvette could take a sip from her drink the Policemen were out on the street, adrenaline rushing through them from what they had just heard. They refrained from talking to each other until a man who was walking a dog passed by.

"Eight fucking million pounds worth of diamonds," Hain whispered in amazement. "But what I can't work out is what Eddie was doing using South London muscle. It don't make no sense."

"Well, he certainly went for the big one before he pulled the suicide scam," said Powell. "But now we've got to find a pilot. Somebody had to bring the contraband in."

"Do you reckon that Tony knows he's alive and kicking?"

"No. If he knew that he wouldn't have been so free with his information. Eddie always knew how to keep people quiet."

"So, what are we going to do tomorrow?"

"I'm not sure what I'm going to do yet. I'll have to sleep on it. But I want you to do something for me in the morning. We've got enough on Davie to haul him in for questioning, so why don't you see about getting us an arrest warrant? When the time's right, you can take Heather with you and bring him in. Then maybe we can find out who this Danny character is."

Powell had a mischievous grin on his face and he blew a few kisses.

Hain smiled. "Those Trident people can certainly get what they want."

"They certainly can, Scott. Makes you wonder, doesn't it? *We* could do what they're doing, and if we crack this Eddie thing the both of us might be up for something good. You never know, soon we might be dishing out orders and walking in suits like what that Wiley wears."

Scott laughed and had a quick thought of one day working for Special Branch, Operation Trident or even with the *spooks* of S.O.10. He hummed the theme to *The Professionals* as they walked back to the car.

Inside the Spotted Dog things were not so jovial. Yvette was gnawing a cuticle while punching holes in the floorboards with her high heels as she prowled back and forth along the length of the bar.

"You're a prick, Tony," she spat. "A no good, dumb-fuck Aussie prick!"

Tony was surprised by her poisonous attitude, so he stopped polishing the beer pumps and paced towards her sheepishly.

"Come on, love," he said.

"Get away from me, you prick!"

He halted as though he'd walked into patio doors, his hands splayed in a gesture of passiveness. "What's up, love?" he asked in his smoothest manner.

"Don't call me '*love*'," Yvette replied. "I'm not your love and I never was. All you ever were to me was someone to flirt with!"

"What?"

"You heard me! I can't believe what you just said. I can't believe that you spilt the beans to the Police about Careful Eddie!"

Having retreated back to the safety of the bar, Tony wondered what Yvette was going on about. Her face was a storm of aggression and her eyes two blue hurricanes that raged fiercely. As he wondered what to say to calm her, she downed the remainder of her drink then threw the empty glass at his head. He ducked and it shattered against a Gin optic noisily, spraying splintered shrapnel all about him.

"Hey, come on, babe," he said, rising up from behind the bar like an infantryman from his foxhole. "I did it for you. *You*. So you and me can be safe together. Back in Oz, I reckon."

"You did it for me? You did it for me?" Her words burned like acid. "Dream on, you prick-brained cowson. What the fuck do you mean, you did it for me? Everything was going fine until you opened your big, fat Aussie gob!" You might have sentenced me to more years in fucking Plaistow, she wanted to add.

"But I had to get Powell away from us. Don't you want those bastards who kidnapped you locked up?"

Yvette's fury was so absolute that she snivelled when she talked. "But you turned the heat on Eddie," she cried. "And I ain't going back to Oz with you. Christ, I haven't fucked you and you're getting delusions of grandeur! *What* have you fucking got that you can offer me?"

"I... I don't understand," Tony pleaded, his face devoid of expression. "I thought you liked me, Yvette. You know, playing hard to get. I thought that was why you worked in the pub with me?"

Yvette's laugh had razors in it. "I didn't come to work in this shit-hole because of *you*," she snarled. She paused to savour what was to come. "I took this shitty job because I was fucking *Eddie!*" Now she had blurted this fact out, she hated herself. Why couldn't Tony be the one to have it all?

The words had the desired effect, and Tony took a step backwards as though stung. "What?" he exclaimed.

"You heard me!" Yvette moved in for the kill, knowing she was vexed with what Tony *wasn't* rather than what he was. "I was fucking Eddie within two months of you bringing me here! I only took the job, because it made my seeing him easier."

"You're kidding me?"

"You think so, *eh*? Well, take a good look at yourself, Buster, and then wonder why I stuck around."

A chilly silence filled the deserted pub that Tony tried to warm up with more conversation. "But he's an old man," he whined helplessly.

"And a fucking *rich* one," came the retort. "We've got four million in the bank and in a few days we're gonna start spending it. Providing, of course, your big mouth hasn't screwed everything up. Talking to Powell, indeed! Weren't the four grand enough to keep your gob quiet?"

Tony saw his life clattering downhill and Yvette had just cut the brakes, but he thought he saw a way of steering it back to level ground. "But Eddie's dead," he managed. "You've got no-one except me, Yvette. We can still make it work, and if the lads find the diamonds we can use our cut to get away from here!"

Another laugh custom-designed by Gillette cut through his desperate smile. "You fool," Yvette mocked cruelly. She sat on a stool near her coat and crossed her long legs. "Eddie isn't dead. And why should I care about your meagre share of the diamonds when Eddie and me already have half?"

If Tony's life was going downhill, he now saw a level crossing at the bottom of it and its lights were on red. His despair was forgotten for a moment as he muttered: "Eddie's *alive*?"

"You bet he is," Yvette replied as she wrestled with putting on her coat. "And I'm meeting up with him tomorrow. We'll be out of the country by Sunday so fuck you, *love*, I'm getting out of here!"

Yvette stood then strode towards the door of the pub, her high heels clicking as she crossed the sawdust-strewn floor. "Goodbye, Tony," she purred, glancing over her shoulder briefly to his distraught, tearful face. "And one last thing. If you or the boys come looking for me, Eddie *or* the diamonds, then you'd better think about leaving your kneecaps at home."

Thursday 6th of December, 2001; 10:27am.

Doctor Khan re-read the chart as though Davie's presence alone could change the news he was about to relate. "I'm sorry, Mr. Thompson. I wish there was something else I could say," Doctor Khan said. "The Lab results confirm our worst suspicion and there is no room for error. You don't have Gulf War syndrome as you claim. The tests prove that you have what is known as Subacute Sclerosing Panencephalitis."

"I… I don't understand," Davie replied nervously. He sat facing the short, Pakistani doctor with his hands folded on his lap. "You mean you've finally found out what's wrong with me? What is this Subacute Sclerosing whatnot?"

"I'm sorry," Doctor Khan resumed, his eyes not flicking up from the chart. "I'm afraid that I have some very bad news for you. There is no other way to tell you this, Mr. Thompson, other than to speak plainly. I'm afraid that the condition you have is terminal and in quite an advanced stage. Our knowledge of the condition suggests that you have between one and three years…"

"What?"

"S.S.P.E., as Subacute Sclerosing Panencephalitis is known, is a mutation of the measles virus that attacks the central nervous system. It's very rare. One in a million. I realise that this must be difficult news for you to hear, Mr. Thompson, so perhaps I could give you the details at another time? Tomorrow, perhaps? I'm afraid that we'll be seeing rather a lot of each other from now on. We'll need to do more tests and establish a drug regime. I'll put you on Isoprinosine for now. It's an immuno enhancer that will help retard the virus' progress, but to give you the most effective treatment there will have to be more tests."

Davie felt as though a giant, invisible hand was pushing him back into his chair. His stomach felt molten while his left arm spasmed with a life of its own; a life he could now attribute to Subacute Sclerosing Panencephalitis.

"But… but…" he managed while his hazy mind groped for some pertinent recollection of his medical training, but he realised after a moment that his stuttered buts were going nowhere. Like the doctor, he had very little to say. "Measles?" he asked eventually.

"Yes, Mr. Thompson, measles. One out of every million of us keeps the measles virus in our system once we have it and after a period of a few years it comes back as S.S.P.E.. The reason why the diagnosis took so long is that S.S.P.E. is so rare, and usually occurs in people a few years younger than yourself. Do you remember ever having measles, Mr. Thompson? You must have been in your twenties."

As the doctor spoke, Davie's mind retreated into his memories; to his time with the British Army when he had fought with the coalition forces that made up operation Desert Storm.

He'd been inoculated against everything that the *Powers That Be* thought Saddam Hussein would throw at him; anthrax, the black death, and even the whooping cough, but now Davie knew that they had not prepared him for the everyday diseases found outside the theatre of war.

The sky had been a clear blue over the Kurdish refugee camp in Northern Iraq where Davie and two other medics had tended to the sick who had fled Saddam's regime. Malnutrition, dehydration and hypothermia had been the main causes for concern, but there was also an outbreak of measles that scythed through the camp's children without mercy. Davie couldn't remember ever having had the disease himself, but as he dabbed the children's itching pox marks with ointment, he thought it can't be all that bad. Most of the children were smiling, after all.

Two weeks later, stationed back at the Field Medical Centre, red marks appeared on his own skin and a case of measles was diagnosed, so he was pulled away from the front line and given a few weeks to Mr. Thompson... Mr. Thompson... *Mr. Thompson*?

Doctor Khan stood over Davie with crow's feet wrinkles emphasising the concern that radiated from his gentle face. He held a torch-pen in his hand and was ready to shine it into Davie's eyes. "Mr. Thompson?"

"*Huh*?" Davie managed, the doctor's face emerging through the miasma of his reverie. "I got measles in nineteen ninety-one," he explained, hoping that this was the answer to the doctor's last question.

Doctor Khan returned to his seat then leant his elbows on his desk. "I'm afraid that the clinical progression of S.S.P.E. is rather daunting," he explained, feeling self conscious about saying '*I'm afraid*' far too much, but knowing of no other way to begin such difficult sentences. "Are you sure you want to hear them now, or can I call a family member to be here with you? Perhaps a friend?"

Davie thought about Danny, who was waiting for him in the hospital car park, and realised that he was the nearest thing to a friend he'd had since the Army. For that matter, he was the nearest thing to *family* he'd had since the Army.

"No, there's no-one," he said after a time. "You'd better just get this over with. I can handle it."

There was a moment of silence while Doctor Khan gathered his thoughts. "You can expect the symptoms that you are showing thus far to continue," he began. "In fact, they will get worse and continue to do so until you are unable to cook and clean for yourself. Have you seen that Stephen Hawkins fellow on the television?"

Davie nodded, barely recognising the words that the doctor uttered. A vision of himself drooling from a wheelchair consumed him. He was too shocked to speak.

"The virus attacks the central nervous system and rapidly overwhelms the brain," the doctor continued. "There will be... *dementia*, Mr. Thompson. It's progress will be swift until eventually you will reach a state of coma. Your respiration will suffer as you lose the ability to control your lungs and this will eventually lead to your death." He paused. "I'm sorry, I wish that there was something else I could say, Mr. Thompson."

The doctor sat back in his chair and waited for Davie to speak, but he said nothing. The left side of his face hung slack.

"Mr. Thompson? Perhaps I can get you a glass of water?"

Davie shook his head and stood, his movements slow, but his eyes glistened as though cut from crystal.

"I know what you're getting at," he growled, his hands clenching into fists. "You think you can fool me like you did all them others? S.S.P.E., my arse! You're working for *them*. The Ministry of Defence, the Home Office or whoever. They've told you to say this so I can keep off of their statistics."

"Mr. Thompson, really I..."

"And you can stop all that malarkey for a start. There's chemicals in the food and genetically modified crops. Livestock were made cannibals to produce B.S.E. and multinationals pump untold chemicals into the air every day. Then you tell me I'm dying of *measles*? Pull the other one, *Doctor*, it's got bells on!"

Davie paused as his breathing grew rapid and the doctor wished he had an emergency buzzer to press. He squirmed further back into his chair as Davie leant forward with his palms on the desk and continued his tirade in a conspiratorial whisper. "Who's paying you off, Doctor?" he demanded slyly. "The Government? Some global petrochemical corporation or other? That oily Texecutor Bush and his dad's sneaky C.I.A.? I bet the Yanks want things kept quiet, don't they? All that compensation to the Gulf servicemen?"

"Mr. Thompson, if you will only let me show you the chart..."

"A chart? A chart?" Davie roared. "You think you can convince me with a chart? Like how McDonalds shows how it's saving the environment while it tears down the rain forests? Are we talking that kind of chart, Doctor? The kind of chart that Governments and companies and newspapers have used to bullshit the population since the dawn of time? I'll give you *chart*, Doctor, and I'll tell you where to stick it too, so help me!"

As Davie ranted he backed off towards the door. His hand trembled as he twisted the doorknob.

"Mr. Thompson, your prescription..."

"My lobotomising tranquillisers more like!" Davie scowled as he finally wrestled the door open. "Some chemical or other to stop me spreading the truth. No thank you, Doctor!"

The door slammed behind him as Davie stomped through the musty corridors of Oldchurch hospital back to the car park. Danny had bought a copy of The Sun and was sitting in the driver's seat reading it peacefully until Davie snatched it from him and threw it out into a puddle. "Evil lies," he snarled. "More programming for the masses! Do you like your bread and circuses?"

"Are you alright, Davie?" Danny asked, knowing he wasn't.

Davie's aggression fled along with the newspaper to be replaced by a cold, contemplative fury. "Sure, Alan," he sighed. "Just drop me off at B&Q."

Danny drove to the hardware store saying nothing in case Davie flew off of the handle then waited for him while he went inside. He returned after ten minutes carrying several bags full of purchases and a length of steel piping that he stowed in the car's boot.

"This should see us sorted," Davie said once he had reclaimed the passenger seat. "Now drive."

A further five minutes of silence saw Danny helping Davie to carry the supplies up to his flat. "What's this lot for?" he asked, hoping to kick-start a conversation, searching for words of comfort.

"Let me show you."

Once Danny and Davie were inside the flat Davie set the bags near his kitchen table then rooted around for his tool box. Like the lounge, the walls of the kitchen were covered in newspaper clippings, but with an emphasis upon the British and American forces stationed in Afghanistan. "You thirsty?" he asked.

Danny nodded. "Sure. I couldn't spit a tanner."

"Then put a brew on while I do this."

Davie walked back to his hallway whereupon he unscrewed a light bulb from its fitting, then while Danny made some tea he heated the metal end of the bulb over his gas cooker.

"What you doing?" Danny asked as he popped two tea bags into a couple of mugs.

"This," Davie replied as he gently peeled the metal cap and filament away from the glass bubble of the bulb. "The heat has softened the glue used to keep this thing together."

"I can see that," Danny acknowledged as he dealt with the milk. "Maybe I should've said 'Why are you doing that?'."

"Because I don't like unwelcome visitors," Davie answered. As he spoke he laid the opened light bulb back on the kitchen table then produced a small can of gasoline from one of his B&Q bags. He then poured some of the gasoline into a saucepan and set it on the cooker, heating it with a low gas.

Danny finished making the tea then watched silently as Davie continued with his bizarre recipe. He wondered if Davie had any family somewhere who could counsel him. Davie took a packet of soap powder from the cupboard under his sink then added some flakes to the heated gasoline, stirring all the while. He muttered to himself as he worked, and did not look up from the pot until its contents had stiffened to a satisfactory goo. "Sorted," he mumbled, setting the mixture aside to cool. "Now I need to bodge up some ball bearings. I know I've kept something in reserve…"

Danny's eyes widened as Davie rummaged around in his tool box. After a while he pulled out a packet of heavy fishing weights that he poured into the broth of soap powder and gasoline. Still muttering to himself he stirred them in, then poured the result into the glass bubble of the bulb until it was half filled.

Danny sipped at his tea feeling a heavy sadness, lost for words as Davie replaced the cap and filament of the light bulb, making certain that the filament was thrust within the concoction, before gluing it in place. He whistled as he wandered back into his hallway and replaced the bulb in its socket. It was the socket above the front door.

"Are you gonna tell me what all this is about?" Danny asked eventually, unable to take the suspense any longer.

"They ain't gonna get me," Davie answered. "And if you wanna stick around I have work to do. Here, make yourself useful with these."

Davie took a household box of friction matches from a kitchen shelf then tossed them for Danny to catch. "Cut the heads from that lot," he commanded distractedly. "There's a Stanley knife in the tool box."

Danny, thinking that if he refused his task, Davie would rant at him and do it anyway, rooted around for the knife while Davie disappeared off into his flat. He returned with a tennis ball and another light bulb. While Danny decapitated the matches, Davie heated the light bulb as before and once he had pulled free its cap and filament he set it upon the table. He then took a box from a kitchen cupboard and spooned its white, powdery contents into the light bulb.

"What's that stuff?" Danny asked fearfully.

"Baking Soda. I'm gonna fill the pipe I bought with vinegar."

The smell of warm gasoline clung to the air giving it a greasy feel, so Danny opened a window to ventilate the kitchen while wondering about Davie's sanity. He had glued the cap of the baking soda-filled bulb back in place and posted it down the end of the steel tube that he had bought from B&Q. When he was happy that the bulb could move freely therein, he attached a screw cap to one end of the pipe then re-inserted the bulb along with a bunch of loose nails that he took from a carton in his tool box. Lastly, he emptied a bottle of vinegar down the tube, then topped it off with the vinegar from a jar of pickled onions.

"I can't take this no more," Danny whined as Davie fitted the remaining screw cap to the free end of the pipe to secure its contents. "You've gotta tell me what's going on."

"Urban warfare," Davie replied. "If I throw this pipe hard enough the bulb inside will break causing the baking soda to mix in with the vinegar." He mimicked a slow motion throwing action then laid the pipe on the table carefully. "When the two chemicals are mixed they produce a gas in a violent reaction, and it's a reaction violent enough to blast this pipe into smithereens; sending nails, glass and bits of pipe all over the place."

"You mean it's a fucking bomb?"

Davie nodded, but his attention was focussed elsewhere. "More of a grenade," he admitted nonchalantly, "although the delay between throwing the thing and its going off is anyone's guess. It can be instantaneous to neigh-on half a minute, depending on how well the baking soda and vinegar mixes. That, of course, is up to God and the laws of physics."

"You're yanking my chain."

"I don't have the time to joke, Danny," said Davie earnestly. "Things have suddenly gotten very serious."

"How so?"

"They're on to me. I found out in the hospital just now."

"Who are on to you?"

"They. They. *They*. The Government. The Police. Who knows? For all I know the S.A.S. could be through that door at any minute with flashbangs and C.S. gas. They kept folks quiet in Ulster, and as sure as eggs is eggs you can bet that they keep folks quiet here too."

"Davie, I..."

"No, Danny. It's a conspiracy and a cover up. They want to keep me from blabbing about the Syndrome to save on servicemen's compensation. But I've got a little surprise in store for them. Oh yes. So long as my hallway is kept nice and dark..."

Davie's eyes narrowed, his mouth stretched into a wide smile and his head tilted back as though he was consumed by the throes of ecstasy.

"The light bulb?" Danny questioned.

"Yeah. You got it. If some idiot touches the switch to throw some light on the subject the bulb will explode over his head and he'll be picking pellets out of his skull for a month."

"But, Davie, you can't do shit like that… You're upset. Let me take you out for a nice Ruby or something. Give yourself time to calm down."

"*No*, Danny. Nothing can calm me now."

While Danny thought about heading for the hills, Davie was tucking the cut-off heads of the matches through a tiny slit he had cut in the tennis ball. A turkey baster served as a narrow-mouthed funnel that he employed to insert fishing weights through the cut. "This is another trick I picked up in Ulster," he went on. "Catholic kids threw these at squaddies all the time. You pack a tennis ball tight with friction matches, and when you bounce the ball the friction matches rub together and ignite. Hey presto, another quick explosion and more shrapnel flies about the place. Not as powerful as the pipe bomb, I grant you, but this one's *instantaneous*."

Once he had finished, Davie took the tennis ball and pipe bomb from the kitchen, leaving Danny to contemplate what he had seen. In their many years of friendship, Danny had seen Davie do some strange things, yet for the first time he wondered about the good sense of his keeping Davie around. His Gulf War Syndrome had tightened its grip in recent months, and Danny realised that it had passed the point where it was safe for Davie to continue in his chosen line of business. It had always been tough for Davie. He *would* rob a clothing chain store if its wares were made in sweatshops, but he would *not* rob a security van that was taking cash from that store since he saw these as '*civilians*' in his one man terror war against the System. He *would* petrol bomb a McDonalds, but he would *not* lean on his local kebab shop for protection. Danny had learned over the years what jobs Davie would consider legitimate '*targets*' and, in truth, he had been surprised that Davie had agreed to work on the jacking. Maybe it was because they had merely blagged blaggers, Danny reasoned.

When Davie returned he was holding a M.S.G.90 sniper's rifle under his arm that he laid on the kitchen table as though it were a bag of groceries. The rifle was long, black and came with a 10x Hensoldt telescopic sight that could find a wasp in a beehive. Its range was close to a mile. Danny felt as though it was staring at him. "I got this smuggled over from the States especially," Davie stated before Danny could ask the obvious question. "I made a few Yank friends out there in the Gulf and one or two of them joined the Militia."

"What? Those fruitcakes you see on telly who go on about the United Nations and Jews taking over the world?" he asked uncertainly.

"If you mean those individuals who don't like corrupt, multinational-financed Governments meddling in their affairs, then yes." Davie paused and cradled the gun in his arms. "This baby took an arm and a leg to get through Customs," he resumed, "and I've been saving it for a special occasion. Not so much as fired a shot. But when I do... boy, a round will blast though at least three brick walls and *still* have enough punch to kill."

Davie took the rifle apart and as he began cleaning its components expertly Danny realised that he might never see Davie again after the completion of this job. He might even give the Police an anonymous tip incriminating him in something minor. At least doing bird he'd have to accept medical aid or some kind of counselling. In fact, he was tempted to leave Davie right there and then, but he kicked that notion aside when he thought of angering a man who owned a sniper's rifle and could build pipe bombs out of kitchen sundries. That wasn't worth Davie's share of the diamonds.

"You know, I had a revelation in the car just now," Davie said conversationally, his mood the calmest and most cheerful since he had left the hospital. "You wanna hear it?"

"Sure," Danny replied, humouring his friend.

"Well, since the Army I'd built up this philosophy about how the World is like a big game of chess," Davie began. "You know, we're all the pawns and the Government is the King, that kind of stuff. It's hardly original. Anyway, the thing is, it's only *now* I realise that that's all bullshit. Life ain't like a game of chess at all. Now I'd say that life is far more like a game of checkers."

Davie paused as he reassembled the rifle, the oiled components clicking back into place smoothly. "The rules to this game are much more simple," he explained as he slipped the rifle's magazine home. "There ain't no moves and counter moves on a grand scale. No strategies. Like the pieces on a checkers board, we all keep our nuts down and just charge straight forward regardless while hoping to jump over some other poor bastard to gain an advantage if we get the chance."

Danny sighed. "So that's all we are? Just a bunch of black and white counters on a board game?"

"Pretty much so. Of course, if you make it to the other side you get made a king, and then it don't matter whether you're black or white, because when you're a king you can go in any direction you want and can fuck over everybody."

"And that's what all this is about? You wanna be made king?"

"No, Danny," Davie replied as he picked up the rifle. His hands shook with the effort, but his smirk of grim determination was set in stone. "I don't wanna be king. I wanna kick over the gaming table and make us *all* kings.'"

Thursday 6th of December, 2001; 11:07am.

As soon as Jasmine departed to attend college, K had hidden all evidence of her presence then called Baron and Colin asking for a meeting. Knowing that mobile calls can be detected by certain authorities, he was careful not to explain what this get together was about. While rinsing the two wine glasses in the sink he thought again about the prospect of having a share of eight million pounds. It was tantalisingly close and he felt sure that a plan was possible. Even if he couldn't find a job teaching in Iran he could live there like a Lord. A forceful knock on the door disturbed his cunning. Baron and Colin entered together. K made a mental note that *this* hadn't happened before. What are these two cooking? he wondered. He led them to his front room where he offered them beers and crisps. Baron declined, deciding to wrap a spliff, but Colin accepted a bottle of Stella.

"K, man," Colin munched. "Dis better be important. Dinging me jus' after nine O'clock. Usually a man would affe get a slap for dat."

K, standing up, sipped from his glass of orange juice and searched the eyes of his gang members. "Say there was a way we could get our hands on those diamonds that Eddie brought in, we could call it a day and retire on the spot. Build new lives."

"But der ain't no way," Colin mocked. "Der not gonna focking roll out de red carpet an' 'ave a welcoming committee if we show our backsides on the east sides again. Nah, man. We should go back to wha' we do best. Bringing in mules on Air Jamaica, credit cards, protection of business an' de odd post office an' t'ing."

Baron lit his joint without taking his eyes off K. "Bwai, yu nuh as bright as yu mek out. Check dis. We kill ah man up dem sides, we tek part inna plane hijack an' de man who set t'ings in motion ketch ah train in 'im bombaclaat - Eddie more dead dan de Igloo man herb plant. Boom boom claat! An' yu t'ink we coulda come up dem side again an' look fe diamond? K, man, it seem yu read too much book dat de word dem spread out an' start mosh up de inside ah yu brain."

"Just think about it," insisted K, admitting to himself that Baron had a point. "Those white guys are just like us. They're in all this because of the money. How would you feel if those white guys got hold of the diamonds and weeks later were driving around in the Costa Del Sol in brand spanking new sports cars?" K directed his spectacles to Colin, for his last sentence was for his benefit, playing on his prejudices. "I for one would be gutted... We deserve some of that cake and I reckon we'd be foolish just to give up on it."

"Well, you'd better come up wid a serious plan," remarked Colin. "I dunno... Maybe we can chat to Tony's bitch an' force her to get some info. I could handle it. You still have her address, K?"

K looked at Baron and they both guessed that Colin had an altogether different motive to involve Yvette again. "No," K said. "We shouldn't put the heat on Yvette until we have to. Remember, she's the only witness to Lee's murder."

Baron toked mightily on his spliff, exhaling through his nose. "Better leave her alone fe de time being, mon. Mebbe some time inna de future we should call 'pon her. Mek sure she don't say nutten. Or even better, we should forward to her mudder an' fader yard an' empty de Uzi 'pon de front door ah night time. Her mout' will staple after dat fe real."

K nodded, liking Baron's idea better than Colin's one. He recognised that Colin didn't really have a plan, he just wanted to rape Yvette. His top priority was still finding a way to get his hands on the diamonds. "You remember the Clint Eastwood film *For A Few Dollars More*?" K received curious nods in response. "Clint Eastwood gained the confidence of the other gang by pretending he could help them in some way. Maybe I could do something like that." He felt a strange urge to tell them the film was based on an earlier Japanese classic, but they wouldn't appreciate that, he thought.

Colin and Baron locked eyeballs of suspicion then returned their attention to K. "You're de so-called brains of dis operation," Colin replied mockingly. "But you're on your own wid dis one. If me and Baron don't hear from you den we'll go to de bitch after we drill untold bullets into her parents' front door an' *den* mek her work for us."

"Alright," K agreed. "Give me two days. I *will* work something out. Perhaps I'll go to Davie or Danny, see one of them on their own so there'll be no need for playing the macho card. Yeah, I'll have to think about what I'm going to say."

"T'ink good," counselled Baron. "Cah any wrong move an' yu gwarn end up dead like fish 'ead dat sell ah Papine market. Boom boom claat!"

Thursday 6th December, 2001; 08:47pm.

An outlay of two hundred quid had seen Matt ready for his night down the pub. His new Doctor Martin boots were a fierce cherry red that matched the Fred Perry jumper and T-shirt he wore. His new olive green bomber jacket was so crisp that it rustled as he walked and his haircut was so short that his hair appeared almost translucent.

This time, when the Saint George's bouncer had cause to frisk him, he found an eight inch bowie knife in Matt's inside jacket pocket that was still damp with the oil used in its manufacture. It was sharp, obsessively so, for Matt had spent many long, contemplative hours honing it.

"Go on through," the bouncer said.

Matt strode through the double doors into the main saloon where he was confronted by a fist of sound that slammed forth from the juke box. He didn't know the band, but he liked what they were promoting with their vinegar-sharp chords and scathing lyrics. It was all about *fear*.

The pub was only half full, because the meeting was still some time away, but Matt recognised a few people whom he had met during his first visit to the Saint George. Spider was playing pool with his cronies and, like before, he was spouting a truckload of jokes that would make Bernard Manning blanche.

Matt ordered himself a Guinness then walked over to the pool table where Spider was taking a shot. He was playing stripes and had three balls to go. "Why don't niggers take aspirin?" he asked, looking up from his cue with a mischievous glint in his eye.

Matt shrugged.

"Because aspirin's white, it works, and niggers refuse to pick the cotton out of the bottle."

Matt's laughter was loud and full. He sipped at his Guinness while he recollected a joke Lee had once told him, then watched Spider take his shot and miss. "What do you do when you see a nigger with one leg?" he asked.

"I dunno," Spider replied. "What do you do when you see a nigger with one leg?"

"Stop laughing and re-load."

Laughter exploded around the pool table. "I ain't never heard that one before," Spider told him. "Here, Gary, you ever hear that one before?"

"No I ain't," came the reply. Gary, Spider's pool opponent, was a tall, lean skinhead with ginger hair, green eyes and freckles. He had four balls to go that reduced to three as one bounced into a pocket from a side cushion. "Gotcha," he said.

Matt watched them play in silence until Gary emerged as the victor.

"Where's your mate?" Spider asked. "The little blond soldier."

Matt had been waiting for this moment, so he chose his words carefully. "He got martyred for the Cause," he mumbled. "You hear about that shooting in Barking last week?"

"Yeah."

"Well, niggers did it."

There was a crack as Spider slapped his cue down on the pool table, his eyes blazing to resemble twin pulsars. "Fucking bastards," he growled. "Right fuckin' nasty, smelly mud bastards!" He paused while he gulped at his lager. "You sure it was niggers?"

"Yeah. I know who it was too. I got his address."

"Nice one," Gary cut in.

Matt went to the bar and bought himself a drink along with two lagers for Spider and Gary. His mentioning Lee's death had fired their blood and they were discussing the merits of lynching when he returned. It was just as Matt had hoped.

"I bought you these," he said, placing the lagers on the edge of the pool table.

"Nice one."

"Sorted."

As the two skinheads took their lagers Matt hoisted his Guinness to indicate a toast. "To the martyrs of our cause," he said, not sure whether he meant a word of it. Spider and Gary raised their glasses and the three men clinked them together. "White power," Gary muttered under his breath.

Three more games of pool were played, and Matt was allowed to join in the last one; playing against Gary, who annihilated him. As they shot pool and chatted Matt bought the drinks, inserting a comment here and there that stirred the hatred of his companions. The pub filled up and soon a band were playing, but Matt was determined to keep his new friends away from the mosh pit of drunken, pogoing Fascists so he could continue working on them.

Spider and Gary seemed only too willing to stick around him while he continued to fork out for their beer, swapping jokes and venting spite. Matt was pleased, but it did not manifest itself in a warm glow of contentment, rather it was the white-heat pleasure of sated determination.

"I tell you," he said. "The nigger what done for my mate should get what's coming to him. There should be a fuckin' lynching."

Spider and Gary indicated their accord by bopping their heads. "A fuckin' lynching," they agreed.

"So," Matt sprang on them, knowing that he now had them where he wanted them. "Are you gonna help me to do it or what?"

Both Spider and Gary knew that to refuse would reflect badly upon them, so they were left with little choice.

"First things first," Spider said, his eyes flicking in the direction of Gary for just a second. "How'd we know you're legit?"

"I'll tell you how we'll know," Gary replied. "He can come on a little trip with us first." He ran a hand through his ginger skinhead and his teeth flashed green. "You up for it, then? Nothing rounds off a night better than a bit of Paki bashing."

Matt thought about it. His mood was fired by drink and the thought of K squirming across the pavement as he and his new friends pummelled him with their boots and fists made his pulse quicken. Sure he didn't mind going on a little late night excursion if it meant that Spider and Gary would help him beat up K. "You're on," he said.

Spider and Gary drained their glasses in a series of noisy gulps them slammed them down on the pool table. "Come on, then," Spider said. "Let's see what you're made of."

Fortunately, Matt had almost finished his Guinness so there wasn't a lot to knock back. He wiped his mouth with the back of his hand when he had finished then followed Spider and Gary out of the pub. The night was damp and puddles reflected the street lights. They had not gone far when Spider spotted their quarry. An elderly Sikh man with a grey beard and baggy white clothing was sitting at a bus stop, its glass kicked out onto the street. He saw the three white youths approaching out of the corner of his spectacles, so he directed his gaze at the floor.

"Oi, Paki-man," Gary jeered. "Been taking any flying lessons lately?"

The elderly Sikh did not look up. He had grown used to bin Laden insults since the atrocities of September 11th. Most Sikhs had.

"Oi, Paki, my mate was talking to *you*!" Spider added in a growl. "Don't you speak no fuckin' English?"

Spider and Gary strode over to the bus stop purposefully as the Sikh rose in an effort to retreat. Matt trailed behind the two skinheads with his fists clenched, but he hoped the trouble would be over before he caught up with them.

Spider grabbed the Sikh by his shoulder as he tried to walk away and spun him around. "Get out of my country," Spider hollered into his face.

"Yeah. Back on yer banana boat," Gary added. He took a hold of the Sikh's grey beard and tugged on it like he expected the butler to arrive. "And learn to fuckin' shave. Filthy bastard."

The scene seemed to accelerate as Matt neared. Without warning, Spider kicked the Sikh's legs from under him and he hit the ground hard. Gary laughed and punched him about the face. "Go home, Paki-man, Paki-man," they chorused.

The elderly Sikh contracted into a tight, pain-wracked ball and said something in a language that Matt did not understand. His glasses were ripped from his face and Gary stamped them into the pavement with his size twelve boot. "Speak English," Spider snarled.

"Sorry, I'm so sorry," the Sikh replied, as though it was his fault that his blood now stained their boots. He groped for his shattered spectacles.

Spider pulled the Sikh up to his knees by tugging at his white turban. It unravelled as he did so to reveal long, grey hair.

"Do you love my country?" Spider demanded.

There was no answer, so a prompt was given that took the form of a fist. "Yes, yes," the old man replied. "I love England. It is the best country."

"Then kiss the ground," Gary commanded him. He pushed the Sikh down until he laid on his belly, then dragged him out into the road until his face touched the kerb. "Kiss the kerb," he specified.

Matt watched, agog, as the old man did just that. He pursed his pale, cracked lips and they brushed against the cold stone of the pavement as though the streets were made of hemlock.

"Now *bite* the kerb," Spider added.

Gary grabbed Matt by the arm and dragged him closer while Spider forced the Sikh's head down onto the road. "Go on – *bite it*," he commanded.

The Sikh's mouth opened as tears pearled down his cheeks. His long hair lay haphazard about his face. Gary laughed; a raw, animal sound as the old man fastened his teeth carefully on the grey concrete that made up the edge of the pavement and as he did so Spider turned to Matt.

"You know what you've gotta do," he hissed.

Matt looked from the two skinheads down to the old man who lay snivelling before him. His hands were behind his back in a gesture of absolute submission. Matt thought about what his companions wanted him to do, but not for too long because if he faltered now he would never get his revenge. He needed Spider and Gary so he could beat up K, and to get them to help he'd have to...

Matt slammed his boot into the back of the old Sikh's head; forcing his face and open mouth forward onto the jagged edge of the kerb. Teeth splintered, blood flowed and a jaw broke with a whip-crack. The old man was unable to scream, his mouth was a tortured ruin and his lower jaw hung slack. He tilted to one side as a bubbling gurgle escaped him, curled up like a baby, and wept.

Teeth and blood adorned the old man's face as Spider and Gary ran away, laughing, and Matt followed them, not daring to look back. They ducked inside a side street once their breath was rasping from their lungs and Spider pulled out his cigarettes. He passed them around. "Man, what a laugh," he chortled.

Matt took a cigarette and lit it with trembling fingers. What had he done?

"We showed him, eh?" Gary burbled, blowing smoke.

Once their cigarettes were lit, the three men strode off into the night while Matt wondered how he would get his new friends to keep their side of the bargain. "So, you're going to help me?" he managed, once he realised that he could think of nothing better to say.

"We're going to help you now," Gary replied.

Matt had lied about having K's address, hoping that he could get that particular piece of information from Davie or Danny later on, so he wondered how the two skinheads could help him *now*. After five minutes of walking they reached a back alley that was lined with Council garages and overflowing dustbins whereupon Spider held up a hand. "You wait here with Gary," he commanded.

Matt did as he asked without comment, while Gary took a can of beer from his pocket and cracked it open. It frothed over where it had been shaken as they ran. After a few minutes Spider returned and he was clutching to his chest a tatty carrier bag that was wrapped up with string.

Matt was getting nervous, so he lit another cigarette. "We can't get the nigger tonight," he said, rapidly growing intimidated by the two crew-cutted young men. They suddenly seemed a lot taller. "Maybe I can arrange to meet you guys next week and we can go give the bastard a real good kick-in?"

Spider vented the cruel, cynical laugh that Matt was growing accustomed to. "Don't be such a queer," he said, and his eyes resembled gravestones. "We ain't going nowhere. You've gotta be a man about this, a white man, and so we'll show you how to do it."

Spider tore a hole in the carrier bag and within Matt could see the cold steel snout of a gun. "You pay like with like in this war," Gary told him. "It's the only language the niggers understand. If one of them sent your mate to Valhalla, then it's only right that you send one of them to nigger hell. Either that, or you're a queer and a traitor to your race."

"You wouldn't be a traitor to your race, now, would you?" Spider asked venomously, thrusting the carrier bag into Matt's skinny chest.

Matt took the carrier bag and looked between Spider and Gary. Their expressions were brick walls displaying graffiti that read 'no compromise'.

"No… no… I'll do it," Matt mumbled, stuffing the carrier bag under his coat. The stench of the dustbins was suddenly overpowering.

"And the bullets come free," Gary told him. "You've got six of them."

Now Matt was confused. "Free?" he questioned.

"Yeah, free," Spider replied. "The gun's gonna cost you two tonne fifty. And you don't need to worry. Me and Gary will walk you to a cash point. We know where all of 'em are around here."

Gary wrapped an arm around Matt's shoulders and steered him back in the direction of the main road, with Spider bringing up the rear. "After all, you wouldn't want to rip off your mates, now, would you?" he cooed silkily. "So, come on, let's get this business sorted and then we can all go home. What bank was it you needed? Let me see your cash card."

The grip on Matt's shoulder tightened as an ambulance drove by. Its siren sounded like the lamentations of the damned. "It's in my pocket," was all that he could think of to say.

Friday 7th December, 2001; 10:27am

Driving rain reflected sharp diamonds of sunlight from the windscreen of her light-blue Ford Focus as Yvette took the Barking turn-off of the A13. The car's wipers swished back and forth in an attempt to clear her view, but their efforts were futile as her eyes were bleary with a wash of stinging tears.

Why had Eddie done it? she wondered, her long fingers gripping the steering wheel tightly. Why had he abandoned her when she had done so much for him? He chucked *me*? she asked herself, not believing this fact.

She had found the note left on the pillow written in Eddie's cumbersome, near-illegible scrawl. *'I've got to go now. Goodbye,'* it said, and Yvette cursed that Eddie's pathological caution meant that he had even written his farewell letter to resemble a suicide note in case the Police found it first.

Yvette's first thought was to search Eddie's hotel room hoping to find some clue to his whereabouts, but the smell of furniture polish that clung to the atmosphere revealed that Eddie had erased his prints, which meant that he had had plenty of time to think of everything else too.

The room was paid up for a further week, but Yvette knew she would not stay. After all, a Southend three star in December certainly wasn't the summit of her ambitions. As she flushed Eddie's crumpled note down the toilet she caught her reflection in the bathroom mirror; the pleasing features, the immaculate hair, then she thought of Eddie with his bald pate, beer belly and wrinkles. Had he really thought she had put up with him for his personality? Yvette guessed not, otherwise he might have stayed.

Well, fuck Eddie, she reasoned sourly as her car pulled up alongside the maisonettes in Barking's Upney Lane. So Eddie had decided to keep his four million share for himself. That was

Okay with her, because all she needed was one phone number and that phone number she had taken from Eddie's mobile just in case of such an eventuality. Yvette laughed despite her angry tears when she remembered how Eddie had always taught her to trust no-one and to think of everything, since it seemed that he was right.

A muttered telephone call to the one number had resulted in an address and now, thirty minutes on, she was at that address and checking her makeup in the rear view mirror to cover up any signs of her distress.

Once she was ready, she swung her long legs out of the car then paced along the road until she found the maisonette she was looking for. Two men admired her as they waited at the zebra crossing and she tossed her hair with the palm of her hand to make a show of it. After all, she needed to make sure that her charm was in full working order before she had to use it. Fuck it! For the life of me I ain't gonna be sentenced to a life in fucking Plaistow, her internal voice yelled.

She managed to whet her lips just before Danny came to the door. "Yvette," he said, beckoning her inside with his hands. What the fuck is she doing here? "This *is* a surprise."

Danny was wearing a West Ham football top and neat blue jeans. His hair clung to his face where he had recently pulled himself from a shower.

"Hi there, Danny," Yvette said as she followed him down the hall to his lounge. It was well kept and tidy, but it smelled of ash trays, reeked of men. "Nice place you have here." Any gaff was nicer than mum's, she thought.

"Yeah – it's about all that the Mrs. left me," came the reply. "Places tend to look tidy when someone else has run off with the telly, video and kids."

"I'm sorry. I didn't know."

"No problem. I wasn't expecting you to."

Yvette leant back in Danny's comfy sofa and crossed her legs. It was time to turn on the charm. He could be the key for me to get out of East London and if I have to fuck him to get it so be it, but that's a last resort. "You look so much nicer fresh out of the shower," she told him. "You should do it more often." Her ruby and pearl smile indicated a joke.

Danny poured two whiskies then handed one to her. Silly tart, he thought. I've come across the likes of you before. The bitch didn't notice me before and now she's giving me the green man at the lights. "So what is it that you want to talk about?" he probed innocently.

Yvette looked over the top of her drink coquettishly while she sipped at it. "Eddie," she replied eventually, smacking her lips. "Or should I say Eddie and how he's screwed you out of eight million in diamonds?"

"Keep talking." Danny leant closer, trying to ignore Yvette's body language.

"Well, he screwed me out of my share too and now I want to get even."

Danny had told the truth about his lack of a television and video, but he *had* been left with an aged Hi-Fi that he switched on to accompany their conversation. *Beatles For Sale* was his current C.D. of choice and it began with Lennon's melancholic *No Reply*.

As the first harmony of the song caressed the room Danny slumped into his floral-pattern single-seater and studied Yvette's lithe frame.

Dressed in a black pencil skirt, white blouse and black suit jacket, she lounged on the sofa nonchalantly with her bestockinged legs crossed and one high heel dangling from the sole of her foot. A slender, gold-braceleted arm was laid across the back of the sofa clutching her drink, while the other toyed with her hair, flicking it back behind her left ear.

"So?" Yvette asked. I could have him like a snack, she thought. They're all the same. Fucking *men*. Even if he was still married he would fuck me at the drop of a hat… If I gave him the chance. Well, Danny-boy, take a good look, because by the time I'm gone you'll be wondering should you keep me on side because there might be a chance of a fuck; and while you're thinking about it you'll give me my ticket out of here and you won't see me again.

Danny was still busy trying to read her face, but her body language was immersed in her sensuality and all Danny could tell from her wide eyes, smooth complexion and full mouth was that he wanted to stick his cock in the latter. His lack of focus angered him, so he bit the inside of his cheek to take his mind from everything except the diamonds. He reasoned that if he couldn't tell her motives from her face, then he'd just have to listen to her voice.

"Keep talking," he said, vexed with something growing in his pants.

Yvette enjoyed watching Danny's eyes flick around every part of the room except for those few square feet that her body occupied and recognised it for the hopeless gesture that it was. Got him, she half-smiled to herself.

"Okay," she began, realising that she was forced to play her hand early on in this game. "What if I told you that the heist was all my idea? What if I told you that it was *me* who introduced the inside man to Eddie?"

"I'd say that ain't enough to help me find the diamonds," Danny replied, satisfied he had managed to quell his erection.

"I know that," Yvette spat, her poise lost momentarily. "I haven't even started yet. Do you want to hear where this is going, or not?"

"I'm all ears."

"Okay," Yvette resumed. "I met this guy out Stepney way who was flashing some cash and, well, after a few hours we got talking." She paused and her lashes tilted to the carpet as her face reddened. "Anyway, his cash came from piloting some guys between here and mainland Europe; drugs, he'd thought at first, but then he learned that one of the crew was stitching up the others by bringing in a load of diamonds as well. The guy was stuffing them in one of the packets of merchandise, but taking them out before the packets were sold on, see?"

Danny nodded. "But this is all useless to me," he said coolly. "I don't give a monkeys how Eddie found out about the diamonds, and I don't need to know the inside man. All I need to know is where Eddie *left* the diamonds."

"Will you shut up so I can get to the point?"

"Be my guest."

"Well, I introduced Eddie to the pilot and they came up with a plan whereby they could nab the diamonds from the other crew. Eddie knew Harry Green, who's plot they were landing on, so it was easy for him to get that side of things sorted. The rest was up to you and the other crew."

"So up comes the Cavalry to complete the job and then your inside man tosses Eddie under a train?"

Yvette's expression betrayed her surprise. "Eddie's dead?" she exclaimed. "Of course he's not, you fool. Didn't you hear from Alan?"

"Alan?"

"Yes. Alan Jones. I thought he'd have spilled the beans to you by now."

Danny recalled Matt's message that Alan had summoned him for a prison visit, but he had assumed incorrectly that it was to do with the death of his only son. "I haven't seen him yet," was his reply, his stomach now awash with guilt.

"Okay," Yvette paused while she collated the relevant information. "I was asked by Eddie to visit your mate Alan in Wandsworth nick so he could arrange a special favour for Eddie. Eddie wanted Alan to sort out a jail bird who looked a bit like himself and was due a stint of parole. Someone who could do with a right good kick-in. Anyway, Alan found some fucked-up nonce or other who turned up at the pub on the day of the heist and it was Eddie who saw *him* under that train at Barking Station, not the other way around."

"So Eddie ain't dead?" stated Danny, trying his best not to look shocked.

"You catch on fast. He's very much alive and well, until I get my hands on him at any rate. He got the nonce dosed up with whisky and dopamine then took him to where he'd get hit by the train. He had some idea about making the corpse unrecognisable, but what that is I cannot say."

"Why not?"

"Because I don't know."

The revaluation of Eddie's good health struck Danny like a hammer blow and he felt the urge to down his drink, but he knew that this would affect business so he forced the impulse aside. I've got to look like this is just another stroll in the park, he told himself.

He wondered what to say while Yvette flamed a cigarette. The lighter she flicked with her red-painted nail was gold and monogrammed. She must have been fucking Eddie, he concluded. Always wondered where she got all her flashy clothes from. And to think I was contemplating on her choking my bishop with her gob after Eddie's been there! Danny recoiled at the thought.

"So tell me," he said, proffering a half-filled ashtray. He now felt in control. "What can you actually offer me that will get me any closer to them diamonds?"

"Now we get down to the nitty-gritty," Yvette replied, blowing a smoke ring with practised skill. "What if I told you that Eddie was leaving the country tomorrow along with the diamonds?"

"I'd say I hope he has a good fake passport."

"He doesn't need one. He's got the inside man, remember? The pilot? I was meant to be flying into Europe with him and Eddie tomorrow, so I know the where and the when."

"And you'll fill in the blanks of the where and when if we cut you in on the pay-off?"

"I can see your mum raised no fools."

Something niggled Danny that made him suspicious. "If you know where Eddie is," he wondered aloud, "then why don't you just turn up at the rendezvous and demand your share? Get him to take you with him to Europe or wherever?"

"Because he fucked me over, Danny. I want more than just the money now. I want to get my own back."

Danny smiled. It was easy to guess how the gorgeous Yvette had wormed herself into Eddie's confidence, but her current plight revealed how Eddie had used her all along; his caution so great that he was able to resist Yvette's considerable appeal while exploiting her for her lucrative contact. Danny had to admire Eddie's style, his having beaten Yvette at her own game while getting free sex into the bargain. No wonder she was angry and prepared to make a deal.

"Okay," he said, lighting a cigarette of his own. "You'll get an equal share of whatever we make providing the where and the when comes off kosher."

"The where is Southend Airport," Yvette replied. "The when is tomorrow. Eddie and the pilot are taking a brief trip to Antwerp. I doubt that Eddie will be coming back."

"What's the pilot's name?"

"Ronnie Thatcher."

"And do you know the time?"

"About seven tomorrow morning."

As Yvette spoke Danny picked up his phone and dialled a number. "Matt," he said, "get your arse in gear. You, me and Davie need to talk pronto." He paused and his face contorted momentarily. "What? The Police Station?," he resumed, then his expression relaxed once more. "Ah – Okay – if it's just questioning about Lee then be sure to keep schtumn and get out of there A.S.A.P.. Meet me in the Abahoni Indian restaurant on Longbridge Road once you're out. I'll grab Davie."

Yvette smiled and blew another smoke ring, amused at Danny's sudden surge of activity. "Can I come?" she asked coyly with one eyebrow raised.

Danny shook his head. "I think I work with you best when I don't have to see you," was his reply.

Yvette presented Danny with a long, slow beat of her eyelashes; trying her best to disguise her offence at Danny's last remark. Danny simply emptied his glass down his throat and smiled.

Friday 7th December, 2001; 11:07am

Matt sat in an interview room of Barking Police Station glaring at D.S. Powell with his solicitor positioned next to him like a hungry Rottweiler. A petite, auburn-haired woman in her early thirties, Serpil Ahmed appeared more of a nursery nurse than a solicitor, but her sharp eyes and acid tongue indicated her keen mind.

"My client has answered these questions already," she purred sibilantly as she twisted her biro around in the corner of her lips. "I really can't see why you should keep him here. After all, he isn't under arrest."

Dudley Powell sighed and wished that Matt wasn't Alan Jones' nephew. Alan had spent enough time in Court to know a good solicitor when he saw one, and Serpil Ahmed had dealt with his last three Court appearances, with only the last one of them not turning out to his liking. Now it seemed that the entire Jones family had the feisty Turk's phone number.

"Ms. Ahmed, Matt has only been brought into the station to help us with our enquiries concerning the death of his cousin," Dudley replied. "I really don't see the need for a solicitor…"

"No, I'm sure you don't, D.S. Powell," Serpil interjected. "Not when you're showing my client autopsy photographs of a man you allege his cousin killed. I agree with you. I'm sure you *don't* want a solicitor around while you browbeat my client into inadvertently, and might I add *falsely*, incriminating himself or his deceased relative in a case of murder." Serpil paused, slid the biro from between her lips, then wagged it at Dudley like an enraged school mistress. "You have nothing more than a sighting of my client in a public house talking with someone who you claim *resembles* a man shot dead last week in Stockwell," she resumed. "Now he's answered your questions and told you that he knows nothing of the black men whom you *allege* he spoke with, so I suggest we bring this interview to an end."

"Not *all* the questions, Ms. Ahmed."

Matt was not the only man in the room with a dedicated, female protectress. D.C.I. Wiley had been good to his word and W.P.C. Heather Golightly had been brought on the case to help Dudley, while Scott Hain liased between both Barking and Brixton nicks and Operation Trident.

Heather glowered from her seat beside Dudley like a cobra with fang-ache, her attention focussed upon the diminutive solicitor. "We haven't asked him about Davie Thompson yet," she stated coolly. "So if you will just be quiet for a moment we can get this over and done with and your client can go home."

Dudley was sure that he could see Heather's fingernails extending to claws as he flipped Davie's photograph down onto the table. "I saw you talking with this man in the Spotted Dog public house the week before last," he stated. "Can you tell me what you were chatting about?"

Matt stared at the photograph of Davie and tried to recollect what he had told him to say on the night of Ali's murder, should the Police question him. Something about car stereos…

"Erm," Matt began, and he could see Serpil's eyelashes batting at him as though she was using them to try and take off. What did she want him to say?

"Car stereos," Matt blurted finally. "I'm sure when I saw that guy talking with the black guys they were talking about car stereos."

Serpil Ahmed looked worried. "I'm sure my client wishes to…"

"…to get everything sorted, so that those who murdered his cousin can face due punishment," Heather interrupted.

"Not to mention your gold-digging for the as-yet unconnected Stockwell Park murder," Serpil sniped back as her retort.

Dudley had to sip at his coffee to hide his smile. Both women were petite, canny and devilishly cute, and there they were having a cat-fight right there in front of him. Man, he thought to himself when he saw Serpil's pouting lips pull back over her brilliantly white teeth in a disdainful sneer, had I known that this was going down I could have sold tickets!

He wished he could just sit back, relax and watch the show, but he knew why Serpil had stamped on Matt's monologue, and he knew that she knew that he knew. Matt had now connected Davie Thompson with the man suspected of Lee's murder, not only that, but the connection was made *before* Dudley himself had turned up on the scene, so Davie had no room for excuses, saying that he had joined in the conversation simply to annoy the Police.

"Are you sure, Matt?" Dudley asked in his most convivial tone. "Was Davie talking with the black men about car stereos?"

Matt nodded before Serpil had the time to hold up a hand and Heather stood before Serpil had the opportunity to complain. "Okay, interview's over," Heather said once she had received non-verbal confirmation from Dudley. "You're free to go, Mr. Jones. Ms. Ahmed, it's been a pleasure."

Dudley opened the door of the interview room and Serpil tottered outside with Matt trailing after her like an errant schoolboy. Dudley was sure that she would clip his ear before they entered the car park.

"Phew, what a bitch," Heather whistled through her teeth as the diminutive solicitor harassed the desk sergeant about something or other.

"Yeah, but we still love you for it, Heth," Dudley replied as he took her up the stairs to the C.I.D. office.

Detective Constable Scott Hain, wearing a new suit, clean shirt and combed hair, was sat at his desk looking industrious and powerful, which was a stance he had maintained since Heather's being brought onto the case.

"I've got some news, Sarge," he said importantly when Dudley neared. His eyes were locked on his superior so that they could not focus upon the bubbly, young W.P.C. who stood next to him. "We've identified the stiff from Barking Station."

"Ah, our bogus Careful Eddie Maynard," Dudley exclaimed as he took his seat. "Heth, why don't you pull up a pew and sit at the desk with Scott here?"

Scott was struck speechless as Heather parked the object of his affection a mere eight inches away from his loins and remained speechless until Dudley flicked an elastic band at him.

"Oh, yes," Scott resumed. "The stiff. I got a call from S.O.4 telling me that they identified it from the finger prints. It seems their owner had some form."

"Nice one," Dudley said, then he waited. "Well spit it out, son."

"A nonce by the name of Richard Keating. He did a stretch in Wandsworth for messing around with young girls, and according to S.O.4 he was only paroled about a week before we found him."

"Hmmm – a revenge attack?" Dudley mused. "A former victim all grown up and angry?" He paused. "I don't see what this Richard Keating bloke has to do with Careful Eddie, but I can think up a long list of people who'd like to see a nonce stuffed under a train. This certainly has broadened the picture."

There wasn't enough room at Scott's desk for Heather to stick her legs under it, so she had to cross them, which only made Scott worse. "Are you suggesting that the corpse being a child abuser means that it's unlikely for his murder to be related to the Jones case?" she asked, eager to make a name for herself in C.I.D..

Dudley shrugged and wished he could say *'fucked if I know'*, but he refused to do that in mixed company. "I haven't a clue," he admitted once he'd found a suitable substitute phrase. "But I can tell you one thing."

"What's that, Sarge?"

"Matt Jones just connected Davie Thompson with that guy we have on the C.C.T.V.. He says they were talking about car stereos, but I know that West Ham will score after Christmas before Davie Thompson ever buys a car to put a stereo in, so it's time for you to go rustle up a warrant."

"A warrant, Sarge?"

"Yep, a warrant so you two can go out and arrest Davie Thompson. I want him banged up here for questioning in connection with the death of Lee Jones and I want him here tonight."

Scott dared a glance at Heather and saw that she was smiling. "You're on," he said.

Friday 7th December, 2001; 07:30pm

Danny and Davie had left Matt after their *eat-all-you-can-for-a-fiver* buffet in the Abahoni Indian restaurant next to Barking Station. During the meal, Danny had explained what he had learned from Yvette, but the explanation was cut short when his mobile chimed out *Jingle Bells*. His face slackened when he heard the voice on the other end of the telecommunications satellite.

"K?" he murmured, his surprise obvious. Davie leant in closer to the phone.

"Sure. We *do* need to talk," Danny breathed into the mouthpiece. "Where? The Barbican? Sure. I know the place. Who's coming? Just you? Alright, but I'm bringing Davie with me, if that's Okay?" There was a pause. "Yeah. There's lots of people there. Yeah. There ain't gonna be no surprises. We can be there in just over an hour."

Danny killed the phone call then glanced around the table while whistling through his teeth. "Well who would Adam and Eve it?" he wondered aloud.

"What did he want?" Davie wanted to know.

Danny drainpiped the last of his Tiger Brew. "Come on, we've gotta hit the tube," he said. "It's time we smoked a peace pipe with the West Indians."

"I hear ya," Davie agreed, fishing out two twenties that he used to pay the bill.

Matt's expression revealed his lack of conviction. "What?" he demanded sourly, his usually pale face flushed Jacobs Creek red. He gulped some lager. "You're going to meet up with those… with those… *niggers*?"

"You betcha ass," Danny replied in a bad American accent as he was tugging on his coat. "I'm way too old to be making moccasins."

"*Eh*?"

"He means fighting," answered Davie.

"Well, I for one ain't going," Matt scowled, his face pulled into a childish sulk. "And you two shouldn't be going neither. Have you forgotten what those cowsons did to Lee?"

"No, I ain't," Danny spat back as his reply. "And that's why I'm going. I don't want my doorstep painted in shades of Danny Red one wet December morning, and I don't want those guys to think that I allow boys in my crew to go gun crazy whenever they feel like it. It's bad for business, and has a tendency of cutting your career real short."

Danny nudged Davie with an elbow as Mr. Mesbahuddin the Bangladeshi manager approached bearing Davie's change on a silver tray along with some mints. Davie took the change, but the mints were left for posterity. "Ready, willing and unstable," he grinned as he groped for his tatty grey trench coat.

Within moments, Danny and Davie were taking the Metropolitan Line to the Barbican having left Matt prodding at his cold prawn biriani.

"You think it's a set-up?" Davie asked as they passed Whitechapel.

Danny thought about it and concluded that K seemed alright in their conversation in the Spotted Dog car park. Social worker, he half grinned. "Nah. K don't wear those glasses for show," he stated. "The Barbican will be full of artsy-fartsy ponces on a Friday evening and there's loads of open spaces to keep a good clock. We're as safe as Cliff Richard on a buggery charge."

"There's high rise Yuppie flats all over the place. *Sniper*?"

Danny checked Davie's facial expression to gauge whether or not he was joking, and was disappointed to find that he wasn't. "You've been watching too many movies," was all he could think of to say, while he worried that Davie's increasing paranoia was getting the better of him. He certainly hadn't thought that way before the Syndrome kicked in. The sooner we get this over with the better, he sighed internally.

The Barbican Centre was only a short walk away from the station, and it was busy despite the cold breeze and drizzle that harassed the day. Danny and Davie entered the main foyer though its large glass doors and found themselves in a spacious, open plan area that was peppered with reception desks that were either selling theatre tickets or giving out leaflets detailing bohemian, South Bank events.

The smell of the nylon carpet singed the air with the portents of a static wake up call as Danny strode across the foyer to where a string quartet were playing a tune that he'd only ever heard before on a soap advert. Gaggles of bespectacled men and women wearing little black numbers loitered around trying to look like they were supposed to be there, but the only pair of spectacles that Danny was interested in were on the little black number who was sitting on his own reading an issue of *New Statesmen*. It was Professor K.

"I'm glad you called," was Danny's introduction when he neared. Glad also to see him alone. Don't need an interpreter with this guy. He realised the futility of offering a hand.

K laid his magazine beside him then looked at Danny over the top of his glasses as though they were a barricade. "Where's Davie?" he asked.

"Gone down to the bar to fetch the pig's ears. He'll be along in a moment."

Rage erupted across K's face like a flash flood. "You mean you've got him wired and you're dumb enough to tell me?" he snarled, rising to leave. "Dumb amateurs."

For a brief moment Danny was poleaxed with confusion, but he managed to grip K by his arm and urge him back to his seat while flashing a weather-beaten smile. "Erm – no, I meant the beer," he managed, forcing a strained laugh. "You know – pig's ear, *beer*. Christ, K, don't get your knickers in a twist. He's only gone off to the bar!"

K was embarrassed by his open display of ignorance and masked it by joining Danny in his counterfeit mirth. "Yeah, it's crazy the things you forget," he grinned, resuming his seat.

Danny pulled up a stool and sat opposite K, hunched forward with his elbows on his knees. He slapped his palms together. "Now where to begin?" he wondered aloud.

K, feeling back in control, had a glass of dry white wine that he sipped from slowly and reasoned that Danny's weakness was his trustful nature. "You can cut to the chase," he answered pragmatically. "I'm not here to listen to any apologies, and you're not here to make them. Your kid cost us dear, but as far as we're concerned that debt is now cleared. All we're interested in is business."

Danny's expression telegraphed his surprise. He thought he was here to make peace with the South Londoner, nothing more. What was this talk of business?

"But you do know that we had nothing to do with… you know… the big fella," he managed while he bought himself some time to think.

"Like that matters?"

The quartet began a slow, solemn piece as Davie appeared bringing with him a lager for Danny and a still water for himself. The tide was out in the lager, but Danny knew not to complain as he guessed that Davie's arm had tremored while he walked.

"K," Davie greeted.

"Hey, man," came the reply.

Danny swigged at his lager while Davie hunted down a stool and when he was seated Danny began the peace process.

"So what do you know already?" he asked eventually, seeing no other way out of the issue.

"Only what we heard from you when you gatecrashed Crumb's blues," K replied. "Something about there being seven million in ice on that plane we jacked."

"Eight million."

K smiled, and Danny knew he had passed the test. "Eight million. The news got a bit fuzzy after that on account of all the gunfire."

Danny opened his mouth to speak, but said nothing when Davie raised a cautionary hand. "Not until we know where this is going first," Davie stated.

K swirled the wine around in his glass, still vexed by the price he had to pay for it. "Simple. We split the haul fifty-fifty."

An uncomfortable gap appeared in the conversation that the string quartet tried to fill, but they were unable to soothe the rising tension. Someone had to speak.

"And what do we get out of the arrangement?" Davie asked eventually. "A Community badge from the Cub Scouts? We have the information, K, so why would we bring you in on the deal?"

K's smile was broad and he hoped his half hour at Brixton library was about to pay off. And Danny would trust him. "So you know where to lay your hands on eight millions worth of ice," he said confidently. "That's all well and groovy, but I'll lay a penny to the pound that you don't have the faintest about where to shift them. You think your local East End fence knows how to punt that much glass? You think your local pawn shop is gonna take an unset stone and give you the market value? I should co-co."

Danny nodded. He had to admit that K had a point. K sipped at his wine then continued in a conspiratorial whisper. He leant in close.

"The thing is," K explained, directing his gaze to Danny. "You reckon that eight million is up for grabs, but the way you're carrying on you'll be lucky to see ten percent of that. Eddie said they were worth eight million. *Eddie*. Get the picture? Eddie was a well connected man and you can bet your bottom dollar that when Eddie says eight million he isn't talking street value. He had the contacts and the patience to get the best deal. But a couple of hustlers like you guys? You ain't even close."

"You've told us what we don't know," Davie told him. "You ain't told us how you know any better."

There was a pause while K closed his eyes and went over the story in his mind. The sound of the string quartet calmed him and his thoughts meandered back to his morning's research at the library. While the remainder of his crew were still in bed, he had been up and alert with only one topic filling his mind, and that topic was *diamonds*.

"You ever heard of a place called Antwerp?" K asked, lifting his head in a superior manner.

Davie nodded. "Yeah – a port in northern Belgium."

K turned to Danny, who he guessed would be the weaker link of the pair when it came to general knowledge. "Know anything about it?"

As expected, Danny shook his head.

"Well, Antwerp is the home of the diamond trade. Every beggar goes there to buy and sell. It's a very Jewish city, but for all that not everyone who's there is kosher. In fact, there are more than enough Fagins for us to shift the glass at almost market value."

"And I take it that you're about to tell us that you have a contact there?" Davie probed, disliking K's haughty manner. "A likely story."

"Oh, I don't, but Baron does," K lied, enjoying his hook. "He's a fly boy, isn't he? He used to ferry some rather lucrative illegal immigrants into the country up until that particular net got tightened. Everyone thinks the immigrants come from France, see? They ain't never expecting them from Belgium. So, the ones with the bulging wallets go there, and that's where Baron offered his first class services."

"And Baron thinks he can shift the ice for top dollars?"

"He knows he can."

Davie looked to Danny and their eyes bespoke their uncertainty. Davie's glass trembled as he raised it to his lips.

"You mind if we talk in private?" Danny asked the South Londoner.

"Sure. Go wear yourselves out."

K picked up his magazine and pretended to read it as Danny and Davie walked away. He knew they'd be back soon, and he also knew what their answer would be. They had no choice but to allow his crew in on the deal if they wanted to get anywhere near the eight million that the diamonds were actually worth. He knew that even with their fifty-fifty split, they would still come out better off. He had to laugh at that, but he sipped at his wine to hide it. As soon as he had enough information from Davie and Danny to make a grab for the diamonds himself, then all they would see was his dust. Like they're gonna find me in a villa in Iran, he reasoned. Fuck them.

A self-satisfied smile caressed the corners of his mouth as he imagined his future life with Jasmine. He took off his glasses and gnawed on one of its arms ponderously, so he did not see the rain-soaked figure who stared at the back of his head through the thick glass of the foyer.

Out on the pavement, Matt observed K though slit eyes that burned with a cold loathing. He saw Davie and Danny return, then their conversation with K. Danny did most of the talking. Spilling his guts as a traitor to his race.

Their conversation ended fifteen minutes later, and as K took the tube back to his South London home he had no idea that a dark cloud of retribution clung to him like a swarm of flies around a plague cart; fuelled up on hatred and in possession of a gun.

K took the lift up to his 14th floor flat still unaware of his pursuer and when he reached his front door he beheld Colin X pulling a face.

"You're focking late," Colin chided him. "I've been freezing my balls off standing here so for ten minutes. Why'd you ding me and say be here so now, when you ain't on time yourself? Black people always 'pon Jamaican time. Char! You sight your watch any time recent? It's gone midnight, y'know!"

"Sorry, Colin," K pacified. "You know how mobiles get funny on the tube. I lost my connection before I could tell you where I was."

Colin's scowl deepened. "Dis better be good. De brethren don't get no raas emancipation so dey could get summoned by a raas claat bell every time uder man feel like it. Business time is dis!"

K unlocked his front door and stepped inside, ushering Colin after him. He could hear footsteps on the stairs accompanied by rasping breath and he didn't want to catch any aggravation from his neighbours about not waiting for them with the lift. He closed the door swiftly once Colin was inside.

"Did you get in touch with Baron?" he asked.

Colin walked through to the lounge, taking off his coat as he did so.

"You never asked me to."

"I did – just as my mobile was conking out."

"Well, me never catch dat. You want me to ding him now?"

"If you would be so kind."

Colin punched a number while K set his own phone on charge from a power point in the kitchen. He poured himself an orange juice and grabbed a lager for Colin, wondering if he had any crisps. When he returned to the lounge, Colin had finished his call and was torching one of Baron's half-smoked spliffs that he'd found in an ashtray next to the sofa.

"So how did de t'ing go with de white man?" Colin asked.

K sat down and digited one of his many remote controls. This one worked the stereo so the multiple C.D. turntable clicked into action. K set it to random and Bob Marley was soon telling him the tale of some buffalo soldiers.

"I know what we need to know," K replied. "It turns out that there was an inside man on the jacking, and the smart money is going on it being the pilot. The stiff they found at Barking ain't Careful Eddie neither. Danny and Davie reckon he faked his own death."

"So dis Eddie gangsta wasted someone who looked like him?"

"It makes sense. Wouldn't you try for a clean start if you had that much money behind you? I sure would."

Colin nodded and grumbled at the same time. He felt uncomfortable, so he removed something heavy from his name-brand tracksuit pocket. K saw it was a pistol. A short, silver and black pistol that Colin laid on his smoked glass coffee table. "I'm gonna keep packing arms 'til dis job is done, brethren," Colin told him. "You t'ink you can fool dem pagan men, an' dey not t'ink de same 'bout you?"

K didn't mind; for if Colin and Baron decided to waste the East London crew, there'd be more money for him. "They can't while they think that Baron can fence the diamonds at near market value."

"So dat's wha' you told dem?"

"Yeah. And they swallowed it quicker than a skint crack whore an hour late for her fix."

Colin grinned and flexed his muscular shoulders. "So de feeling is good! Allah be praised, dem pagan men will accept anyt'ing if you wrap it in enough dollars."

He chugged on his near-dead spliff contentedly until his mobile beeped. "Yo, bwai," he crooned into the mouthpiece. "He's at de top of the block. Come up quick time an' me gi' you de rocks myself."

K put his hand over Colin's mobile and mouthed the word "Who?"

"It's sweet," Colin whispered back. "Me set up a t'ing wid a brudder fe him to pick up some Crispies, an' when you set me 'pon a different mission me tell him to meet me here so."

"He isn't coming inside," K stressed, shocking Colin with his tone.

"Char!"

Colin resumed his conversation. "Sorry 'bout dat, my brethren start going on weird, raas claat. I'll meet you outside in de car park. Gi' me liccle time to catch de lift. You better 'ave de pussy'ole currency."

Colin was pulling on his coat as he finished his conversation. "Dis will only tek me about a minute," he said, tossing a jeweller's bag in his hand that held two rocks of crack cocaine. "But dis is wha' you get when you ding me during business hours."

K opened the front door for him and smiled when Colin slapped the lift button in an overtly aggressive manner. Colin's machismo never took a day off.

Once the steel doors of the lift had swallowed Colin, K closed his front door, contemplating on whether he had enough time in Colin's absence to call Jasmine. He wanted to hear her voice, a voice that promised a good future away from South London and the likes of Colin and Baron. He failed to see the crouched figure who was pressed tight against the wall of the stairwell. Matt thrust his hand in his pocket and felt the coldness of the pistol as his fingers enclosed its wooden stock. His heart fluttered in his chest like a caged bird and his breathing raced. As he fought for inner calm he stared out of a stairwell window and could see the myriad lights of South London far below him. For a moment he wondered what he was doing here and a small voice in his head reminded him that what he was about to do was wrong. He could turn back now, he reasoned, and no-one would ever know that he had been here. He could go back to Danny and Davie, work with the South Londoners, then live the life of Riley with his share of the loot. After all, he hadn't wanted to shoot K – just to beat him up a little, but he couldn't beat up K on his own, but he *did* have a gun. Surely this must all be fate or something?

Bile rose in Matt's throat, but he forced it back down with a gulp. No, he realised. This was a situation that was far beyond his control. The actions of others had put him on this stairwell with a gun, and the enormity of the pressure of this combination of events overwhelmed him. Whether or not he wanted to kill K was irrelevant. Any notion of the choice between right and wrong had fled; evicted by opinions and actions that were so much stronger than his own, and all that Matt knew was that he was here, now, and that there was only one thing left for him to do. There was no longer any choice in the matter.

In three strides Matt was at the top of the stairwell and in another two he was outside K's front door, the pistol in his hand. A mist swirling around inside his head fenced off his sense of reasoning, swathing him in a warm glow of tranquillity, and he never heard the sound of the gun as he shot the lock from K's front door.

Inside the flat, K, who had decided to ring Jasmine later on, was emptying an ashtray in the kitchen's peddle bin when he heard the bang. At first he thought one of his speakers had blown, but when Coolio continued to rap his *Gangster's Paradise* K knew that he was mistaken. Another thought crossed his mind, but he shooed it away as nonsense. Had he really heard a gun? There was more noise and any doubts about the origin of the sound were dispersed as K recognised the squeal of his front door being pushed open. Had Colin's drug deal gone sour? He moved into his lounge and saw Colin's gun resting on the coffee table. With cat-like silence he made a grab for it and clicked off the safety. Booted footsteps could be heard crunching on broken glass in the hall. He crouched down beside his armchair and raised his gun at the doorway. A pale tongue licked at his drying lips. This is all I need, he thought. A pissed off addict who probably thinks I've got crack all over the flat.

Matt continued along the hallway in a daze, his gun pointed to four O'clock. When he reached the open door to the lounge K was taken aback by the haircut and clothes. Had Lee come back from the dead to haunt him? His pistol was trained on the intruder's chest, his wrist shaking, then he saw the sullen, melancholy eyes and he realised that the unwelcome interloper was Matt.

"Matt," K said, standing. He was relieved because he felt sure that he could reason with the youngster. "What the hell…"

As he stood, Matt raised his weapon slowly and shot Professor K in the abdomen. The force of the bullet punched him back into the kitchen and his own pistol span from his grip to skid across the lino next to his peddle bin.

Matt lurched through the lounge with the indomitable persistence of an ice flow, kicking aside the coffee table as he did so. K put a hand to his belly as his teeth clenched with the pain. Blood welled up from between his fingers as he crawled backwards away from the door. "Matt, man!" he managed.

Matt paused when he reached the kitchen doorway. He looked down at K as he writhed around in his own blood and held the gun like it was a bunch of flowers.

"Do you remember when we were waiting in the car for the plane, you tried to tell me all about shooting?" he asked, his elbow leant on the door frame and the gun rubbing against his temple. "About how you shouldn't hesitate. About how you should go for the body rather than the head?"

K was distracted by the pain, but he knew that for every second that he kept Matt talking the closer Colin would be to rescuing him. He gasped a few times before he managed a tearful "Yeah?".

"Well, you shoulda taken your own advice. *You* hesitated, so now I get to do *both*," Matt told him as he readied his pistol and shot K square in the face. The back of K's head was slammed down into the lino as blood, flesh and half his jawbone sprayed in a crimson arc across the fridge and up the walls. His glasses were spun under the cooker where they came to rest by some pipes. Matt paced forward slowly leaving sanguine boot-prints on the white flooring and as he did so he emptied his weapon into K's gasping form. It twitched with the impact of the bullets and when there were no more bullets to be fired Matt stood, staring; his body more still than the gurgling wreck who sprawled before him.

Colin X heard the first gunshot as he was about to step out of the lift. "Bloodclaat!" he exclaimed, jabbing the lift button that would take him back to where he had come from. As the little lights blinked on and off telling him how far he had ascended Colin cursed himself for having left his weapon up with K. Had the fool shot himself? he wondered. Was his mind playing tricks on him, or was some wannabe gangster firing blanks, with the rest being filled in by Colin's own paranoia?

The smashed front door dispelled any illusions Colin may have had about the origin of the gunfire. "K? K?" he called into the hallway from the safety of the front door. No reply came. Colin flexed his shoulders and wondered what he should do. No sounds came from inside the flat, so whoever had been there must have gone. After all, who would be daft enough to stay after making that much noise?

Colin thought about dialling nine-nine-nine from his mobile, then heading for the hills, but the silence of the flat hailed him like a siren's song. All he could hear was Coolio and the wind rattling the windows.

Inch by nervous inch, Colin crept inside. He was careful not to tread on anything that would make a sound, then he peeped into the lounge and saw the kicked-over coffee table. Its glass had cracked. There was nowhere for a gunman to hide, so he continued with his stealthy advance until he came to the kitchen.

What he saw therein startled him. K was laying flat on his back with most of his lower face missing, while Matt stood over him like a jackbooted colossus, a gun hanging limp in his pale, twitching hand. The nauseating stench of pooled blood slammed into his nostrils like a blackjack.

Matt turned when Colin reached the blood-smeared lino and he saw in Matt's sunken eyes the tortured insanity of the damned. His complexion was bloodless, his mouth hanging open in a stupefied 'O', and he made no effort to defend himself as Colin approached. It was as though K had been shot, and yet Matt had arisen as the undead.

The two men stared at each other for a time, Colin wondering whether the gun was still loaded and whether Matt had enough sense remaining to use it, while Matt looked through Colin to whatever hell he envisioned behind him.

The scene may have continued indefinitely, had a siren not fired up in the distance that called Colin to action. Like an eccentric school master he grabbed Matt by his collar and dragged him out of the flat towards the lift, still clutching the gun. The young skinhead offered no resistance. Colin recalled K pulling him away from Ali's body outside Crumb's blues, telling him to make haste, and recognised he didn't have the same tug of emotion when abandoning K. "He weren't a brudder," he muttered under his breath.

As the lift doors opened Colin thrust Matt inside then pulled out his mobile phone. The number he dialled was answered immediately. "Baron," he panted, noticing for the first time that he now had K's blood on his hands. "You in some wheels? How far away are you from K's gates? Two minutes? You better hit de raas turbo button an' mek it here so in seconds. Shit, man, you ain't gonna focking believe wha's been going on up here!"

Saturday 8th December, 2001; 12:17am

"It's too bloody brass monkeys to be buggering about at this time of night," D.C. Scott Hain complained as he tugged on his black leather gloves and glowered out of the window of the squad car to the rainswept streets of Barking town centre.

W.P.C. Heather Golightly had opted to drive and as she shifted gear she risked a swift glance in Scott's direction. "I don't know, I could get used to this C.I.D. lark," she replied. "I don't have to wear a hat, so I can do more things with my hair."

Scott had to admit that he preferred Heather in civilian clothing too. Her skirts were shorter and her blouses tighter when she picked her own glad rags. With her petite, auburn-bobbed frame clad in an above-the-knee grey skirt, loosely-buttoned white blouse and patent leather shoes she resembled a convent schoolgirl on her first night away from the nuns.

"Turn into the next left," Scott pointed out as they neared the Gascoigne council estate. "Davie's in that block over there."

Heather did as he asked, slotting the vehicle into a disabled parking space so they could be nearer the main doors. "Let's get this show on the road," she grinned.

Scott wagged the arrest warrant against his palm for a few seconds then stepped from the squad car out into the rain. When Heather was ready, he followed the hypnotic sway of her backside into the tower block then jabbed at a button for the lift. "Here we go," Scott said.

While the duo waited for the lift's arrival Scott felt his stomach tighten. They had perhaps another minute or so alone together, and this was his first time alone with Heather since her transfer from Stratford nick. If he was to ask her out for dinner then the time had to be now. After all, he reasoned, he couldn't do it later with Davie Thompson handcuffed between them, and he sure as hell wouldn't do it with Dudley around. He'd never live it down if she declined.

"Heth," he mumbled nervously as they stepped into the piss-reeking lift. "There's something I wanna ask you before we get to Davie's."

Heather poked the appropriate button and she turned to face Scott as they ascended to the heavens. Her head was tilted to one side in expectation.

Suddenly Scott's mouth felt dry and he had to lick his lips. For a brief moment he wondered whether his hair had been messed up by the rain.

"Well?" Heather asked as the lift's maw opened. Someone had smashed the corridor's light, so their only illumination came from street lights through the windows. After adjusting to the near-total darkness, she took the five paces needed to be outside Davie's front door then waited.

"Erm… well… well…" Scott began, his world suddenly a chaotic, swirling maelstrom of anxiety and messed-up hormones. "Would you like to come out to dinner some time?"

"What? You mean like on a date?"

Scott didn't know whether to nod or not, so Heather put him out of his misery with a smile. "Sure," she said. "Any time. Where are you going to take me?"

Scott hadn't thought that far ahead, in the same way that he hadn't prepared his flat for a deluge of frogs. This simply was not meant to happen.

"Erm… erm…" he managed.

"Okay, my place tonight at eight," Heather decreed, neatly side-stepping Scott's neuroses-impaired perspicacity with direct action. "I hope you like home cooked Italian."

Before Scott could vocalise his everlasting gratitude, Heather ignored the tatty notice on Davie's front door that foreboded bad tidings to any mortal who dared cross the threshold of his demesne and rapped his letter box. "Mr. Thompson. Mr. *David* Thompson," she called. "This is the Police. Please open up at once."

Inside the flat, Davie awoke and slipped from his sleeping bag noiselessly. He was already dressed in camouflaged combat trousers, white T-shirt and socks, and his boots were close at hand with their laces loosened so he could tug them on quickly. He snarled as the letter box clapped again. His flat was darker than a mineshaft in a blackout, deliberately so; with thick blankets covering all the windows that shed light into the hall, but he found the bag with the rifle and bombs instinctively.

His camouflage jacket was flung next to the bag and he struggled to thread his twitching arm through its sleeve as Scott readied his truncheon to smash the door's window. "We're coming in, Mr. Thompson," Heather called when the truncheon crashed down and glass splintered.

Davie crouched down behind a box of yellowed newspapers where he had a darkness-hindered view of the doorway and considered drawing his rifle, but Scott Hain thrust his arm through the broken window and opened the latch before he had the chance. With the door opened, Scott led the assault, stomping into Davie's hermitage with the gung-ho attitude of a white-armoured stormtrooper heading into a Rebel base until his new boots skidded on some shards of glass and he slipped flat on his face.

Heather stepped over him then pulled him to his feet. "I think you'll be safer with the lights on," she said.

As her hand reached the switch, Davie ducked his head so he did not see the firestorm that ballooned along the hallway. Glass, lead fishing weights and plaster from the ceiling blasted in all directions directly above the heads of the two Police officers and Heather was cannoned into the floor, her face awash with blood. Scott was flung back against a wall, which he slid down unceremoniously as unconsciousness slipped him a greetings card. Through his tunnelling vision, he saw Heather laying a few feet away with glass and lead pellets dotted like freckles about her face, and he could not tell whether she was alive or dead.

The gasoline and soap flakes concoction was splashed about the ceiling and the walls burning fiercely, filling the hallway with grey, choking smoke. Davie watched dispassionately as Scott Hain dragged himself forward to lay on top of Heather Golightly, shielding her with his own body and limbs, before he, too, lost his battle against creeping unconsciousness.

When he saw that no more movement came from the two crumpled, bloodied forms, Davie rose and stepped over the pair, walking to the lift with the canvas bag slung over his shoulder.

Saturday 8th December, 2001; 12:24am

Colin X was waiting behind a bush with Matt's head viced under one arm and a pistol levelled at his head when Baron pulled up outside K's block.

"Are yu focking mad?" Baron charged. "People der 'bout an' yu drag de white bwai wet up inna blood where nuff people coulda see it?"

Matt's feet barely touched the ground as Colin dragged him towards the car. K's blood was splattered over his right sleeve, hand and face, while his eyes were vacant and seemed immune to any feeling. Baron opened a rear passenger door and stilled his tongue until Colin bundled Matt inside before clambering in himself; slamming the door shut after him.

"Him kill off K. Half of his bloodclaat head is missing," Colin grimaced as the image of K's broken form mushroomed into his mind.

He beat Matt about the side of the head with his pistol as he spoke and only stopped when Matt swung senseless onto his side; his erratic breathing alone indicating his tentative grip on life. "It made me feel sick," Colin admitted.

The proximity of wailing sirens prompted Baron to bottom the accelerator and they were soon lost to the night. "So why yu drag de bwai to de car?" Baron asked as Colin took out a knife and proceeded to hack through a rear seat belt. He used the cut-off belt to tie Matt's hands. "Yu shoulda kill 'im when yu find him. An' yu lucky me even find car fe drive. Me bredrin will ah wonder why me 'ave blood all 'bout inna 'im car."

"I'm gonna mek him talk," X replied as he stared into Matt's blank, unseeing eyes. "K tell me dat de white bwai dem know de programme of the diamond t'ing. An' dis pagan's gonna tell me wha' I don't know. I'm gonna get brutal like ancient Apache on his pagan backside an' by de time I finish wid him his overseer ancestors will wake up from deat' feeling pussyclaat pain! I'm gonna find out 'bout de diamonds if it kills me! Now drive de rarse car!"

"Where?" Baron asked, more than willing to drive now that he could see blue flashing lights in his rear-view mirror.

"The railway arches near Loughborough Junction. Where Pinchers has his joinery business t'ing."

Baron nodded and while Colin spent his time eyeballing their hostage with his gun poised the London streets flashed by. Within a few minutes they reached the lock-up and Colin tossed Baron a set of keys.

Baron stepped out of the car and fingered through them. He was content that there were no street lights about and the place seemed to be isolated from passers by. "It's the small brass-looking one," Colin advised, keeping a close watch on his semi-conscious prey.

Baron negotiated the padlock and pulled the blue-painted doors open to the sound of wood scraping against concrete. Taking a torch out of his pocket, he showered light on three work benches with wood-gripping vices in-situ, then, pointing the torch to his right, he saw that finished cabinets and coffee tables were placed on brown paper on the floor at the rear of the shop, while saws, hammers, pliers and other tools were hanging on a board of nails.

Power tools were kept in a large wooden box in the corner of the lock-up and the shelves that were fixed to the side walls held pots of varnish, sandpaper, metal G-clamps and other carpentry sundries. Sawdust and paper-thin, curled strips of wood covered the ground and the smell of pine tinted the dank air.

Colin hauled a dazed Matt into the workshop, while Baron went outside and locked the car. When he returned he found a light switch and thumbed it on. A fluorescent bulb spluttered and flickered into life, splashing a sharp yellow light across the cream-painted brickwork. He switched off the torch and glanced at the pitiful figure of Matt, making a mental note that on no circumstances should he take his gloves off. A freight train rumbled overhead, vibrating the foundations of the workshop.

Still holding Matt around his neck, Colin launched him onto one of the work benches; Matt's head hitting the unforgiving wood. "Hol' on," demanded Baron. "Nuh touch 'im yet. Me affe gi' back de car an' find ah nex' one. Tie 'im up wid somet'ing 'til me reach."

Baron looked around the shop floor and spotted a few rolls of masking tape in a corner. "Cover 'im mout' wid dat," he commanded. He then noticed a dust sheet covering a newly-built cabinet, so he walked over to it and sliced a strip from the white material using his Stanley knife. "Use dis`fe tie up 'im arms," he continued. He tossed it over to Colin, who caught it, then he departed closing the blue double doors behind him; leaving Colin glaring at his quarry with his thoughts fuelled by a black panther's feral cunning.

It took almost two hours for Baron to clean the car, return it, then steal another. When he returned to the arches he found Colin still leaning over Matt like a lion sizing up a young wildebeest. Matt had masking tape plastered over his mouth and eyes and Colin had exploited the spare time and Matt's borderline-consciousness to tie his arms back onto the benches with his wrists held between the jaws of two steel vices.

Colin ripped off the tape and Matt exhaled vigorously, his eyes squirming from the light. Colin turned to Baron. "You get another car alright?"

"Yeah, mon. Me 'ad fe t'ief one… But get dis t'ing over an' done wid, mon. Morning light soon come."

"Get me dat jigsaw," ordered Colin. "I'm gonna do somet'ing Viking-like to his pagan arse."

Baron collected the powertool from the large wooden carton in the corner and wondered what Colin intended to do with it.

Me nuh see too much torture inna Jamaica, he thought. We jus' killed dem. Me hope 'im nuh get too messy cah me nuh wipe up nuh blood or bits of 'ead. He gave the jigsaw to Colin and stepped back two paces. "'ear me, English bwai, me nuh care wha' yu do to de white bwai, but let me tell yu from now me nuh clear up nutten. If blood ah run den yu will affe tek up de mop. Boom boom claat! Me already swab de raas wheels."

Colin slapped Matt on his head. "Wake up, you bloodclaat pagan!"

Matt murmured something and moved his head slightly, but his eyes were somewhere far from home. "Der's a bucket in the corner, Baron, and a sink t'rough dat side door. Fill it up wid nuff water."

Moments later, Baron loomed over Matt with the water. "Fling it over him," ordered Colin. For a strange reason, Colin found himself thinking about Ali's funeral and whether it would be Islamic or Pentecostal. It was strange how shit like that didn't matter now. He thought of Ali's mother and what type of black outfit she would wear and wondered if she would ever get over her son's death. Well, Ali was always going on about how she wants to go back to Jamaica, he recalled. By the time I'm finished she could go on a round the world trip first.

Baron emptied the bucket and Matt, reacting to the coldness of the water, contorted in a rapid spasm and tried to sit up, but the teeth of the vices that lock-jawed into his wrists kept him on his back.

Colin slapped him about the face. "Now, do I have your attention?"

Matt blinked rapidly, focused and saw the definition of diabolical portent staring over him. He felt his head throb and wondered what caused this pain. He realised something thicker than water was lubricating the back of his head and his wrists felt like they were wrapped in torqued barbed wire. He could now smell the alcohol wafting from Colin's breath and wondered where he was. He thought of Lee and decided he wouldn't give the fuckin' niggers any information. Spider would be proud of him. When Spider got news about his slaying of K he'd be the toast of the Saint George. Yeah, *that* one was for Lee. His thoughts became a blur as the pain from the back of his head pulsed through his whole being and his wrists protested at the crushing weight of the vices. He looked into the eyes of Colin and a realisation came to him that he had witnessed his last dawn. The blood now gorging through his rapid-beating heart was cold. Matt also felt the wintry drafts on his skin that swirled around the workshop. He shivered.

"Wha' do you know 'bout de pilot?" Colin insisted, his face desperate, the image of Ali's dead body in his mind.

"That… That… he… he hates niggers just… just as much as I…"

Colin twisted the handle on the vice that held Matt's right wrist in place and continued to do so until he heard a bone snap over the wail of Matt's screams. "Alright, so you wanna be brave."

Colin turned to Baron. "I'm gonna inject dis focking pagan wid so much shit he'll be crapping crack 'til his nineties."

"Nuh, mon," Baron rejected. "If yu do dat de white bwai will nuh feel de pain. We 'ave 'im where we waan 'im, so der's nuh need fe waste decent Crispies dat cyan sell anoder day."

Colin pulled on the left-hand vice until he had achieved the same result as with the first. A scream punctuated the silence of the night and Matt's hands were turning purple where the vices had starved them of blood. "I get wid de programme, Baron," said Colin. "T'reaten dat we'll cut off his focking 'ands."

"Nuh, mon," Baron shook his head. "Bruk one ah 'im toes an' den t'reaten 'im dat if 'im nuh gi' us wha' we waan, bruk ah next toe."

Colin apparently didn't hear Baron's last piece of advice. Fuelled by his vengeance for Ali and intoxicated with his addiction of violence, he revved up the jigsaw then set its juddering blade against Matt's left hand, just below the bases of the fingers. Dark, oxygen-starved blood spurted across his T-shirt as he drove the powertool forward and he did not relent despite Matt's plaintive wails until four fingers dropped to the workshop floor, leaving behind a gnawed palm and a twitching thumb.

Him as crazy wid hate as de white bwai who kill Ali, Baron realised as Matt's yelps of anguish ricocheted off the walls.

Yout' don't affe be white to hate anudder man's skin. Dem all racist pussies.

"Now, do me 'ave to do dat shit again, or you gwarn talk?"

"Alright! Alright!" Matt submitted between pain-wracked gasps.

"If you tell me any fuckery I'm gonna rip you up from de bottom crease to your white pencil-dick. Now, who's de focking pilot?"

Matt couldn't answer instantly as saliva was building up in his mouth. Colin hit him in the face with the business end of the jigsaw, causing a welt to appear below Matt's right eye. *"Who?"*

Matt made a gurgling sound and then attempted to clear his throat. "It was an... an inside job... the pilot knew he... he was gonna be jacked."

Colin exchanged glances with Baron then revved up the jigsaw once more *"Name!"*

"Ronnie... Ronnie Thatcher. He..." Matt paused while he screamed his anguish. "He was the pilot wearing glasses... blond hair."

Colin's memory rewound back to the time of the initial heist and recollected that one of their victims did wear glasses and had blond hair. He also felt safe that the information was bona-fide since Matt had not been there to see the pilot for himself. Nevertheless, Colin pushed the whirring jigsaw forward until it bit into the bone of Matt's remaining hand. This wasn't to facilitate a confession, this time it was just for kicks.

"What's Eddie's plan?" he demanded.

"Uuurr." Matt was on the verge of insensibility. He had come to the point where his body could take no more pain, and his nervous system debated whether or not to switch off all the lights. Colin pulled the blade of the jigsaw free of Matt's wrist, while Baron toked on his spliff; the fluorescent light illuminating its smoke.

"Eddie... Eddie's gonna try and make for... for..."

"Where?"

"Southend airport... Then Antwerp... That's all I know..."

For a short second, Colin thought of K and how shrewd he was. *"When?"*

"Sat... Uuurrr... Saturday morning... at sev... seven ..."

Matt's head tilted to one side and a long, drawn-out breath rattled past his pale lips. His eyes closed and his face appeared as if at rest.

Baron shook his head while taking stock of the large pool of blood that had been soaked up by the sawdust. "Me tell yu before dat me nuh clear up nutten. An' 'im coulda tell us more, mon," he said. "Yu mek 'im lose blood too fas'."

"Gimmi your Stanley, 'cos Ah wanna rip off 'is trousers," Collin demanded. "Ah wanna see his shrivelled Nazi balls when Ah jigsaw dem."

Baron shook his head and tucked his Stanley knife away. "Yu t'ink yu nah a racist an' a Nazi jus' 'cos yu black?" he sneared. "Nuh skin-colour 'as de raas copywrite on dat. Yu cyan hide it 'ere in Inglan' jus' 'cos yu in de minority, but yu jus' anudder butcher Mugabe in de making." He paused so that he could freeze Colin with his authoritative stare. "Me spill blood fe business, nuh fe fun," he resumed, "an' me see nuff carnage back ah yard to know dat yout' like yu would do de same as dem der Nazi white bwais if yu 'ad de raas chance. So, do wha' yu mus', but *don't* try an' fool me dat yu any better dan dat der ball 'ead. Yu all as messed up wid hate as each udder."

Colin recoiled at Baron's blunt assertion and fought to rid the uncomfortable truth from his mind. He noticed that Matt was still just about breathing and with his lust for violence cooling, a spec of unaccustomed pity crept into his mind. "I'll put him out of his misery now," he murmured.

"Nuh, mon," Baron advised, raising a hand. "Not 'ere. Der's ah place we could tek 'im, an' if we get stopped by Babylon on de way dey can't slap us fe 'is murder. Jus' off Garratt Lane inna Wandswort' dey 'ave ah liccle industrial estate where de small river run under ah liccle bridge. We'll tek 'im der alive an' fling 'im off."

Colin nodded and in a matter of moments they had carried Matt's limp body into the rear of the stolen car. Baron reached the industrial estate in twelve minutes and Colin nodded, appreciating that this was indeed a good spot to get rid of their hostage. The main building housed a storage business; the phone number in big red letters covering high windows. To the left of the entrance was an electrical cable company with a factory-like roof. Satellite buildings of small businesses filled the rest of the area. Fifty yards through the entrance, a small bridge arched over rushing water that journeyed its way to the Thames. It was wider than a stream, but not as broad as a river. Soiled rubbish was caught by sticks and other objects on the banks. Baron pulled up, climbed out of the car and looked around. "Nobody 'der 'bout." He was still wearing his gloves.

As they dragged Matt's unconscious body out of the car, Colin recoiled when he saw that Matt still clung on to life. He hoped Baron hadn't seen his startled reaction. "Me hope de water is cold enough to wake you when you hit it, white bwai," Colin said when he and Baron levered Matt's body up onto the bridge's handrail.

Matt coughed; a wretched, gurgling sound, then Colin pushed him forward so that he tumbled head-first into the inky, cold water; his handless arms flailing about him like broken wings.

As he sank below the surface, Baron went back to the car where he picked up a blood-stained plastic bag that contained Matt's severed fingers, then tossed it casually into the water. The pair waited until they were certain that Matt's body would not re-surface, then they turned and walked back to the car.

"Yu'd better clean de bloodclaat arches," ordered Baron. "Nuff D.N.A. der-ya."

Saturday 8th December, 2001; 03:13am

The rattle of rain pattering against a window greeted Danny as his eyes slid open to behold the new day, but that was not the sound that had roused him. He crooked his head so that his ears were free of his pillow and listened until he heard the sound again. Was someone coming up the stairs?

Danny was naked save for his West Ham tattoo and he cursed that he didn't own a gun. An intruder was in his home and in his present condition he knew that he was helpless. After all, the only weapons at hand were an ageing clock radio and a hair brush.

He slithered from his bed as footfalls padded on the landing and tugged a belt from his jeans to improvise a knuckle-duster when he saw the knob turn on his door. It opened slowly, silently, and as the interloper came into view Danny's fear turned to anger.

"Davie," he croaked, his voice choked with adrenaline. "What the fuck?"

Davie was dressed like a paintballer on angel dust; with a camouflaged jacket and trousers, black woolly hat and black gloves. Shades hid his eyes despite the early hour and black boots shod his feet. "We've gotta split," he said insouciantly, hefting his bulging canvas bag over his shoulder.

"But how'd you get in?"

"Don't talk – get dressed. I'll explain on the hoof."

While Danny rooted around hurriedly for his clothes, Davie prowled through the upper rooms of the maisonette peering out of windows into the streets and gardens. His arm twitched with the life that Subacute Sclerosing Panencephalitis had given it and his face wore the gaunt cloak of a stroke victim. His canvas bag never left his side.

Within a few minutes Danny was ready, having donned a black leather jacket, jeans and an un-ironed England football shirt. He's done something bad, he reasoned. Don't think I wanna know what it is. "Change the shirt," Davie told him. "You make too easy a target. Wear something black."

"But this strip brings me luck. It's Beckham's shirt."

"Then you won't be wanting any bullet holes in it. Go change."

Danny was wearing a dark blue polo neck *over* his England shirt as he ducked into his car and a strange thought came over him that he wouldn't see his maisonette for a long time. Davie only abandoned the safety of the hallway when the passenger's door was opened and the car's engine grumbling. "Time to set up an obbo at the airport," he said.

"What about Matt?"

"He ain't at home. I checked."

Danny wondered how Davie had checked during the night when he did not own a phone, nor know Matt's number, but then he remembered how *he* had been introduced to Davie this morning and decided not to ask. He took the Upney Lane turn-off onto the A13 heading towards Southend and as they approached Dagenham he turned on the radio. Sixties hits tingled the air.

"Southend airport will be a subterfuge nightmare," Davie said suddenly as they passed by Fords. "From the car park, the entrance is just a big glass door set into a big glass wall that leads to an open plan departure lounge. The far wall of the lounge is also made of glass and it leads directly onto the air strip."

"I didn't realise it was *that* small an airfield," replied Danny, wondering where Matt could be.

"Just weekend pilots and flights to Jersey and Guernsey. The open plan feel means everyone has a clear view of the landing field even if they're standing outside the airport in the car park, so we've gotta keep good clocks once we get there. Once we're inside the lounge there ain't no place to hide."

"We've got to contact K, right? They're meeting us at the airport."

Danny pulled out his mobile and keyed K's number. It was answered after a few rings and his face sagged within moments. He killed the call without speaking. "Christ on a bike!" he exclaimed. "His phone was answered by the Law and some copper started asking me questions. K musta been nabbed."

"No – he's dead," Davie stated unconcernedly. "If he'd been arrested they woulda just let the phone ring."

Davie took the mobile and wiped it clear of prints on his jacket before throwing it out of a window into the street. His expression did not change.

"Who'd you think popped him?" Danny asked, realising he was way out of his depth. "Colin? Baron?"

"Maybe Eddie," Davie replied. "But whoever it is, they're gonna be pissed at us, so we can't expect a welcome reception once we see them at the airport. That's why I wanted to be there first. That way we keep the initiative."

Danny went to answer, but stopped when a news bulletin came on the radio. A bomb had gone off in central Barking and two Policemen were in hospital. A manhunt was underway and a suspect was being sought. He looked at Davie as if he was someone else.

Davie slapped home a tape and Billy Bragg's *A New England* silenced the newscaster. "You don't wanna believe everything that you hear," he said.

Saturday 8th December, 2001; 03:32am

Baron climbed the steps to the fifth floor of his own block of flats. He was weary, but he knew he had no time to sleep. Before opening his front door he peered into the brightening sky, sure that he would soon be airborne again and on his way to Miami. His vantage point offered him a view of Clapham Junction train station and he spotted maintenance crews tending the platforms. "Pussies," he whispered. "If me programme go right me will 'ave more dan wha' dey could earn in fifty raas years."

With two heavy-duty mortice keys he turned the locks of his reinforced front door and entered his flat, kicking away the mail that was resting on the door mat. "Me nuh affe answer yu," he grinned.

Walking through the hallway, he turned left into the kitchen. The cooker was spotless, and the pots and pans hanging off pegs from the walls appeared as though they had never encountered food nor seen a scouring pad. Empty take-away food cartons were piled up on the rubbish bin in a corner precariously and on the Formica-topped table, next to the sink, was a selection of drinks. Baron screwed off the top of the rum bottle and took a gentle swig before shaking his head vigorously in order to rouse himself from tiredness. "Aaaahhh. Dat better."

He went to his bedroom and headed for the telephone that was sitting on a bedside cabinet. A picture of the Jamaican D.J. Ninja Man, torn out from a magazine, looked over his single bed; untold bed sheets compensated for the lack of any blankets. There was no pillow. Numerous cassette tapes formed pillars on Baron's dressing table and keeping them company were loose cigarette papers, various lighters, a greyed glass ashtray, C.D.s and loose change. A top of the range portable hi-fi system was in the corner of the room, its digital display informing Baron that the time had just nudged 03:40am. Underneath the phone was an international calling card. He picked it up, read the dialling code and punched in the number. Then he dialled a Miami Dade-County number.

"It's Malakai, mon.... Wha' yu mean yu jus' went to bed? Wake up nuh! Me know yu been working 'ard shifts an' it's almost ten your time, but yu affe listen... Nuh, mon, me nuh get meself involve wid dem t'ing der... Me jus' co-operating wid de Police dem fe get me visa... Nuh worry yuself, me soon come... Nuh, mon, dey will affe gi' de visa to me cah me 'elp dem nuff... Nuh, mon. Nobody after me an' when me gone ah Miami dem bad man will never know where me der-ya... Jamaica? 'ave some fait', mon... Dem cyan't sen' me der... T'ings will be irie an' boderation will be nuh more... Yeah, mon, me 'ave ah liccle money... Nuh worry yuself me tek control ah dat... Yu coulda see me in de nex' few days... Of course me tell yu de flight number... How de pickney dem? Good fe 'ear... Yeah, mon, it'll be ah good Christmas... Jus' tell dem daddy soon come wid nuff t'ings fe dem... Me affe go now an' deal wid de programme... Yeah, mon, walk safe an' live good 'til me reach... Later will be greater."

Baron placed the phone down and stared at it for a few seconds before rummaging under his bed. His hand emerged with a mobile phone and before he dialled he composed himself, preparing his story.

"Hooker? We affe meet... Fock de raas hour an' open dem ears wide! Me 'ave ah liccle information fe yu... But me nuh tell yu nutten if yu nuh get out ah your crib dis minute an' set up de visa t'ing... Early as possible... Now is good. Yeah, mon, but not too far... Somewhere inna Battersea... Yeah, mon, me know it... Clove Hitch Quay by de riverside near de 'copter landing somet'ing... Four ah clock... It's bona-fide... Mek sure yu der-ya."

A short while later, Baron found Detective Sergeant Michael Hooker standing by rails that protected pedestrians from the soiled and mud-coloured Thames. A block of expensive apartments looked over him as he sucked on a cigarette, the smoke mingling with his cold breath. He was dressed casually in a tanned leather jacket, jeans and name brand trainers. Up river, high in the sky, a helicopter emerged out of the cloud cover flashing its lights. Baron acknowledged him with his eyes before stepping over. "So, Hooker, yu reach," he greeted. "Nuh res' fe de raas wicked, eh?"

Hooker's tired face morphed into one of vexation as he grabbed the lapels of Baron's jacket and yanked him nearly off his feet towards him where their heads almost collided. He then bent Baron's spine backwards across the rail so that he leant over the lapping water of the Thames. The cigarette dropped out of Hooker's mouth. "How many times do I have to tell you *never* use that name when I'm with you. Me name's Spinner for the streets!"

Baron wrestled himself away. "Boom boom claat! Yu sight anybody der 'bout? Mon, 'andle me once more an' see me don't rip out yu bloodclaat!"

Hooker knew there was no such thing as paranoia for an undercover cop, and that loose jaws like Baron's could get him killed. Not even the surveillance team knew his real name, listening in to the wire that he wore. He walked away a few paces, lighting himself another cigarette to calm himself down. He tailed a boat for a few seconds before returning to Baron, an apology written on his face to smooth the deal. He spoke quietly. "Well, I hope you've finally got something for me. It better be good 'cos we're losing our patience."

Baron kissed his teeth. "Me cyan't mek it too obvious dat me waan information, y'understand? Dangerous business. But me find somet'ing out, mon, fe real... Me waan yu fe promise dat if me gi' yu somet'ing, leading to nuff arrests an' t'ing, yu gwarn set me up wid de visa."

"Depends on what your information is," returned Hooker, blowing his smoke over the river.

Baron leaned closer to the officer and seized him with his eyes. "*Don't* pussyclaat fock wid me. Now, me 'ave bona-fide information an' me be saving yu nuff Police time. An' fe get it me affe risk me bloodclaat life."

"And so do *I*," Hooker countered. "*Every* fucking day."

Baron didn't show too much concern about the daily perils for Hooker and resumed. "An' true dem bad man t'ink me is ah terrorist dem try fe impress me wid bragga talk or dey woulda shoot me widout any raas claat apology. Me done me part."

"Baron, if the information leads to arrests and is a help to our investigation, then I'm sure you'll get your visa. But it's not up to me. My superiors will have to rubber stamp it then the application will have to be signed by the Home Office and the American Embassy." Hooker checked himself, using the pause to take another toke of his cigarette. "It'll just be a matter of time if we can show these people evidence of how you have helped us… So if *you* have something to say, *say* it and stop wasting my time."

Baron thought about it. "Alright." He leaned closer still to Hooker and spoke in a whisper. "It was never ah black on black t'ing dat killed de brudder named Ali. Me find out dis Ali was part of ah Brixton crew, crack an' t'ing dem ah deal wid. Dem bring in nuff mule 'pon Air Jamaica. But white mon kill 'im, mon. Drive by shooting… Two crews, one from Brixton side an' de uder from East London set up ah drug deal. Somet'ing went wrong… Me even know two ah de white bwai name."

"Go on," said Hooker.

"Davie an' Danny. An' de leader fe de Brixton crew, people call 'im Professor K. Some mon say 'im come from Yard an' some say 'im come from States. 'im ah dangerous mon, believe it. Me 'ear so 'im kill nuff people, an' me 'ear so 'im kill off ah white mon from East London recently. Me nuh know if it all connected. But dis Brixton crew, all ah dem born ah England an' dem nuh 'fraid fe use gun. Der's somet'ing going down, mon. Somet'ing big. Some kinda meeting. Yu affe gi' me more time fe find out where de meeting ah der-ya. Y'understand?"

"This Professor K, do you know his first name?"

"Nuh, mon. But 'im short an' stocky... Wears glasses. Me 'ear say 'im dog-hearted, but 'im know how fe use 'im brain. Police never ketch 'im fe anyt'ing yet so me 'ear."

Hooker adjusted his jacket in the hope that it would improve the reception of his wire. He could imagine the surveillance team taking notes and making frantic phone calls in his mind's eye. "What do you think this meeting is about?"

"Me nuh really sure. Could be some kinda peace t'ing fe stop de killing. Or to split up de drugs dem. Yu affe gi' me more time... Den me could ah set yu up neatly, informing yu where de killers ah der-ya... Mebbe yu cyan gi' me some information?"

"Oh, what?"

"Me 'ear ah name mention. Ronnie T'atcher. 'im ah small plane pilot. Me nuh know how 'im involve in all dis, but 'im get ah mention plenty time when me talk to people. Yu know 'im? Yu know where 'im der-ya?"

"Doesn't ring a bell. I'll call you after I follow it up."

"Anyway, dat's all me know. Me call yu when me find out more."

Baron watched a helicopter take off and for a moment stared skywards blankly, then without even presenting Hooker a farewell glance, he walked away; not wanting to stand in the wind-chilled morning too long. On his way home, Baron decided that he didn't want to wait on a chance for Hooker to come up with the visa. Me gwarn get de diamonds, he thought. Yeah mon. Fock de Police. Kill off dis Ronnie T'atcher an' fly de plane to Antwerp. Shame Hooker could nuh tell me anyt'ing 'bout dis mon or where 'im ah live. Oderwise me would 'ead straight fe 'im, kill 'im bloodclaat, an' Eddie would affe use me. Boom boom claat.

Baron reached his flat in fifteen minutes and headed straight for his land-line phone. "Yo, X mon... Look ah different car fe today... Mek sure yu 'ave nuff petrol an' carry yu arms... Yu better find your passport too... Yeah, mon, me gwarn fly dat bloodclaat plane to de continent an' anybody who get inna me way dem gwarn taste me Uzi... Boom boom claat! Collect me ah de Chopper pub... Near de 'copter pad... Say five t'irty... Yeah, mon... Me signing off now."

Baron dropped the phone into its cradle and immediately lifted his mattress off the bed, revealing wads of ten and twenty pound notes secured by elastic bands. He collected them all and placed them on his dressing table. "Eleven gran'," he whispered to himself. "If me come t'rough tonight me affe look ah mon ah foreign who cyan set me up neatly wid ah visa. Boom boom claat. Den Miami me forward. But how me gwarn carry de bloodclaat money?"

Saturday 8th December, 2001; 04:42am

An air of sickly silence choked the air of Oldchurch Hospital's intensive care unit that was only broken by the metronome beeps of various life support machines.

Nurses padded back and forth wearing soft-soled shoes, doctors frowned as they examined charts, and a porter pushed a large, v-shaped broom along a dimly-lit corridor that led to the operating theatres.

Dudley Powell sat alone on a rack of orange plastic chairs with his face cradled in his hands. He lifted his feet for the broom as the porter passed.

Scott Hain was undergoing emergency surgery to remove a dozen or more slithers of shrapnel from his skull. The doctor had said that Scott had sustained severe burns. Heather Golightly had been transferred from the hospital to a specialist burns unit for emergency plastic surgery and according to her parents the doctors said that she may need to lose an eye. Dudley had been woken at 02:30 by a phone call from D.S. Mike Conway at Barking Police Station bearing the bad news, and he had been sat in the hospital since 03:00.

"I just spoke to the head nurse," came a gentle voice at his side. "Don't worry, D.S. Powell, we will get the monster who did this."

Dudley looked up to see the broad face of William Wiley smiling down at him in a manner that was supposed to be upbeat under difficult circumstances. "You bet we will," Dudley replied.

William sat down next to Dudley then knitted his thick fingers together as he balanced his elbows upon his knees. He hated these moments in his line of work, but knew the investigation had to proceed, with or without Dudley's colleagues. Wiley placed his conscience to the back of his priorities. "I also got a wake-up call in the middle of the night," he said. "But my call was for better news, if we can call it that given the circumstances. Are you up for hearing it?"

Dudley nodded, but his face displayed a lack of enthusiasm for the investigation. "Shoot."

"One of S.O.10's spooks made contact with a grass by the name of Malakai Perry a few hours back," Wiley began. "He says the Stockwell Park hit was undertaken by an I.C.1 East London crew and gave us two names into the bargain – Danny and Davie."

"Yeah – Davie fucking Thompson," Dudley sneered.

William nodded. "Quite possibly. He also said that the hit was avenged with an East London death and that, we can assume, was Lee Jones who, once again, you saw talking in the pub with Davie Thompson and the I.C.3s."

As William's deep bass reverberated along the corridor Dudley looked up slowly. Now, he thought, this is getting somewhere.

William pulled out his note pad to kick-start his memory; turning over the front page quickly as it was covered with doodled smiling faces that were drawn at a more relaxed time.

"Another I.C.3 was mentioned with the street name of Professor K," he continued. "We didn't have a handle on him, but a man fitting his description was blasted into a coma in the wee hours of this morning and his first name begins with a K - Keith."

"We don't know whether Davie was at his flat when Scott and Heather turned up," Dudley interrupted. "They haven't regained consciousness to tell us. I guess it could have been him."

"Or this Danny character. However, I have saved the best piece of information until last. The informant told my undercover man that the remainder of the two crews are going to be meeting up soon to write up a peace treaty and he's going to give us the where and when, but the best part is that he asked about a con named Ronnie Thatcher. He got busted a few years back for smuggling immigrants into the country using light aircraft."

"I don't know him."

"That's Okay – neither did I until an hour ago – but since then I've kept my people busy and they've worked at double pace since they heard about Heather and Scott. Ronnie Thatcher is a Southend lad, so I had one of them check out Southend airport and you'll never guess what. It just so happens that Ronnie Thatcher submitted a flight plan to Jersey two days ago. Leaving in a few hours."

"What's that when it's at home?"

"A flight plan is a notification that pilots give to control towers letting them know of their route when they fly. It's a legal requirement safety thing."

"So this Ronnie Thatcher may be part of one of the crews? You think he's doing a runner?"

"Better than that. When my plod spoke to whoever it was they spoke to, the guy said it was funny that Ronnie Thatcher had put in a flight plan." He paused while he scanned his notes. "Apparently, they only have to be submitted an hour or so before a plane is due to hit the wide blue yonder, so getting one three days in advance is less common than a South London day free of mobile phone robberies. It just doesn't happen."

Dudley's eyes brightened when he saw Wiley smile; guessing what he was driving at. "But it wouldn't be unusual for a psychotically mindful bastard like our one and only Careful Eddie Maynard," he exclaimed excitedly. "If he doesn't have things done and dusted to the letter he tends to have people killed!"

"Exactly. And if we can nab Eddie Maynard we get one step closer to tracking down Davie Thompson, even if the two crews *don't* meet up." Wiley paused. "Either way, it's worth our taking a look."

Dudley looked around for his coat, then realised that in his rush to see Scott he hadn't brought one. "You say it's this morning?" he asked, rising.

Wiley nodded then rose to his impressive six foot four. "We can be at the airport in just over an hour," he said.

Saturday 8th December, 2001; 06:05am

Baron clambered into the passenger seat of Colin's stolen Land Rover with his Uzi 9mm hidden beneath a tracksuit top that was folded over his arm. As he made himself comfortable Colin spotted a bulging, leather money belt concealed beneath his T-shirt and wondered how much it contained.

The Battersea streets were dark and deserted and streetlights reflected from puddles like pools of molten gold.

Colin slapped home a tape and Ice T's *Colors* blasted out of the car's impressive stereo system with window-shaking ferocity. In his back trouser pocket he could feel his passport pressed against his backside. Inside this was a slip of paper where he had earlier written down Ali's mother's address. "This track always helps me to get into the mood for butchery," he grinned.

Baron nodded his approval and continued to bop his head along with the music as London streets fled by. The early hour made for easy traffic and within thirty minutes the Land Rover was harassing the tarmac of the A127 heading towards Southend.

"Yu know where de airport der-ya?" Baron asked as the first shreds of daylight grew visible along the horizon.

Colin handed him an A-Z. "No – but me know a man who does," was his reply. "I'm de pilot of dis vehicle, so you get to play de rarse navigator."

Baron kissed his teeth and scoured the A-Z until he had located Southend airport. "We almost reach," he stated. "An' look, bloodfire! Read dat road sign, mon. Wha' does it say?"

"Sout'end airport," Colin acknowledged, clicking the indicator. "Looks like me no need a navigator at all." Endgame, he thought. I could be rich or I could be dead. No way I'm going back to jailhouse. He glanced at Baron and wondered how he was feeling, wanting to detect any nerves in him so he would feel better.

"Yu gwarn need one if yu nuh recognise de raas signs," Baron smiled.

As they pulled up in the deserted airport car park, Davie lowered the scope of his M.S.G.90 sniper's rifle and nudged Danny in the side. "It's Colin and Baron," he said matter of factly.

They were parked a hundred metres down the road from the car park and Davie had removed the M.S.G.90's 10x Hensoldt telescopic sight so that he could survey all who neared the airport.

"Shall we go in?" Danny asked when he saw the Brixtonians park their Land Rover and walk into the airport's glass-fronted Departures lounge. He felt *that* buzz again and for a short second regretted K's death, which was now a very good guess. He might've smoothed things over.

Davie shook his head. "There's no point when Eddie ain't shown up. What's the point of rumbling with these guys if we don't get no pay-off?"

"But they might get to Eddie before we can."

"In which case we nab 'em when they come out. Leave Colin and Baron to fight Eddie, then *we* pick off the winner."

Davie returned the scope to his right eye, while Danny craned his neck to make sure that no-one came up on their car from the rear.

There was a wait of ten minutes before another car turned into the car park and Davie's gaunt face grinned when he recognised the rotund form of Careful Eddie. A lean, blond man wearing glasses was with him and Davie recognised him as the pilot of the plane that they had hijacked ten days before. "That confirms our inside man," he said coolly. "Come on – let's get this show on the road."

Danny had been unable to get his hands on a gun, so the only weapon he had with him was a carving knife that he had taken from his kitchen drawer. He also knew that Davie's rifle, although formidable at assassinating opponents from a mile distant, was ill-prepared for the rigours of close quarters combat. Lee Jones had been murdered with a submachine gun, and it was unlikely that the South Londoners had left it at home, which meant that they were at a definite advantage when it came to firepower.

With the thought of imminent combat against a stronger foe Danny felt his intestines somersault, and he debated asking Davie to down their quarry there and then at long range, but then he glanced at Davie's twitching, spasming hands and knew that the time had long gone where Davie would make an effective sniper. If he was to use the weapon he would need to be up close and personal.

"Is that thing easy to shoot?" he asked, thinking that maybe *he* could take the shot himself, but Davie's expression indicated his slim chance of success.

"We've got to hurry," Davie said, stashing the scope back into his bag then stepping free of the car.

The airport Departures lounge was an open-plan L-shape with one glass wall facing the car park and another leading out onto the landing strip. A steamy cafeteria served coffee to its two patrons and double doors led into the airport's other areas. One led to a reception, another was restricted to pilots and air crews only, while lavatories were positioned near the front door.

"Bwai, dis place empty like dancehall back ah Jamaica when bad-mon fire dem gun salute fe wicked D.J.," Baron noted as he stared out of a window to the airfield. Light aircraft for joyriding and larger, commercial craft for flights to the Channel Islands could be seen. "We're gwarn control one easy raas snatch." He thought of seeing his kids soon.

Colin X kissed his teeth and fastened his gaze on the car park. "Eddie an' 'is flyboy come," he said once he clocked the advancing duo. "Keep your face set that way. Man an' man don't wanna be recognised before our time."

The weight of the pistol in his pocket suddenly felt very heavy and Colin wondered why there was no sign of security in the airport while the British still fought the Taliban in Afghanistan. Hadn't they learned after the Twin Towers? His brothers in

Islam could be anywhere, ready to take out a flight full of white pussies.

Baron still cradled his Uzi hidden under his folded tracksuit jacket, but the cafeteria's two occupants were not paying them enough attention to notice it.

"That's the target," Dudley exclaimed excitedly as he compared the mug-shot of Ronnie Thatcher to the man who was advancing upon the airport. "And that's Careful Eddie with him."

William Wiley slowed his Rover so he could turn into the car park. From the corner of his eye he spied two men who were walking across a patch of grass in the direction of the airfield, one of whom was wearing combat fatigues and carrying a large canvas bag. "The I.C.1s at two O'clock," he stated.

Dudley swivelled his head and his face set into a grim sneer. "Davie Thompson," he hissed sourly. "We'd better call for backup."

As Wiley digited his mobile, Dudley watched as Eddie and Ronnie entered the lounge with Danny and Davie trailing a hundred metres or so behind them. His rage at the incapacitation of Heather and Scott boiled acrid and furious in his stomach and he felt the urge to abandon the car and set about the mad bomber with his feet and fists. His Police training overwhelmed by his anger, his hand stretched out to caress the cool plastic of the door handle, but Wiley's huge paw stretched out to grip his wrist and render any attempt at departure futile.

"Wait," he said. "An Armed Response team is coming."

As Eddie and Ronnie entered the Departures lounge, Colin X observed their movements through their reflection upon a window. The pair were talking, but separated once they were inside. Ronnie walked through the door that was marked for flight crews while Eddie angled towards the toilets.

"Me gwarn silence him bloodclaat inna de shit'ouse," Colin explained, his hand sliding into the pocket that held his pistol.

Baron nodded his approval as Colin stepped away then returned his attention to the white Cessna 182 that was being refuelled by an orange-jacketed attendant. "Dat der kite is mine," he muttered to himself contentedly. "Me cyan mek me way to de Continent in dat fe certainty."

Glass double doors led onto the airfield and the only barricade between Baron and the Cessna was a sticker on the doors that read *'Unauthorised Passage Beyond This Point is Prohibited'*. The fuel attendant turned around and Baron flashed him his teeth as he coiled the fuel pipe away. "Dis jus' *too* raas easy," he concluded.

The door to the Gent's lavatory closed slowly on an oiled spring and Colin found Eddie Maynard with his prick in his hands standing in front of a urinal.

"You got somet'ing fe me, Eddie?" Colin asked as he pulled the gun from his pocket. "A liccle somet'ing you forgot to mention wha' was 'pon de rarse plane?"

Eddie turned slowly and beheld the gun, but he did not recognise Colin. "What's with the fuckin' hardware?" he demanded, still painting the porcelain, but his aim went askew as Colin shot him in the groin.

The sound of the gunshot echoed about the tiled lavatory and Eddie was punched backwards into the door of a cubicle. It smashed inward with the impact and Eddie hit his head on a toilet bowl before slipping to the ground.

"Pagan shit," Colin scowled, shooting Eddie again at point blank range. "Me can search you for de glass easier if you're *bombaclaat* dead."

Dark blood welled from wounds in Eddie's abdomen and chest and he was too weak to protest as Colin X ransacked his pockets. "Where's de fockin' diamonds?" Colin demanded.

"Fuck you," Eddie retorted, spitting blood into Colin's face. His head twitched and spasmed before his chin found a final resting place upon his collar bone. His eyes were half closed, as if caught in mid-blink, and Eddie's mouth was slightly open, still. He had already expelled his last breath.

When the sound of gunshots ricocheted around the airport, Danny and Davie knew they had arrived too late for the kick-off. With his expression radiating grim resignation, Danny thrust open the double doors of the Departures lounge as Davie pulled the rifle free from his canvas bag. They appeared to be moving in slow motion.

"I heard a shot! It's a shot," Dudley exclaimed from the passenger seat of Wiley's Rover.

"Where's that A.R.V.?" Wiley hollered into his cell phone. "Shots have been fired. I repeat: shots have been fired. We need S.O.19 *now!*"

Colin cursed when he found Eddie's pockets empty save for his passport and a packet of Bensons. Surely Eddie had the diamonds? Would he really have left them with the pilot? He pulled a handful of bullets from his pocket and yanked free his pistol's magazine. Law are on the loose now, he realised. The clock is ticking.

"Alright, everybody up 'gainst de wall!" Baron ordered, pulling the jacket off of his Uzi and pointing its angry snout at the occupants of the tiny cafeteria. Remembering his training, he east-wested his eyes for any peril, the gun pointed above his head in readiness, U.S. Army style. His voice was authoritative and not tinged with panic. "Yu," he growled, his bloodshot eyes directed at the woman who was serving. "Get 'pon dis side ah de counter an' place your 'ands where me cyan sight dem. Me nuh waan nuh Rambo business or yu gwarn end up seriously dead."

The woman joined her two patrons and Baron herded them together and up against the nearest wall by prodding them with his weapon. He put their hands behind their heads roughly and kept them facing the wall.

Danny and Davie saw Baron dart into the cafeteria with his Uzi drawn, so they hid around the corner of the L-shaped lounge. Davie kicked over a table and crouched behind it, dragging Danny after him as Colin leapt out of the lavatory, while thrusting the magazine of his pistol home. He did not see the East Londoners and ran towards Baron shouting: "Eddie don't 'ave de rarse diamonds, man! We have to move seriously!"

Davie readied his weapon, but he was too slow to take a shot.

"Where's the pilot?" Danny wondered aloud.

"My bet is in there," Davie answered.

Screams and sobs filled the lounge as Davie jerked his head in the direction of the door that read *Flight Crews Only*. "Eddie will have given the glass to the pilot as they don't get so much hassle from Customs," he explained, then he stood and backed towards the door with his rifle clutched at his side and pointed in the direction of the cafeteria. He could hear Colin X and Baron shouting, then the sound of running footsteps. "They've cottoned on too," he suggested.

Danny rose and ran at a crouch towards the door while Davie kept him covered with the rifle. Both men entered the restricted area just as Colin and Baron sped around the corner, Jamaican expletives following them like a cloud.

"Quick," Davie said, grabbing a chair and throwing it in front of the door. "Stop them getting in."

They were in a corridor with doors on either side of them. A young woman wearing a terrified expression stuck her head out of one of them. "Fuck off!" Danny screamed as he hefted a pinewood coffee table from one room and manhandled it in front of the door. "Keep out our fuckin' way!"

With the table in place, Danny and Davie backed into a side room and listened to the sirens that were now discernible in the distance. "Shit, why did the silly bastards have to make so much noise?" Danny shrieked. "We coulda done this without a shot being fired."

Davie smirked mischievously as he took the match-filled tennis ball from his canvas bag. His rifle was slung over his shoulder. On the opposite side of the corridor he saw a room that was marked *Pilots' Lounge* and he indicated it to Danny with his eyes.

Danny nodded and as Colin X thrust his shoulder against the door that lead in from the Departures lounge, Danny kicked open the pilots' lounge door an instant before Davie threw the tennis ball inside.

A dull, fizzing crack like the sound of a firework sizzled the air as the tennis ball exploded in a blaze of combusting sulphur. Davie hefted his rifle into the ready position and ducked inside followed immediately after by Danny, who had now pulled his knife.

Two stunned men were inside; Ronnie Thatcher and a short, swarthy man who Danny kicked into silence before he had time to recover from the blast.

Davie strode over to Ronnie and slapped him about the face with the butt of his rifle. Teeth splintered and blood geysered from his mouth. "The diamonds," Davie demanded, his gaunt face a pale death mask. "Hand them over."

Before Ronnie could move, the rifle connected with the side of his head and he was pitched sideways to the floor, where his head hit a wall; cracking the plaster.

"Me know you in der, pagan!" Colin X shouted as he thrust his muscular shoulders up against the door. "Me coming to waste your white arse!"

"Boom boom chaat!" Baron scowled, pushing Colin out of the way. "Ah yout' waan tek over ah mon job." He levelled his Uzi at the door and emptied its magazine in one long, rattling burst. "Now, bus' 'im bloodclaat."

Colin tried again and the wood splintered. The table behind the door moved. "Pagan! Don't boder try any brave shit. If you 'ave de diamonds you'd better gi' me dem now if you don't want *dead!*"

"Gotcha," Danny exclaimed as he pulled a velvet bag from Ronnie's trouser pocket. He jingled its contents in his hands. His eyes widened. *Eight million quid!* "It's the ice alright."

The smell of smouldering tennis ball and spent cartridges polluted the air making Davie's eyes water as he kept his rifle levelled at their two captives. "Now we need to get out of here in one piece," he stated, one hand dipping down into his canvas bag.

As Colin continued to harass the door Baron glanced out of the window to the armoured Police van that had pulled up outside. "De beastman come," he said. "Time fe ah liccle action." He crawled along the floor on his belly away from the door until he was ensconced behind a table then changed his magazine with professional haste. "Bloodfire," he hissed. He could see men wearing black flak jackets and visored helmets streaming from the back of the vehicle with rifles in their hands. A tall, black man wearing a suit made directional gestures with his arms. He recognised the giant form of D.C.I. Wiley.

"Time fe me fe drill ah coconut," Baron whispered as he readied his Uzi to fire three-shot bursts then pointed its snout over the top of the table. He thought of his seemingly-impossible-to-get visa "'im mudder mus' feel ah great shame de way 'im turn out."

He pressed the trigger and the wide glass window of the Departures lounge shattered to spray glittering diamonds of glass in all directions. The bullets missed Wiley by inches and slammed into his Rover, where they lodged in its engine.

"Jesus Christ!" Wiley cried as his beloved Rover developed a sudden case of the pox. "Get down!"

Dudley was still sitting in its passenger seat roaring instructions into Wiley's mobile when the bullets hit, but he got out of the vehicle quickly and threw himself to the ground. "Where are the fucking snipers?" he demanded.

William rolled across the asphalt to lay next to him then pointed with a finger. "The shooters' team leader said he's posting the guns around there," he said, indicating various points along the perimeter of the airfield. "They'll be in position within two minutes."

Another report from Baron's Uzi caused William and Dudley to retreat to behind the Rover and they knew that they were pinned down. "Shit, I wasn't expecting *this* before breakfast," Dudley squealed. "Who the fuck's the gunman?"

Wiley's face looked grim. "I have a pretty good idea," he answered. "And if it is who I think it is don't pop up your head to take a look... He's C.I.A. trained."

Disbelief at their predicament swarmed over Powell's face like thrown custard.

"Alright, me affe reach de plane," Baron hissed through his teeth as he spied around himself. He saw an S.O.19 rifleman getting into position on the roof of a house opposite the airfield and knew that he could not reach him with his own weapon. "Too raas bad," he complained, shouldering his Uzi, then he crawled along the floor tipping over tables and chairs to hamper the view of any would-be snipers. "Yu t'ink me don't survive tougher shit dan yu back ah yard?" he snarled, knowing his foe couldn't hear him, but saying it lent himself confidence.

While Baron continued to topple furniture, Colin succeeded in breaking through the barricaded door. He kicked the table used to jam it aside then readied his pistol.

Still in the pilots' lounge, Davie heard Colin's advance, so he delved into his canvas bag and produced his home-made pipe bomb. He tapped it forcibly on the ground then shook it near his ear, whereupon he heard the tinkling sound of smashed glass. The light bulb keeping the baking soda from the vinegar had shattered.

"Fire in the hole," he whispered to Danny as he threw the pipe outside. Colin saw the missile and gave a toothy sneer of contempt. "You t'ink you can scare me by flinging de plumbing?" he scoffed, stepping towards the length of pipe and scooping it up in his hand. "Rarse pussies!"

The pipe bomb exploded as he prepared to throw it back and the force of the blast tore his arm from its shoulder. Nails and lead piping fountained around Colin's head ripping the flesh from his bones and scoring puncture marks all over his body. He remained standing for an instant, his swaying corpse displaying a scornful grimace of denial, but then his body tipped backwards to rest in an ever-expanding pool of his own blood.

"What the hell was *that*?" Dudley shouted as the explosion shook the dull Essex scenery. "Has someone set off a bomb?"

Wiley ignored him and thumbed the Police radio he had taken from the Armed Response team leader. "Okay, we don't have time to wait for a trained negotiator," he said. "Let the snipers do the talking."

A static-drenched 'affirmative' indicated that all was ready, so William and Dudley crouched lower behind the Rover and prepared for the showdown. "Good luck, lads," Dudley said.

Smoke from the pipe bomb obscured the view inside the airport despite the smashed windows, but it did highlight the red laser trails of the snipers' targetting aids. Baron glanced to where he could see what remained of Colin's head; his face resting on one side covered in soot and blood. He knew that the fuelled Cessna was waiting only a few metres outside on the airstrip, but with so many snipers around it may as well have been half a mile away and across a minefield.

The screams of the people whom he had locked in the cafeteria had intensified since the explosion and they were beginning to singe Baron's nerves. He had to think quickly.

A red laser tongue licked close by, so Baron shifted his position and he realised to his dismay that the snipers were inadvertently pushing him closer towards Danny and Davie. "Me nuh waan fe end up like me bredren der," Baron admitted to himself as he spied once again Colin X's mangled corpse. "Me t'ink it's time fe ah liccle understanding."

Still inside the pilots' lounge, Danny and Davie were wondering how to escape from the airport with their lives. "Yo, Danny, Davie," Baron called through the smoke. "X dead. An' if yu waan live yu gwarn affe follow me to de plane. Nuff sniper der-bout. Y'understand?"

Davie and Danny locked glances whereupon Danny shrugged. They had no other options. "Get talking," he called.

"Der's a bucket outside me see fuelled up neatly an it cyan tek us far inna de Continent. Me 'ave room fe yu, but de price is ah cut of dem diamonds. Wha' yu ah say?"

"What proof can you give that we'll be safer with you than the Law?" Davie asked.

"Me gi' yu dis," Baron replied, skidding his empty Uzi across the floor into the corridor. "But yu mus' mek up your mind quick-time as dem Police nuh set dem phaser fe stun. Me gwarn move inna count ah ten."

As Baron counted, Danny weighed the bag of diamonds in his hand, while Davie continued to scrutinise their concussed captives. "Let's do it," he said.

Danny left the pilots' lounge, crawling into the corridor, and Davie followed him with the rifle. Baron was good to his word and soon all three men were skimming along the floor of the Departures lounge towards the airstrip while laser beams glistened in the smoke overhead.

Once they were at the door that faced the airstrip Baron let out a curse. "Me sight dem sniper inna de field," he stated, indicating a cluster of trees with his hand. "When we forward to dat Cessna over der yu better run like Linford Christie or de Police pepper yu quick-time... Yu ready?"

Danny nodded, closing his eyes for a short second and muttering something under his breath. He lurched into a crouch in preparation to flee, but Davie shook his head. "There ain't enough fuel in a Cessna to get three people to the

Continent, and we'll be toast before we get to it anyway," he said. "You two go and I'll keep you covered."

"What?" Danny cried suddenly. "Don't be so fuckin' stupid."

"Go, Danny," Davie pleaded, his eyes wide in desperation. "Remember what I said about life being like a game of checkers? Well, it's time for you to hop over me, son. Go on, you've always deserved to be one of the kings."

Davie's arm spasmed and he turned his attention in the direction of the trees. "Be quick about it," he said.

Danny placed an arm on his friend's shoulder and went to say something, but Baron kicked the door leading to the airstrip open before he had the chance.

With Baron's movement Davie rose, levelled his rifle and a barking report shattered the silence of the early morning as a heavy calibre bullet ripped through the bay window and out into the dawn. "Go!" he shouted.

Davie let off another round as Danny and Baron raced towards the Cessna and discharged a shuddering breath of release when he saw them both clamber into its cabin. As the plane's engine fired up Davie wondered how much time his share of the diamonds would have bought him fighting against Subacute Sclerosing Panencephalitis, then he realised that he would trade his share of the loot along with the prolonged, undignified death that awaited him for a quick shot in the head any day. "I call that a bargain," he said aloud.

With hands that trembled, Davie removed the magazine from his rifle and tossed it aside, then he watched the Cessna taxi along the runway, picking up speed all the while.

A flak-jacketed Policeman ran out from a hanger and Davie looked to the trees where he knew a sniper waited. Then, as the Cessna took to the air on its way to Antwerp or somewhere, Davie stood up from behind his cover and slowly raised his empty weapon at the running Policeman.

"Game over," he said.

THE END

www.xpress.co.uk

For the full range of titles published
by The X Press

www.xpress.co.uk

For the full range of titles published
by The X Press

www.xpress.co.uk

For the full range of titles published
by The X Press

www.xpress.co.uk

For the full range of titles published
by The X Press

www.xpress.co.uk

For the full range of titles published
by The X Press

www.xpress.co.uk

For the full range of titles published
by The X Press

www.xpress.co.uk

For the full range of titles published
by The X Press

www.xpress.co.uk

For the full range of titles published
by The X Press